BAD SEEDS:
EVIL PROGENY

OTHER BOOKS EDITED BY STEVE BERMAN

So Fey: Queer Fairy Fiction

Magic in the Mirrorstone

Wilde Stories: The Year's Best Gay Speculative Fiction

Heiresses of Russ: The Year's Best Lesbian Speculative Fiction

The Touch of the Sea

Bad Seeds: Evil Progeny

Where Thy Dark Eye Glances: Queering Edgar Allan Poe

Zombies: Shambling Through the Ages

Shades of Blue and Gray: Ghosts of the Civil War

Handsome Devil: Tales of Sin and Seduction

BAD SEEDS: EVIL PROGENY

EDITED BY STEVE BERMAN

PRIME BOOKS

BAD SEEDS: EVIL PROGENY

Prime Books
www.prime-books.com

For more information, contact Prime Books:
prime@prime-books.com

ISBN: 978-1-60701-393-8

CONTENTS

"I see no hope for the future of our people if they are dependent on frivolous youth of today, for certainly all youth are reckless beyond words . . . " —**Hesiod**

"A child is a curly dimpled lunatic."
—**Ralph Waldo Emerson**

INTRODUCTION

I was a teen when I read *Lord of the Flies* for the first time. High school English class reading assignments had varied between *Romeo and Juliet* (burdened by innumerable footnotes to allow a twentieth-century adolescent some comprehension of Renaissance English and quips) and Salinger's *The Catcher in the Rye*, which, written in 1951, seemed as oddly dated to me as Shakespeare's plays even though less than three decades had passed since it was published. But then I found myself lost, adrift, on the island with those British boys.

Goldman's novel was also a product of the 1950s, also a commentary on adolescence and the truth between the perceptions of adults and the realities of youth. But what left me rapt, what kept me reading until well past any reasonable bedtime, was the terrors wrought by Jack Merridew, a choirboy, on fair Ralph and poor Piggy. As a child, I had known bullying all my life (a list of playground sins: asthmatic, bespectacled, scrawny, unathletic, and a definite sissy), but in the 1970s and 1980s no one addressed the constant taunting and menacing as they do now. I found Jack the embodiment of all the cruelties I knew. Jack Merridew was evil, more so than any boogeyman found in the works of fantasy authors I'd read—worse than Lloyd Alexander's Horned King or John Bellairs's Selenna Izard—because in the real world Jack Merridews preyed on boys like me.

Once you have been haunted by a childhood bully, you never quite recover. Storytellers know this, as much as they know that the nineteenth-century nursery rhyme "What Are Little Boys Made Of?" offers still a popular misconception of "puppy-dogs' tails" and "sugar and spice" for little girls. Laird Koenig's eerie Rynn Jacobs from *The Little Girl Who Lives Down the Lane* or Kubrick's infamous staging of the haunting Grady girls from *The Shining* challenge that.

There are stories here that suggest children return in spades the violence

STEVE BERMAN

inflicted upon them by adults. Sharper than a serpent's tooth? Perhaps. Or perhaps the hand that feeds them deserves to be bitten.

Many of the stories in this book are set during Halloween, when children are encouraged to revel in monster costumes, demand treats from their elders or inflict mayhem on their property. Perhaps what we think of as costume is really the outward expression of the inner bête noire hidden away during the rest of the year. Except, of course, during recess on the playground.

Of course, not everyone's son or daughter, niece or nephew, is a terror. Remind yourself of that next time you witness a tantrum, the thrashing of limbs and high-pitched yowls. Remind yourself of that next time the little one says with utter seriousness "I hate you" or "I wish you were dead." Remind yourself that when you shut the door to the bedroom and realize how few short steps it is through the darkened hall to your own door, to your own bed, when you'll be asleep. And helpless against the Jack Merridews and Rynn Jacobses that we have inadvertently raised.

Now remember to play nice.

Steve Berman
Spring 2013

IF DAMON COMES
CHARLES L. GRANT

Fog, nightbreath of the river, luring without whispering in the thick crown of an elm, huddling without creaking around the base of a chimney; it drifted past porch lights, and in passing blurred them, dropped over the street lights, and in dropping grayed them. It crept in with midnight to stay until dawn, and there was no wind to bring the light out of hiding.

Frank shivered and drew his raincoat's collar closer around his neck, held it closed with one hand while the other wiped at the pricks of moisture that clung to his cheeks, his short dark hair. He whistled once, loudly, but in listening heard nothing, not even an echo. He stamped his feet against the November cold and moved to the nearest corner, squinted and saw nothing. He knew the cat was gone, had known it from the moment he had seen the saucer still brimming with milk on the back porch. Damon had been sitting beside it, hands folded, knees pressed tightly together, elbows tucked into his sides. He was cold, but refused to acknowledge it, and Frank had only tousled his son's softly brown hair, squeezed his shoulder once and went inside to say good-bye to his wife.

And now . . . now he walked, through the streets of Oxrun Station, looking for an animal he had seen only once—a half-breed Siamese with a milk-white face—whistling like a fool afraid of the dark, searching for the note that would bring the animal running.

And in walking, he was unpleasantly reminded of a night the year before, when he had had one drink too many at someone's party, made one amorous boast too many in someone's ear, and had ended up on a street corner with a woman he knew only vaguely. They had kissed once and long, and once broken, he had turned around to see Damon staring up at him. The boy had turned, had fled, and Frank had stayed away most of the night, not knowing what Susan had heard, fearing more what Damon had thought.

It had been worse than horrid facing the boy again, but Damon had acted as though nothing had happened; and the guilt passed as the months passed, and the wondering why his son had been out in the first place.

He whistled. Crouched and snapped his fingers at the dark of some shrubbery. Then he straightened and blew out deeply held breath. There was no cat, there were no cars, and he finally gave in to his aching feet and sore back and headed for home. Quickly. Watching the fog tease the road before him, cut it sharply off behind.

It wasn't fair, he thought, his hands shoved in his pockets, his shoulders hunched as though expecting a blow. Damon, in his short eight years, had lost two dogs already to speeders, a canary to some disease he couldn't even pronounce, and two brothers stillborn—it was getting to be a problem. *He* was getting to be a problem, fighting each day that he had to go to school, whining and weeping whenever vacations came around and trips were planned.

He'd asked Doc Simpson about it when Damon turned seven. Dependency, he was told; clinging to the only three things left in his life—his short, short life—that he still believed to be constant: his home, his mother . . . and Frank.

And Frank had kissed a woman on a corner and Damon had seen him.

Frank shuddered and shook his head quickly, remembering how the boy had come to the office at least once a day for the next three weeks, saying nothing, just standing on the sidewalk looking in through the window. Just for a moment. Long enough to be sure that his father was still there.

Once home, then, Frank shed his coat and hung it on the rack by the front door. A call, a muffled reply, and he took the stairs two at a time and trotted down the hall to Damon's room set over the kitchen.

"Sorry, old pal," he said with a shrug as he made himself a place on the edge of the mattress. "I guess he went home."

Damon, small beneath the flowered quilt, innocent from behind long curling lashes, shook his head sharply. "No," he said. "This is home. It is, Dad, it really is."

Frank scratched at the back of his neck. "Well, I guess he didn't think of it quite that way."

"Maybe he got lost, huh? It's awfully spooky out there. Maybe he's afraid to come out of where he's hiding."

"A cat's never—" He stopped as soon as he saw the expression on the boy's thin face. Then he nodded and broke out a rueful smile. "Well, maybe you're right, pal. Maybe the fog messed him up a little." Damon's hand crept into his, and he squeezed it while thinking that the boy was too thin by far; it made his head look ungainly. "In the morning," he promised. "In the morning. If he's not back by then, I'll take the day off and we'll hunt him together."

Damon nodded solemnly, withdrew the hand and pulled the quilt up to his chin. "When's Mom coming home?"

"In a while. It's Friday, you know. She's always late on Fridays. And Saturdays." And, he thought, Wednesdays and Thursdays, too.

Damon nodded again. And, as Frank reached the door and switched off the light: "Dad, does she sing pretty?"

"Like a bird, pal," he said, grinning. "Like a bird."

The voice was small in the dark: "I love you, Dad."

Frank swallowed hard, and nodded before he realized the boy couldn't see him. "Well, pal, it seems I love you, too. Now you'd better get some rest."

"I thought you were going to get lost in the fog."

Frank stopped the move to close the door. He'd better get some rest himself, he thought; that sounded like a threat.

"Not me," he finally said. "You'd always come for me, right?"

"Right, Dad."

Frank grinned, closed the door, and wandered through the small house for nearly half an hour before finding himself in the kitchen, his hands waving at his sides for something to do. Coffee. No. He'd already had too much of that today. But the walk had chilled him, made his bones seem brittle. Warm milk, maybe, and he opened the refrigerator, stared, then took out a container and poured half its contents into a pot. He stood by the stove, every few seconds stirring a finger through the milk to check its progress. Stupid cat, he thought; there ought to be a law against doing something like that to a small boy that never hurt anyone, never had anyone to hurt.

He poured himself a glass, smiling when he didn't spill a drop, but he refused to turn around and look up at the clock; instead, he stared at the flames as he finished the second glass, wondering what it would be like to stick his finger into the fire. He read somewhere . . . he thought he'd read

CHARLES L. GRANT

somewhere that the blue near the center was the hottest part and it wasn't so bad elsewhere. His hand wavered, but he changed his mind, not wanting to risk a burn on something he only thought he had read; besides, he decided as he headed into the living room, the way things were going these days, he probably had it backward.

He sat in an armchair flanking the television, took out a magazine from the rack at his side and had just found the table of contents when he heard a car door slam in the drive. He waited, looked up and smiled when the front door swung open and Susan rushed in. She blew him a distant kiss, mouth *I'll be back in a second*, and ran up the stairs. She was much shorter than he, her hair waist-long black and left free to fan in the wind of her own making. She'd been taking vocal lessons for several years now, and when they'd moved to the Station when Damon was five, she'd landed a job singing at the Chancellor Inn. Torch songs, love songs, slow songs, sinner songs; she was liked well enough to be asked to stay on after the first night, but she began so late that Damon had never heard her. And for the last six months, the two-nights-a-week became four, and Frank became adept at cooking supper.

When she returned, her makeup was gone and she was in a shimmering green robe. She flopped on the sofa opposite him and rubbed her knees, her thighs, her upper arms. "If that creep drummer tries to pinch me again, so help me I'll castrate him."

"That is hardly the way for a lady to talk," he said, smiling. "If you're not careful, I'll have to punish you. Whips at thirty paces."

In the old days—the very old days, he thought—she would have laughed and entered a game that would last for nearly an hour. Lately, however, and tonight, she only frowned at him as though she were dealing with a dense, unlettered child. He ignored it, and listened politely as she detailed her evening, the customers, the compliments, the raise she was looking for so she could buy her own car.

"You don't need a car," he said without thinking.

"But aren't you tired of walking home every night?"

He closed the magazine and dropped it on the floor. "Lawyers, my dear, are a sedentary breed. I could use the exercise."

"If you didn't work so late on those damned briefs," she said without

14

looking at him, "and came to bed on time, I'd give you all the exercise you need."

He looked at his watch. It was going on two.

"The cat's gone."

"Oh, no," she said. "No wonder you look so tired. You go out after him?"

He nodded, and she rolled herself suddenly into a sitting position. "Not with Damon."

"No. He was in bed when I came home."

She said nothing more, only examined her nails. He watched her closely, the play of her hair falling over her face, the squint that told him her contact lenses were still on her dresser. And he knew she meant: *did you take Damon with you?* She was asking if Damon had followed him. Like the night in the fog, with the woman; like the times at the office; like the dozens of other instances when the boy just happened to show up at the courthouse, in the park while Frank was eating lunch under a tree, at a nearby friend's house late one evening, claiming to have had a nightmare and the sitter wouldn't help him.

Like a shadow.

Like a conscience.

"Are you going to replace it?" He blinked. "The cat, stupid. Are you going to get him a new cat?"

He shook his head. "We've had too much bad luck with animals. I don't think he could take it again."

She swung herself off the sofa and stood in front of him, her hands on her hips, her lips taut, her eyes narrowed. "You don't care about him, do you?"

"What?"

"He follows you around like a goddamn pet because he's afraid of losing you, and you won't even buy him a lousy puppy or something. You're something else again, Frank, you really are. I work my tail trying to help—"

"My salary is plenty good enough," he said quickly.

"—this family and you're even trying to get me to stop that, too."

He shoved himself to his feet, his chest brushing against hers and forcing her back. "Listen," he said tightly, "I don't care if you sing your heart out a million times a week, lady, but when it starts to interfere with your duties here—"

"My *duties?*"

"—then yes, I'll do everything I can to make sure you stay home when you're supposed to."

"You're raising your voice. You'll wake Damon."

The argument was familiar, and old, and so was the rage he felt stiffening his muscles. But this time she wouldn't stop when she saw his anger. She kept on, and on, and he didn't even realize it when his hand lifted and struck her across the cheek. She stumbled back a step, whirled to run out of the room, and stopped.

Damon was standing at the foot of the stairs.

He was sucking his thumb.

He was staring at his father.

"Go to bed, son," Frank said quietly. "Everything's all right."

For the next week the tension in the house was proverbially knife-cutting thick. Damon stayed up as late as he could, sitting by his father as they watched television together or read from the boy's favorite books. Susan remained close, but not touching, humming to herself and playing with her son whenever he left—for the moment—his father's side; each time, however, her smile was more forced, her laughter more strained, and it was apparent to Frank that Damon was merely tolerating her, nothing more. That puzzled him. It was he who had struck her, not the other way around, and the boy's loyalty should have been thrown into his mother's camp. Yet it hadn't. And it was apparent that Susan was growing more resentful of the fact each day. Each hour. Each time Damon walked silently to Frank's side and slid his hand around the man's waist, or into his palm, or into his hip pocket.

He began showing up at the office again, until one afternoon when Susan skidded the car to a halt at the curb and ran out, grabbed the boy and practically threw him, arms and legs thrashing, into the front seat. Frank raced from his desk and out the front door, leaned over and rapped at the window until Susan lowered it.

"What the hell are you doing?" he whispered, with a glance to the boy.

"You hit me, or had you forgotten," she whispered back. "And there's my son's alienation of affection."

He almost straightened. "That's lawyer talk, Susan," he said.

16

"Not here," she answered. "Not in front of the boy."

He stepped back quickly as the car growled away from the curb, walked in a daze to his desk and sat there, chin in one palm, staring out the window as the afternoon darkened and a faint drizzle began to fall. His secretary muttered something about a court case the following morning, and Frank nodded until she stared at him, gathered her purse and raincoat and left hurriedly. He continued to nod, not knowing the movement, trying to understand what he had done, what both of them had done to bring themselves to this moment. Ambition, surely. A conflict of generations where women were homebodies and women had careers; where men tried to adjust when they couldn't have both. But he had tried, he told himself . . . or he thought he had, until the dishes began to pile up and the dust stayed on the furniture and Damon said *does she sing pretty?*

It's always the children who get hurt, he thought angrily.

Held that idea in early December when the separation papers had been prepared and he stood on the front porch watching his car, his wife, and his son drive away from Oxrun Station south toward the city. Damon's face was in the rear window, nose flat, palms flat, hair pressed down over his forehead. He waved, and Frank answered.

I love you, Dad.

Frank wiped a hand under his nose and went back inside, searched the house for some liquor and, in failing, went straight to bed where he watched the moonshadows make monsters of the curtains.

"Dad," the boy said, "do I have to go with Mommy?"

"I'm afraid so. The judge . . . well, he knows better, believe it or not, what's best right now. Don't worry, pal. I'll see you at Christmas. It won't be forever."

"I don't like it, Dad. I'll run away."

"No! You'll do what your mother tells you, you hear me? You behave your-self and go to school every day, and I'll . . . call you whenever I can."

"The city doesn't like me, Dad. I want to stay at the Station."

Frank said nothing.

"It's because of the lady, isn't it?"

He had stared, but Susan's back was turned, bent over a suitcase that would not close once it had sprung open again by the front door.

"What are you talking about?" he'd said harshly.

"I told," Damon said as though it were nothing. "You weren't supposed to do that."

When Susan straightened, her smile was grotesque.

And when they had driven away, Damon had said *I love you, Dad.*

Frank woke early, made himself breakfast and stood at the back door, looking out into the yard. There was a fog again, nothing unusual as the Connecticut weather fought to stabilize into winter. But as he sipped at his coffee, thinking how large the house had become, how large and how empty, he saw a movement beside the cherry tree in the middle of the yard. The fog swirled but he was sure . . .

He yanked open the door and shouted: "Damon!"

The fog closed and he shook his head. Easy, pal, he told himself; you're not cracking up yet.

Days.

Nights.

He called Susan regularly, twice a week at pre-appointed times. But as Christmas came and Christmas went, she became more terse, and his son more sullen.

"He's getting fine grades, Frank, I'm seeing to that."

"He sounds terrible."

"He's losing a little weight, that's all. Picks up colds easily. It takes a while, Frank, to get used to the city."

"It's his home. He will."

In mid-January Susan did not answer the phone and finally, in desperation, he called the school, was told that Damon had been in the hospital for nearly a week. The nurse thought it was something like pneumonia.

When he arrived that night, the waiting room was crowded with drab bundles of scarves and overcoats, whispers and moans and a few muffled sobs. Susan was standing by the window, looking out at the lights far colder than stars. She didn't turn when she heard him, didn't answer when he demanded to know why she had not contacted him. He grabbed her shoulder and spun her around; her eyes were dull, her face pinched with red hints of cold.

"All right," she said. "All right, Frank, it's because I didn't want you to upset him."

"What in hell are you talking about?"

"He would have seen you and he would have wanted to go back to Oxrun." Her eyes narrowed. "This is his home, Frank! He's got to learn to live with it."

"I'll get a lawyer."

She smiled that. "Do that. You do that, Frank."

He didn't have to. He saw Damon a few minutes later and could not stay more than a moment. The boy was in dim light and almost invisible, too thin to be real beneath the clear plastic tent and the tubes and the monitors . . . too frail, the doctor said in professional conciliation, too frail for too long, and Frank remembered the day on the porch with the saucer of milk when he had thought the same thing and had thought nothing of it.

He returned after the funeral, all anger gone. He had accused Susan of murder, knowing at the time how foolish it had been, but feeling better for it in his own absolution. He had apologized. Had been, for the moment, forgiven.

Had stepped off the train, had wept, had taken a deep breath and decided to live on.

Returned to the office the following day, piled folders onto his desk and hid behind them for most of the morning. He looked up only once, when his secretary tried to explain about a new client's interest, and saw around her waist the indistinct form of his son peering through the window.

"Damon," he muttered, brushed the woman to one side and ran out to the sidewalk. A fog encased the street whitely, but he could see nothing, not even a car, not even the blinking amber light at the nearest intersection.

Immediately after lunch he dialed Susan's number, stared at the receiver when there was no answer and returned it to the cradle. Wondering.

"You look pale," his secretary said softly. She pointed with a pencil at his desk. "You've already done a full day's work. Why don't you go home and lie down? I can lock up. I don't mind."

He smiled, turned as she held his coat for him, touched her cheek . . . and froze.

Damon was in the window.

No, he told himself . . . and Damon was gone.

He rested for two days, returned to work and lost himself in a battle over a will probated by a judge he thought nothing less than senile, to be charitable. He tried calling Susan again, and again received no answer.

And Damon would not leave him alone.

When there was fog, rain, clouds, wind . . . he would be there by the window, there by the cherry tree, there in the darkest corner of the porch.

He knew it was guilt, for not fighting hard enough to keep his son with him, thinking that if he had the boy might still be alive; seeing his face everywhere and the accusations that if the boy loved him, why wasn't he loved just as much in return?

By February's end he decided it was time to make a friendly call on a fellow professional, a doctor who shared the office building with him. It wasn't so much the faces that he saw—he had grown somewhat accustomed to them and assumed they would vanish in time—but that morning there had been snow on the ground; and in the snow by the cherry tree the footprints of a small boy. When he brought the doctor to the yard to show him, they were gone.

"You're quite right, Frank. You're feeling guilty. But not because of the boy in and of himself. The law and the leanings of most judges are quite clear—you couldn't be expected to keep him at his age. You're still worrying yourself about that woman you kissed and the fact that Damon saw you; and the fact that you think you could have saved his life somehow, even if the doctors couldn't; and lastly, the fact that you weren't able to give him things, like pets, like that cat. None of it is your fault, really. It's merely something unpleasant you'll have to face up to. Now."

Though he didn't feel all that much better, Frank appreciated the calm that swept over him when the talk was done and they had parted. He worked hard for the rest of the day, for the rest of the week, but he knew that it was not guilt and it was not his imagination and it was not anything the doctor would be able to explain away when he opened his door on Saturday morning and found, lying carefully atop his newspaper, the white-face Siamese. Dead. Its neck broken.

He stumbled back over the threshold, whirled around and raced into the downstairs bathroom where he fell onto his knees beside the bowl and lost his breakfast. The tears were acid, the sobs like blows to his lungs and stomach, and by the time he had pulled himself together, he knew what was happening.

The doctor, the secretary, even his wife . . . they were all wrong.

There was no guilt.

There was only . . . Damon.

A little boy with large brown eyes who loved his father. Who loved his father so much that he would never leave him. Who loved his father so much that he was going to make sure, absolutely sure, that he would never be alone.

You've been a bad boy, Daddy.

Frank stumbled to his feet, into the kitchen, leaned against the back door. There was a figure by the cherry tree dark and formless; but he knew there was no use running outside. The figure would vanish.

You never did like that cat, Daddy. Or the dogs. Or Mommy.

The telephone rang. He took his time getting to it, stared at it dumbly for several moments before lifting the receiver. He could see straight down the hall and into the kitchen. He had not turned on the overhead light and, as a consequence, could see through the small panes of the back door to the yard beyond. The air outside was heavy with impending snow. Gray. Almost lifeless.

"Frank? Frank, it's Susan. Frank, I've been thinking . . . about you and me . . . and what happened."

He kept his eyes on the door. "It's done, Sue. Done."

"Frank, I don't know what happened. Honest to God, I was trying, really I was. He was getting the best grades in school, had lots of friends . . . I even bought him a little dog, a poodle, two weeks before he . . . I don't know what happened, Frank! I woke up this morning and all of a sudden I was so damned *alone*. Frank, I'm frightened. Can . . . can I come home?"

The gray darkened. There was a shadow on the porch, much larger now than the shadow in the yard.

"No," he said.

"He thought about you all the damned time," she said, her voice rising into hysteria. "He tried to run away once, to get back to you."

The shadow filled the panes, the windows on either side, and suddenly there was static on the line and Susan's voice vanished. He dropped the receiver and turned around.

In the front.

Shadows.

He heard the furnace humming, but the house was growing cold.

The lamp in the living room flickered, died, shone brightly for a moment before the bulb shattered.

He was . . . wrong.

God, he was wrong!

Damon . . . Damon didn't love him.

Not since the night on the corner in the fog; not since the night he had not really tried to locate a cat with a milk-white face.

Damon knew.

And Damon didn't love him.

He dropped to his hands and knees and searched in the darkness for the receiver, found it and nearly threw it away when the bitterly cold plastic threatened to burn through his fingers.

"Susan!" he shouted. "Susan, damnit, can you hear me?"

A bad boy, Daddy.

There was static, but he thought he could hear her crying into the wind.

"Susan . . . Susan, this is crazy, I've no time to explain, but you've got to help me. You've got to do something for me."

Daddy.

"Susan, please . . . he'll be back, I know he will. Don't ask me how, but I know! Listen, you've got to do something for me. Susan, damnit, can you hear me?"

Daddy, I'm—

"For God's sake, Susan, if Damon comes, tell him I'm sorry!"

home.

TREATS

NORMAN PARTRIDGE

Monsters stalked the supermarket aisles.

Maddie pushed the squeaky-wheeled cart past a pack of werewolves, smiling when they growled at her because that was the polite thing to do. She couldn't help staring at the bright eyes inside the plastic masks. Brown eyes, blue and green eyes. Human eyes. Not the eyes that she couldn't see. Not the black eyes that stared at her from Jimmy's face, so cold, ordering her here and there without a glint of compassion or love.

"Jimmy, get away from that candy!"

Maddie covered her mouth, fearful that she'd spoken. No, she hadn't said anything. Besides, Jimmy was at home with them. He'd said that they were preparing for Operation Trojan Horse and he had to speak to them before—

"Jimmy, I'm telling you for the last time . . . "

A little ghoul clutching a trick-or-treat bag scampered down the aisle. He tore at the wrapping of a Snickers bar and gobbled a big bite before his mother caught his tattered collar.

"I warned you, young man," she said, snatching away the bright-orange treat sack. "You're not going to eat this candy all at once and make yourself sick. You're allowed one piece a day, remember? That way your treats will last for a long, long time."

Maddie saw the little boy's shoulders slump. Her Jimmy had done the same thing last Halloween when Maddie had given him a similar speech, except her Jimmy had been a sad-faced clown, not a ghoul.

And not a general. Not *their* general.

Maddie raised her hand, as if she could wave off the boy's mother before she made the same mistake Maddie had made a year earlier. She saw lipstick smears on her fingers and imagined what her face must look like. It had been so long since they'd allowed her to wear cosmetics that she'd made a mess of herself without realizing it. The boy's mother would see that, and she wouldn't listen. She'd rush away with her son before Maddie could warn her.

Defeated, the boy stared down at his ghoul-face mirrored in the freshly waxed floor. His mother crumpled his trick-or-treat bag closed, and the moment slowed. Maddie saw herself reaching into her shopping cart, watched her lipstick-smeared fingers tear open a bag of Milk Duds and fling the little yellow boxes down the aisle in a slow, scattering arc. She saw the other Jimmy's mother yelling at her, the boxes bouncing, the big store windows behind the little ghoul and the iron-gray clouds boiling outside. Wind-driven leaves the color of old skin crackling against the glass.

And then Maddie was screaming at the little ghoul. "Eat your candy! Eat it now! Don't let them come after it!"

• • •

She paid for the Milk Duds, of course, and for all the other candy that she had heaped into the shopping cart. The manager didn't complain. Maddie knew that the ignorant man only wanted her out of his store.

He thought that she was crazy.

Papery leaves clawed at her ankles as she loaded the candy into the back of the station wagon. She smiled, remembering the other Jimmy, the ghoul Jimmy, gobbling Milk Duds. Other monsters had joined in the feast. Werewolves, Frankensteins, zombies. Maddie prayed that they'd all have awful stomachaches. Then they'd stay home, snuggled in front of their television sets. They wouldn't come knocking at her door tonight. They'd be safe from her Jimmy and his army.

Maddie climbed into the station wagon and slammed the door. She pretended not to notice Jimmy's friends in the back seat. It was easy, because she couldn't see them, couldn't see their black eyes. But she could feel their presence nonetheless.

Slowly, Maddie drove home. Little monsters stood on front porches and watched the gray sky, waiting intently for true darkness, when they would descend on the neighborhood in search of what Jimmy wanted to give them. Maddie glanced in the rearview mirror at the grocery bags in the back of the station wagon. Even in brown paper, even wrapped in plastic, she could smell the sugar. It was the only smell she knew anymore, and she tasted it in the back of her throat.

God, she'd been tasting it for a year now.

"*Mommy*," Jimmy had cried, "you said my candy would last. Now look at it. Look at *them*. They ruined it. I want new candy. I want it now!"

But Jimmy's whining had been a lie. Maddie knew that now. Jimmy hadn't wanted the candy. *They* had wanted it, and they'd coaxed Jimmy into getting it for them. And they scared her, even if they didn't scare her son. They'd always scared her.

Because they were everywhere. In the cupboards. Under the floor. In the garden and under the rim of the toilet seat. Maddie's house swelled with them. And when she went to work, they were there, too, watching her through the windows. Black eyes she couldn't see, staring. Through the winter cold, through the summer heat, they were always there. Studying her. Never resting.

They had her son, too. He had a million fathers now, all who cared for him more than the man who'd given him his face and his last name before disappearing beneath a wave of unpaid bills. They nested in Jimmy's room and traveled in his lunch box. Jimmy took them places and showed them things. He taught them about the town, and they told him how smart he was. They made him a general and swore to obey his commands.

Maddie pulled into the driveway and cut the engine. She sat in the quiet car, dreading the house. Inside, Jimmy's legions waited. Jimmy waited, too. But Jimmy wasn't a sad-faced clown anymore. Now he was a great leader, and he was about to attack.

The sky rumbled.

Heavy raindrops splattered the windshield.

Maddie almost smiled but caught herself just in time. She glanced in the rearview mirror and pretended to wipe at her smeared lipstick, but really she was looking for Jimmy's spies.

She wished that she could see their eyes.

• • •

Jimmy was in the basement, telling the story of the Trojan horse. They stood at attention in orderly black battalions, listening to every word. Maddie didn't know how they tolerated it. Jimmy had told them the story at least a hundred times.

"The candy's upstairs, Jimmy. I left it on the kitchen table."

Jimmy thumbed the brim of a military cap that was much too large for his head. He'd made Maddie buy the cap at an army surplus store, and it was the smallest size available. "I'll grow into it." That's what he'd said, smiling, but he wasn't smiling now.

Maddie managed a grin. "The candy, Jimmy. You remember—"

"Of course I remember! I only wish that you'd remember to call me the right thing!"

"I'm sorry, general." Maddie straightened. "The candy—the supplies—are upstairs in the mess hall."

Jimmy seemed pleased. "Very good. Bring the supplies down here, and we'll begin Operation Trojan Horse."

Maddie stared at the black sea on the cement floor, imagining a million eyes focused on her. She wouldn't walk among them. Not when she could see them clearly, not when she could feel them scuttling over her feet.

"I don't want to do that," she said.

The boy's lips twisted into a cruel smile. "Maybe you'd rather have me send a few squads to your bedroom tonight, like the last time you disobeyed a direct order. You won't get much sleep with a jillion little feet crawling all over you . . . "

"Jimmy!" She stared at him, revolted by his black insect eyes, and then turned away.

She got the candy.

Jimmy used a penknife to make tiny holes in the packages. His troops climbed inside, listening to their leader talk of conquest and the Trojan Horse and the birth of a new order. He told them the best places to hide in a house and reminded the scouts that he must be kept informed at all times concerning the progress of their mission.

And when they were all in place, why then . . .

Silently, Maddie climbed the stairs. Rainwater ran down the front window, drooling from the rusty gutters above. The street outside was slick and black. The sidewalks were empty, gray; a flotilla of fallen leaves swam in the cement gutters. Maddie watched the leaves and imagined hundreds of little monsters washed into their homes by a great wave.

She looked down and saw her son's face mirrored in the window. His reflection was smeared with rain, sad, his straight lips twisted into a dripping frown, his black eyes deep pools overflowing high cheekbones. He exhaled sharply and the image fogged over.

"They just told me," he whispered. "It took them a long time to get out of the car. I guess you think that was pretty smart, closing the vents and all."

Maddie said nothing. She stared at the foggy spot on the window. *Just a glimpse,* she thought. *Just a glimpse, but it was a clown's face I saw.*

"I never thought about this." Jimmy stared out at the rain. "They aren't coming, are they?"

"Not tonight."

Jimmy whispered, "Not tonight, troops. Operation Trojan Horse is scrubbed."

Maddie took a deep breath, hating the air, hating the stink of sugar. She thought about the little clown she'd seen mirrored in the rain-washed window, and she thought about the other Jimmy, the little ghoul, safe and dry in front of a TV set.

Tiny antennae probed Maddie's heel. Tiny feet, sticky with chocolate, marched over her toes.

The rain came harder now, in sheets. Jimmy brushed his troops away from his mother's feet. He rose and took her hand. Mirrored in the window, his lips were straight, his jaw firm.

God, it's been so long since he touched me, she thought, but she said, "Jimmy, let's watch television."

He nodded, studying the rain, not really listening.

His eyes narrowed until Maddie couldn't see them anymore.

"Next year," he said, his grip tightening.

THE FAMILY

HALLI VILLEGAS

The family's house was a rambling white-frame farmhouse set on a hill. It had attics and dormers and porches. To her it seemed like there were twenty, forty, even fifty children in the family, but the actual count was thirteen. Like a family of rabbits in a warren on the hill, instead of underneath it. Not all the children lived at home; a few were off at university or had jobs in the city, but there were still enough to make the house feel perpetually in chaos.

Adelaide was a distant cousin, spending the summer with the family ostensibly as a sort of babysitter, but the parents were never far from home. The children's parents, Ruth and Jim, spent a good deal of their time in the outbuildings that served as their business, where they spun and dyed the wool from their own sheep, and then knit it into fabulous and bizarre sweaters, hats, scarves. Their company, Au Natural, was known for its striking colour combinations and the way they had of constructing the knit pieces so that they seemed to float, or to hang just ready to fall apart. They'd even had designers from Europe and fashion editors at the farm to see the pieces and order things for collections. These fashionable people always left delighted with the modesty of Ruth and Jim, who ran Au Natural like they ran their family, with a charming negligence and trust in the ability of everyone to pull their own weight. They were known as good neighbours, unpretentious successes, and the best of the new-era hippies who combined style with eco-awareness.

• • •

Adelaide had to admit that the children, despite their absolute lack of respect for her or any other authority figure except their parents, kept themselves constructively busy. They built tree forts, put together little books with their own drawings and collages, knitted doll clothes under the trees in the orchard, rode their horses wildly, but not recklessly, and cared for their rabbits, ducks, dogs, and cats without being reminded to. They were polite to Adelaide, but sometimes cut their eyes away when she was talking to them, to indulge in a secret amusement amongst themselves. Sometimes they would stare with wide-open eyes at her, as if she were speaking a foreign language when she tried to direct them to sit down at the table for lunch, or some such thing.

Then one of them would shout, "A picnic!" And before she could say anything they would grab blankets and pillows, the older children filling a large willow basket with leftovers and bottles of lemonade. A picnic would be spread beside the brook that meandered behind the house, under a tree, the children eating, talking about books they had read or the antics of their pets, while Adelaide sat helpless a way off on a large pillow thoughtfully set by them in the shade of the tree and watched. Often their parents would stumble on these idyllic scenes and smile and the children would surround them vying for attention, and Ruth or Jim would tell Adelaide she was doing a really terrific job, they were so happy she had joined them that summer and the children would look at her with their secretive eyes to see what she would say.

If she began to say, "Oh, it wasn't . . . " they would roar and start some sort of noisy sport, or begin to tickle her until everyone was laughing, but Adelaide could feel their hard fingers scratching at her under the guise of play and she wished that the summer was over.

• • •

One of the children in particular regarded Adelaide with absolute disdain. Her name was Mary Matilda, and she was sometimes called Mattie, and sometimes Mary Mat, or just M. Adelaide, in her own fit of rebelliousness, called her nothing but Mary Matilda. The little girl was about nine or ten, with a dark fringe of hair over her forehead and her mother's blue eyes in a face still round with baby fat. But her skin, a matte white under the dark hair, and the eyebrows like a raven's feather promised beauty later on. She never spoke to Adelaide unless pressed and always refused to do whatever Adelaide said—not with any anger, but with the calm assurance of authority. She would turn on her heel and go out to the stables or the yard, leaving Adelaide speechless. Adelaide didn't dare grab hold of her arm or shoulder and call her back, because Mary Matilda was a great favourite among her siblings and they watched after one another with unusual devotion.

• • •

All the children were good riders, but Mary Matilda was the best of all. That summer she generally rode bareback. Adelaide would stand by the house while the children raced down the long winding drive overhung with trees on their horses. One of the boys, Edward, would lie along one of the long tree limbs and wave a flag for them to start. The children would gallop down the drive, coming to such an abrupt stop at the end that their horses' hindquarters, foamed with sweat, would seem to almost crumple under the effort.

Mary Matilda almost always won. The only one who could beat her was her older brother Matthew.

Adelaide complained to Ruth and Jim, worried that the children would get hurt.

Ruth laughed, and said, "The children have been riding since they were born."

"Before, honey, before they were born. You were riding horses into your third trimester." Jim laid his arm along his wife's shoulders. "Just about gave old Doc Johnston a heart attack." He looked at Adelaide and winked. "Don't worry, Adelaide, we won't hold you responsible if anyone breaks their neck on your watch." Then he leaned over and kissed Ruth in a way that made Adelaide blush.

• • •

Matthew, at sixteen, was the oldest of the boys still at home. His eyes were reddish brown and quite large. He used them a lot when begging favours for himself: to go down to the creek at night, to sleep on the porch when it got too hot in his attic bedroom, favours that Adelaide knew he only asked her permission for as a courtesy. He would have done what he wanted anyway.

Matthew would throw his long legs and arms into various attitudes of supplication as he lay down beside Adelaide on the grass and asked her what she was reading, or if she wanted lemonade, he grinned at her with white teeth, his eyes peering from beneath a flop of sandy curls. He asked Adelaide about her friends and the city where she went to school, propped his chin in his long-fingered hands while he listened, his oddly delicate wrist bones sticking well out from his too-small jersey sleeves.

Matthew was considerate of the younger children and played their games, let them sit on his knee while he read to them. On rainy days Mary Matilda and the others would fall in a heap on him while he sat on the old sofa in front of the fireplace in the living room and told stories.

Often while he was playing hide or seek with the children or croquet, he would leave the game and come and sit beside Adelaide to talk. Once he showed her a poem he had written, another time, he put an arm around her when they looked at a book Adelaide had brought from home. When she shrugged out from underneath, he had looked at her with the same wide eyes all the children had, guileless.

Adelaide did nothing to encourage his puppy crush, but admitted to herself she found it comforting amidst the general disregard the others treated her with.

• • •

The only house rule was that two hours in the afternoon, at the height of the day, was to be quiet time. The children were expected to go to their bedrooms and read, or sleep. None of the children ever disobeyed this rule and Adelaide was always surprised at how quietly and quickly they went up to their rooms and shut the doors. The house would fall silent, except for the sonorous ticking of the grandfather clock that stood in the entryway. Adelaide usually went out to the kitchen porch and sat on the porch swing, where she read, or looked out over the well-tended gardens and land of the family's farm. Sometimes Matthew would join her, bringing a drink or a book and they would talk until the first of the children came down. He didn't come all the time, not too often, because he said his parents would be disappointed if he did not set a good example for the younger children by keeping the one house rule.

When he did come, Adelaide found herself having fun for the first time that summer while she watched him goof around for her, imitating visitors to the farm, or when she caught him staring at her with his wide brown eyes, eager for her approval.

• • •

One night near the end of the summer, as the family sat at the long trestle table having dinner in the farmhouse kitchen, Ruth and Jim announced they had some news to share with them. The children, polite, attentive, listened while their parents told them that Marcus and Jane, their oldest siblings, would be coming home tomorrow. Secondly, Au Natural had just signed a contract with Devaughn, the British rock star, to provide dyed wools for the line of eco-correct clothing he and his wife had started, called Gardun, which would mean a trip to London for the whole family. Lastly, Ruth and Jim had decided to adopt a baby from Africa, a little girl whose father was dead from AIDS and whose mother could not afford to keep her any longer.

The children broke out in their own carefully controlled uproar, which always struck Adelaide as being somehow scripted.

"A baby? Can I name her?"

"I can't wait to see Marcus and show him the new pony."

"Is Jane bringing her boyfriend?"

"Are we going to be rich, Mummy?"

"Do you think we can go backstage to Devaughn's show?"

Jim and Ruth laughed and answered questions animatedly, the fingers flying as they described various things, their arms flung out in gestures, with much theatrical hugging of the children closest to them.

Matthew winked at Adelaide, and she noticed that only Mary Matilda sat silent.

• • •

The next day during the quiet hours, Adelaide sat on the porch and waited for Matthew. She assumed his wink meant he wanted to talk to her about his parents' news, that they shared a secret amusement at the whole thing. As she looked out over the garden and watched the small figure of Jim or Ruth, hard to tell from this distance, walk from shed to barn, she heard a step behind her. Adelaide turned and smiled, but it was Mary Matilda.

"Mary Matilda, it's quiet time." Adelaide felt a little tremor go through her—what if Matthew came down now and Mary Matilda saw and started a general mutiny? Matthew would never come down again during quiet time.

"I'm not sleepy." Adelaide's worry deepened. For that matter, what if Ruth or Jim came and saw Mary Matilda on the porch instead of in her room? They would know she had failed, that she had no authority over their so-well-behaved children.

"Mary Matilda, you don't have to sleep. Just lie there and read. You know the rules." Adelaide stood up.

Mary Matilda looked at her. "My necklace is caught in my hair and it pulls. Can you come upstairs and fix it."

"I can fix it here, turn around."

"No, upstairs." Mary Matilda went in the house and Adelaide followed, knowing Mary Matilda was quite capable of causing uproar if it would make Adelaide look bad. She knew in that moment that the child in front of her, with the straight dark hair almost to her waist, the firm legs of an outdoor girl burnished with tan, the childish shoulder blades that fluttered under her striped t-shirt, hated Adelaide. Adelaide knew she hated this little girl right back, she wanted to slap her for her insolence. There was no corporal punishment allowed of course, but Adelaide felt that Mary Matilda and her attitude would only benefit from a few well-placed spankings.

When they came to Mary Matilda's small room, a little cubby hole really, with roses on the wallpaper and a small bed with a chenille coverlet, an overflowing bookcase and dresser, a closet door ajar, she lost her temper.

"Mary Matilda, lie down right now."

"My hair, it's caught. It pulls. It hurts."

Adelaide wheeled Mary Matilda around quickly, lifted her hair and saw that, just as she thought, the child wasn't wearing a necklace.

"Get in that bed, or I'll tell your parents."

Mary Matilda's face closed like a flower shutting for the night and she lay down rigid on her bed. Adelaide left the room and pulled the door almost shut behind her, not closing it so she could see if Mary Matilda was going to stay in her room. Adelaide would look for Matthew and tell him what happened so that if Mary Matilda made any more trouble, maybe he could stop it. She could see the little girl motionless on the bed, her white arm rigid at her side, and after a heartbeat, Adelaide began to walk down the hall.

Then she heard whispers.

• • •

Walking back silently to Mary Matilda's door, wondering what trick the brat was playing on her now, she stopped just outside it and listened.

"Don't worry, the bitch went back downstairs. Come on, M, I'll let you win the next race."

Through the crack she saw his long limbs climbing on the narrow bed, the long-fingered hands tugging at something.

Standing in the hall frozen, her hand at her mouth, now she heard whispers all around her, heard the soft noises, like animals in their secret places, where there wasn't any light.

THE HORSE LORD

LISA TUTTLE

The double barn doors were secured by a length of stout, rust-encrusted chain, fastened with an old padlock.

Marilyn hefted the lock with one hand and tugged at the chain, which did not give. She looked up at the splintering gray wood of the doors and wondered how the children had gotten in.

Dusting red powder from her hands, Marilyn strolled around the side of the old barn. Dead leaves and dying grasses crunched beneath her sneakered feet, and she hunched her shoulders against the chill in the wind.

"There's plenty of room for horses," Kelly had said the night before at dinner. "There's a perfect barn. You can't say it would be impractical to keep a horse here." Kelly was Derek's daughter, eleven years old and mad for horses.

This barn had been used as a stable, Marilyn thought, and could be again. Why not get Kelly a horse? And why not one for herself as well? As a girl, Marilyn had ridden in Central Park. She stared down the length of the barn: for some reason, the door to each stall had been tightly boarded shut.

Marilyn realized she was shivering, then, and she finished her circuit of the barn at a trot and jogged all the way back to the house.

The house was large and solid, built of gray stone 170 years before. It seemed a mistake, a misplaced object in this cold, empty land. Who would choose to settle here, who would try to eke out a living from the ungiving, stony soil.

The old house and the eerily empty countryside formed a setting very much like one Marilyn, who wrote suspense novels, had once created for a story. She liked the reality much less than her heroine had liked the fiction.

The big kitchen was warm and felt comforting after the outside air. Marilyn leaned against the sink to catch her breath and let herself relax. But she felt tense. The house seemed unnaturally quiet with all the children away at school. Marilyn smiled wryly at herself. A week before, the children had been driving her crazy with their constant noise and demands, and now that they were safely away at school for six hours she felt uncomfortable.

From one extreme to another, thought Marilyn. The story of my life.

Only a year ago she and Derek, still newly married, were making comfortable plans to have a child—perhaps two—"someday."

Then Joan—Derek's ex-wife—had decided she'd had her fill of mothering, and almost before Marilyn had time to think about it, she'd found herself with a half-grown daughter.

And following quickly on that event—while Marilyn and Kelly were still wary of each other—Derek's widowed sister had died, leaving her four children in Derek's care.

Five children! Perhaps they wouldn't have seemed like such a herd if they had come in typical fashion, one at a time with a proper interval between.

It was the children, too, who had made living in New York City seem impossible. This house had been in Derek's family since it was built, but no one had lived in it for years. It had been used from time to time as a vacation home, but the land had nothing to recommend it to vacationers: no lakes or mountains, and the weather was unusually unpleasant. It was inhospitable country, a neglected corner of New York state.

It should have been a perfect place for writing—their friends all said so. An old house, walls soaked in history, set in a brooding, rocky landscape, beneath an unlittered sky, far from the distractions and noise of the city. But Derek could write anywhere—he carried his own atmosphere with him, a part of his ingrained discipline—and Marilyn needed the bars, restaurants, museums, shops and libraries of a large city to fill in the hours when words could not be commanded.

The silence was suddenly too much to bear. Derek wasn't typing—he might be wanting conversation. Marilyn walked down the long dark hallway—thinking to herself that this house needed more light fixtures, as well as pictures on the walls and rugs on the cold wooden floors.

Derek was sitting behind the big parson's table that was his desk, cleaning one of his sixty-seven pipes. The worn but richly patterned rug on the floor, the glow of lamplight and the books which lined the walls made this room, the library and Derek's office, seem warmer and more comfortable than the rest of the house.

"Talk?" said Marilyn, standing with her hand on the doorknob.

"Sure, come on in. I was just stuck on how to get the chief slave into bed with the mistress of the plantation without making her yet another clichéd nymphomaniac."

"Have him comfort her in time of need," Marilyn said. She closed the door on the dark hallway. "He just happens to be on hand when she gets a letter informing her of her dear brother's death. In grief, and as an affirmation of life, she and the slave tumble into bed together."

"Pretty good," Derek said. "You got a problem I can help you with?"

"Not a literary one," she said, crossing the room to his side. Derek put an arm around her. "I was just wondering if we shouldn't get a horse for Kelly. I was out to look at the barn. It's all boarded and locked up, but I'm sure we could get in and fix it up. And I don't think it could cost that much to keep a horse or two."

"Or two," he echoed. He cocked his head and gave her a sly look. "You sure you want to start using a barn with a rather grim history?"

"What do you mean?"

"Didn't I ever tell you the story of how my, hmmm, great-uncle, I guess he must have been—my great-uncle Martin, how he died?"

Marilyn shook her head, her expression suspicious.

"It's a pretty gruesome story."

"Derek . . . "

"It's true, I promise you. Well . . . remember my first slave novel?"

"How could I forget. It paid for our honeymoon."

"Remember the part where the evil boss-man who tortures his slaves and horses alike is finally killed by a crazed stallion?"

Marilyn grimaced. "Yeah. A bit much, I thought. Horses aren't carnivorous."

"I got the idea for that scene from my great-uncle Martin's death. His horses—and he kept a whole stable—went crazy, apparently. I don't know if they actually *ate* him, but he was pretty chewed up when someone found his body." Derek shifted in his chair. "Martin wasn't known to be a cruel man. He didn't abuse his horses; he loved them. He didn't love Indians, though, and the story was that the stables were built on ground sacred to the Indians, who put a curse on Martin or his horses in retaliation."

Marilyn shook her head. "Some story. When did all this happen?"

"Around 1880."

"And the barn has been boarded up ever since?"

"I guess so. I remember the few times Anna and I came out here as kids we could never find a way to get inside. We made up stories about the ghosts of the mad horses still being inside the barn. But because they were ghosts, they couldn't be held by normal walls, and roamed around at night. I can remember nights when we'd huddle together, certain we heard their ghosts neighing . . . " His eyes looked faraway. Remembering how much he had loved his sister, Marilyn felt guilty about her reluctance to take in Anna's children. After all, they were all Derek had left of his sister.

"So this place *is* haunted," she said, trying to joke. Her voice came out uneasy, however.

"Not the house," said Derek quickly. "Old Uncle Martin died in the barn."

"What about your ancestors who lived here before that? Didn't the Indian curse touch them?"

"Well . . . "

"Derek," she said warningly.

"OK. Straight dope. The first family, the first bunch of Hoskins who settled here were done in by the Indians. The parents and the two bond-servants were slaughtered, and the children were stolen. The house was burned to the ground. That wasn't this house, obviously."

"But it stands on the same ground."

"Not exactly. That house stood on the other side of the barn—though I doubt the present barn stood then—Anna and I used to play around the foundations. I found a knife there once, and she found a little tin box which held ashes and a pewter ring."

"But you never found any ghosts."

Derek looked up at her. "Do ghosts hang around once their house is burned?"

"Maybe."

"No, we never did. Those Hoskins were too far back in time to bother with, maybe. We never saw any Indian ghosts, either."

"Did you ever see the ghost horses?"

"See them?" He looked thoughtful. "I don't remember. We might have. Funny what you can forget about childhood. No matter how important it seems to you as a child . . . "

"We become different people when we grow up," Marilyn said.

Derek gazed into space a moment, then roused himself to gesture at the wall of books behind him. "If you're interested in the family history, that little set in dark green leather was written by one of my uncles and published by a vanity press. He traces the Hoskinses back to Shakespeare's time, if I recall. The longest I ever spent out here until now was one rainy summer when I was about twelve . . . it seemed like forever . . . and I read most of the books in the house, including those."

"I'd like to read them."

"Go ahead." He watched her cross the room and wheel the library ladder into position. "Why, are you thinking of writing a novel about my family?"

"No. I'm just curious to discover what perversity made your ancestor decide to build a house *here*, or all godforsaken places on the continent."

• • •

Marilyn thought of Jane Eyre as she settled into the window seat, the heavy green curtains falling back into place to shield her from the room. She glanced out at the chilly gray land and picked up the first volume.

James Hoskins won a parcel of land in upstate New York in a card game. Marilyn imagined his disappointment when he set eyes on his prize, but he was a stubborn man and frequently unlucky at cards. This land might not be much but it was his own. He brought his family and household goods to a roughly built wooden house. A more permanent house, larger and built of native rock, would be built in time.

But James Hoskins would never see it built. In a letter to relatives in Philadelphia, Hoskins related:

"The land I have won is of great value, at least to a poor, wandering remnant of Indians. Two braves came to the house yesterday, and my dear wife was nearly in tears at their tales of powerful magic and vengeful spirits inhabiting this land.

"Go, they said, for this is a great spirit, as old as the rocks, and your God cannot protect you. This land is not good for people of any race. A spirit (whose name may not be pronounced) set his mark upon this land when the earth was still new. This land is cursed—and more of the same, on and on until I lost patience with them and told them to be off before I made powerful magic with my old Betsy.

"Tho' my wife trembled, my little daughter proved fiercer than her Ma, swearing she would chop up that old pagan spirit and have it for her supper— which made me roar with laughter, and the Indians to shake their heads as they hurried away."

Marilyn wondered what had happened to that fierce little girl. Had the Indians stolen her, admiring her spirit?

She read on about the deaths of the unbelieving Hoskinses. Not only had the Indians set fire to the hasty wooden house; they had first butchered the inhabitants.

"They were disemboweled and torn apart, ripped by knives in the most hungry, savage, inhuman manner, and all for the sin of living on land sacred to a nameless spirit."

Marilyn thought of the knife Derek said he'd found as a child.

Something slapped the window. Marilyn's head jerked up, and she stared out the window. It had begun to rain, and a rising wind slung small fists of rain at the glass.

She stared out at the landscape, shrouded now by the driving rain, and wondered why this desolate rocky land should be thought of as sacred. Her mind moved vaguely to thought of books on anthropology which might help, perhaps works on Indians of the region which might tell her more. The library in Janeville wouldn't have much—she had been there, and it wasn't much more than a small room full of historical novels and geology texts—but the librarian might be able to get books from other libraries around the state, perhaps one of the university libraries . . .

She glanced at her watch, realizing that school had let out long before; the children might be waiting at the bus stop now, in this terrible weather. She pushed aside the heavy green curtains.

"Derek—"

But the room was empty. He had already gone for the children, she thought with relief. He certainly did better at this job of being a parent than she did.

Of course, Kelly was his child; he'd had years to adjust to fatherhood. She wondered if he would buy a horse for Kelly and hoped that he wouldn't.

Perhaps it was silly to be worried about ancient Indian curses and to fear that a long-ago even would be repeated, but Marilyn didn't want horses in a barn where horses had once gone mad. There were no Indians here now, and no horses. Perhaps they would be safe.

Marilyn glanced down at the books still piled beside her, thinking of looking up the section about the horses. But she recoiled uneasily from the thought. Derek had already told her the story; she could check the facts later, when she was not alone in the house.

She got up. She would go and busy herself in the kitchen, and have hot chocolate and cinnamon toast waiting for the children.

. . .

The scream still rang in her ears and vibrated through her body. Marilyn lay still, breathing shallowly, and stared at the ceiling. What had she been dreaming?

It came again, muffled by distance, but as chilling as a blade of ice. It wasn't a dream; someone, not so very far away, was screaming.

Marilyn visualized the house on a map, trying to tell herself it had been nothing, the cry of some bird. No one could be out there, miles from everything, screaming; it didn't make sense. And Derek was still sleeping, undisturbed. She thought about waking him, then repressed the thought as unworthy and sat up. She'd better check on the children, just in case it was one of them crying out of a nightmare. She did not go to the window; there would be nothing to see, she told herself.

Marilyn found Kelly out of bed, her arms wrapped around herself as she stared out the window.

"What's the matter?"

Kelly didn't shift her gaze. "I heard a horse," she said softly. "I heard it neighing. It woke me up."

"A horse?"

"It must be wild. If I can catch it and tame it, can I keep it?" Now she looked around, her eyes bright in the moonlight.

"I don't think . . . "

"Please?"

"Kelly, you were probably just dreaming."

"I heard it. It woke me up. I heard it again. I'm not imagining things," she said tightly.

"Then it was probably a horse belonging to one of the farmers around here."

"I don't think it belongs to anyone."

Marilyn was suddenly aware of how tired she was. Her body ached. She didn't want to argue with Kelly. Perhaps there had been a horse—a neigh could sound like a scream, she thought.

"Go back to bed, Kelly. You have to go to school in the morning. You can't do anything about the horse now."

"I'm going to look for it, though," Kelly said, getting back into bed. "I'm going to find it."

"Later."

As long as she was up, Marilyn thought as she stepped out into the hall, she would check on the other children, to be sure they were all sleeping.

To her surprise, they were all awake. They turned sleepy, bewildered eyes on her when she came in and murmured broken fragments of their dreams as she kissed them each in turn.

Derek woke as she climbed in beside him. "Where were you?" he asked. He twitched. "Christ, your feet are like ice!"

"Kelly was awake. She thought she heard a horse neighing."

"I told you," Derek said with sleepy smugness. "That's our ghost horse, back again."

• • •

The sky was heavy with the threat of snow; the day was cold and too still. Marilyn stood up from her typewriter in disgust and went downstairs. The house was silent except for the distant chatter of Derek's typewriter.

"Where are the kids?" she asked from the doorway.

Derek gave her a distracted look, his hands still poised over the keys. "I think they all went out to clean up the barn."

"But the barn is closed—it's locked."

"Mmmm."

Marilyn sighed and left him. She felt weighted by the chores of supervision. If only the children could go to school every day, where they would be safe and out of her jurisdiction. She thought of how easily they could be hurt or die, their small bodies broken. So many dangers, she thought, getting her coral-colored coat out of the front closet. How did people cope with the tremendous responsibility of other lives under their protection? It was an impossible task.

The children had mobilized into a small but diligent army, marching in and out of the barn with their arms full of hay, boards or tools. Marilyn looked for Kelly, who was standing just inside the big double doors and directing operations.

"The doors were chained shut," she said, confused. "How did you—"

"I cut it apart," Kelly said. "There was a hacksaw in the toolroom." She gave Marilyn a sidelong glance. "Daddy said we could take any tools from there that we needed."

Marilyn looked at her with uneasy respect, then glanced away to where the other chilren were working grimly with hands and hammers at the boards nailed across the stall doors. The darkness of the barn was relieved by a storm lantern hanging from a hook.

"Somebody really locked this place up good," Kelly said. "Do you know why?"

Marilyn hesitated, then decided. "I suppose it was boarded up so tightly because of the way one of your early relatives died here."

Kelly's face tensed with interest. "Died? How? Was he murdered?"

"Not exactly. His horses killed him. They . . . turned on him one night, nobody every knew why."

Kelly's eyes were knowing. "He must have been an awful man, then. Terribly cruel. Because horses will put up with almost anything. He must have done something so—"

"No. He wasn't supposed to have been a cruel man."

"Maybe not to *people*."

"Some people thought his death was due to an Indian curse. The land here was supposed to be sacred; they thought this was the spirit's way of taking revenge."

Kelly laughed. "That's some excuse. Look, I got to get to work, OK?"

• • •

Marilyn dreamed she went out one night to saddle a horse. The barn was filled with them, all her horses, her pride and delight. She reached up to bridle one, a sorrel gelding, and suddenly felt—with disbelief that staved off the pain—powerful teeth bite down on her arm. She heard the bone crunch, saw the flesh tear, and then the blood . . .

She looked up in horror, into eyes which were reddened and strange.

A sudden blow threw her forward, and she landed face-down in dust and straw. She could not breathe. Another horse, her gentle black mare, had kicked her in the back. She felt a wrenching, tearing pain in her leg: when finally she could move she turned her head and saw the great yellow teeth, stained with her blood, of both her horses as they fed upon her. And the other horses, all around her, were kicking at their stalls. The wood splintered and gave, and they all came to join in the feast.

• • •

The children came clattering in at lunchtime, tracking snow and mud across the redbrick floor. It had been snowing since morning, but the children were oblivious to it. They did not, as Marilyn had expected, rush out shrieking to play in the snow but went instead to the barn, as they did every weekend now. It was almost ready, they said.

Kelly slipped into her chair and powdered her soup with salt. "Wait will you see what we found," she said breathlessly.

"Animal, vegetable, or mineral?" Derek asked.

"Animal *and* mineral."

"Where did you find it?" Marilyn asked.

The smallest child spilled soup in her lap and howled. When Marilyn got back to the table, everyone was talking about the discovery in the barn: Derek curious, the children mysterious.

"But what is it?" Marilyn asked.

"It's better to see it. Come with us after we eat."

• • •

The children had worked hard. The shrouded winter light spilled into the empty space of the barn through all the open half-doors of the stalls. The rotting straw and grain was all gone, and the dirt floor had been raked and swept clear of more than an inch of fine dust. The large design stood out clearly, white and clean against the hard earth.

It was not a horse. After examining it more closely, Marilyn wondered how she could have thought it was the depiction of a wild, rearing stallion. Horses have hooves, not three-pronged talons, and they don't have such a feline snake of a tail. The proportions of the body were wrong, too, once she looked more carefully.

Derek crouched and ran his fingers along the outline of the beast. It had been done in chalk, but it was much more than just a drawing. Lines must have been deeply scored in the earth, and the narrow trough then filled with some pounded white dust.

"Chalk, I think," Derek said. "I wonder how deep it goes?" He began scratching with a forefinger at the side of the thick white line.

Kelly bent and caught his arm. "Don't ruin it."

"I'm not, honey." He looked up at Marilyn, who was still standing apart, staring at the drawing.

"It must be the Indian curse," she said. She tried to smile, but she felt an unease which she knew could build into an open dread.

"Do you suppose this is what the spirit who haunts this land is supposed to look like?" Derek asked.

"What else?"

"Odd that it should be a horse, then, instead of some animal indigenous to the area. The legend must have arisen after the white man—"

45

"But it's not a horse," Marilyn said. "Look at it."

"It's not a horse exactly, no," he agreed, standing and dusting his hands. "But it's more a horse than it is anything else."

"It's so fierce," Marilyn murmured. She looked away, into Kelly's eager face. "Well, now that you've cleaned up the barn, what are you going to do?"

"Now we're going to catch the horse."

"What horse?"

"The wild one, the one we hear at night."

"Oh . . . that. Well, it must be miles away by now. Someone else must have caught it."

Kelly shook her head. "I heard it last night. It was practically outside my window, but when I looked it was gone. I could see its hoofprints in the snow."

• • •

"You're not going out again?"

The children turned blank eyes on her, ready to become hostile, or tearful, if she were going to be difficult.

"I mean," Marilyn said apologetically, "you've been out all morning, running around. And it's still snowing. Why don't you just let your food digest for a while—get out your coloring books, or a game or something, and play in here where it's warm."

"We can't stop now," Kelly said. "We might catch the horse this afternoon."

"And if you don't, do you intend to go out every day until you do?"

"Of course," Kelly said. The other children nodded.

Marilyn's shoulders slumped as she gave in. "Well, wrap up. And don't go *too* far from the house in case it starts snowing harder. And don't stay out too long, or you'll get frostbite." The children were already moving away from her as she spoke. They live in another world, Marilyn thought, despairing.

She wondered how long this would go on. The barn project had held within it a definite end, but Marilyn could not believe the children would ever catch the horse they sought. She was not even certain there was a horse out in that snow to be caught, even though she had been awakened more than once by that shrill, distant screaming that might have been a horse neighing.

Marilyn went to Derek's office and climbed again into the hidden window seat. The heavy curtains muffled the steady beat of Derek's typewriter, and the falling snow muffled the country beyond the window. She picked up another of the small green volumes and began to read.

"Within a month of his arrival, Martin Hoskins was known in Janeville for two things. One: he intended to bring industry, wealth, and population to upstate New York, and to swell the tiny hamlet into a city. Second: A man without wife or children, Hoskins' pride, passion, and delight was in his six beautiful horses.

"Martin had heard the legend that his land was cursed, but, as he wrote to a young woman in New York City, 'The Indians were driven out of these parts long ago, and their curses with them, I'll wager. For what is an Indian curse without an Indian knife or arrow to back it?'

"It was true that the great Indian tribes had been dispersed or destroyed, but a few Indians remained: tattered and homeless in the White Man's world. Martin Hoskins met one such young brave on the road to Janeville one morning.

"'I must warn you, sir,' said the ragged but proud young savage. 'The land upon which you dwell is inhabited by a powerful spirit.'

"'I've heard that tale before,' responded Hoskins, shortly but not unkindly. 'And I don't believe in your heathen gods; I'm not afraid of 'em.'

"'This spirit is no god of ours, either. But my people have known of it, and respected it, for as many years as we have lived on this land. Think of this spirit not as a god, but as a force . . . something powerful in nature which cannot be reasoned with or fought—something like a storm.'

"'And what do you propose I do?'

"'Leave that place. Do not try to live there. The spirit cannot follow you if you leave, but it cannot be driven out, either. The spirit belongs to the land as much as the land belongs to it.'

"Martin Hoskins laughed harshly. 'You ask me to run from something I do not believe in! Well, I tell you this: I believe in storms, but I do not run from them. I'm strong; what can that spirit do to me?'

"The Indian shook his head sorrowfully. 'I cannot say what it may do. I only know that you will offend it by dwelling where it dwells, and the more you offend it, the more certainly will it destroy you. Do not try to farm there, nor keep animals. That land knows only one master and will not take to another. There is only one law, and one master on that land. You must serve it, or leave.'

"'I serve no master but myself—and my God,' Martin said."

Marilyn closed the book, not wanting to read of Martin's inevitable, and terrible, end. He kept animals, she thought idly. What if he had been a farmer? How would the spirit of the land have destroyed him then?

She looked out the window and saw with relief that the children were playing. They've finally given up their hunt, she thought, and wondered what they were playing now. Were they playing follow-the-leader? Dancing like Indians? Or horses, she thought, suddenly, watching their prancing feet and tossing heads. They were playing horses.

• • •

Marilyn woke suddenly, listening. Her body strained forward, her heart pounding too loudly, her mouth dry. She heard it again: the wild, mad cry of a horse. She had heard it before in the night, but never so close, and never so human-sounding.

Marilyn got out of bed, shivering violently as her feet touched the cold, bare floor and the chilly air raised bumps on her naked arms. She went to the window, drew aside the curtains, and looked out.

The night was still and clear as an engraving. The moon lacked only a sliver more for fullness and shone out of a cloudless, star-filled sky. A group of small figures danced upon the snowy ground, jerking and prancing and kicking up a spray of snow. Now and again one of them would let out a shrill cry: half a horse's neigh, half a human wail. Marilyn felt her hairs rise as she recognized the puppetlike dancers below: the children.

She was tempted to let the curtains fall back and return to bed—to say nothing, to do nothing, to act as if nothing unusual had happened. But these were *her* children now, and she wasn't allowed that sort of irresponsibility.

The window groaned as she forced it open, and at the faint sound the children stopped their dance. As one, they turned and looked up at Marilyn.

The breath stopped in her throat as she stared down at their upturned faces. Everything was very still, as if that moment had been frozen within a block of ice. Marilyn could not speak; she could not think of what to say.

She withdrew back into the room, letting the curtains fall back before the open window, and she ran to the bed.

"Derek," she said, catching hold of him. "Derek, wake up." She could not stop her trembling.

His eyes moved behind their lids.

"Derek," she said urgently.

Now they opened and, fogged with sleep, looked at her.

"What is it, love?" He must have seen the fear in her face, for he pushed himself up on his elbows. "Did you have a bad dream?"

"Not a dream, no. Derek, your Uncle Martin—he could have lived here if he hadn't been a master himself. If he hadn't kept horses. The horses turned on him because they had found another master."

"What are you talking about?"

"The spirit that lives in this land," she said. She was not trembling, now. Perspiration beaded her forehead. "It uses the . . . the servants, or whatever you want to call them . . . it can't abide anyone else ruling here. If we . . . "

"You've been dreaming, sweetheart." He tried to pull her down beside him, but she shook him off. She could hear them on the stairs.

"Is our door locked?" she suddenly demanded.

"Yes, I think so." Derek frowned. "Did you hear something? I thought . . . "

"Children are a bit like animals, don't you think? At least, people treat them as if they were—adults, I mean. I suppose children must . . . "

"I *do* hear something. I'd better go—"

"Derek— No—"

The doorknob rattled, and there was a great pounding at the door.

"Who is that?" Derek said loudly.

"The children," Marilyn whispered.

The door splintered and gave way before Derek reached it, and the children burst through. There were so many of them, Marilyn thought, as she waited on the bed. And all she could seem to see was their strong, square teeth.

MY NAME IS LEEJUN
JOHN SCHOFFSTALL

I heard dad swearing as his boots stamped up the steps. I scooted under my bed and hid among the socks and the dust balls, like a cockroach would. I'm good at hiding. You can learn a lot from a cockroach.

The screen door slammed. "Janice!"

Mom and I are always done with lessons by the time dad gets home, because he doesn't like to wait for supper. Mom's voice was from far away. That means she's in their bedroom, up at other end of the trailer.

"Dinner's in the oven, hon! It's a pot roast."

"Janice, you still on the computer? Have you even been outside today?"

"What's wrong, baby?"

"I said, look outside. I'm calling the county. They think they can ignore us, just 'cause it's a goddamned trailer park. You better believe they spray in Woodbridge and Chestnut Run. I hear those people on the radio news complaining when they don't."

The screen door latch clicked again. Mom's voice said, "What's wrong, baby? It's a beautiful day outside."

"Janice, will you look? Dead birds all over the place. Dead crow in the car-port, another one on the walk, one on the lawn. You know what that means? It means West Nile. The county needs to spray. Folks will start turning up sick any day." The phone slammed down. "Answering machine, and it's not even five o'clock. I'll call 'em tomorrow."

Mom's voice, fainter, from outside. "Baby, it was probably just a cat. Don't call the county, they'll send a sheriff's deputy around again, the way they did about the Davisons' dog. He scared Bobby. Bobby had nightmares for weeks."

"Janice," dad yelled, "for chrissakes, don't touch that bird, you don't know what it's got. It's not a cat doing it. A cat wouldn't kill three birds and not eat any."

"Please don't call the county," mom said. "I'll just keep Bobby inside. We'll keep the screen door closed. We'll keep screens on the windows all the time. Nobody will get the West Nile. Don't call the county. Please?"

The screen door opened and closed again, and I heard mom walk across the living room. She came into my room. I saw her shoes walk across the floor. "Bobby? Bobby, where are you? Rick, he's hiding again. You scared him with all that yelling. I wish you wouldn't do that."

• • •

We had pot roast for dinner. I like pot roast. The Davisons' dog Rowfy wants to stick his whole head in, and go *glosp, glosp, glosp*, and come up wagging his tail. When I did that with pot roast once, mom laughed until she peed her pants, but dad was really mad. Since then I ignore Rowfy and just eat with a knife and fork like mom and dad want me to.

"What did you learn today, Bobby?" dad asked, the way he does every night at supper.

"I read about the Ant and the Grasshopper," I said.

"Bugs," dad said. "Janice, don't encourage him to eat bugs again."

"It's just a story," mom said. "It has a moral. Tell your dad about it, Bobby."

"Well," I said, "the ant spent all summer storing food and stuff for the winter, but the grasshopper just hopped around. Then the grasshopper asked the ant for food, but the ant said he should dance instead."

"Pretty mean ant," dad said. He dished more pot roast onto my plate.

"What's the moral?" mom said.

"Um," I said. "I think . . . it's to gets lots of stuff and save it, so it's still there when you need it."

"Good!" Mom gave me a kiss on the cheek. "Every story has a moral that helps you learn right from wrong. Right?"

"Right!" I said.

"Did you read that story yourself, or did your mom read it for you?" dad asked.

"He read some of it himself," mom said. "He's starting to write, too. He can write his name. He wrote, 'I am Bobby' today. He got most of the letters right. He's a quick learner, Rick. He takes after you."

Dad pointed his finger at me. "And I don't eat bugs. Remember that."

"You don't need to keep reminding him," mom said. "He only ate one bug."

"It was more than one."

"And he doesn't do it anymore."

Dad forked another piece of pot roast into his mouth and chewed on it. "Do we really need to home-school him?"

Mom nodded. "Honey, they'd put him in the Beech Valley district. You know those schools aren't very good."

Dad sighed. He said, "I wish you didn't have to stay home all day. It would help a lot if you could cashier at McDonald's or the dollar store or something. But with Bobby, I don't know." He stared at me with that way he has. "There might be bugs in school. He might eat more bugs. Or something else."

"Rick! He doesn't."

"How about it, son?" dad asked. "Are you going to eat bugs, ever again?"

I shook my head.

I don't eat bugs any more. Really I don't. It was a mistake to eat bugs. You can learn everything a bug knows without eating it.

• • •

I stayed awake after they sent me to bed. When there was no more TV noise, I snuck out of my bedroom.

The living room was dark except for stripes of moonlight through the blinds. I walked very slowly towards the door, keeping near the walls. I stayed away from the center of the room. That's so you don't make noise from the floor squeaking, especially in house trailers like this that ain't built for shit. That's what Howie Lackmann says, and Howie's a burglar, so he knows. You can learn a lot from a burglar.

I opened the front door and went down the steps, keeping near the edges again. I looked all over in the moonlight, but I couldn't see any dead birds.

They keep the trash cans under the carport, next to where dad parks his pickup. I took the lid off one trash can, and there they were: three big black crows. Crows had been hanging around in the pine trees for a couple of days. They're almost tame. The day before yesterday I sat on the steps and fed them pieces of bread. One came so close I could nearly touch him, but not quite. Mom came out and told me not to touch them. She made me go back in the house.

I reached down and touched the crow lying on top of the trash. The feathers on its tummy were soft and nice to feel, but its body was stiff and cold. The crow part was gone. You can't learn anything from a dead crow.

• • •

Mom made me stay inside all the next day. In the morning I learned how to add numbers with two places. It's harder, because you have to carry. While mom was eating lunch, I found a mosquito that got in even though we have window screens. I caught it in my hands. There's not much you can learn from a mosquito, though.

"What have you got in your hands?" Mom asked. "Let me see."

"Mosquito."

"Let it go."

I opened my hands, and let the mosquito fall into the wastebasket.

Mom didn't let me out of the house all day, but through the screen door I saw another dead crow in the yard, and one more across the drive in the Davisons' yard.

In the afternoon a truck stopped out front and a man in a brown uniform knocked at the door. Mom let him in, and they talked for a while. He left some papers on the kitchen table. After he was gone, Mom sat at the kitchen table and cried for a while.

When dad got home, he picked up the papers on the table. He said, "What's this?" He shuffled through them. "This is stuff about West Nile."

"A man from Public Health came," mom said.

"I thought you didn't want to call the county," dad said.

"Maybe someone else called," mom said. Dad shrugged.

A week later the sheriff's deputies came.

• • •

Some of them wore uniforms, and some were in yellow coveralls. It was after dinner, while mom and dad were watching TV. The deputies crowded into the trailer. I stood in a corner by mom and held onto her hand.

The deputies said it was about the dead birds. They took all the cleaning stuff from under the counters and put it in plastic tubs and carried it away. They took everything out of the medicine cabinets in the bathrooms. They took the stuff dad uses to work on the pick-up. They opened all the drawers everywhere, and turned over all the furniture, even my bed and dresser. Rowfy is barking, and Howie the burglar is very nervous. He hates the fucking cops. He says, get the fuck out until LEO is out of the fucking house. He says he knows a girl in Conway we can crash with.

Mom kept saying, "I don't believe this is happening. I don't believe this is happening."

"Mom," I said. "Mom." I tugged on her hand.

"What, Bobby?"

"We should get the fuck out until LEO is out of the fucking house," I said. "A girl named Connie . . . her car crashed . . . I think."

She went, "Sh-sh-shhhhh," and put her fingers over my mouth. She hugged me to her. Then she began to sob again. A couple of the deputies were looking at us.

"What does this have to with West Nile?" dad said. "We keep screens up. The house isn't infected or anything."

"It's not West Nile," one of the deputies said. "West Nile didn't kill the crows. The state lab says they were poisoned."

Dad got a look on his face like someone ran over his dog. "Poisoned . . . " He stared at the deputies carting stuff away. "Tom," he said to one of the deputies. "You know us. We don't cause trouble. You think we poisoned a bunch of birds? C'mon."

Tom shrugged. "Rick, it's not up to me. You can talk to the detective if you want. You know we've gotten calls to your house before. Like that thing with the Davisons' dog."

"A dead dog, for chrissakes. They investigated it, it wasn't poisoned. Just a dead dog. How's that our fault?"

"And the guy from Conway with a warrant on him. When a dead burglar turns up in your kid's bedroom, it makes people spit out their chew."

"It was a heart attack," dad said. "He was on cocaine, the coroner said. He had already hit two other places, he just happens to have his goddamn heart attack in my goddamn house."

"I know, I know," Tom the deputy said, "but that kind of stuff draws attention to you, so the next time something happens in the neighborhood—"

A deputy came out of mom and dad's bedroom. "Who uses the computer in here?" he asked.

Mom and dad looked at each other. Finally, mom said, "I do. Mostly."

"Someone's been doing searches on how to poison birds," the deputy said.

Mom put her arms around me and hugged me hard. "God forgive me," she said. She looked down at me. "I was only trying to help you."

Dad said, "Janice. What the hell."

Tom the deputy said, "Ms. Douglas, I'm going to ask you to go down to the office with me and give a statement."

Mom shook her head rapidly back and forth. "No, no . . . "

Another deputy in a black leather jacket stepped up beside her and took her arm. Tom said, "Things will go better for everyone if you cooperate, Ms. Douglas."

"Are you arresting me?" Mom asked.

Howie the burglar is frantic. Shit's goin' down, he says, fuckin' hogs are gonna to put the old lady away. Call a bail bondsmen, he says, I got a name for you in Little Rock. I didn't know what that meant. Howie isn't helping, Rowfy is just barking his head off so I couldn't think, the cockroaches and silverfish and Penny's goldfish and the crayfish from the creek are telling me to scuttle under the bed, dig under a rock, swim, hide, but I knew I shouldn't do that. I had to stay and save mom and dad.

The sheriff's deputies knew what to do. They were in charge. They were the ones I needed to learn from.

I squeezed out of mom's arms. I put my hands on the deputy who was holding her. I opened him up like a book and read him in, until everything he knew was inside me. Like when I read the Ant and the Grasshopper.

I learned everything I could from him until there wasn't any more of him left.

• • •

The empty part of the deputy fell down with a bang that shook the floor. Mom gasped, "Bobby, no!" Everyone was yelling.

"Jake! Jake!"

"What the hell happened?"

"Is he breathing?"

"No pulse. Start CPR."

"Christ almighty."

"Ed, call for EMS."

One man started kissing what used to be Jake, and another was doing push-ups on its chest.

Goddamn, Jake says. Goddamn. What is this? I never been like this before.

"Did anyone hear a shot?" one of the deputies said.

"Uh-uh."

"No shot."

"Anyone know how to reach Jake's wife?"

"It's like that death from before, the guy with the warrant on him."

"You don't think the suspect poisoned him? Hey, nobody ate anything, did they? Nothing off the counter, or anything? Since we been here?"

Tom yelled, "Cut the chatter. Everybody out, except the CPR. Secure the family in a vehicle."

A deputy took us outside. Mom and dad and I sat in the back of a police car. Jake wants to fight with Howie, he doesn't like him at all. I had to keep them apart. I said to Jake, tell me how to help mom and dad. Jake says I should do whatever the deputies wanted. He says that mom is in trouble, and there isn't anything I can do about it right now. He says that dad and I will probably be released later.

I looked out the window. The Dixons and the Davisons were in their yards, watching. I waved to Peggy Davison, but I don't think she saw me. Or maybe she did, and still didn't wave back. She's been scared of me since Rowfy.

I heard a siren coming. An ambulance pulled up. Men in orange clothing got out and went into our trailer. They had a metal table with cross legs that rolled on squeaky wheels.

Mom hugged me. "Bobby," she said, "I want you to know that I love you, baby. I saw you with the crows, and I was afraid you'd touch them, and they'd die like Rowfy. And I was afraid people would see, and they'd find out about you ... and you'd be ... they'd hurt you ... you got to understand, baby, I was trying to help you." She started crying instead of talking.

It's not safe to talk here, Jake said. The car is wired. There's a voice-activated digital recorder.

"It's not safe to talk here," I said to mom. "The car is wired. There's a voice, something-something corduroy."

Mom stared at me, then started crying even harder. She hugged me some more. Dad just looked confused.

A sheriff's deputy got in the car, and we drove to a place that Jake says is the Sheriff's Office. The deputies took mom away. Dad and I sat around on plastic chairs for a long time. They gave me a sandwich. Dad said he wasn't hungry. A sheriff's deputy took dad and me into a little room and asked a lot of questions. Dad said he wanted a lawyer. Howie says, don't say nothin' till they get you a public defender. Jake says, don't lie, but don't volunteer anything. Don't say anything about killing people.

I don't kill people, I told him. They're all right here.

• • •

I didn't see mom again that night. Dad said she had to stay at the Sheriff's Office. One of the deputies drove us home.

Dad said I could sleep in the bed with him. I said I'd be okay in my own room. Dad is scary when he yells. He seemed all nervous tonight, and I thought maybe he'd yell. I went in my room, put on my pajamas, and scuttled under the bed like I learned from the cockroaches. People are afraid of the dark, but cockroaches know that dark places are safest.

I couldn't get to sleep for a long time because Howie and Jake started fighting again. Jake really doesn't like Howie. I finally told Jake that he had to shut up, or I'd get rid of him.

You should get rid of that stupid crackhead, instead, Jake says. He's nothing but trouble.

No, I say to him, Howie has taught me lots of neat stuff. You have to be nice to him.

JOHN SCHOFFSTALL

Jake isn't listening, so I pick one of the silverfish from long ago, from when I first discovered how to read things. I've learned all I can from silverfish, and I didn't need it any more. Getting rid of the silverfish is like rubbing it between my hands, until there is nothing left but silvery dust. I hold up my palms and blow the dust away. Where the silverfish had been, there's nothing. Where its whispery voice had been, there's only silence.

You have to be nice, I say, or that's what I'll do to you.

Jake doesn't say anything after that.

I missed mom. I wanted her back.

I curled up and put my thumb in my mouth, and went to sleep.

• • •

Dad stayed home with me for a few days, but then he had to go to work, and big girls came over to watch me. All of them seemed scared, at least at first.

"What's wrong?" I asked one girl.

"What do you think?" she said. "Two people have *died* in this house. Just dropped dead for no reason."

Most of the girls just watched TV all the time and played with their hair. One of them helped me read books, but it wasn't like with mom.

It took forever before I saw mom again. We had to drive for hours and hours in the pick-up. Mom wasn't in the Sheriff's Office any more, she was in a place called Hawkins. Dad had to drive through Little Rock to get there. Little Rock has tall buildings. I saw a jet plane take off from the airport.

Hawkins had a high wire fence around it, and lots of buildings inside. There was a big gate, but we didn't drive through it. Dad parked the pickup, and we went in through a door beside the gate. Dad had to talk to policemen who let us in. They're not police, Jake says, they're prison guards. Screws, says Howie. I hate screws. The guards searched us with their hands, and made us walk through scanner to look for guns. That's what Jake says it was. I ask Howie, and he says yeah. I like it when they agree. Sometimes they don't, and then I have to decide.

Inside it smelled like floor wax. A lady guard walked in front of us. She smelled nice. Look at that butt, says Howie.

Just agree to everything they want, Jake says. Don't do anything funny or they won't let you see mom.

This here sketches me out, Howie says. I don't never want to be in a jailhouse again.

The lady guard took dad and me into a little room with chairs. Then she brought mom in through another door in the back. Mom had on a gray dress I hadn't seen her wear before. Mom picked me up and hugged me and kissed me, then she hugged and kissed dad.

Mom and dad talked a long time, about things like bail and probation and getting the hearing moved up. Jake tries to explain to me. It's hard to understand. Howie says, it don't matter, it's always a set-up, they're always out to screw you over.

Mom asked how I'm doing. I told her about the girls who come over.

"Are they nice to you?"

"They're okay, I guess."

"Is he learning anything, Rick?" Mom asked.

Dad shrugged. "I tell them to read to him."

"They don't do it as good as you do," I said.

"Oh, baby," mom said.

"I'm going to have to put him in public school in the fall," dad said. "The lawyer says you're not going to be out by then, even if the plea bargain goes through."

"You couldn't get bail money?"

"I called both families. They ask why, and when they hear it's about poisoning birds, no one wants to help. Why'd you do it, Janice? You're so impulsive."

"I won't have him in public school," mom said. Mom never gets angry, but her voice was closer to being angry than I had ever heard before. "Not where there's a lot of people and I can't watch over him. Something might happen."

"Like what? Like he might eat another bug?"

"You know."

Dad looked away.

"You *know*, Rick. Like what happened with the deputy. If Bobby does it again, they'll hurt him. He doesn't know any better. He can't help himself. Not unless I'm there to stop him."

The door behind her opened. The lady guard looked in. "Time's up, Ms. Douglas."

"Rick, promise me you won't put him in public school."

Dad's voice was like a trapped bug that can't escape. "Babe, I can't keep him home, the county will come and take him."

"*Promise me.*"

"Ms. Douglas, we have to go. Right now."

"Okay, okay, I promise," dad said.

"You're lying to me," mom said.

"Janice—"

"Ms. Douglas, time's up," the lady guard said, "You have to return to your cell now, or I will call another guard."

Mom grabbed my hands and squeezed them. Her fingers were dry, and cold. She stared in my eyes, and I couldn't look away. "Bobby, they're trying to take me away from you. Do you want me to be with you, and help you, all the time, forever and ever?"

Of course I did.

"Then take me with you now."

"Janice!" dad yelled. "What the hell are you doing?"

The guard was talking on her walkie-talkie. "Assistance in Visit 4 for an unruly prisoner."

"But . . . " I said. "But . . . "

"This is the only way I can be with you," Mom said. "Please. Like you did with Rowfy and the burglar." Dad was trying to pull her away from me.

Mom's hands tightened on my fingers so much that it hurt. "Please, Bobby. So we can be together forever."

So I opened mom up like a book, and read every last bit of her. Because she wanted me to.

• • •

The thing that used to be mom fell down, half over a chair. I think its head hit something. Blood came out. Everyone was yelling. Dad started yelling at what was left of mom, and shaking it. The lady guard was yelling for medical on her walkie-talkie. Oh christ, oh christ, oh christ, Howie says. Don't do anything crazy, Jake says, there'll be an investigation, but I think we can wiggle our way out.

It's okay, baby, mom says. I'm here. Everything's okay, now.

But everything wasn't okay. Dad screamed, "Janice! Janice! *Janice!*" Then he stopped and looked at me. His mouth hung open, and he was panting. "You crazy little fucker," he yelled, "put her back!" He grabbed me by the shirt and slapped my face, hard. "Put her back, goddamn you!" He slapped me again. Hot pain burned my face. "Give me Janice back!"

The lady guard said, "Mister, don't do that." She tried to hold his arm back. "Don't hurt the little boy." Dad shook her off. He kept hitting me and yelling. I started to cry. Every slap hurt worse and worse.

All of a sudden, I knew how to stop it.

No! says mom. Bobby, no, please!

But it hurt bad. It had to stop. It had to.

I touched dad, opened him up, and read every bit of him into me. What was left of him fell on the floor.

What's this, dad says. What happened? Howie keeps saying, Oh christ, oh christ, oh christ. Mom says, oh, baby, I'm so sorry.

The lady guard looked back and forth at the empty parts of mom and dad. "What on earth," she said. She said into her walkie-talkie, "Medical! Where are you? We've got two down in Visit 4." She offered me her hand. "Little boy, we have to get out while the medics help your parents. Okay?"

"I want to go home," I said. "I don't like it here." My face still hurt, and everything was blurry with tears. I wiped my nose with my hand.

"I know, honey, but right now we have to—"

"I want to go home!"

"We need to let the medics work." She put her arm around me and hoisted me up on her hip.

I knew she wasn't going to take me home. So I opened her up, and read her in.

Her name is Kaysha.

• • •

The empty part of her fell to the floor. I fell, too. I got some bumps, but I was okay.

I want to go home, I say to them all. I tell Kaysha to show me the way out. She's still all confused and afraid. She doesn't want to talk.

Better talk, lady, Howie says, or he'll blow you out like a match. I seen him done it.

Mom says, please help us, Miss Kaysha.

Finally Kaysha says, the staff won't let an unaccompanied child be in the building by himself, and they won't let us out the sally port. She says, we're in the soup.

I'm going home, I say. If anyone tries to stop me, I'll read them in, and the empty part will fall down.

Fucking hell, Howie says. We're a goddamn machine of destruction. Let's go fuck 'em up.

No, baby, please, mom says.

Jake says, It won't work. They'll figure it out. They'll shoot us. We'll die.

I give up, dad says. I just give up. This is all crap.

How about this, Jake says. Tell them Kaysha smelled carbon monoxide fumes.

I practiced the words a couple of times.

Men and women in uniforms tried to crowd in the back door of the room. They had one of those rolling metal tables. Stretcher, says Kaysha. "Holy christ, what happened here," one of the men said.

"She said it smelled like carbon monoxide fumes," I said. I pointed to the empty part that used to be Kaysha. "Before she fell down."

The men and women were yelling into their walkie-talkies. "Get out that door, kid," the woman said.

I ran into the hall. Lights were going around and flashing on the ceiling. A fire alarm bell started clanging. It rang so loud it hurt my ears.

Do what they tell you, mom says. Don't make anyone else fall down.

The guards are going to take you outside, Jake says. Go along with them.

Just like Jake says, another lady guard took my hand, and we went down the hall and through the metal scanner and the door to the outside. It was bright sunshine. Men in suits and uniforms and pretty women walked around and talked and and pointed at the building we were just in. People were still hurrying out of the door.

I heard sirens. Two ambulances and a police car pulled up outside the big gate over the road. The gate swung up.

Now run for it, Jake says. This is it! Howie says. Run like hell!

I yanked my hand free from the lady guard, and ran past the ambulances. I heard people shouting behind, but I kept on running. I ran as fast as I could across the parking lot, and across the highway. A car honked at me. There was a field on the other side of the highway. I ran through the high corn. The edges of the leaves cut my arms and my face as I ran. At the end of the field there were woods, and I ran into them.

• • •

When I came to a creek, Howie showed me how to take off my shoes and socks and wade downstream to confuse the dogs. The water was cold, and the stones were hard and slippery. After a long time the stream came to a culvert. I got out on the other side, put my shoes back on, and climbed up to the road above the culvert. A couple of cars came by before one stopped, and the man gave me a ride.

Tell him to stop, Howie says, eat him up, get his money.

Don't do that, mom says, it isn't right.

Nothing's right or wrong any more, dad says. The world's gone crazy, he says.

Don't do it, Jake says, someone will find him soon, it'll be a point the police can track you from.

I know a place we can go, Howie says. Jake and Howie and mom talk a long time. Yeah, Jake says finally, it'll do. Howie tells me where to have the man let me out of the car.

In the woods by the road there was a path. After walking for a long time, I found some people under a railroad bridge. Most were grown-up men, but there were also some boys older than me. They were really dirty. "Hey, who's the baby," they said. "What'cha doing, out here without your mommy?" They were cooking in a can hanging over fire. I was really hungry, and they gave me some beans and syrup. They asked me where I came from. I told them about dad, and mom, and the birds, and the prison. "Crazy shit," one boy said. After they finished eating, they were drinking. They gave me some in a plastic coffee cup, but it burned my mouth and my nose and I didn't like it. One boy was smoking from a glass straw. He said I should try some.

Howie and Jake say it'll probably be safe here for a few days, but then I'll have to move on.

I don't know what to do about dad. He won't help. He won't talk to me, or the others. He just complains. I told him I might get rid of him. Mom begged me not to, so I didn't. For now.

My face still hurts. I wish dad hadn't hit me.

Mom, Howie, Jake, Kaysha, they all help me plan what to do next. It'll be tough at first, everyone says, because people don't like to see a kid running around without parents.

When I get older, they say, things will be easier. There are people I can learn a lot from. People in banks. People in government. Scientists. Generals. I could read in the smartest people in the world. I could have them all inside me.

But meanwhile, we have to be careful, they say. We have to keep moving. We have to keep out of sight. We have to hide.

That's okay. I'm good at hiding. You can learn a lot from a cockroach.

PRINCESS OF THE NIGHT
MICHAEL KELLY

Warren heard it, quite plainly, outside his front door; a faint stirring, a sigh, a melancholy moan. He waited . . . waited . . . but no knock came. Then another sound, like shuffling feet.

Warren groaned, dropped the magazine, and lifted his tired bones from the rocker. He shuffled over to the door and pulled it open.

"Trick or treat."

Warren looked down, puzzled. The first thing he noticed about her was the scar: a livid line that zigzagged from the corner of her mouth to her earlobe. In the wan light of the full moon it pulsed, as if alive. She was a wee pale thing with fine blond hair and cool blue eyes that gazed flatly at him. Couldn't have been more than nine or ten years old, Warren thought. She was dressed in a purple robe, trimmed in gold. A tiara sat on her head. A little princess. She clutched an orange plastic pumpkin that grinned blackly.

Dead leaves skittered on the porch. The wind rushed in, carrying a touch of frost. It smelled like earth and worms and rain. It snatched at his sweater, the wind. It swirled around him, whispering secrets only he knew.

Warren breathed deeply. Burning leaves and peppermint rain. Autumn! A half-smile creased his face. Once—long, long ago—he'd been an autumn person. Once, long ago, he'd been a man who'd smiled.

"*Trick or treat.*" Her voice was an autumn voice, a voice of fog and rain and green mystery. And Warren hadn't seen her mouth move.

Warren sighed. He hadn't left the porch light on, hadn't left a Jack-O-Lantern in the window. Didn't they know he never celebrated Halloween? He hadn't celebrated Halloween in a very long time, not since . . . since . . . Why were they knocking at his door? Then he remembered that there hadn't actually been a knock. And another memory came bubbling to the surface, one that had lain hidden like a dark stone in a cool riverbed: wet and foggy night; a sudden blur of blond hair; hiss of tires: a faint *thump*; and Warren—before driving away—watching through the rain-blurred window as a plastic pumpkin bumped and rolled down the dark, almost empty street.

"*Trick or treat.*" Her voice was an autumn voice—dead leaves, rich earth, and green menace.

Warren shuddered, took a step back. Though her mouth didn't move, Warren heard a sigh, a miserable moan. And as the little princess took a slow step forward, one dim thought entered Warren's head: It wasn't Halloween.

DUCK HUNT

JOE R. LANSDALE

There were three hunters and three dogs. The hunters had shiny shotguns, warm clothes, and plenty of ammo. The dogs were each covered in big, blue spots and were sleek and glossy and ready to run. No duck was safe.

The hunters were Clyde Barrow, James Clover, and little Freddie Clover, who was only fifteen and very excited to be asked along. However, Freddie did not really want to see a duck, let alone shoot one. He had never killed anything but a sparrow with his BB gun and that had made him sick. But he was nine then. Now he was ready to be a man. His father told him so.

With this hunt he felt he had become part of a secret organization. One that smelled of tobacco smoke and whiskey breath; sounded of swear words, talk about how good certain women were, the range and velocity of rifles and shotguns, the edges of hunting knives, the best caps and earflaps for winter hunting.

In Mud Creek the hunt made the man.

Since Freddie was nine he had watched with more than casual interest, how when a boy turned fifteen in Mud Creek, he would be invited to the Hunting Club for a talk with the men. Next step was a hunt, and when the boy returned he was a boy no longer. He talked deep, walked sure, had whiskers bristling on his chin, and could take up with the assurance of not being laughed at, cussing, smoking, and watching women's butts as a matter of course.

Freddie wanted to be a man too. He had pimples, no pubic hair to speak of (he always showered quickly at school to escape derisive remarks about the size of his equipment and the thickness of his foliage), scrawny legs, and little, gray, watery eyes that looked like ugly planets spinning in white space.

And truth was, Freddie preferred a book to a gun.

But came the day when Freddie turned fifteen and his father came home from the Club, smoke and whiskey smell clinging to him like a hungry tick, his face slightly dark with beard and tired-looking from all-night poker.

He came into Freddie's room, marched over to the bed where Freddie was reading *Thor,* clutched the comic from his son's hands, sent it fluttering across the room with a rainbow of comic panels.

"Nose out of a book," his father said. "Time to join the Club."

Freddie went to the Club, heard the men talk ducks, guns, the way the smoke and blood smelled on cool morning breezes. They told him the kill was the measure of a man. They showed him heads on the wall. They told him to go home with his father and come back tomorrow bright and early, ready for his first hunt.

His father took Freddie downtown and bought him a flannel shirt (black and red), a thick jacket (fleece lined), a cap (with earflaps), and boots (water-proof). He took Freddie home and took a shotgun down from the rack, gave him a box of ammo, walked him out back to the firing range, and made him practice while he told his son about hunts and the war and about how men and ducks died much the same.

Next morning before the sun was up, Freddie and his father had breakfast. Freddie's mother did not eat with them. Freddie did not ask why. They met Clyde over at the Club and rode in his jeep down dirt roads, clay roads and trails, through brush and briars until they came to a mass of reeds and cattails that grew thick and tall as Japanese bamboo.

They got out and walked. As they walked, pushing aside the reeds and cattails, the ground beneath their feet turned marshy. The dogs ran ahead.

When the sun was two hours up, they came to a bit of a clearing in the reeds, and beyond them Freddie could see the break-your-heart blue of a shiny lake. Above the lake, coasting down, he saw a duck. He watched it sail out of sight.

"Well, boy?" Freddie's father said.

"It's beautiful," Freddie said.

"Beautiful, hell, are you ready?"

"Yes, sir."

On they walked, the dogs way ahead now, and finally they stood within ten feet of the lake. Freddie was about to squat down into hiding as he had heard of others doing, when a flock of ducks burst up from a mass of reeds in the lake and Freddie, fighting off the sinking feeling in his stomach, tracked them with the barrel of the shotgun, knowing what he must do to be a man.

His father's hand clamped over the barrel and pushed it down. "Not yet," he said.

"Huh?" said Freddie.

"It's not the ducks that do it," Clyde said.

Freddie watched as Clyde and his father turned their heads to the right, to where the dogs were pointing noses, forward, paws upraised—to a thatch of underbrush. Clyde and his father made quick commands to the dogs to stay, then they led Freddie into the brush, through a twisting maze of briars and out into a clearing where all the members of the Hunting Club were waiting.

In the center of the clearing was a gigantic duck decoy. It looked ancient and there were symbols carved all over it. Freddie could not tell if it were made of clay, iron, or wood. The back of it was scooped out, gravy bowl-like, and there was a pole in the center of the indention; tied to the pole was a skinny man. His head had been caked over with red mud and there were duck feathers sticking in it, making it look like some kind of funny cap. There was a ridiculous, wooden duck bill held to his head by thick elastic straps. Stuck to his butt was a duster of duck feathers. There was a sign around his neck that read DUCK.

The man's eyes were wide with fright and he was trying to say or scream something, but the bill had been fastened in such a way he couldn't make any more than a mumble.

Freddie felt his father's hand on his shoulder. "Do it," he said. "He ain't nobody to anybody we know. Be a man."

"Do it! Do it! Do it!" came the cry from the Hunting Club.

Freddie felt the cold air turn into a hard ball in his throat. His scrawny legs shook. He looked at his father and the Hunting Club. They all looked tough, hard, and masculine.

"Want to be a titty baby all your life?" his father said.

That put steel in Freddie's bones. He cleared his eyes with the back of his sleeve and steadied the barrel on the derelict's duck's head.

"Do it!" came the cry. "Do it! Do it! Do it!"

At that instant he pulled the trigger. A cheer went up from the Hunting Club, and out of the clear, cold sky, a dark blue norther blew in and with it came a flock of ducks. The ducks lit on the great idol and on the derelict. Some of them dipped their bills in the derelict's wetness.

When the decoy and the derelict were covered in ducks, all of the Hunting Club lifted their guns and began to fire.

The air became full of smoke, pellets, blood, and floating feathers.

When the gunfire died down and the ducks died out, the Hunting Club went forward and bent over the decoy, did what they had to do. Their smiles were red when they lifted their heads. They wiped their mouths gruffly on the backs of their sleeves and gathered ducks into hunting bags until they bulged. There were still many carcasses lying about.

Fred's father gave him a cigarette. Clyde lit it.

"Good shooting, son," Fred's father said and clapped him manfully on the back.

"Yeah," said Fred, scratching his crotch, "got that sonofabitch right between the eyes, pretty as a picture."

They all laughed.

The sky went lighter, and the blue norther that was rustling the reeds and whipping feathers about blew up and out and away in an instant. As the men walked away from there, talking deep, walking sure, whiskers bristling on all their chins, they promised that tonight they would get Fred a woman.

THE CHOIR

JOEL D. LANE

The Rat Burglar was the start of it, I suppose. Creeping through open windows in the stillness of late summer, while people were asleep or in the next room. Couldn't have been older than nine. A few people saw him, but he was too quick for them. Got away with jewellery boxes, phones, wallets. One woman saw only the light of his tiny torch nosing around the bedroom. She thought she was dreaming, but in the morning her purse was gone.

There were worse crimes after that. Someone smashed the back window of a teacher's car in a primary school playground and emptied a bag of rotten meat over the seats. In another school, dead mice kept turning up in teachers' handbags. And one evening, young kids in masks swarmed into a newsagent's and robbed him at knifepoint. He said their leader's voice hadn't even broken. Worst of all, a ten-year-old girl whose parents were being arrested for drug dealing clawed a police officer's face with bleach under her fingernails. He lost his sight.

It was as if the younger generation had declared war on us. Not teenagers, that's only to be expected, but the kind of little creatures our local paper was more used to calling *innocent*. What the police couldn't find was any sign of an adult gang using kids in an organised way for theft or drug-running. They were freelance. We ran a feature on the city's "feral children," though I wasn't sure exactly what that meant. Kids raised by wolves were supposed to have built a city, not torn one down.

We got a few of the usual idiot letters blaming the offences on recent cuts in family benefits and social services. Apparently some government department had said we had the worst child welfare record of any major city, as if that meant anything. Our editorials (which I usually wrote) took a clear line: it was the whole culture of "support," of living cap in hand, that was to blame for these sickening crimes. If people relied on themselves, they'd turn out honest. We called for a level of discipline that matched the nature of the offenders.

A week later, I got an e-mail from a police contact saying *This might interest you.* There was a link to a local blog called *Newtown Crier*. The anonymous writer had been ranting for weeks about juvenile crime, calling for the sterilisation of single mothers and the banning of interracial marriage. Neither of which ideas we were likely to touch with a barge-pole, thank you. But that day, he'd posted a short message: *The feral children are getting under the radar of police—but now they'd better watch out. The Chosen Few are on their trail. No taller, no older—but better armed and with right on their side. Make no mistake, they will win.*

I replied to my contact, asking: *Is he talking about some kind of child militia?* He didn't reply at once. Then, after a few days when the level of juvenile crime seemed higher than ever, he invited me to a "press conference" at the Steelhouse Lane police station. That was his code for an exclusive story. These days I rarely leave the office—there's more information online than on the streets, and the paper's staff is barely a tenth of what it was in the old days—but something told me this was not one to miss. Though autumn had just given way to the bitter nights of winter.

• • •

The station was nested among the gaunt brick buildings of the old hospital, some crusted with scaffolding. Inside, it was barely warmer. My contact—I'll call him Ian, though I never knew his first name—led me down a narrow concrete staircase to a corridor whose floor-tiles gleamed with moisture. The doors, which were all shut, had spy-holes. He stopped at the last one. "Meet the Chosen Few," he said quietly to me before unlocking the heavy door. A group of some fifteen children were standing inside. They were all dressed in white, like a choir. White ceramic masks covered their upper faces, but even so I was sure none of them could be over twelve years old.

That impression was confirmed when they began to sing, or rather chant. Their untrained voices had a shrill purity that put my teeth on edge. It was like the sound made by striking a wine-glass with a tuning fork. But in such a limited space, and with so many children, it could have been a whole pub's worth of wine-glasses. I had no idea what they were singing or in what language. Some of them were holding coshes, some handcuffs or lengths of rope. I couldn't see any adult in charge of them. There was something in their eyes, a kind of calm directness, that made me wish they couldn't see me.

"Take a picture," Ian said, sounding annoyed that I hadn't done so. I whipped out my digital camera, focused it and took three hasty shots. The singing ceased. Ian yanked me back out of the cell and slammed the door. "There's your front page," he said as we walked back to the ground floor. There was no sound from any cell we passed.

"I need more than that," I complained. "Where are they from, what are they trained for, and why do—"

"You don't need any of that. Just publish the photo. What they do, you'll find out soon enough." He walked me briskly to the exit and patted my arm. "Watch yourself out there."

The streets were blurred with mist. I hurried back to my car. Could have done with a drink, but for some reason I didn't feel very safe. Instead, I drove to the *Mercury* office and started working on the story. There was only me and the website girl there. Sometimes I flirted with her, but that night I knew I'd want more, so left her alone. Back at my desk I checked the *Newtown Crier* blog again, but the only update was a single quotation: "*Virtue without terror is ineffective.*" —*Robespierre.*

· · ·

Our front-page story, two days later, was headlined "Youth Squad." I thought "The Chosen Few" was a bit tacky somehow. We cropped the image so the children weren't so obviously small. The accompanying text was brief—it had to be, given the lack of information. A boxed-out paragraph:

This is the new generation of law enforcers. A radical initiative in North Birmingham to counter the horrific recent wave of juvenile crimes, the youth police squad are being trained to enforce the law in our schools and on our streets. Young offenders will have nowhere to hide. The Mercury *supports the new squad and hopes it will do what needs to be done.*

We expected a tidal wave of liberal condemnation, but the reaction was muted. We had more letters about the Blues squad (Birmingham City FC) than the youth police squad. But the story did seem to have an impact: the juvenile crime statistics fell almost at once, and reports of offences by pre-teens stopped entirely. It didn't occur to me that the children I'd photographed might themselves have had a real impact, until another police story came to my attention. Across the city, but mostly in Newtown, a number of "problem" children had gone missing.

Needless to say, these were just the kind of scrotes who were likely to go on the run or get knocked off or sold by criminal associates or their own families (if the distinction was even valid). But there were so many in a few weeks that a parents' group started in Ward End, asking why the police weren't doing more. They too went quiet after a little while. Perhaps they found the answer, or it found them.

In early December, when the petrol-tinged rain gave way to a calming stillness, I walked home from the office. It was just after midnight; we'd put the morning edition of the *Mercury* to bed too late for our usual Friday night drink. The roads were coated with frost. Outside the city centre, traffic sped down the expressways and a few beggars poked at the litter bins. Otherwise, the streets were empty and silent. I had the sensation of being watched.

Two days later I got a call from Ian on my mobile, also shortly after midnight. He was very drunk. I didn't catch most of what he said—only the phrase *never thought of this* and the final statement: *There's a choir practice tomorrow night, late, at St Francis' Church in Bordesley.* Then his voice broke up into hoarse wordless sounds, as if he was crying or in pain. When I asked him what was wrong, he rang off.

• • •

St Francis' wasn't in the phone book, but I found a reference to it at the Council House. It was part of an old street awaiting demolition, due to the subsidence common in that area. The church had been derelict for twenty years. I wasn't sure what "late" meant, but doubted the bedtime of youngsters was a factor.

Shortly after ten, I parked my car on the main road in Bordesley and walked to the condemned backstreet. It was the kind of slum that had mostly been replaced by tower blocks in the sixties: terraced houses barely wider than their front doors, with a single window on the first floor. Every house was boarded or bricked up. The church itself had suffered storm damage, and seemed in addition to be slightly tilted—but the light was poor, and I couldn't swear to it. However, it seemed clear that the door was securely locked. I walked up and down the ruined street a few times, sipping at my hip flask of Maker's Mark. There was no sign of life anywhere in the street.

Eventually I went back to my car, but felt too wound up to leave. I flicked back and forth between local radio channels for over an hour, hoping to catch something about the Chosen Few. But all the conversations seemed artificially bright, like a game played under floodlights. My hunger for the story was mixed with a growing concern at what I might have helped to set in motion. There had to be an answer. Near midnight, I got out of my car and walked back to St Francis'. There was no sign of life.

The moon was higher now, and it was a clear night. I was able to make out something I'd missed before: a side door to the church whose lock had been smashed. It was held shut by a pile of bricks. As quietly as possible, I shifted the bricks aside and pushed open the rotting door. Inside, the dark was pregnant with a smell I could neither bear nor understand. It seemed to be a combined reek of ammonia, shit and decay, but with something else—some diseased animal, perhaps. I fished in my jacket pocket for my tiny pocket torch—probably not unlike the one used by the Rat Burglar months before—and switched it on.

The walls and furnishings were smeared with black mould and laced with cobwebs. Water had pooled in the nave, where the swollen and torn remains of a few hymn-books were scattered on the floor. The altar bore an unusually large cross of twisted iron, slightly at an angle. My nose told me more than my eyes. The ammonia smell—rats, of course—was everywhere, and so was the smell of rotting wood and stone. But the strange, terrible disease smell, tinged with excrement, came from one place: the altar. I walked around it and saw that at the back, an area of cobweb had recently been cleared away. And standing there, I became aware of a sound: a faint, uneven chorus of high voices. They weren't singing. They were screaming in pain and terror. Even in the chilly air, I began to sweat.

A light flickered in the corner of my eye. Suddenly the nave was filled with small figures clothed in white, some of them holding lit candles. Those with free hands rushed at me and smashed into my legs, knocking me to the cobwebbed floor. Two of them cuffed my hands behind my back, then tied my legs with wire. I tried to tell them I was only here as a reporter, but a child blocked my mouth with a small hand, pinching my nose until I almost blacked out. They dragged me to the side of the altar, so I could see what they did next.

The Chosen Few were no longer masked. Their small faces had the calm serenity of prayer. Silently, they pulled away the moth-eaten rug behind the altar and lifted the trapdoor they had exposed. The stench of disease became stronger, and so did the cries from below. A rat crawled up through the black space and ran beyond the light. Most of the children went down beneath the floor. A few minutes later, they returned with their prisoners.

The figures they dragged up from the vault were no bigger than themselves—but filthy, smeared with blood and excrement, their wrists and ankles chained, their hair bound in veils of cobweb, their faces bruised and grey. It was like a medieval painting of angels guiding the dead up to Heaven. At least they'd given up trying to scream.

When the prisoners were gathered in a heap, still chained, before the altar, the Chosen Few formed a semicircle around them. Threads of pale smoke rose from the candles, which didn't seem to have made the church any warmer. Then the choir began to sing. Louder and harsher than before, the sound filled the nave and made every muscle in my trapped body tense. Their voices merged into a single note that rose until its pitch was unbearable. Then, all at once, they stopped.

The giant cross on the damp-stained altar crumpled as if its arms had been broken. Something began to take shape around it, like mould around a skeleton. A grey figure, bent over but with obvious vigour, jumped down to the floor. The long, yellow teeth that filled its face gleamed in the candlelight. Between its stumpy legs, something thickened and rose. Slowly, almost playfully, it reached out to the nearest of the prisoners and began to feed, while the Chosen Few—looking, for the first time, like the children they were—curled happily on the floor around its taloned feet.

CHILDREN OF THE CORN
STEPHEN KING

Burt turned the radio on too loud and didn't turn it down because they were on the verge of another argument and he didn't want it to happen. He was desperate for it not to happen.

Vicky said something.

"What?" he shouted.

"Turn it down! Do you want to break my eardrums?"

He bit down hard on what might have come through his mouth and turned it down.

Vicky was fanning herself with her scarf even though the T-Bird was air-conditioned. "Where are we, anyway?"

"Nebraska."

She gave him a cold, neutral look. "Yes, Burt. I know we're in Nebraska, Burt. But where in hell *are* we?"

"You've got the road atlas. Look it up. Or can't you read?"

"Such wit. This is why we got off the turnpike. So we could look at three hundred miles of corn. And enjoy the wit and wisdom of Burt Robeson."

He was gripping the steering wheel so hard his knuckles were white. He decided he was holding it that tightly because if he loosened up, why, one of those hands might just fly off and hit the ex-Prom Queen beside him right in the chops. We're saving our marriage, he told himself. Yes. We're doing it the same way us grunts went about saving villages in the war.

"Vicky," he said carefully. "I have driven fifteen hundred miles on turnpikes since we left Boston. I did all that driving myself because you refused to drive. Then—"

"I did not refuse!" Vicky said hotly. "Just because I get migraines when I drive for a long time—"

"Then when I asked you if you'd navigate for me on some of the secondary roads, you said sure, Burt. Those were your exact words. Sure, Burt. Then—"

"Sometimes I wonder how I ever wound up married to you."

"By saying two little words."

She stared at him for a moment, white-lipped, and then picked up the road atlas. She turned the pages savagely.

It *had* been a mistake leaving the turnpike, Burt thought morosely. It was a shame, too, because up until then they had been doing pretty well, treating each other almost like human beings. It had sometimes seemed that this trip to the coast, ostensibly to see Vicky's brother and his wife but actually a last-ditch attempt to patch up their own marriage, was going to work.

But since they left the pike, it had been bad again. How bad? Well, terrible, actually.

"We left the turnpike at Hamburg, right?"

"Right."

"There's nothing more until Gatlin," she said. "Twenty miles. Wide place in the road. Do you suppose we could stop there and get something to eat? Or does your almighty schedule say we have to go until two o'clock like we did yesterday?"

He took his eyes off the road to look at her. "I've about had it, Vicky. As far as I'm concerned, we can turn around right here and go home and see that lawyer you wanted to talk to. Because this isn't working out—"

She had faced forward again, her expression stonily set. It suddenly turned to surprise and fear. *"Burt, look out, you're going to—"*

He turned his attention back to the road just in time to see something vanish under the T-Bird's bumper. A moment later, while he was only beginning to switch from gas to brake, he felt something thump sickeningly under the front and then the back wheels. They were thrown forward as the car braked along the centerline, decelerating from fifty to zero along black skidmarks.

"A dog," he said. "Tell me it was a dog, Vicky."

Her face was a pallid, cottage-cheese color. "A boy. A little boy. He just ran out of the corn and . . . congratulations, tiger."

She fumbled the car door open, leaned out, threw up.

Burt sat straight behind the T-Bird's wheel, hands still gripping it loosely. He was aware of nothing for a long time but the rich, dark smell of fertilizer.

Then he saw that Vicky was gone and when he looked in the outside mirror he saw her stumbling clumsily back toward a heaped bundle that looked like a pile of rags. She was ordinarily a graceful woman but now her grace was gone, robbed.

It's manslaughter. That's what they call it. I took my eyes off the road.

He turned the ignition off and got out. The wind rustled softly through the growing man-high corn, making a weird sound like respiration. Vicky was standing over the bundle of rags now, and he could hear her sobbing.

He was halfway between the car and where she stood and something caught his eye on the left, a gaudy splash of red amid all the green, as bright as barn paint.

He stopped, looking directly into the corn. He found himself thinking (anything to untrack from those rags that were not rags) that it must have been a fantastically good growing season for corn. It grew close together, almost ready to bear. You could plunge into those neat, shaded rows and spend a day trying to find your way out again. But the neatness was broken here. Several tall cornstalks had been broken and leaned askew. And what was that further back in the shadows?

"Burt?" Vicky screamed at him. "Don't you want to come see? So you can tell all your poker buddies what you bagged in Nebraska? Don't you—" But the rest was lost in fresh sobs. Her shadow was puddled starkly around her feet. It was almost noon.

Shade closed over him as he entered the corn. The red barn paint was blood. There was a low, somnolent buzz as flies lit, tasted, and buzzed off again . . . maybe to tell others. There was more blood on the leaves further in. Surely it couldn't have splattered this far. And then he was standing over the object he had seen from the road. He picked it up.

The neatness of the rows was disturbed here. Several stalks were canted drunkenly, two of them had been broken clean off. The earth had been gouged. There was blood. The corn rustled. With a little shiver, he walked back to the road.

Vicky was having hysterics, screaming unintelligible words at him, crying, laughing. Who would have thought it could end in such a melodramatic way?

He looked at her and saw he wasn't having an identity crisis or a difficult life transition or any of those trendy things. He hated her. He gave her a hard slap across the face.

She stopped short and put a hand against the reddening impression of his fingers. "You'll go to jail, Burt," she said solemnly.

"I don't think so," he said, and put the suitcase he had found in the corn at her feet.

"What—?"

"I don't know. I guess it belonged to him." He pointed to the sprawled, face-down body that lay in the road. No more than thirteen, from the look of him.

The suitcase was old. The brown leather was bettered and scuffed. Two hanks of clothesline had been wrapped around it and tied in large, clownish grannies. Vicky bent to undo one of them, saw the blood greased into the knot, and withdrew.

Burt knelt and turned the body over gently.

"I don't want to look," Vicky said, staring down helplessly anyway. And when the staring, sightless face flopped up to regard them, she screamed again. The boy's face was dirty, his expression a grimace of terror. His throat had been cut.

Burt got up and put his arms around Vicky as she began to sway. "Don't faint," he said very quietly. "Do you hear me, Vicky? Don't faint."

He repeated it over and over and at last she began to recover and held him tight. They might have been dancing, there on the noon-struck road with the boy's corpse at their feet.

"Vicky?"

"What?" Muffled against his shirt.

"Go back to the car and put the keys in your pocket. Get the blanket out of the back seat, and my rifle. Bring them here."

"The rifle?"

"Someone cut his throat. Maybe whoever is watching us."

Her head jerked up and her wide eyes considered the corn. It marched away as far as the eye could see, undulating up and down small dips and rises of land.

"I imagine he's gone. But why take chances? Go on. Do it."

She walked stiltedly back to the car, her shadow following, a dark mascot who stuck close at this hour of the day. When she leaned into the back seat, Burt squatted beside the boy. White male, no distinguishing marks. Run over, yes, but the T-Bird hadn't cut the kid's throat. It had been cut raggedly and inefficiently—no army sergeant had shown the killer the finer points of hand-to-hand assassination—but the final effect had been deadly. He had either run or been pushed through the last thirty feet of corn, dead or mortally wounded. And Burt Robeson had run him down. If the boy had still been alive when the car hit him, his life had been cut short by thirty seconds at most.

Vicky tapped him on the shoulder and he jumped.

She was standing with the brown army blanket over her left arm, the cased pump shotgun in her right hand, her face averted. He took the blanket and spread it on the road. He rolled the body onto it. Vicky uttered a desperate little moan.

"You okay?" He looked up at her. "Vicky?"

"Okay," she said in a strangled voice.

He flipped the sides of the blanket over the body and scooped it up, hating the thick, dead weight of it. It tried to make a U in his arms and slither through his grasp. He clutched it tighter and they walked back to the T-Bird.

"Open the trunk," he grunted.

The trunk was full of travel stuff, suitcases and souvenirs. Vicky shifted most of it into the back seat and Burt slipped the body into the made space and slammed the trunklid down. A sigh of relief escaped him.

Vicky was standing by the driver's side door, still holding the cased rifle.

"Just put it in the back and get in."

He looked at his watch and saw only fifteen minutes had passed. It seemed like hours.

"What about the suitcase?" she asked.

He trotted back down the road to where it stood on the white line, like the focal point in an Impressionist painting. He picked it up by its tattered handle and paused for a moment. He had a strong sensation of being watched. It was a feeling he had read about in books, mostly cheap fiction, and he had always doubted its reality. Now he didn't. It was as if there were people in the corn,

STEPHEN KING

maybe a lot of them, coldly estimating whether the woman could get the gun out of the case and use it before they could grab him, drag him into the shady rows, cut his throat—

Heart beating thickly, he ran back to the car, pulled the keys out of the trunk lock, and got in.

Vicky was crying again. Burt got them moving, and before a minute had passed he could no longer pick out the spot where it had happened in the rearview mirror.

"What did you say the next town was?" he asked.

"Oh." She bent over the road atlas again. "Gatlin. We should be there in ten minutes."

"Does it look big enough to have a police station?"

"No. It's just a dot."

"Maybe there's a constable."

They drove in silence for a while. They passed a silo on the left. Nothing else but corn. Nothing passed them going the other way, not even a farm truck.

"Have we passed anything since we got off the turnpike, Vicky?"

She thought about it. "A car and a tractor. At that intersection."

"No, since we got on this road. Route 17."

"No. I don't think we have." Earlier this might have been the preface to some cutting remark. Now she only stared out of her half of the windshield at the unrolling road and the endless dotted line.

"Vicky? Could you open the suitcase?"

"Do you think it might matter?"

"Don't know. It might."

While she picked at the knots (her face was set in a peculiar way—expressionless but tight-mouthed—that Burt remembered his mother wearing when she pulled the innards out of the Sunday chicken), Burt turned on the radio again.

The pop station they had been listened to was almost obliterated in static and Burt switched, running the red marker slowly down the dial. Farm reports. Buck Owens. Tammy Wynette. All distant, nearly distorted into babble. Then, near the end of the dial, one single word blared out of the speaker, so loud and

82

clear that the lips which uttered it might have been directly beneath the grille of the dashboard speaker.

"*Atonement!*" this voice bellowed.

Burt made a surprised grunting sound. Vicky jumped.

"*Only by the blood of the Lamb are we saved!*" the voice roared, and Burt hurriedly turned the sound down. This station was close, all right. So close that . . . yes, there it was. Poking out of the corn at the horizon, a spidery red tripod against the blue. The radio tower.

"Atonement is the word, brothers 'n' sisters," the voice told them, dropping to a more conversational pitch. In the background, off-mike, voices murmured amen. "There's some that thinks it's okay to get out in the world, as if you could work and walk in the world without being smirched by the world. Now is that what the word of God teaches us?"

Off-mike but still loud: "No!"

"*Holy Jesus!*" the evangelist shouted, and now the words came in a powerful, pumping cadence, almost as compelling as a driving rock-and-roll beat: "When they gonna know that way is death? When they gonna know that the wages of the world are paid on the other side? Huh? Huh? The Lord has said there's many mansions in His house. But there's no room for the fornicator. No room for the coveter. No room for the defiler of the corn. No room for the hommasexshul. No room—"

Vicky snapped it off. "That drivel makes me sick."

"What did he say?" Burt asked her. "What did he say about corn?"

"I didn't hear it." She was picking at the second clothesline knot.

"He said something about corn. I know he did."

"I got it!" Vicky said, and the suitcase fell open in her lap. They were passing a sign that said: *Gatlin 5 Mi. Drive Carefully Protect our Children.* The sign had been put up by the Elks. There were .22 bullet holes in it.

"Socks," Vicky said. "Two pairs of pants . . . a shirt . . . a belt . . . a string tie with a—" She held it up, showing him the peeling gilt neck clasp. "Who's that?"

Burt glanced at it. "Hopalong Cassidy, I think."

"Oh." She put it back. She was crying again.

After a moment, But said, "Did anything strike you funny about that radio sermon?"

"No. I heard enough of that stuff as a kid to last me forever. I told you that."

"Didn't you think he sounded kind of young? That preacher?"

She uttered a mirthless laugh. "A teen-ager, maybe, so what? That's what's so monstrous about that whole trip. They like to get hold of them when their minds are still rubber. They know how to put all the emotional checks and balances in. You should have been at some of the tent meetings my mother and father dragged me to . . . some of the ones I was 'saved' at.

"Let's see. There was Baby Hortense, the Singing Marvel. She was eight. She'd come on and sing 'Leaning on the Everlasting Arms' while her daddy passed the plate, telling everybody to 'dig deep, now, let's not let this little child of God down.' Then there was Norman Staunton. He used to preach hellfire and brimstone in this Little Lord Fauntleroy suit with short pants. He was only seven."

She nodded at his look of unbelief.

"They weren't the only two, either. There were plenty of them on the circuit. They were good *draws*." She spat the word. "Ruby Stampnell. She was a ten-year-old faith healer. The Grace Sisters. They used to come out with little tin-foil haloes over their head and—*oh!*"

"What is it?" He jerked around to look at her, and what she was holding in her hands. Vicky was staring at it raptly. Her slowly seining hands had snagged it on the bottom of the suitcase and had brought it up as she talked. Burt pulled over to take a better look. She gave it to him wordlessly.

It was a crucifix that had been made from twists of corn husk, once green, now dry. Attached to this by woven cornsilk was a dwarf corncob. Most of the kernels had been carefully removed, probably dug out one at a time with a pocketknife. Those kernels remaining formed a crude cruciform figure in yellowish bas-relief. Corn-kernel eyes, each slit longways to suggest pupils. Outstretched kernel arms, the legs together, terminating in a rough indication of bare feet. Above, four letters also raised from the bone-white cob: I N R I.

• • •

"That's a fantastic piece of workmanship," he said.

"It's hideous," she said in a flat, strained voice. "Throw it out."

"Vicky, the police might want to see it."

"Why"

"Well, I don't know why. Maybe—"

"Throw it out. Will you please do that for me? I don't want it in the car."

"I'll put it in back. And as soon as we see the cops, we'll get rid of it one way or the other. I promise. Okay?"

"Oh, do whatever you want with it!" she shouted at him. "You will anyway!"

Troubled, he threw the thing in the back, where it landed on a pile of clothes. Its corn-kernel eyes stared raptly at the T-Bird's dome light. He pulled out again, gravel splurting from beneath the tires.

"We'll give the body and everything that was in the suitcase to the cops," He promised. "Then we'll be shut of it."

Vicky didn't answer. She was looking at her hands.

A mile further on, the endless cornfields drew away from the road, showing farmhouses and outbuildings. In one yard they saw dirty chickens pecking listlessly at the soil. There were faded cola and chewing tobacco ads on the roofs of barns. They passed a tall billboard that said: *Only Jesus Saves*. They passed a café with a Conoco gas island, but Burt decided to go on into the center of town, if there was one. If not, they could come back to the café. It only occurred to him after they had passed it that the parking lot had been empty except for a dirty old pickup that looked like it was sitting on two flat tires.

Vicky suddenly began to laugh, a high, giggling sound that struck Burt as being dangerously close to hysteria.

"What's so funny?"

"The signs," she said, gasping and hiccupping. "Haven't you been reading them? When they called this the Bible Belt, they sure weren't kidding. Oh Lordy, there's another bunch." Another burst of hysterical laughter escaped her, and she clapped both hands over her mouth.

Each sign had only one word. They were leaning on white-washed sticks that had been implanted in the sandy shoulder, long ago by the looks; the whitewash was flaked and faded. They were coming up at eighty-foot intervals and Burt read:

A . . . Cloud . . . By . . . Day . . . A . . . Pillar . . . Of . . . Fire . . . By . . . Night

"They only forgot one thing," Vicky said, still giggling helplessly.

"What?" Burt asked, frowning.

"Burma Shave." She held a knuckled fist against her open mouth to keep in the laughter, but her semi-hysterical giggles flowed around it like effervescent ginger-ale bubbles.

"Vicky, are you all right?"

"I will be. Just as soon as we're a thousand miles away from here, in sunny sinful California with the Rockies between us and Nebraska.

Another group of signs came up and they read them silently.

Take . . . This . . . And . . . Eat . . . Saith . . . The . . . Lord . . . God

Now why, Burt thought, should I immediately associate that indefinite pronoun with corn? Isn't that what they say when they give you communion? It had been so long since he had been to church that he really couldn't remember. He wouldn't be surprised if they used cornbread for holy wafer around these parts. He opened his mouth to tell Vicky that, and then thought better of it.

They breasted a gentle rise and there was Gatlin below them, all three blocks of it, looking like a set from a movie about the Depression.

"There'll be a constable," Burt said, and wondered why the sight of that hick one-timetable town dozing in the sun should have brought a lump of dread into his throat.

They passed a speed sign proclaiming that no more than thirty was now in order, and another sign, rust-flecked, which said: *You are now entering Gatlin, nicest little town in Nebraska—or anywhere else! Pop. 5431.*

Dusty elms stood on both sides of the road, most of them diseased. They passed the Gatlin Lumberyard and a 76 gas station, where the price signs swung slowly in a hot noon breeze: *Reg 35.9 Hi-Test 38.9*, and another which said: *Hi truckers diesel fuel around back.*

They crossed Elm Street, then Birch Street, and came up on the town square. The houses lining the streets were plain wood with screened porches.

Angular and functional. The lawns were yellow and dispirited. Up ahead a mongrel dog walked slowly out into the middle of Maple Street, stood looking at them for a moment, then lay down in the road with its nose on its paws.

"Stop," Vicky said. "Stop right here."

Burt pulled obediently to the curb.

"Turn around. Let's take the body to Grand Island. That's not too far, is it? Let's do that."

"Vicky, what's wrong?"

"What do you mean, what's wrong?" she asked, her voice rising thinly. "This town is empty, Burt. There's nobody here but us. Can't you feel that?"

He had felt something, and still felt it. But—

"It just seems that way," he said. "But it sure is a one-hydrant town. Probably all up in the square, having a bake sale or a bingo game."

"*There's no one here.*" She said the words with a queer, strained emphasis. "Didn't you see that 76 station back there?"

"Sure, by the lumberyard, so what?" His mind was elsewhere, listening to the dull buzz of a cicada burrowing into one of the nearby elms. He could smell corn, dusty roses, and fertilizer—of course. For the first time they were off the turnpike and in a town. A town in a state he had never been in before (although he had flown over it from time to time in United Airlines 747s) and somehow it felt all wrong but all right. Somewhere up ahead there would be a drugstore with a soda fountain, a movie house named the Bijou, a school named after JFK.

"Burt, the prices said thirty-five-nine for regular and thirty-eight-nine for high octane. Now how long has it been since anyone in this country paid those prices?"

"At least four years," he admitted. "But, Vicky—"

"We're right in town, Burt, and there's not a car! *Not one car!*"

"Grand Island is seventy miles away. It would look funny if we took him there."

"I don't care."

"Look, let's just drive up to the courthouse and—"

"*No!*"

There, damn it, there. Why our marriage is falling apart, in a nutshell. No

I won't. No siree. And furthermore, I'll hold my breath till I turn blue if you don't let me have my way.

"Vicky," he said.

"I want to get out of here, Burt."

"Vicky, listen to me."

"Turn around. Let's go."

"Vicky, will you stop a minute?"

"I'll stop when we're driving the other way. Now let's go."

"*We have a dead child in the trunk of our car!*" he roared at her, and took a distinct pleasure at the way she flinched, the way her face crumbled. In a slightly lower voice he went on: "His throat was cut and he was shoved out into the road and I ran him over. Now I'm going to drive up to the courthouse or whatever they have here, and I'm going to report it. If you want to start walking back toward the pike, go to it. I'll pick you up. But don't you tell me to turn around and drive seventy miles to Grand Island like we had nothing in the trunk but a bag of garbage. He happens to be some mother's son, and I'm going to report it before whoever killed him gets over the hills and far away."

"You bastard," she said, crying. "What am I doing with you?"

"I don't know," he said. "I don't know anymore. But the situation can't be remedied, Vicky."

He pulled away from the curb. The dog lifted its head at the brief squeal of the tires and then lowered it to its paws again.

They drove the remaining block to the square. At the corner of Main and Pleasant, Main split in two. There actually was a town square, a grassy park with a bandstand in the middle. On the other end, where Main Street became one again, there were two official-looking buildings. Burt could make out the lettering on one: *Gatlin Municipal Center.*

"That's it," he said. Vicky said nothing.

Halfway up the square, Burt pulled over again. They were beside a lunchroom, the Gatlin Bar and Grill.

"Where are you going?" Vicky asked with alarm as he opened his door.

"To find out where everyone is. Sign in the window there says 'open.'"

"You're not going to leave me here alone."

"So come. Who's stopping you?"

She unlocked her door and stepped out as he crossed in front of the car. He saw how pale her face was and felt an instant of pity. Hopeless pity.

"Do you hear it?" she asked as he joined her.

"Hear what?"

"The nothing. No cars. No people. No tractors. Nothing."

And then, from a block over, they heard the high and joyous laughter of children.

"I hear kids," he said. "Don't you?"

She looked at him, troubled.

He opened the lunchroom door and stepped into dry, antiseptic heat. The floor was dusty. The sheen on the chrome was dull. The wooden blades of the ceiling fans stood still. Empty tables. Empty counter stools. But the mirror behind the counter had been shattered and there was something else . . . in a moment he had it. All the beer taps had been broken off. They lay along the counter like bizarre party favors.

Vicky's voice was gay and near to breaking. "Sure. Ask anybody. Pardon me, sir, but could you tell me—"

"Oh, shut up." But his voice was dull and without force. They were standing in a bar of dusty sunlight that fell through the lunchroom's big plate-glass window and again he had that feeling of being watched and he thought of the boy they had in their trunk, and of the high laughter of children. A phrase came to him for no reason, a legal-sounding phrase, and it began to repeat mystically in his mind: *Sight unseen. Sight unseen. Sight unseen.*

His eyes traveled over the age-yellowed cards thumb-tacked up behind the counter: *Cheeseburg 35¢ World's Best Joe 10¢ Strawberry Rhubarb Pie 25¢ Today's Special Ham & Red Eye Gravy w/ Mashed Pot 80¢.*

How long since he had since lunchroom prices like that?

Vicky had the answer. "Look at this," she said shrilly. She was pointing at the calendar on the wall. "They've been at that bean supper for twelve years, I guess." She uttered a grinding laugh.

He walked over. The picture showed two boys swimming in a pond while a cute little dog carried off their clothes. Below the picture was the legend: *Compliments of Gatlin Lumber & Hardware You Breakum, We Fixum.* The month on view was August 1964.

"I don't understand," he faltered, "but I'm sure—"

"You're sure!" she cried hysterically. "Sure, you're sure! That's part of your trouble, Burt, you've spent your whole life being *sure*!"

He turned back to the door and she came after him.

"Where are you going?"

"To the Municipal Center."

"Burt, why do you have to be so stubborn? You know something's wrong here. Can't you just admit it?"

"I'm not being stubborn. I just want to get shut of what's in the trunk."

They stepped out onto the sidewalk, and Burt was struck afresh with the town's silence, and with the smell of fertilizer. Somehow you never thought of that smell when you buttered an ear and salted it and bit in. Compliments of sun, rain, all sorts of man-made phosphates, and a good healthy dose of cow shit. But somehow this smell was different from the one he had grown up with in rural upstate New York. You could say whatever you wanted to about organic fertilizer, but there was something almost fragrant about it when the spreader was laying it down in the fields. Not one of your great perfumes, God no, but when the late-afternoon spring breeze would pick up and waft it over the freshly turned fields, it *was* a smell with good associations. It meant winter was over for good. It meant that school doors were going to bang closed in six weeks or so and spill everyone out into summer. It was a smell tied irrevocably in his mind with other aromas that *were* perfume: timothy grass, clover, fresh earth, hollyhocks, dogwood.

But they must do something different out here, he thought. The smell was close but not the same. There was a sickish-sweet undertone. Almost a death smell. As a medical orderly in Vietnam, he had become well versed in that smell.

Vicky was sitting quietly in the car, holding the corn crucifix in her lap and staring at it in a rapt way Burt didn't like.

"Put that thing down," he said.

"No," she said without looking up. "You play your games and I'll play mine."

He put the car in gear and drove up to the corner. A dead stoplight hung overhead, swinging in a faint breeze. To the left was a neat white church. The grass was cut. Neatly kept flowers grew beside the flagged path up to the door. Burt pulled over.

"What are you doing?"

"I'm going to go in and take a look," Burt said. "It's the only place in town that looks as if there isn't ten years' dust on it. And look at the sermon board."

She looked. Neatly pegged white letters under glass read: *The Power and Grace of He Who Walks Behind the Rows.* The date was July 24, 1976—the Sunday before.

"He Who Walks Behind the Rows," Burt said, turning off the ignition. "One of the nine thousand names of God only used in Nebraska, I guess. Coming?"

She didn't smile. "I'm not going in with you."

"Fine. Whatever you want."

"I haven't been in a church since I left home and don't want to be in *this* church and I don't want to be in *this town*, Burt. I'm scared out of my mind, can't we just *go*?"

"I'll only be a minute."

"I've got my keys, Burt. If you're not back in five minutes, I'll just drive away and leave you here."

"Now just wait a minute, lady."

"That's what I'm going to do. Unless you want to assault me like a common mugger and take my keys. I suppose you could do that."

"But you don't think I will."

"No."

Her purse was on the seat between them. He snatched it up. She screamed and grabbed for the shoulder strap. He pulled it out of her reach. Not bothering to dig, he simply turned the bag upside down and let everything fall out. Her keyring glittered amid tissues, cosmetics, change, old shopping lists. She lunged for it but he beat her again and put the keys in his own pocket.

"You didn't have to do that," she said, crying. "Give them to me."

"No," he said, and gave her a hard, meaningless grin. "No way."

"Please, Burt! I'm scared!" She held her hand out, pleading now.

"You'd wait two minutes and decide that was long enough."

"I wouldn't—"

"And then you'd drive off laughing and saying to yourself, 'That'll teach Burt to cross me when I want something.' Hasn't that pretty much been your motto during our married life? That'll teach Burt to cross me?"

He got out of the car.

"Please, Burt!" she screamed, sliding across the seat. "Listen . . . I know . . . we'll drive out of town and call from a phone booth, okay? I've got all kinds of change. I just . . . we can . . . *don't leave me alone, Burt, don't leave me out here alone!*"

He slammed the door on her cry and then leaned against the side of the T-Bird for a moment, thumbs against his closed eyes. She was pounding on the driver's side window and calling his name. She was going to make a wonderful impression when he finally found someone in authority to take charge of the kid's body. Oh yes.

He turned and walked up the flagstone path to the church doors. Two or three minutes, just a look-around, then he would be back out. Probably the door wasn't even unlocked.

But it pushed in easily on silent, well-oiled hinges (reverently oiled, he thought, and that seemed funny for no really good reason) and he stepped into a vestibule so cool it was almost chilly. It took his eyes a moment to adjust to the dimness.

The first thing he noticed was a pile of wooden letters in the far corner, dusty and jumbled indifferently together. He went to them, curious. They looked as old and forgotten as the calendar in the bar and grill, unlike the rest of the vestibule, which was dust-free and tidy. The letters were about two feet high, obviously part of a set. He spread them out on the carpet—there were eighteen of them—and shifted them around like anagrams. *Hurt Bite Crag Chap CS.* Nope. *Crap Target Chibs Huc.* That wasn't much good either. Except for the *Ch* in *Chibs.* He quickly assembled the word *Church* and was left looking at *rap taget cibs.* Foolish. He was squatting here playing idiot games with a bunch of letters while Vicky was going nuts out in the car. He started to get up, and then saw it. He formed *Baptist*, leaving *rag ec*—and by changing two letters he had *Grace. Grace Baptist Church.* The letters must have been out front. They had taken them down and had thrown them indifferently in the corner, and the church had been painted since then so that you couldn't even see where the letters had been.

Why?

It wasn't the Grace Baptist Church anymore, that was why. So what kind of church was it? For some reason that question caused a trickle of fear and he stood up quickly, dusting his fingers. So they had taken down a bunch of letters, so what? Maybe they had changed the place into Flip Wilson's Church of What's Happening Now.

But what had happened then?

He shook it off impatiently and went through the inner doors. Now he was standing at the back of the church itself, and as he looked toward the nave, he felt fear close around his heart and squeeze tightly. His breath drew in, loud in the pregnant silence of this place.

The space behind the pulpit was dominated by a gigantic portrait of Christ, and Burt thought: If nothing else in this town gave Vicky the screaming meemies, this would.

The Christ was grinning, vulpine. His eyes were wide and staring, reminding Burt uneasily of Lon Chaney in *The Phantom of the Opera*. In each of the wide black pupils someone (a sinner, presumably) was drowning in a lake of fire. But the oddest thing was that this Christ had green hair . . . hair which on closer examination revealed itself to be a twining mass of early-summer corn. The picture was crudely done but effective. It looked like a comic-strip mural done by a gifted child—an Old Testament Christ, or a pagan Christ that might slaughter his sheep for sacrifice instead of leading them.

At the foot of the left-hand rank of pews was a pipe organ, and Burt could not at first tell what was wrong with it. He walked down the left-hand aisle and saw with slowly dawning horror that the keys had been ripped up, the stops had been pulled out . . . and the pipes themselves filled with dry cornhusks. Over the organ was a carefully lettered plaque which read: *Make no music except with human tongue saith the Lord God.*

Vicky was right. Something was terribly wrong here. He debated going back to Vicky without exploring any further, just getting into the car and leaving town as quickly as possible, never mind the Municipal Building. But it grated on him. Tell the truth, he thought. You want to give her Ban 5000 a workout before going back and admitting she was right to start with.

He would go back out in a minute or so.

He walked toward the pulpit, thinking: People must go through Gatlin all the time. There must be people in the neighboring towns who have friends and relatives here. The Nebraska SP must cruise through from time to time. And what about the power company? The stoplight had been dead. Surely they'd know if the power had been off for twelve long years. Conclusion: What seemed to have happened in Gatlin was impossible.

Still, he had the creeps.

He climbed the four carpeted steps to the pulpit and looked out over the deserted pews, glimmering in the half-shadows. He seemed to feel the weight of those eldritch and decidedly unchristian eyes boring into his back.

There was a large Bible on the lectern, opened to the thirty-eighth chapter of Job. Burt glanced down at it and read: "Then the Lord answered Job out of the whirlwind, and said, Who is this that darkeneth counsel by words without knowledge? . . . Where wast thou when I laid the foundations of the earth? declare, if thou hast understanding." The Lord. He Who Walks Behind the Rows. Declare if thou hast understanding. And please pass the corn.

He fluttered the pages of the Bible, and they made a dry whispering sound in the quiet—the sound that ghosts might make if there really were such things. And in a place like this you could almost believe it. Sections of the Bible had been chopped out. Mostly from the New Testament, he saw. Someone had decided to take on the job of amending Good King James with a pair of scissors.

But the Old Testament was intact.

He was about to leave the pulpit when he saw another book on a lower shelf and took it out, thinking it might be a church record of weddings and confirmations and burials.

He grimaced at the words stamped on the cover, done inexpertly in gold leaf: *Thus let the iniquitous be cut down so that the ground may be fertile again saith the Lord God of Hosts.*

There seemed to be one train of thought around here, and Burt didn't care much for the track it seemed to ride on.

He opened the book to the first wide, lined sheet. A child had done the lettering, he saw immediately. In places an ink eraser had been carefully used, and while there were no misspellings, the letters were large and childishly made, drawn rather than written. The first column read:

Amos Deigan (Richard), b. Sept. 4, 1945	Sept. 4, 1964
Isaac Renfrew (William), b. Sept 19, 1945	Sept. 19, 1964
Zepeniah Kirk (George), b. Oct. 14, 1945	Oct. 14, 1965
Mary Wells (Roberta), b. Nov. 12, 1945	Nov. 12, 1964
Yemen Hollis (Edward), b. Jan 5, 1946	Jan. 5, 1965

Frowning, Burt continued to turn through the pages. Three-quarters of the way through, the double columns ended abruptly:

Rachel Stigman (Donna), b. June 21, 1957	June 21, 1976
Moses Richardson (Henry), b. July 29, 1957	
Malachi Boardman (Craig), b. August 15, 1957	

The last entry in the book was for Ruth Clawson (Sandra), b. April 30, 1961. Burt looked at the shelf where he had found this book and came up with two more. The first had the same *Iniquitous be cut down* logo, and it continued the same record, the single column tracing birth dates and names. In early September of 1964 he found Job Gilman (Clayton), b. September 6, and the next entry was Eve Tobin, b. June 16, 1965. No second name in parentheses.

The third book was blank.

Standing behind the pulpit, Burt thought about it.

Something had happened in 1964. Something to do with religion, and corn . . . and children.

Dear God we beg thy blessing on the crop. For Jesus' sake, amen.

And the knife raised high to sacrifice the lamb—but had it been a lamb? Perhaps a religious mania had swept them. Alone, all alone, cut off from the outside world by hundreds of square miles of the rustling secret corn. Alone under seventy million acres of blue sky. Alone under the watchful eye of God, now a strange green God, a God of corn, grown old and strange and hungry. He Who Walks Behind the Rows.

Burt felt a chill creep into his flesh.

Vicky, let me tell you a story. It's about Amos Deigan, who was born Richard Deigan on September 4, 1945. He took the name Amos in 1964, fine Old Testament name, Amos, one of the minor prophets. Well, Vicky, what happened—don't laugh—is that Dick Deigan and his friends—Billy Renfrew, George Kirk, Roberta Wells, and Eddie Hollis among others—they got religion and they killed off their parents. All of them. Isn't that a scream? Shot them in their beds, knifed them in their bathtubs, poisoned their suppers, hung them, or disemboweled them, for all I know.

Why? The corn. Maybe it was dying. Maybe they got the idea somehow that it was dying because there was too much sinning. Not enough sacrifice. They would have done it in the corn, in the rows.

And somehow, Vicky, I'm quite sure of this, somehow they decided that nineteen was as old as any of them could live. Richard "Amos" Deigan, the hero of our little story, had his nineteenth birthday on September 4, 1964— the date in the book. I think maybe they killed him. Sacrificed him in the corn. Isn't that a silly story?

But let's look at Rachel Stigman, who was Donna Stigman until 1964. She turned nineteen on June 21, just about a month ago. Moses Richardson was born on July 29—just three days from today he'll be nineteen. Any idea what's going to happen to ole Mose on the twenty-ninth?

I can guess.

Burt licked his lips, which felt dry.

One other thing, Vicky. Look at this. We have Job Gilman (Clayton) born on September 6, 1964. No other births until June 16, 1965. A gap of ten months. Know what I think? They killed all of the parents, even the pregnant ones, that's what I think. And one of *them* got pregnant in October of 1964 and gave birth to Eve. Some sixteen- or seventeen-year-old girl. *Eve. The first woman.*

He thumbed back through the book feverishly and found the Eve Tobin entry. Below it: Adam Greenlaw, b. July 11, 1965.

They'd be just eleven now, he thought, and his flesh began to crawl. And maybe they're out there. Someplace.

But how could such a thing be kept secret? How could it go on?

How unless the God in question approved?

"Oh Jesus," Burt said into the silence, and that was when the T-Bird's horn began to blare into the afternoon, one long continuous blast.

Burt jumped from the pulpit and ran down the center aisle. He threw open the outer vestibule door, letting in hot sunshine, dazzling. Vicky was bolt upright behind the steering wheel, both hands plastered on the horn ring, her head swiveling wildly. From all around the children were coming. Some of them were laughing gaily. They held knives, hatchets, pipes, rocks, hammers. One girl, maybe eight, with beautiful long blond hair, held a jackhandle. Rural weapons. Not a gun among them. Burt felt a wild urge to scream out: *Which of you is Adam and Eve? Who are the mothers? Who are the daughters? Fathers? Sons?*

Declare, if thou hast understanding.

They came from the side streets, from the town green, through the gate in the chain-link fence around the school playground a block further west. Some of them glanced indifferently at Burt, standing frozen on the church steps, and some nudged each other and pointed and smiled . . . the sweet smiles of children.

The girls were dressed in long brown wool and faded sunbonnets. The boys, like Quaker parsons, were all in black and wore round-crowned flat-brimmed hats. They streamed across the town square toward the car, across lawns, a few came across the front yard of what had been the Grace Baptist Church until 1964. One or two of them almost close enough to touch.

"The shotgun!" Burt yelled. "Vicky, get the shotgun!"

But she was frozen in her panic, he could see that from the steps. He doubted if she could even hear him through the closed windows.

They converged on the Thunderbird. The axes and hatchets and chunks of pipe began to rise and fall. My God, am I seeing this? he thought frozenly. An arrow of chrome fell off the side of the car. The hood ornament went flying. Knives scrawled spirals through the sidewalls of the tires and the car settled. The horn blared on and on. The windshield and side windows went opaque and cracked under the onslaught . . . and then the safety glass sprayed inward and he could see again. Vicky was crouched back, only one hand on the horn ring now, the other thrown up to protect her face. Eager young hands reached in, fumbling for the lock/unlock button. She beat them away wildly. The horn became intermittent and then stopped altogether.

The beaten and dented driver's side door was hauled open. They were trying to drag her out but her hands were wrapped around the steering wheel. Then one of them leaned in, knife in hand, and—

His paralysis broke and he plunged down the steps, almost falling, and ran down the flagstone walk, toward them. One of them, a boy of about sixteen with long red hair spilling out from beneath his hat, turned toward him, almost casually, and something flicked through the air. Burt's left arm jerked backward, and for a moment he had the absurd thought that he had been punched at long distance. Then the pain came, so sharp and sudden that the world went gray.

He examined his arm with a stupid sort of wonder. A buck and half Pensy jackknife was growing out of it like a strange tumor. The sleeve of his J.C. Penney sport shirt was turning red. He looked at it for what seemed like forever, trying to understand how he could have grown a jackknife . . . was it possible?

When he looked up, the boy with the red hair was almost on top of him. He was grinning, confident.

"Hey, you bastard," Burt said. His voice was creaking, shocked.

"Remand your soul to God, for you will stand before His throne momentarily," the boy with the red hair said, and clawed for Burt's eyes.

Burt stepped back, pulled the Pensy out of his arm, and stuck it into the red-haired boy's throat. The gush of blood was immediate, gigantic. Burt was splashed with it. The red-haired boy began to gobble and walk in a large circle. He clawed at the knife, trying to pull it free, and was unable. Burt watched him, jaw hanging agape. None of this was happening. It was a dream. The red-haired boy gobbled and walked. Now his sound was the only one in the hot early afternoon. The others watched, stunned.

This part of it wasn't in the script, Burt thought numbly. Vicky and I, we were in the script. And the boy in the corn, who was trying to run away. But not one of their own. He stared at them savagely, wanting to scream, *How do you like it?*

The red-haired boy gave one last weak gobble, and sank to his knees. He stared up at Burt for a moment, and then his hands dropped away from the haft of the knife, and he fell forward.

A soft sighing sound from the children gathered around the Thunderbird. They stared at Burt. Burt stared back at them, fascinated . . . and that was when he noticed that Vicky was gone.

"Where is she?" he asked. "Where did you take her?"

One of the boys raised a blood-streaked hunting knife toward his throat and made a sawing motion there. He grinned. That was the only answer.

From somewhere in back, an older boy's voice, soft: "Get him."

The boys began to walk toward him. Burt backed up. They began to walk faster. Burt backed up faster. The shotgun, the goddamned shotgun! Out of reach. The sun cut their shadows darkly on the green lawn . . . and then he was on the sidewalk. He turned and ran.

"*Kill him!*" someone roared, and they came after him.

He ran, but not quite blindly. He skirted the Municipal Building—no help there, they would corner him like a rat—and ran on up Main Street, which opened out and became the highway again two blocks further up. He and Vicky would have been on that road now and away, if only he had listened.

His loafers slapped against the sidewalk. Ahead of him he could see a few more business buildings, including the Gatlin Ice Cream Shoppe and—sure enough—the Bijou Theater. The dust-clotted marquee letters read *Now howing l mited en agemen Eli a Taylor Cleopa ra.* Beyond the next cross street was a gas station that marked the edge of town. And beyond that the corn, closing back in to the sides of the road. A green tide of corn.

Burt ran. He was already out of breath and the knife wound in his upper arm was beginning to hurt. And he was leaving a trail of blood. As he ran he yanked his handkerchief from his back pocket and stuck it inside his shirt.

He ran. His loafers pounded the cracked cement of the sidewalk, his breath rasped in his throat with more and more heat. His arm began to throb in earnest. Some mordant part of his brain tried to ask if he thought he could run all the way to the next town, if he could run twenty miles of two-lane blacktop.

He ran. Behind him he could hear them, fifteen years younger and faster than he was, gaining. Their feet slapped on the pavement. They whooped and shouted back and forth to each other. They're having more fun than a five-alarm fire, Burt thought disjointedly. They'll talk about it for years.

STEPHEN KING

Burt ran.

He ran past the gas station marking the edge of town. His breath gasped and roared in his chest. The sidewalk ran out under his feet. And now there was only one thing to do, only one chance to beat them and escape with his life. The houses were gone, the town was gone. The corn had surged in a soft green wave back to the edges of the road. The green, swordlike leaves rustled softly. It would be deep in there, deep and cool, shady in the rows of man-high corn.

He ran past a sign that said: *You are now leaving Gatlin, nicest little town in Nebraska—or anywhere else! Drop in anytime!*

I'll be sure to do that, Burt thought dimly.

He ran past the sign like a sprinter closing on the tape and then swerved left, crossing the road, and kicked his loafers away. Then he was in the corn and it closed behind him and over him like the waves of a green sea, taking him in. Hiding him. He felt a sudden and wholly unexpected relief sweep him, and at the same moment he got his second wind. His lungs, which had been shallowing up, seemed to unlock and give him more breath.

He ran straight down the first row he had entered, head ducked, his broad shoulders swiping the leaves and making them tremble. Twenty yards in he turned right, parallel to the road again, and ran on, keeping low so they wouldn't see his dark head of hair bobbing among the yellow corn tassels. He doubled back toward the road for a few moments, crossed more rows, and then put his back to the road and hopped randomly from row to row, always delving deeper and deeper into the corn.

At last, he collapsed onto his knees and put his forehead against the ground. He could only hear his own taxed breathing, and the thought that played over and over in his mind was: *Thank God I gave up smoking, thank God I gave up smoking, thank God—*

Then he could hear them, yelling back and forth to each other, in some cases bumping into each other ("Hey, this is my row!"), and the sound heartened him. They were well away to his left and they sounded very poorly organized.

He took his handkerchief out of his shirt, folded it, and stuck it back in after looking at the wound. The bleeding seemed to have stopped in spite of the workout he had given it.

He rested a moment longer, and was suddenly aware that he felt *good*, physically better than he had in years . . . excepting the throb of his arm. He felt well exercised, and suddenly grappling with a clear-cut (no matter how insane) problem after two years of trying to cope with the incubus gremlins that were sucking his marriage dry.

It wasn't right that he should feel this way, he told himself. He was in deadly peril of his life, and his wife had been carried off. She might be dead now. He tried to summon up Vicky's face and dispel some of the odd good feeling by doing so, but her face wouldn't come. What came was the red-haired boy with the knife in his throat.

He became aware of the corn fragrance in his nose now, all around him. The wind through the tops of the plants made a sound like voices. Soothing. Whatever had been done in the name of this corn, it was now his protector.

But they were getting closer.

Running hunched over, he hurried up the row he was in, crossed over, doubled back, and crossed over more rows. He tried to keep the voices always on his left, but as the afternoon progressed, that became harder and harder to do. The voices had grown faint, and often the rustling sound of the corn obscured them altogether. He would run, listen, run again. The earth was hard-packed, and his stockinged feet left little or no trace.

When he stopped much later the sun was hanging over the fields to his right, red and inflamed, and when he looked at his watch he saw that it was quarter past seven. The sun had stained the corn tops a reddish gold, but here the shadows were dark and deep. He cocked his head, listening. With the coming of sunset the wind had died entirely and the corn stood still, exhaling its aroma of growth into the warm air. If they were still in the corn they were either far away or just hunkered down and listening. But Burt didn't think a bunch of kids, even crazy ones, could be quiet for that long. He suspected they had done the most kidlike thing, regardless of the consequences for them: they had given up and gone home.

He turned toward the setting sun, which had sunk between the raftered clouds on the horizon, and began to walk. If he cut on a diagonal through the rows, always keeping the setting sun ahead of him he would be bound to strike Route 17 sooner or later.

The ache in his arm had settled into a dull throb that was nearly pleasant, and the good feeling was still with him. He decided that as long as he was here, he would let the good feeling exist in him without guilt. The guilt would return when he had to face the authorities and account for what had happened in Gatlin. But that could wait.

He pressed through the corn, thinking he had never felt so keenly aware. Fifteen minutes later the sun was only a hemisphere poking over the horizon and he stopped again, his new awareness clicking into a pattern he didn't like. It was vaguely . . . well, vaguely frightening.

He cocked his head. The corn was rustling.

Burt had been aware of that for some time, but he had just put it together with something else. The wind was still. How could that be?

He looked around warily, half expecting to see the boys in their Quaker coats creeping out of the corn, their knives clutched in their hands. Nothing of the sort. There was still that rustling noise. Off to the left.

He began to walk in that direction, not having to pull through the corn anymore. The row was taking him in the direction he wanted to go, naturally. The row ended up ahead. Ended? No, emptied out into some sort of clearing. The rustling was there.

He stopped, suddenly afraid.

The scent of the corn was strong enough to be cloying. The rows held on to the sun's heat and he became aware that he was plastered with sweat and chaff and thin spider strands of cornsilk. The bugs ought to be crawling all over him . . . but they weren't.

He stood still, staring toward that place where the corn opened out onto what looked like a large circle of bare earth.

There were no midges or mosquitoes in here, no blackflies or chiggers— what he and Vicky had called "drive-in bugs" when they had been courting, he thought with sudden and unexpectedly sad nostalgia. And he hadn't seen a single crow. How was that for weird, a corn patch with no crows?

In the last of the daylight he swept his eyes closely over the row of corn to his left. And saw that every leaf and stalk was perfect, which was just not possible. No yellow blight. No tattered leaves, no caterpillar eggs, no burrows, no—

His eyes widened.

My God, there aren't any weeds!

Not a single one. Every foot and a half the corn plants rose from the earth. There was no witchgrass, jimson, pikeweed, whore's hair, or poke salad. Nothing.

Burt stared up, eyes wide. The light in the west was fading. The raftered clouds had drawn back together. Below them the golden light had faded to pink and ocher. It would be dark soon enough.

It was time to go down to the clearing in the corn and see what was there—hadn't that been the plan all along? All the time he had thought he was cutting back to the highway, hadn't he been being led to this place?

Dread in his belly, he went on down to the row and stood at the edge of the clearing. There was enough light left for him to see what was here. He couldn't scream. There didn't seem to be enough air left in his lungs. He tottered in on legs like slats of splintery wood. His eyes bulged from his sweaty face.

"Vicky," he whispered. "Oh, Vicky, my God—"

She had been mounted on a crossbar like a hideous trophy, her arms held at the wrists and her legs at the ankles with twists of common barbed wire, seventy cents a yard at any hardware store in Nebraska. Her eyes had been ripped out. The sockets were filled with the moonflax of cornsilk. Her jaws were wrenched open in a silent scream, her mouth filled with cornhusks.

On her left was a skeleton in a moldering surplice. The nude jawbone grinned. The eye sockets seemed to stare at Burt jocularly, as if the onetime minister of the Grace Baptist Church was saying: *It's not so bad, being sacrificed by pagan devil-children in the corn is not so bad, having your eyes ripped out of your skull according to the Laws of Moses is not so bad—*

To the left of the skeleton in the surplice was a second skeleton, this one dressed in a rotting blue uniform. A hat hung over the skull, shading the eyes, and on the peak of the cap was a greenish-tinged badge reading *Police Chief.*

That was when Burt heard it coming: not the children but something much larger, moving through the corn and toward the clearing. Not the children, no. The children wouldn't venture into the corn at night. This was the holy place, the place of He Who Walks Behind the Rows.

Jerkily, Burt turned to flee. The row he had entered the clearing by was gone.

Closed up. All the rows had closed up. It was coming closer now and he could hear it, pushing through the corn. An ecstasy of superstitious terror seized him. It was coming. The corn on the far side of the clearing had suddenly darkened, as if a gigantic shadow had blotted it out.

Coming.

He Who Walks Behind the Rows.

It began to come into the clearing. Burt saw something huge, bulking up to the sky . . . something green with terrible eyes the size of footballs.

Something that smelled like dried cornhusks years in some dark barn.

He began to scream. But he did not scream long.

Some time later, a bloated orange harvest moon came up.

• • •

The children of the corn stood in the clearing at midday, looking at the two crucified skeletons and the two bodies . . . the bodies were not skeletons yet, but they would be. In time. And here, in the heartland of Nebraska, in the corn, there was nothing but time.

"Behold, a dream came to me in the night, and the Lord did shew all this to me."

They all turned to look at Isaac with dread and wonder, even Malachi. Isaac was only nine, but he had been the Seer since the corn had taken David a year ago. David had been nineteen and he had walked into the corn on his birthday, just as dusk had come drifting down the summer rows.

Now, small face grave under his round-crowned hat, Isaac continued:

"And in my dream the Lord was a shadow that walked behind the rows, and he spoke to me in the words he used to our older brothers years ago. He is much displeased with this sacrifice."

They made a sighing, sobbing noise and looked at the surrounding walls of green.

"And the Lord did say: Have I not given you a place of killing, that you might make sacrifice there? And have I not shewn you favor? But this man has made a blasphemy within me, and I have completed this sacrifice myself. Like the Blue Man and the false minister who escaped many years ago."

"The Blue Man . . . the false minister," they whispered, and looked at each other uneasily.

"So now is the Age of Favor lowered from nineteen plantings and harvestings to eighteen," Isaac went on relentlessly. "Yet be fruitful and multiply as the corn multiplies, that my favor may be shewn you, and be upon you."

Isaac ceased.

The eyes turned to Malachi and Joseph, the only two among this party who were eighteen. There were others back in town, perhaps twenty in all.

They waited to hear what Malachi would say, Malachi who had led the hunt for Japheth, who evermore would be known as Ahaz, cursed of God. Malachi had cut the throat of Ahaz and thrown his body out of the corn so the foul body would not pollute it or blight it.

"I obey the word of God," Malachi whispered.

The corn seemed to sigh its approval.

In the weeks to come the girls would make many corncob sacrifices to ward off further evil.

And that night all of those now above the Age of Favor walked silently into the corn and went to the clearing, to gain the continued favor of He Who Walks Behind the Rows.

"Goodbye, Malachi," Ruth called. She waved disconsolately. Her belly was big with Malachi's child and tears coursed silently down her cheeks. Malachi did not turn. His back was straight. The corn swallowed him.

Ruth turned away, still crying. She had conceived a secret hatred for the corn and sometimes dreamed of walking into it with a torch in each hand when dry September came and the stalks were dead and explosively combustible. But she also feared it. Out there, in the night, something walked, and it saw everything . . . even the secrets kept in human hearts.

Dusk deepened into night. Around Gatlin the corn rustled and whispered secretly. It was well pleased.

YELLOWJACKET SUMMER
ROBERT R. McCAMMON

"Car's comin', Mase," the boy at the window said. "Comin' lickety-split."

"Ain't no car comin'," Mase replied from the back of the gas station. "Ain't never no cars comin'."

"Yes there is! Come look! I can see the dust risin' off the road!"

Mase made a nasty sound with his lips and stayed where he was, sitting in the old cane chair Miss Nancy had said she wouldn't befoul her behind to sit on. Mase was kinda sweet on Miss Nancy, the boy knew, and he was always asking her to come over for a cold CoCola but she had a boyfriend in Waycross so that wouldn't do. The boy felt a little sorry for Mase sometimes, because nobody in town liked being around him much. Maybe it was because Mase was mean when he got riled, and he drank too much on Saturday nights. He smelled of grease and gasoline too, and his clothes and cap were always dark with stains.

"Come look, Mase!" the boy urged, but Mase shook his head and just sat watching the Braves baseball game on the little portable TV.

Well, there *was* a car, after all, trailing plumes of dust from its tires. But not exactly a car, the boy saw; it was a van with wood trim on its sides. The van had been white before it had met up with four unpaved miles of Highway 241, but now it was reddened by Georgia clay and there were dead bugs spotting the windshield. The boy wondered if any of them were yellowjackets. It was a yellowjacket summer for sure, he thought. Them things were just *everywhere!*

"They're slowin' down, Mase," the boy told him. "I think they're gonna pull in here."

"Lord A'mighty!" He smacked his knee with one hand. "There's three men on base! You go out and see what they want, hear?"

"Okay," he agreed, and he was almost out the screen door when Mase called, "All they want's a roadmap! They gotta be lost to be in this neck o' nowhere! And tell 'em the gas truck's not due till tomorrow, Toby!"

The screen door slammed shut behind him, and Toby ran out into the steamy July heat as the van pulled up to the pumps.

"There's somebody!" Carla Emerson said as she saw the boy emerged from the building. She released the breath she'd been holding for what seemed like the last five miles, since they'd passed a road sign pointing them to the town of Capshaw, Georgia. The ancient-looking gas station, its roof covered with kudzu and its bricks bleached yellow by a hundred summer suns, was a beautiful sight, especially since the Voyager's tank was getting way too low for comfort. Trish had been driving Carla crazy by saying, "It's on the E, Momma!" every minute or so, and Joe made her feel like a twerp with his doomy pronouncement of "Should've pulled over at the rest stop, Mom."

In the back seat, Joe put aside the *Fantastic Four* comic he'd been reading. "I sure do hope they've got a bathroom," he said. "If I can't pee in about five seconds I'm gonna go out in a burst of glory."

"Thanks for the warning," she told him as she stopped the van next to the dusty pumps and cut the engine. "Go for it!"

He opened his door and scrambled out, trying to keep his bladder from bouncing around too much. He was twelve years old, skinny, and wore braces on his teeth, but he was as intelligent as he was gawky and he figured that someday God would give him a better chance with girls; right now, though, computer games and superhero comics took most of his attention.

He almost ran right into the boy who had hair the color of fire.

"Howdy," Toby said, and grinned. "What can I do for you?"

"Bathroom," Joe told him, and Toby motioned with a finger toward the back side of the gas station. Joe took off at a trot, and Toby called, "Ain't too clean in there, though. Sorry!"

That was the least of Joe Emerson's worries as he hurried around the small brick building, back to where kudzu and stickers erupted out of the thick pine forest. There was just one door, and it had no handle on it, but it was mercifully unlocked. He went in.

Carla had her window rolled down. "Could you fill us up, please? With unleaded?"

Toby kept grinning at her. She was a pretty woman, maybe older than Miss Nancy but not *too* old; her hair was light brown and curly, and she had steady

107

gray eyes set in a high-cheekboned face. Perched in the seat next to her was a little brown-haired girl maybe six or seven. "No gas," he told the woman. "Not a drop."

"Oh." The nervous clenching sensation returned to her stomach. "Oh, no! Well . . . is there another station around here?"

"Yes, ma'am." He pointed in the direction the van was facing. "Halliday's about eighteen or twenty miles. They've got a real nice gas station."

"We're on E!" Trish said.

"Shhhh, honey." Carla touched the little girl's arm. The boy with red, close-cropped hair was still smiling, waiting for Carla to speak again. Through the station's screen door Carla could hear the noise of a crowd roaring on a TV set.

"Bet they got a run," the boy said. "The Braves. Mase is watchin' the game."

Eighteen or twenty miles! Carla thought. She wasn't sure they had enough gas to make it that far, and she sure would hate to run out on a country road. The sun was shining down hot and bright from the fierce blue sky, and the pine woods looked like they went on to the edge of eternity. She cursed herself as a fool for not stopping at that rest station on Highway 84, where there was Shell gasoline and a Burger King, but she'd thought they could fill up ahead and she was in a hurry to get to St. Simons Island. Her husband, Ray, was a lawyer and had flown on to Brunswick for a business meeting several days ago; she and the kids had left Atlanta yesterday morning to visit her parents in Valdosta, then were supposed to swing up through Waycross and meet Ray for a vacation. Stay on the main highway, Ray had told her. You get off the highway, you can get lost in some pretty desolate country. But she thought she'd known her own state, particularly the area she'd grown up in! When the pavement had stopped and Highway 241 had turned to dust a ways back, she'd almost stopped and turned around—but then she'd seen the sign to Capshaw, so she'd kept on going and hoped for the best.

But if this was the best, they were sunk.

In the bathroom, Joe had learned that you spell relief p-e-e. It was not a clean bathroom, true, and there were dead leaves and pinestraw on the floor and the single window was broken, but he would've gone in an outhouse if he'd had to. The toilet hadn't been flushed for a long time, though, and the smell wasn't too pleasant. Through the thin wall he could hear a TV set on. The crack of a bat and the roar of a crowd.

And another sound too. Something that he couldn't identify at first.

It was a low droning noise. Somewhere close, he thought, as he stood at the end of an amber river.

Joe looked up, and his hand abruptly squeezed the river off.

Above his head, the bathroom's ceiling crawled with yellowjackets. Hundreds of them. Maybe thousands. The little winged bodies with their yellow-and-black-striped stingers crawled over and around each other, making a weird droning noise that wounded like a hushed, distant—and dangerous—whisper.

The river would not be denied. It kept streaming. As Joe stared upward with widened eyes, he saw maybe thirty or forty of the yellowjackets take off, buzz curiously around his head, and then fly away through the broken window. A few of them—ten or fifteen, Joe realized—came in for a closer look. His skin crept as the yellowjackets hummed before his face, and he heard their droning change pitch, become higher and faster—as if they knew they'd found an intruder.

More left the ceiling. He felt them walking in his hair, and one landed on the edge of his right ear. The river would not stop, and he knew he must not cry out, *must not must not*, because the noise in this confined place might send the whole colony of them into a stinging frenzy.

One landed on his left cheek and walked toward his nose. Five or six of them were crawling on his sweaty Conan the Barbarian T-shirt. And then he felt some of them land on his knuckles and—yes—even *there* too.

He fought back a sneeze as a yellowjacket probed his left nostril. A dark, humming cloud of them hung waiting over his scalp.

"Well," Carla said to the red-haired boy, "I don't guess we've got much choice, do we?"

"But we're on E, Momma!" Trish reminded her.

"You 'bout empty?" Toby asked.

"I'm afraid so. We're on our way to St. Simons Island."

"Long way from here." Toby looked off to the right, where a battered old pickup truck with red plastic dice hanging from the rearview mirror was parked. "That's Mase's truck. Maybe he'd drive over to Halliday for you and get you some gas."

"Mase? Who's that?"

"Oh, he owns this place. Always has. Want me to ask him if he'll do it?"

"I don't know. Maybe we could make it ourselves."

Toby shrugged. "Maybe you could, at that." But the way he smiled told Carla that he didn't believe she would, and she didn't believe it herself. Lord, Ray was going to pitch a fit about this!

"I'll ask him, if you like." Toby kicked a stone with the toe of one dirty sneaker.

"All right," Carla agreed. "Tell him I'll pay him five dollars, too."

"Sure thing." Toby walked back to the screen door. "Mase? Lady out here needs some gas pretty bad. Says she'll pay you five dollars to bring her back a few gallons from Halliday."

Mase didn't answer. His face was blue from the TV screen's glow.

"Mase? Did you hear me?" Toby prodded.

"I'm not goin' a damn place until this damn baseball game is over, boy!" Mase finally said, with a terrible scowl. "Been waitin' all week for it! Score's four to two, bottom of the fifth!"

"She's a looker, Mase," Toby said, casting his voice lower. "Almost as pretty as Miss Nancy."

"I said leave me be!" And for the first time Toby saw that Mase had a bottle of beer on the little table beside his chair. It wouldn't do to get Mase riled up, not on a hot day like this in the middle of yellowjacket summer.

But Toby screwed up his courage and tried once more. "*Please,* Mase. The lady needs help!"

"Oh . . ." Mase shook his head. "All right, if you'll just let me finish watchin' this damn game! I'll drive over there for her. God A'mighty, I thought I was gonna have me a peaceful day."

Toby thanked him and walked back to the van. "He says he'll go, but he wants to watch the baseball game. I'd drive myself, but I just turned fifteen and Mase would whip my tail if I had a wreck. If you like, you can leave the van here. Café to get sandwiches and stuff is just around the bend, walkin' distance. That suit you?"

"Yes, that'd be fine." Carla wanted to stretch her legs, and something cold to drink would be wonderful. But what had happened to Joe? She honked the horn a couple of times and rolled up her window. "Probably fell in," she told Trish.

The yellowjacket had decided not to enter Joe's nostril. Still, there were thirty or more of them on his T-shirt, and he could feel the damned things all in his hair. His teeth were clenched, his face pale and sweating, and yellowjackets were crawling over his hands. Chills ran up and down his spine; he'd read somewhere about a farmer who had disturbed a yellowjacket nest, and by the time they got through with him he was a writhing mass of stung flesh and he'd died on the way to the hospital. At any second he expected a dozen stingers to rip through the skin at the back of his neck. His breathing was harsh and forced, and he was afraid that his knees would buckle and his face would fall into that filthy toilet and then the yellowjackets would go to w—

"Don't move," the red-haired boy said, standing in the bathroom's doorway. "They're all over you. Don't move, now."

Joe didn't have to be told twice. He stood frozen and sweating, and then he heard a low, trilling whistle that went on for maybe twenty seconds. It was a soothing, calming sound, and the yellowjackets started leaving Joe's shirt and flying out of his hair. As soon as they were off his hands, he zipped himself up and he got out of the bathroom with yellowjackets buzzing curiously over his head. He ducked and batted at them, and they flew away.

"Yellowjackets!" he gasped. "Must've been a million in there!"

"Not that many," Toby told him. "It's yellowjacket summer. But don't worry about 'em now. You're safe." He was smiling, and he lifted his right hand.

The boy's hand was covered with them, layer upon layer of them, until it looked as if the hand grown to grotesque proportions, the huge fingers striped with yellow and black.

Joe stood staring, openmouthed and terrified. The other boy whistled again—this time a short, sharp whistle—and the yellowjackets stirred lazily, humming and buzzing and finally lifting off from his hand in a dark cloud that rose up and flew away into the woods.

"See?" Toby slid his hand into his jeans pocket. "I said you were safe, didn't I?"

"How . . . how . . . did you do—"

"Joe!" It was his mother, calling him. "Come on!"

He wanted to run, wanted to leave tornadoes whirling under his sneakers, but he forced himself to walk at a steady pace around the gas station to where his mother and Trish were out of the Voyager and waiting for him. He could hear the crunch of the other boy's shoes on the gravel, following right behind him. "Hey!" Joe said, his face tightening as he tried to smile. "What's goin' on?"

"We thought we'd lost you! What took you so long?"

Before Joe could answer, a hand was placed firmly on his shoulder. "Got hisself stuck in the bathroom," Toby told her. "Old door oughta be fixed. Ain't that right?" The pressure of his hand increased.

Joe heard a thin buzzing. He looked down, saw that the hand clamped to his shoulder had a yellowjacket lodged between the first and second fingers.

"Mom?" Joe said softly. "I was—" He stopped, because beyond his other and sister he could see a dark banner—maybe two or three hundred yellow-jackets—slowly undulating in the bright sunshine over the road.

"You okay?" Carla asked. Joe looked like he was about to upchuck.

"I think he'll live, ma'am," Toby said, and he laughed. "Just scared him a little, I guess."

"Oh. Well . . . we're going to get a bite to eat and something cold to drink, Joe. He says there's a café right around the bend."

Joe nodded, but his stomach was churning. He heard the boy give a low, weird whistle, so soft that his mother couldn't possibly have heard; the yellowjacket flew off from between the boy's fingers, and the awful waiting cloud of them began to break apart.

"Just 'bout lunchtime!" Toby announced. "Think I'll walk thataway with ya'll."

The sun burned down. A layer of yellow dust seemed to hang in the air. "It's hot, Momma!" Trish complained before they'd walked ten yards away from the gas station, and Carla felt sweat creeping down her back under her pale blue blouse. Joe followed further behind, with the red-haired boy named Toby right on his heels.

The road curved through the pine woods toward the town of Capshaw. It wasn't much of a town, Carla saw in another couple of minutes; there were a few unkempt-looking wooden houses, a general store with a *Closed Please Come Again* sign in the front window; a small whitewashed church, and white stone building with a rust-eaten sign that announced it as the *Clayton Café*. In the gravel parking lot were an old gray Buick, a pickup truck of many colors, and a little red sports car with the convertible top pulled down.

The town was quiet except for the distant cawing of a crow. It amazed Carla that such a primitive-looking place should exist just seven or eight miles off the main highway. In an age of interstates and rapid travel, it was easy to forget that little hamlets like this still stood on the back roads—and Carla felt like kicking herself in the butt for getting them into this mess. Now they were really going to be late getting to St. Simons Island!

"Afternoon, Mr. Winslow!" Toby called, and waved to someone off to the left.

Carla looked. On the front porch of a rundown old house sat a white-haired man in overalls. He sat without moving, and Carla thought he looked like a wax dummy. But then she saw a swirl of smoke rise from his corncob pipe, and he lifted a hand in greeting.

"Hot day today!" Toby said. "It's lunchtime! You comin'?"

"Directly," the man answered.

"Best fetch Miss Nancy, then. Got some tourists passin' through!"

"I can see," the white-haired man said.

"Yeah." Toby grinned at him. "They're goin' to St. Simons Island. Long way from here, huh?"

The man stood up from his chair and went into the house.

"Mom?" Joe's voice was tense. "I don't think we ought to—"

"Like your shirt," Toby interrupted, plucking at it. "It's nice and clean."

And then they were at the Clayton Café and Carla was going inside, her hand holding Trish's. A little sign said *We're Air-Conditioned!* But if that was so, the air-conditioning was not functioning; it was as hot in the café as it was on the road.

The place was small, with a floor of discolored linoleum and a counter colored mustard yellow. There were a few tables and chairs and a jukebox pushed back against the wall.

"Lunchtime!" Toby called merrily as he followed Joe through the door and shut it behind them. "Brought some tourists today, Emma!"

Something rattled back in the kitchen. "Come say hello, Emma!" Toby urged.

The door to the kitchen opened, and a thin woman with gray hair, a deeply wrinkled face, and somber brown eyes came out. Her gaze went to Carla first, then to Joe, finally lingered on Trish.

"What's for lunch?" Toby asked her. Then he held up a finger. "Wait! I bet I know! Uh . . . alphabet soup, potato chips, and peanut-butter-and-grape-jelly sandwiches! Is that right?"

"Yes," Emma replied, and now she stared at the boy. "That's right, Toby."

"I knew it! See, folks around here used to say I was special. Used to say I knew things that shouldn't be known." He tapped the side of his skull. "Used to say I had the beckonin' touch. Ain't that right, Emma?"

She nodded, her arms limp at her sides.

Carla didn't know what the boy was talking about, but his tone of voice gave her the creeps. Suddenly it seemed way too cramped in this place, too hot and bright, and Trish said, "Ow, Mommy!" because she was squeezing the child's hand too tightly. Carla loosened her grip. "Listen," she said to Toby. "Maybe I should call my husband. He's at the Sheraton on St. Simons Island. He'll be real worried if I don't check in with him. Is there a phone I can use somewhere?"

"Nope," Emma said. "Sorry." Her gaze slid toward the wall, and Carla saw an outline there where the pay phone had been removed.

"There's a phone at the gas station." Toby sat down at one of the stools facing the counter. "You can call your husband after lunch. By that time Mase'll be back from Halliday." He began to spin himself around and around on the stool. "I'm hungry hungry hungry!" he said.

"Lunch is comin' right up." Emma returned to the kitchen.

Carla herded Trish toward one of the tables, but Joe just stood there staring at Toby; then the red-haired boy got off his stool and joined them at the table, turning his chair around so he rested his elbows on the back. He smiled, watching Carla with steady pale green eyes. "Quiet town," she said uneasily.

"Yep."

"How many people live here?"

"A few. Not too many. I don't like crowded places. Like Halliday and Double Pines."

"What does your father do? Does he work around here?"

"Naw," Toby replied. "Can you cook?"

"Uh . . . I guess so." The question had taken her by surprise.

"Raisin' kids, you'd have to cook, wouldn't you?" he asked her, his eyes opaque. "Unless you're rich and you go out to fancy restaurants every night."

"No, I'm not rich."

"Nice van you got, though. Bet it cost a lot of money." He looked over at Joe and said, "Why don't you sit down? There's a chair for you, right beside me."

"Can I get a hamburger, Momma?" Trish asked. "And a Pepsi?"

"Alphabet soup's on the menu today, little girl. Gonna get you a peanut-butter-and-jelly sandwich, too. That suit you?" Toby reached out to touch the child's hair.

But Carla drew Trish closer to her.

The boy stared at her for a moment, his smile beginning to fade. The silence stretched.

"I don't like 'phabet soup," Trish said softly.

"You will," Toby promised. And then his smile came back again, only this time it hung lopsided on his mouth. "I mean . . . Emma makes the best alphabet soup in town."

Carla could not stand to look into the boy's eyes any longer. She shifted her gaze, and then the door opened and two people came into the café. One was the old white-haired man in overalls, and the other was a skinny girl with dirty-blond hair and a face that might've been pretty if it was clean. She was about twenty or twenty-five, Carla thought, and she wore stained khaki slacks, a pink blouse that had been resewn in many places, and a pair of Top Siders on her feet. She smelled bad, and her blue eyes were sunken and shocked. Winslow helped her to a chair at another table, where she sat muttering to herself and staring at her filthy hands.

Neither Carla nor Joe could help but notice the swollen bites that pocked her face, the welts going right up into her hairline.

"My God," Carla whispered. "What . . . *happened* to—"

"Mase called on her," Toby said. "He's sweet on Miss Nancy."

Winslow sat down at a table by himself, lit his pipe, and smoked it in grave silence.

Emma came out with a tray, carrying bowls of soup, little bags of potato chips, and the sandwiches. She began to serve Toby first. "Have to go to the grocery store pretty soon," she said. "We're runnin' low on near 'bout everythin'."

Toby started chewing on his sandwich and didn't reply.

"My bread's got crust," Trish whispered to her mother; sweat clung to her face and her eyes were round and frightened.

It was so hot in the café that Carla could hardly bear it. Her blouse was soaked with sweat, and now the unwashed smell of Miss Nancy almost sickened her. She felt Toby watching her, and suddenly she found herself wanting to scream. "Excuse me," she managed to say to Emma, "but my little girl doesn't like to eat the crust on bread. Do you have a knife?"

Emma blinked, did not answer; her hand hesitated as she put a bowl of soup in front of Joe. Winslow laughed quietly, a laugh devoid of mirth.

"Sure thing," Toby said as he reached into his jeans pocket. He brought out a folding knife, got the blade extended. "I'll do it," he offered, and started carving the crust away.

"Ma'am? Here's your soup." Emma put a bowl in front of her.

Carla knew she couldn't take a bite of hot soup, not in this already-steaming place. "Can we . . . have something cold to drink, please?"

"Nothin' but water here," Emma said. "Ice machine's broke. Hush up and eat your soup." She moved away to serve Miss Nancy.

And then Carla saw it.

Right there. Spelled out in letters, floating on the top of her alphabet soup.

Boys crazy.

The knife was at work, carving, carving.

Carla's throat was dust-dry, but she swallowed anyway. Her eyes watched the moving blade, so terribly close to her little girl's throat.

"I said, *eat it!*" Emma almost shouted.

Carla understood. She put her spoon into the bowl, churned up the letters so he wouldn't see, then took a mouthful that all but seared her tongue.

"Like it?" Toby asked Trish, holding the blade before her face. "Look at it shine! Ain't it a pretty th—"

He did not finish his sentence, because in that instant hot alphabet soup had been flung into his eyes. But not by Carla. By Joe, who had come out of his daze and now grabbed at the knife as Toby cried out and fell backward from his chair. Even blinded, Toby held off Joe as they fought on the floor, and Carla sat transfixed while precious seconds ticked past.

"Kill him!" Emma screamed. "Kill the little bastard!" She began beating Toby with the tray she held, but in the confusion most of her blows were hitting Joe. Toby flailed out with the knife, snagging Joe's T-shirt and ripping a hole in it. Then Carla was on her feet too, and Miss Nancy was screaming something unintelligible. Carla tried to grab the boy's wrist, missed, and tried again. Toby shouted and writhed, his face a twisted and terrible rictus, but Joe was holding on to him with all his dwindling strength. "Momma! Momma!" Trish was crying—and then Carla put her foot down on Toby's wrist and pinned the knife hand to the linoleum.

The fingers opened, and Joe snatched up the knife.

Both he and his mother stepped back, and Toby sat up with the fury of hell on his face.

"Kill him!" Emma shouted, red to the roots of her hair. "Put that knife right through his evil heart!" She started to grab the blade, but Joe moved away from her.

Winslow was standing up, still calmly smoking his pipe. "Well," he said quietly, "now you done it. Now you gone and done it."

Toby crawled away from then toward the door, wiping his eyes clear with his forearm. He sat up on his knees, then slowly got to his feet.

"He's crazy as hell!" Emma said. "He's killed everybody in this damned town!"

"Not everybody, Emma," Toby replied. The smile had returned. "Not yet."

Carla had Trish in her arms, and she was so hot she feared she might pass out. All the air was heavy and stagnant, and now Miss Nancy was grinning into her face and pulling at her with her filthy hands.

"I don't know what's going on here," Carla finally said, "but we're getting out. Gas or not, we're leaving."

"Are you? Really?" Toby suddenly inhaled, and let the air out in a long, trilling whisper that made Carla's skin creep. The whistling went on and on. Emma screamed, "Shut him up! Somebody shut him up!"

The whistling abruptly stopped, on an ascending note.

"Get out of our way," Carla said. "We're leaving."

"Maybe. Maybe not. It's yellowjacket summer, lady. Them things are just *everywhere*."

Something touched the café's window. A dark cloud began to grow, to spread across the outside of the glass.

"Ever been stung by a yellowjacket, lady?" Toby asked. "I mean bad, *deep* stung? Stung right to the bone? Stung so bad that you'd scream for somebody to cut your throat and end the misery?"

The windows were darkening. Miss Nancy whimpered, and began to cower under a table.

"It's yellowjacket summer," Toby repeated. "They come when I call 'em. They do what I want 'em to do. Oh, I speak their tongue, lady. I've got the beckonin' touch."

"Oh, Jesus." Winslow shook his head. "Now you've gone and done it."

The bright sunlight was going away. Darkness was falling fast. Carla heard the high, thin droning noise from the thousands of yellowjackets that were collecting on the windows, and a trickle of sweat ran down her face.

"State trooper come here once. Lookin' for somebody. I forget who. He says, 'Boy? Where's your folks? How come ain't nobody around here?' And he was gonna put a call through on his radio, but when he opened his mouth I sent 'em in there. They went right smack down his throat. Oh, you should've seen that trooper dance!" Toby giggled at the obscene memory. "They stung him to death from the inside out. But they won't sting me, 'cause I speak their tongue."

The light was almost gone, just a little shard of red-hot sun breaking through when the mass of yellowjackets shifted.

"Well, go on, then," Toby said, and motioned toward the door. "Don't let me stop you."

Emma said, "Kill him right now! Kill him and they'll fly right off!"

"Touch me," Toby warned, "and I'll make 'em squeeze through every damned chink in this place. I'll make 'em sting your eyeballs and go up your ears. And I'll make 'em kill the little girl first."

"Why? For God's sake . . . *why?*"

"Because I *can*," he answered. "Go on. Your van's just a short walk."

Carla set Trish down. She looked into the boy's face for a moment, then took the knife from Joe's hand.

"Give it here," Toby ordered.

She hesitated in the twilight, ran her forearm across her face to mop up some of the sweat, and then she walked to Toby and pressed the blade against his throat. His smile faltered.

"You're going to walk with us," she said, her voice quavering. "You're going to keep them off, or I swear to God that I'll shove this right through your neck."

"I ain't goin' nowhere."

"Then you'll die here with us. I want to live, and I want my children to live, but we're not staying in this . . . this insane asylum. I don't know what you had planned for us but I think I'd rather die. So which is it?"

"You won't kill me, lady."

Carla had to make him believe she would, though she didn't know what she'd do if the time came. She tensed, drove her hand forward in a short, sharp jab. Toby winced, and a little drop of blood ran down his throat.

"That's it!" Emma crowed. "Do it! Do it!"

A yellowjacket suddenly landed on Carla's cheek. Another on her hand. A third buzzed dangerously close to her left eye.

The one on her cheek stung her, the pain searing and vicious. It seemed to make her entire spine vibrate as if she'd suffered an electric shock, and tears came to her eyes, but she kept the blade against his throat.

"One for one," he said.

"You're going to walk with us," Carla repeated as her cheek started swelling. "If either of my children is hurt, I'll kill you." And this time her voice was steady, though four yellowjackets crawled over knuckles.

Toby paused. Then he shrugged and said, "Okay. Sure. Let's go."

"Joe, hold onto Trish's hand. Then grab my belt. Don't let go, and for God's sake don't let her go either." She prodded Toby with the knife. "Go on. Open the door."

"*No!*" Winslow protested. "Don't go out there! You're crazy, woman!"

"*Open it.*"

Toby slowly turned, and Carla pressed the blade against the pulsing vein in his neck while she grasped his collar with her other hand. He reached out—slowly, very slowly—and turned the doorknob. He pulled the door open, the harsh sunlight blinding Carla for a few seconds. When her vision had returned, she saw a dark, buzzing cloud waiting in the doorway.

"I can put this in your neck if you try to run," she warned him. "You remember that."

"I don't have to run. You're the one they want." And he walked into the cloud of yellowjackets with Carla and her children right behind her.

It was like stepping into a black blizzard, and Carla almost screamed, but she knew that if she did they were all lost; she kept one hand closed around Toby's collar and the knife digging into his neck, but she had to squeeze her eyes shut because the yellowjackets swarmed at her face. She couldn't find a breath, felt a sting and then another on the side of her face, heard Trish cry out as she was stung too. "Get them away, damn it!" she shouted as two more stung her around the mouth. The pain ripped through her face; she could already feel it swelling, distorting, and at that instant panic almost swept her senses away. "Get them away!" she told him, shaking him by the collar. She heard him laugh, and she wanted to kill him.

They came out of the vicious cloud. Carla didn't know how many times she'd been stung, but her eyes were still okay. "You all right?" she called. "Joe? Trish?"

"I got stung in the face," Joe said, "but I'm okay. So is Trish."

"Hush crying!" she told the little girl. Carla's right eyelid had been hit, and the eye was starting to swell shut. More yellowjackets kept humming around her head, pulling at her hair like little fingers.

"Some of 'em don't like to listen," Toby said. "They do as they please."

"Keep walking. Faster, damn you!"

Someone screamed. Carla looked over her shoulder, saw Miss Nancy running in the opposite direction with a swarm of several hundred yellowjackets enveloping her. The younger woman flailed madly at them, dancing and jerking. She took three more steps and went down, and Carla quickly looked away because she'd seen that the yellowjackets completely covered Miss Nancy's face and head. The screams were muffled. In another moment they ceased.

A figure stumbled toward Carla, clutching at her arm. "Help me . . . help me," Emma moaned. The sockets of her eyes were crawling with yellowjackets. She started to fall, and Carla had no choice but to pull away from her. Emma lay twitching on the ground, feebly crying for help.

"You've gone and done it now, woman!" Winslow was standing untouched in the doorway as the thousands of yellowjackets flew in a storm around him. "Damn, you've done it!"

But Carla and the kids were out of the worst of it. Still, whining currents of yellowjackets followed them. Joe dared to look up, and he could no longer see the sun directly overhead.

They reached the gas station, and Carla said, "Oh, my God!"

The van was a solid mass of yellowjackets, and the gas station's sagging old roof was alive with them.

The pickup truck was still there. Over the whining and humming, Carla heard the sound of the baseball game on TV. "Help us!" she cried. "Please! We need help!"

Toby laughed again.

"Call him! Tell him to come out here! Do it *now!*"

"Mase is watchin' the baseball game, lady. He won't help you."

She shoved him toward the screen door. A few yellowjackets were clinging to the screen, but they took off as Toby approached. "Hey, Mase! Lady wants to see you, Mase!"

"Mom," Joe said, his lips swollen and turning blue. "Mom . . . "

She could see a figure in there, sitting in front of the glowing TV screen. The man wore a cap. "Please help us!" she shouted again.

"Mom . . . listen . . . "

"HELP US!" she screamed, and she kicked the screen door in. It fell from its hinges to the dusty floor.

"Mom . . . when I was in the bathroom . . . and he talked to somebody in there . . . I didn't hear anybody *answer* him."

And then Carla understood why.

A corpse sat before the TV. The man was long dead—many months, at least—and he was nothing but a red clay husk with a grinning, eyeless face.

"GET 'EM, MASE!" the boy wailed, and he tore away from Carla's grip. She struck with the blade, caught him across the throat, but not enough to stop him. He shrieked and jumped like a top gone crazy.

Yellowjackets began streaming from the corpse's eye sockets, the cavity where the nose had been, and the straining, terrible mouth. Carla realized with soul-numbing horror that the yellowjackets had burrowed a nest inside the dead man, and now they were pouring out of him by the thousands. They swarmed toward Carla and her children with relentless fury.

She whirled around, picked up Trish under one arm, and shouted, "Come on!" to Joe. She raced toward the van, where thousands more yellowjackets were stirring, starting to fly up and merge into a yellow-and-black-striped wall.

Carla had no choice but to thrust her hand into the midst of them, digging for the door handle.

They covered her hand in an instant, plunged their stingers deep, as if directed by a single malevolent intelligence. Howling with pain, Carla searched frantically for the handle. The sea of yellowjackets flowed up her forearm, up over her elbow, and toward her shoulder, stinging all the way.

Her fingers closed around the handle. She got the door open as yellowjackets attacked her neck, cheeks, and forehead. Both Trish and Joe were sobbing with pain, but all she could do was to throw them bodily into the ban. She grabbed up handfuls of yellowjackets and crushed them between her fingers, then struggled in and slammed the door.

Still, there were dozens of them inside. Enraged, Joe started swatting them with his comic book, took off one sneaker and used that as a weapon too. His face was covered with stings, both eyes badly swollen.

Carla started the engine. Used the windshield wipers to brush a crawling mass of the insects aside. And through the windshield she saw the boy, his arms uplifted, his flame-colored hair now turned yellow and black with the yellowjackets that clung to his skull, his shirt covered with them, and blood leaking from the gash on the side of his neck.

Carla heard herself roar like a beast. She sank her foot to the floorboard.

The Voyager leapt forward, through the storm of yellowjackets.

Toby saw, and tried to jump aside. But his twisted, hideous face told Carla that he knew he was a step too late.

The van hit him, knocking him flat. Carla twisted the wheel violently to the right and felt a tire wobble as it crunched over Toby's body. Then she was away from the pumps and speeding through Capshaw with Joe hammering at yellowjackets inside the van.

"We made it!" she shouted, though the voice from her mangled lips did not sound human anymore. "We made it!"

The van streaked on, throwing up plumes of dust behind its tires. The treads of the right-front tire were matted with blood.

The odometer rolled off the miles, and through the slit of her left eye Carla kept watching the gas gauge's needle as it vibrated over the E. But she did not let up on the accelerator, taking the van around the sudden curves so fast it threatened to fly off the road into the woods. Joe killed the last of the yellowjackets, and then he sat numbly in the back, holding Trish close.

Finally, pavement returned to the road and they came out of the Georgia pines at a three-way intersection. A sign said *Halliday* . . . 9. Carla sobbed with relief and shot the van through the intersection at seventy miles an hour.

One mile passed. A second, a third, and a fourth. The Voyager started up a hill—and Carla felt the engine kick.

"Oh . . . God," she whispered. Her hands, clamped to the steering wheel, were inflamed and horribly swollen. "No . . . no . . . "

The engine stuttered, and the van's forward progress began to slow.

"*No!*" she screamed, throwing herself against the wheel in an effort to keep the van going. But the speedometer's needle was falling fast, and then the stuttering engine went silent.

The van had enough steam left to make the top of the hill, and it rolled to a halt about fifteen feet from the declining side. "Wait here!" Carla said. "Don't move!" She got out, staggered on swollen legs to the rear of the van, and put her weight against it, trying to shove it over the hill. The van resisted her. "Please . . . *please*," she whispered, and kept pushing.

Slowly, inch by inch, the Voyager started rolling forward.

She heard a distant droning noise, and she dared to look back.

About four or five miles away, the sky had turned dark. What resembled a massive yellow-and-black-streaked thundercloud was rolling over the woods, bending the pine trees before it.

Sobbing, Carla looked down the long hill that descended in front of the van. At its bottom was a wide S-curve, and off in the green forest were the roofs of houses and buildings.

The droning noise was approaching, and twilight was falling fast.

She heard the muscles of her shoulder crack as she strained against the van. A shadow fell upon her.

The van rolled closer to the decline; then it started rolling on its own, and Carla hobbled after it, grabbed the open door, and swung herself up into the seat just as it picked up real speed. She gripped the wheel, and she told her children to hang on.

What sounded like hail started pelting the roof.

The van hurtled down the hill as the sun went dark in the middle of yellowjacket summer.

THE STUFF THAT GOES ON IN THEIR HEADS

MICHAEL MARSHALL SMITH

I first heard the name on Monday night, when I was putting him to bed. Kathy was out for an early dinner and catch-up with a friend, and so it had been the Ethan-and-Daddy Show from late afternoon. The recurring plot of this regular series boils down to me preparing one of the pasta dishes which have gained my son's tacit approval (and getting him to focus on eating it before it turns into a congealed mass), the two of us then watching his allotted one-per-day ration of *Ben 10: Alien Force*. After its conclusion I coax him up to the bathroom, and into the bath—usually against sustained and imaginative resistance—followed by the even more protracted process of getting him to leave the bath once more, Ethan having in the interim realized that the nice, warm tub is the best place in the world to be, and one he is not prepared to leave at any cost. Then there's the putting-on-of-pajamas and the brushing-of-the-teeth and various other tasks which sound (and should be) simple and quick but always seem to end up taking forever—little tranches of time which add up to really quite a lot of time when taken together, time that I'll never get back. We had Ethan relatively late in life (he's six, making me exactly forty years his senior) but what the older parent may lack in energy and vim is hopefully tempered by what they bring in terms of perspective, and so I understand well enough that it won't be so very long before my presence in the bathroom (or anywhere else) will not be enjoyed or even tolerated by a child who'll grow up faster than seems possible. Two more lots of six years, and he'll be leaving home. I get that. I try, therefore, to take all these little tribulations in good spirit, and to enjoy their fleeting presence in my life. But still, at the end of a long day, you do kind of wish they'd just brush their bloody teeth, by themselves, without all the stalling and prevarication.

For the love of god.

Eventually we got clear of the bathroom and processed in state to Ethan's bedroom—him leading the way, regal in pint-sized dressing gown, chattering about this and that. He resisted getting into bed for a while, but without any real purpose, and in a pro forma manner, as if he knew this part was merely part of a ritual, and he was doing it for my sake more than for himself.

Eventually he yawned massively and headed toward the bed.

He was tired. He always is on Mondays and Wednesdays, because of after-school club. The trick with tired children is to resist in a passive, judo-style fashion, putting up no specific barriers for them to kick against, instead letting them use their own strength against themselves. This, at least, I have learned.

When he was finally tucked up under the covers I asked him how his day had been. I'd meant to do it earlier, but forgot, which meant the enquiry was doomed to failure. Ethan appears to blank the working day within minutes of leaving the school gates, as if what happens within has no more reality than a dream, and melts like ice under the fierce sun of the Outside World. Or perhaps the opposite is true: a fundamental reality about the universe of the school that is impossible to convey to us shades who live in the unconvincing hinterland outside.

Either way, he appeared as usual to have zero recollection of what had occurred between nine a.m. and four p.m. that day. When pushed for a definitive account, however, he issued a brief statement saying that it had been "fine."

"And how was after-school club?"

Many of the kids who go to the Reynolds School have parents who both work. This means the school runs a slick and profitable range of activities to tide tots over from the end of actual school to the point where their stressed-out handlers can pick them up. Ethan's after-school diversion on Mondays is swimming. This is a bit pointless, I can't help thinking. Partly because Monday happens also to be when his class does swimming anyway—and so all his piscine endeavors are concentrated on the same day; and mainly because said classes seem to boil down to the children spending most of the half hour shivering on the edge of the pool, waiting for their brief turn to splash about. Ethan's already pretty confident in the water—courtesy of a vacation in Florida last year—but untutored in terms of strokes, beyond a hectic doggy-paddle that is full of sound and fury but conveys little in the way of forward motion. We hoped the after-school club would help refine this. So far, he seems to be going backwards.

"Terrible," Ethan said.

"Terrible?" This is strong for him. He usually confines pronouncements of quality to "fine" or "okay," occasionally peaking in a devil-may-care "good." I suspect the deployment of "great" would require the school suddenly deciding to hand out free chocolate. I'd never heard "terrible" before, either. "Why?"

"Arthur Milford was mean to me again."

I snorted. "Arthur Milford? What the hell kind of name is that?"

Ethan turned his head in bed to look at me. "What?"

"How old is this kid?"

"Six," Ethan said, with gentle care, as if I was crazy. "He's six. Like me."

"Sorry, yes," I said. I tend to talk to my son as if he's a miniature adult for much of the time—too much of it, perhaps—but there was no way of explaining to him that the name "Arthur Milford," while theoretically acceptable, seemed more appropriate to a music hall comedian of the 1930s than a six year old in 2011. "What do you mean, he was mean to you again?"

"He's always mean to me."

"Really? In what way?"

"Telling me I'm stupid."

"You're not stupid," I said, crossly. "He's stupid, if he goes around calling people names. Just ignore him."

"I can't ignore him." Ethan's voice was quiet. "He's always doing it. He pushes me in the corridor, too. Today he said he was going to throw me out of a window."

"What? He actually said that?"

Ethan looked up at me solemnly. After a moment he looked away. "He didn't actually say it. But he meant it."

"I see," I said, suddenly unsure how much of the entire account was true. "Well, look. If he says mean things to you, just ignore him. Mean boys say mean things. That's just the way it is. But if he pushes you, tell a teacher about it. Immediately."

"I do. They don't do anything about it."

"Well, if it happens again, then tell them again. And tell me, too, okay?"

"Okay, Daddy."

And then, as so often in such conversations, the matter was dismissed as if it had never been of import—instead, something I'd been rather tediously insisting on discussing—and my son asked me a series of apparently random questions about the world, which I did my best to answer, and I read him a story and filled up his water cup and read more story, and eventually he went to sleep.

We tend to alternate in picking Ethan up (as with most parenting duties), and so Tuesday was Kathy's turn. I had a deadline to chase and so—bar him dashing into my study to say hello when they got back—I barely saw Ethan before I kissed him on the head and said goodnight as Kathy led him up toward bath and bedtime.

Fifty minutes later, by which time I'd made a start on cooking, my wife appeared in the kitchen with the cautiously relieved demeanor of someone who believes they've wrangled an unpredictable child into bed.

"Is he down?"

"I'm not enumerating any domesticated, egg-producing fowl," she said, reaching into the fridge for the open bottle of wine, "but he might be. God willing."

She poured herself a glass and took a long sip before turning to me. "God, I'm tired."

"Me too," I said, without a lot of sympathy.

"I know. I'm just saying. By the way—has Ethan mentioned some kid called Arthur to you?"

"Arthur Milford?"

"So he has?"

"Once. Last night. Why—did he come up again?"

"Mmm. And it's not the first time, either."

"Really?"

"Ethan mentioned him last week, and I think the week before, too. They're in after-school swimming together."

"I know. Last night he said this Arthur kid had been mean to him. In fact, he said he'd been mean 'again.'"

"Mean in what way?"

"Pushed him in the corridor. Called him stupid." I thought about mentioning the threat to throw Ethan through a window, but decided not to. I didn't think Kathy needed to hear that part, especially as the telling had subsequently made it unclear whether that had taken place in what Ethan called "real life."

"Pushed him in the corridor? That means it's not just happening during swimming class."

"I guess. If it's happening at all."

"You don't believe him?"

"No, no, I do. But you know what he's like, Kath. He's all about the baddies and the goodies. It just sounds to me a bit like this Arthur Milford kid is in the script as Ethan's dread Nemesis. And that maybe not all of his exploits are directly related to events in what we'd think of as reality."

"Doesn't mean there isn't a real problem there."

"I know," I said, a little irritated that Kathy seemed to be claiming ownership of the issue, or implying that I wasn't taking it seriously enough. "I told him to talk to the teachers if this kid is mean to him again. And to tell me about it, too."

"Okay."

"But ultimately, that's just the way children are. Boys especially. They give each other grief. They shove. Little girls form cliques and get bitchy and tell other girls they're not their friends. Boys call each other names and thump each other. It has been thus since we lived in caves. It will be so until the sun explodes."

"I know. It's just . . . Ethan's such a cute kid. He can be a total pain, of course, but he's . . . so sweet, really, underneath. He doesn't know about all the crap in life yet. I want to protect him from it. I don't want him being hit, just because that's what happens. I don't want him being hurt in any way. I just want . . . everything to be nice."

"I know," I said, relenting. "Me too."

I rubbed her shoulder on the way over to supervise the closing stages of cooking, and privately raised my State of Awareness of the Arthur Milford situation from DefCon 4 to DefCon 3. Despite what everyone seems to think, the readiness-for-conflict index increases in severity from five to one, with one being the highest level (the highest level ever officially recorded is DefCon 2, which obtained for a while during the Cuban Missile Crisis. I knew all this from some half-hearted research for an article I was drafting on Homeland Security).

Be all which as it may, and despite my pompous such-is-life declaration, Kathy was right. I didn't want anyone hassling my kid. Much more of it, and words would need to be spoken.

I picked Ethan up the next day, and remembered to ask him about his day as soon as we got into the car. Ethan proved surprisingly well-informed on his own doings, and filled me in on a variety of Montessori-structured activities he'd undertaken (neither Kathy nor I truly understand what Montessori is about, but we believe/hope that it's generally agreed to be A Good Thing, like lower CO_2 levels and being kind to dogs). There was no mention of Arthur Milford. I thought about asking a direct question, but decided that if Ethan hadn't deemed him worth mentioning, there was probably nothing to say.

Ethan went to bed easily that night, in the unpredictable way he sometimes did. We had a laugh during bath-time, he brushed his own teeth without being asked, and then—after quite a short reading—he drifted off to sleep before I was even ready for it. I sat there for five minutes afterwards, enjoying the peace of quietly being in the same space as someone you love very much.

There's usually a hidden edge to the observation that nothing's as beautiful as a sleeping child (the point being it's all too often nicer than them being awake), but the fact is . . . there really isn't. To watch your son, asleep in his comfortable bed, with a tummy full of food that you made him, and a head full of story, arm gripping a furry polar bear you bought him on a whim but to which he'd taken as if they'd been separated at birth . . . that's why we're born. That's why everything else is worth it.

Yet sometimes I get so angry with him that I don't know what to do with myself. And he knows it. He must do.

About six hours later I woke slowly in my own bed, dimly aware I could hear a noise that shouldn't exist in a house in the middle of the night. By the time I'd opened my eyes, it was quiet. But as I started to relax back into oblivion, I heard it again.

A quiet sob.

I hauled myself quickly upright, staggered out of bed. Kathy lay dead to the world, which was unusual. She generally sleeps on far more of a hair trigger than me. She evidently was really tired, and I blearily regretted my snipe before dinner the evening before.

I went into the hallway to stand outside Ethan's room and listen. Nothing for a minute, but then I heard the sound again. I opened the door. Before I even got to the side of his bed, I could tell how hot he was. Children beam their heat out in the night, like little suns. I squatted down and put my hand on his head.

"Ethan," I said. "It's okay. It's just a dream."

He sobbed once more, very quietly.

"Ethan, it's okay."

He opened his eyes suddenly. He looked scared.

Scared of me.

"It's Daddy," I said, disconcerted. "Just Daddy, okay?"

His eyes seemed to swim into focus. "Daddy?"

"Yes. It's okay. Everything's okay."

Ethan's eyes swiveled. "Is he still here?"

"Who?"

"Arthur Milford."

The back of my neck tickled. "No. Of course not."

"He was here. He came up the stairs and stood outside my room saying things. Then he came in. He stood by my bed and said he was going to . . . "

"No, he didn't," I said, firmly.

"He did."

"Ethan, it was just a dream. No-one's in the house apart from you and me and Mummy. Nobody can get in. The doors are locked. The alarm system's on."

"Are you sure?"

"I'm sure," I said. "I did it myself. I promise you. It's just the three of us, and everything's okay."

Ethan's eyelids were already starting to drift downward. "Okay." He was asleep five minutes later. I went back to bed, and lay there for an hour before I could get under again. Once I've been woken, I find it hard to get back to sleep.

The next morning I was irritable, and snapped pretty badly at Ethan when he made a laboriously annoying job of putting on his school shoes. I shouldn't have, but I was tired, and for fuck's sake—he should be able to put on his own shoes.

But as I watched him and Kathy walk down the path toward the car, the wailing over and a new détente being hammered out between them, I realized that at some point after coming back to my bed in the night, I'd raised the Arthur Milford Awareness Level to DefCon 2.

On Thursday evening Kathy has yoga, and so the Ethan-Going-to-Bed Show featured daddy in a co-starring role (or supporting actor, more likely, my name below the title and in a notably smaller typeface) for the second night in a row. Bedtime did not, of course follow the same course as the night before. That's not how the shorties roll. Like some snappy young boxer on the way up, they'll pull you in, fake like they're running out of steam, and then unleash a brutal combination that will leave you glancing desperately back at your corner, as you take a standing eight count. I'm getting better at rolling with the punches, shifting the conflict to safer ground and letting the passion defuse, but that night I went back at Ethan like some broken-down old scrapper who knew this was his last chance in the ring, and wanted to go out with a bare knuckles slugfest.

He wouldn't eat his pasta, instead deliberately distributing it over the floor—meanwhile looking me steadily in the eye. He wouldn't come upstairs. He wouldn't get into the bath, and then wouldn't get out, and broke a soap dish. I had to brush his teeth for him, and did it none too gently. He wouldn't get into his pajamas because they "always itched"—the very same pair that he'd cheerfully gone to sleep in the previous night.

He wouldn't get into bed, instead breaking out of the room and stomping downstairs, wailing dismally for Kathy, though he knew damned well she was out.

By the time I'd recaptured him, harsh words had been spoken on both sides. I had been designated an "idiot" and a "doofus," and been informed that I was no longer loved. I had likened his behavior to that of a significantly younger child, and had threatened to inform the world at large of this maturity shortfall: his friends, grandparents, and Father Christmas had all been invoked as potential recipients of the information. I'd said he was being childish and stupid, and had even called him the very worst word I (or you) know, though thankfully I'd managed to throttle my voice down into inaudibility at the last moment. So he hadn't caught the word. The anger had sure as hell made it through, though. The anger, and probably the pitiful level of powerlessness, too.

I did however finally manage to get him into bed. He lay there, silently. I sat equally silently in the chair, both of us breathing hard, wild-eyed with silent fury and sour adrenaline.

"Arthur Milford was mean to me today, too," Ethan muttered, suddenly.

I was still pretty close to the edge, and the "too" at the end of his pronouncement nearly pushed me over it into somewhere dark and bad.

I took a breath, and bit my tongue. "Mean in what way?" I managed, eventually.

"In the upstairs corridor. On the third floor."

"Okay—so now I know where the alleged event occurred. But how was he mean? In what actual way?"

"Why are you being so mean to me tonight?"

"I'm . . . Just tell me, okay? What did he do?"

"He pushed me again. Really hard. Into the wall. And then . . . against the window."

"Really?"

"Yes."

"Did you tell a teacher? Like I told you?"

"No."

"Why? That's what you've got to do. You have to tell a teacher."

"He said . . . he said that if anyone told a teacher about what he was doing, he'd throw me out of the window for sure."

"Really? He actually said it this time?"

"Yes."

"But you've just told me about it—so why not a teacher?"

"Arthur said telling you didn't matter. You can't do anything. Only the teachers can."

"I see. How interesting."

I decided then and there that I'd had quite enough of Arthur sodding Milford. I'd like to think this was solely because of the evident discomfort he was causing Ethan, during both waking and sleeping hours, but I know some of it was due to pathetic outrage at hearing myself thus dismissed. As a parent, you often encounter moments when you feel impotent, and may often be genuinely unable to affect events. I had to take crap from my own child, evidently: that didn't hold true for someone else's. It was time for Arthur, and his parents, if necessary, to learn that the world did not stop at the school gates.

As Ethan and I moved on to talking about other things, gradually opening doors to each other once more, and calming down, I silently determined that the Arthur Milford situation had finally reached DefCon 1.

I got to the school a little after two o'clock. My appointment would mean that I'd have time to kill in the area afterwards, before picking Ethan up, but it was the only time the headmistress/owner would deign to see me. It's a small school, privately-owned, and to be fair, I imagine Ms. Reynolds is pretty busy. I was shown to a little office, part of the recent extension on the ground floor, and given a cup of coffee. I sat sipping it, looking up through the glass roof at the side of the building. Two further storeys, grey brick, with long bands of windows.

Schools, even small and bijou ones like this, all feel the same. They take you back. I knew that when Ms. Reynolds arrived I'd stand up slightly too quickly, and be excessively deferential, though she was ten years younger than me and effectively ran a service industry, in which the customer should always be right. None of that matters. School is where you learn the primal things, the big spells, the place where you become versed in the eternal hierarchies and are appraised of our species' hopes and fears. Being back in one as an adult is like returning in waking hours to some epic battleground in the dreamscape—even if, like me, you had a pretty decent time during your formative years.

It was quiet as I waited, all the little animals corralled into classrooms for the time being, having information and cultural norms stuffed into their wild and chaotic heads.

Eventually the door opened, and the trim figure of Ms. Reynolds entered. "Sorry I'm late."

I stood. "No problem."

She smiled briefly, and perched at an angle on the chair on the other side of the desk. I tried hard not to take against her posture, and the way it signaled a confident belief that this was going to be a short conversation. I sat back down, square-on to the table.

"So. How can I help?"

"I wanted a quick word. About Ethan."

"I'm sure it's temporary," she said, briskly. "I honestly don't think it's anything to worry about."

"What is?" I asked, thrown. "Worry about what?"

"Ah," she said, smoothly covering a moment of confusion. "I talked with your wife about this, yesterday, at the end of school. I assumed she'd mentioned it to you."

"Mentioned what?"

"Ethan's schoolwork. It's taken a dip recently, that's all. Nothing major. It happens with most of them, the boys. From time to time. But we're aware of it, and we're working with Ethan to lift things back up. I can appreciate your concern, but I really . . . "

"That's not why I'm here."

"Oh. So . . . "

"I am concerned if there's an issue with his work," I said. I was also a little ticked that Kathy hadn't mentioned it to me when she got back from yoga the night before. "But I wanted to talk about the bullying."

"Bullying?"

"For the last week, maybe two, Ethan's been talking about being bullied."

Ms. Reynolds swiveled to sit square in her chair. It was clear I'd got her full attention now. "If that's the case, it's a very serious matter," she said.

"It's the case."

She frowned. "One of the teachers did notice a mark on his arm this morning. Very minor. It looked as though someone had gripped his arm. Is that what you're referring to?" Her eyes were on me. There was probably no way she could know that the mark, which I'd noticed myself when helping Ethan to get dressed that morning, was the result of me shoving him into bed the night before. Not so very hard, but children's skins are sensitive.

And my own father raised me to tell the truth. "No," I said. "That was me."

"You?"

"There was a disagreement over getting into bed last night. I ended up guiding him into it."

She nodded, a minimalist raise of the chin. "So then what are you referring to?"

"One of the other boys has been picking on him. Muttering things in after-school swimming class, calling him stupid. Shoving him in the corridors."

"Ethan told you this?"

"Yes. And this boy's even threatened to throw Ethan out of a window."

"Throw him out of a window?" Ms. Reynolds now looked stricken. "When? When did this happen?"

"Last Monday. And again yesterday." I'd forgotten, for the moment, that this threat hadn't actually been made on Monday—only implied, or intuited (or fabricated) by Ethan. It didn't matter. Yesterday, it had been said. "I'm not happy about this. At all."

"Well, of course not," the headmistress said, putting her hands out flat on the table in front of her. "And who does Ethan say is doing all this?"

"Arthur Milford," I said, feeling heavy satisfaction as I handed up the name. Not just at finally stepping up to the plate on behalf of my son, but also through disproving what Arthur had told him—that it was only teachers that could do anything about a situation. Learn this, you little shit: stuff that happens in the outside world counts, too.

"Arthur Milford?"

"Yes."

"It can't be," she said.

"I'm sure he behaves perfectly when teachers are around."

"No, that's not what I mean. I mean . . . we don't have an Arthur Milford at this school. Are you sure that's the name?"

"Absolutely sure. I've heard it every day this week, including in the middle of Wednesday night, when Ethan had a nightmare about this boy coming into his room and threatening him. Kathy's heard the name too."

The teacher looked baffled. "We did have an Arthur Ely in the school, a few years ago, who was quite big, and boisterous, but he left well before Ethan joined us. And there was a Patrick Milford, I think. . . . Yes. He was here even before Arthur. But again, he's moved on. There's no Milfords here now. No Arthurs either."

"That's the name Ethan used."

"I'm afraid . . . he may just have made it up. Or one of the other children did."

"What—and the fact there have been kids here with very similar names is just a coincidence?"

"No. Making something up doesn't mean it isn't real. I know this is hard to hear, but. . . . Their parents, everything out there in the world. . . . They're important, of course, you're important. But still not as real to the children as what happens in here."

I nodded, remembering the thoughts I'd had while sitting in the chair waiting, and how it had been when I was a child. "Facts, too," she went on. "Children can get them muddled up. Or half-hear things. Or add two and two and make twenty eleven and a half. Perhaps Ethan got shoved, by accident. Or he and another boy really aren't getting on—or perhaps he's having arguments with a someone who is his friend, and so Ethan doesn't want to use his real name. Children remember the names of those who have gone before. Perhaps they use them, too, sometimes. Like mythological figures. I spend all my working hours in this place, but it doesn't mean I understand everything that goes on."

"So you don't think anyone's actually bullying Ethan?"

"I really doubt it—and not just because we do a lot to make sure this kind of thing doesn't happen. None of the other boys or girls have said anything. None of the teachers, either. But trust me, I'll look into it. The moment you've gone. And if there's anything—anything at all—to be concerned about, I'll call you right away. I promise."

"Thank you," I said. I didn't know what to feel. A little foolish, certainly.

She stood up, and reached out her hand. I did the same, and we shook.

"I hope I haven't wasted your time."

"No time spent talking about a child is wasted," she said, and I felt a little less silly. "But do you mind if I offer you a piece of advice?"

"Go ahead," I said, assuming it would be some way of helping Ethan move past this, or of helping him to get his schoolwork back on track.

"Do be careful about . . . the ways in which you have physical contact with your son."

I froze, indignation and guilt melting together. The room seemed suddenly larger, and very cold. "What do you mean?"

She looked steadily at me. Her eyes were clear, and kind, and for a moment she didn't looked like a teacher, or Ethan's headmistress, just a woman who meant well and cared about her charges a great deal.

"I know what it's like," she said. "What they can be like. I don't have a child of my own, not yet, but I spend a lot of time with them. Which is why, every day after I leave here, I go to the gym and get it out of my system for an hour. I kickbox. I'm not very good, but boy do I give those punch bags a thump. And then I go home and have a gin and tonic that would make most people's eyes water. That information is not for general consumption, okay?"

"Okay," I said, smiling.

"Loving children can be hard work. But it's what we do. I know you love Ethan, very much. I'm just saying . . . be careful. Because of the assumptions others might make, if they see a mark on him. And also because of how you feel, about yourself, and about how he'll feel too. Boys need strong fathers. Men who are strong, and kind . . . and not full of anger and guilt."

I nodded, knowing she was right.

"There's evidently something going on in Ethan's universe, and it's good that I know about it. You did the right thing coming in to tell me about it."

"I hope so," I said, anxious now to lighten the mood. "Ethan said last night that's it was okay to tell me about it, but teachers couldn't know. Otherwise, Arthur would, you know."

Ms. Reynolds smiled, and rolled her eyes, as she started to lead me toward the door. "The stuff that goes on in their heads," she said, with just the right amount of irony, and affection.

I realized that I'd started to like Ms. Reynolds, and respect her, and that perhaps I'd start to take a more active role in Ethan's schooling, and that would be good.

She walked with me out of the doors and to the waiting area outside. I had an hour to kill, and had decided to go find a coffee somewhere. To think through what had been said, to find a way of accessing a calm which must still exist somewhere inside me. To lighten up. To remember how to be strong, and kind.

"You did the right thing," she said, once more.

As we shook hands again, there was the sound of glass breaking, somewhere high above. We looked up and saw the third floor, and the broken window there. Saw the small, boy-shaped figure that came out of it, and started to fall.

SECOND GRADE
CHARLES ANTIN

When the Army recruiter comes to my second grade class, I want to grab his arm and twist it behind his back and say something highfalutin and holier-than-thou as I toss him from the classroom. Instead I say, "Sir, these kids are seven years old," and retreat behind my desk.

He's unfazed. He cocks a 9mm handgun and the kids ooh and aah and before I know what's happening, Aidan, the four foot seven, proud, mature-for-his-age star of my class, steps up. Aidan's my favorite. Thoughtful and handsome, kind but not sentimental, popular yet humble. He's the kind of kid that second grade teachers dream of. I remind him of the sacrifices he'll have to make should he enlist (no more Legos, no more read aloud, no more show and tell, etc.) but I can tell by the look in his still-innocent doe eyes that he's already gone. The recruiter gives him a Crayola magic marker and points to the dotted line. Aidan waves me off like he barely knows me and carefully writes his name in newly-learned handwriting. Aidan's the ringleader so when he signs up, the rest of the boys follow suit.

Some of the girls decide they're being left out and move to sign up too. The recruiter stops them and makes it clear that while they're technically allowed to enlist, they're unwanted. This isn't something that women of any age like to hear. I'm against discrimination but I can't say I'm disappointed.

"Child warfare," says the recruiter. "Little guns, big terror. It's a brave new world. God bless America."

Then he ushers the boys onto a yellow school bus and salutes as they drive out of the parking lot. There's nothing I can do. The boys are ripped from me, their daytime father. I'm helpless. Castrated by Uncle Sam's Bowie knife. Dramatic, I know, but that's what it feels like. I'm left standing there with the girls and the one boy forbidden to enlist: George, our exchange student. George looks at me, the metaphorical eunuch, then at the veritable harem of teary-eyed females, and smiles.

• • •

Back in the classroom, I make an effort to return to business as usual, but things just aren't the same. I return to my curriculum, to the sharing, to the reading aloud, to the other things that seemed quaint and necessary before, but now seem trite. When I take roll call any doubts disappear: I've failed as a teacher. One look at Maggie's big blue eyes, silently asking what I've done, and I almost lose it. I want to scream:

It's not my fault! It's a free country!

Instead, I internalize. Depression sets in. I assign naptime. The children balk, claiming that naps haven't been required of them in years. I'm the teacher, I snap, and leave it at that. There's some crying, some whimpering, some refusal to nap as instructed. I turn down the lights and lie on a rubber mat, too guilty to even move.

The only one who gives me no trouble is George. He curls up on his mat and falls immediately to sleep, as if there's nothing in this world that troubles him. Sleep, George, sleep, like you haven't a care in the world. George George George George. I repeat it over and over under my breath like a dirge. Where did he get this name? The name George is English, and my George is not English. It's clearly a pseudonym, an attempt on his part to "fit in." George is a foreigner, that much is clear, but his exact provenance is unknown. His skin is brown, or perhaps yellow-hazel or burnt orange or umber, and his accent is nondescript, as if he grew up in several places, or perhaps had an English-speaking au pair. His file is classified. This is highly irregular, but then, so is George.

• • •

In the few quiet hours of solitude that I've got after the two p.m. bell, I finger paint. At first, I find it rejuvenating; the cold wet paint between my fingers reminds me that I'm still alive. Each time I finish a painting I'm reassured that I can still produce something ex nihilo. I still have an imagination, perhaps a soul.

I stare at the finger paintings for so long that I start to see things in these impromptu Rorschachs. This one is Aidan coming home with third-degree burns and no lips. That one is Aidan in a wheelchair, drinking vodka from the bottle on skid row. Another is George, sleeping quietly and mockingly on a rubber mat, while I toss and turn in a feather bed. When laid out side by side, the paintings recall an amateur *Guernica* in brown. I stop finger painting for good.

. . .

At lunch the next day, Eliza says she won't eat until I get the boys back. In practice, a hunger strike, she just doesn't know the term. I'm in no shape to deal with her; I haven't eaten in a day.

Her unopened Lunchables, once the envy of the class, remain perfectly preserved in their compartmentalized plastic container. I put them in the fridge, in case she changes her mind. I hand out Otis Spunkmeyer cookies in three-packs to the rest of the class. The girls are unimpressed.

"At what cost?" their frowns seem to say. "At what cost do we have these delicious cookies?"

They're right: there is a surplus of cookies thanks to our reduced number. But it would be a strong-willed second grader who could turn down cookies. George scarfs down his and the girls abandon their frowns and follow his lead. There's a moment of relief but it disappears almost as quickly as it came. The cookies weren't enough. As soon as they're eaten, the children ask for more, and this time with a very off-putting sense of entitlement. You gave us back what was already ours, their outstretched palms seem to say. Now give us more.

. . .

When the first letters come, it's like rain after a drought. I flip through them, scanning the return addresses for Aidan's name. At first, I can't believe that he hasn't written, so I scan the pile one more time. When reality sets in, I turn over the letters to the girls, who descend upon them like a pack of hyenas on a wounded gazelle.

The girls are indiscriminate in their joy. This sort of non-specific happiness troubles me. It seems capitalist, consumerist, super-size, "American." George remains silent and, even though I fault the girls for their over-exuberance, I fault George even more for his placidity. Has he no emotions?

The letters are, for the most part, illegible and nonsensical. The boys, despite their new profession, can't hide the fact that they are still only second graders. In fact, most of the "letters" are nothing more than crude drawings, made cruder by the desert's unforgiving shades of tan and shadowless sandscapes. Trees, houses, the odd crossing guard or stop sign are the things that make up a second grader's repertoire. In the desert, they are artistically adrift. The drawings consist of squares that signify tanks, squiggly lines that (I'm guessing here) represent snakes and, in the best examples, a few cactuses.

The girls love the pictures. They exhaust half a dozen glue sticks covering the walls with them. Once they're hung it's apparent that the pictures are more numerous than I first thought. They cover the walls of the classroom like evil wallpaper in Bic blue.

During all this, George paints quietly at his desk. I steal up behind him and glance over his shoulder. He catches me and, though I politely avert my gaze, invites me to take a look. George, it turns out, is no slouch with the watercolors. On a regular 8.5 x 11 sheet of printer paper is what appears to be a family of four: a father, tall, broad-shouldered, with a mustache and black hair, a mother with a round face punctuated by a slender aquiline nose and almond-shaped eyes and a daughter with chubby cheeks and black corkscrew curls. Next to them is a boy. George, I presume. They are standing in front of a house, but the architecture provides no clues to their whereabouts. There is a bird and a tree, but they are stylized and abstract. The clothing, too, is unfamiliar, so other than "not America" it's impossible to place. The brushwork, however, is immaculate. I think back to my own finger painting and grimace. George gives me the painting: a gift. I take it and tell him I plan to hang it on my refrigerator at home. When his back is turned, I fold it over and over and over until it is the size of half a credit card and stick it in the bottom drawer of my desk.

• • •

The girls love George. He has replaced Aidan completely in their eyes. His foreignness adds to his cachet. He sashays about the class in corduroy pants and linen shirts—clothing not quite familiar but not quite foreign—exuding pure confidence.

The confidence is because George is the heir to a glue fortune. Rubber cement, paste, epoxy, you name it. If it's sticky, George's family makes it. It's rumored, via Lindsay, the exchange student coordinator and my ex-girlfriend, that George's family produces enough glue each year to fill the Great Lakes, and that he's worth over a billion dollars. This potential for bequeathment is no small thing at this school.

Without the other boys, George takes on a more alpha role. Things begin to change. Eliza returns to her Lunchables. The others go about their business, napping, snacking, teasing one another, as best they know how. Before long, it's almost as if nothing has changed. They're aware of their counterparts' disappearance, but they seem to accept it as inevitable.

Though I am skeptical of his motives, I'm thankful for this change in the collective mood and George knows it. He begins to take small liberties in the classroom—taking extra cookies during snack time, and always making sure he's first in line for recess (we usually line up alphabetically).

I'm lenient, for now.

• • •

Then comes the Pinky fiasco. Pinky is our hamster and mascot. He's also an emotional barometer for the class. One day, Eliza goes to feed Pinky and finds him cowering in the corner of his cage. This isn't abnormal behavior for Pinky so I shrug it off. But Pinky refuses to eat. Soon he's pressing his little hamster nose between the bars of the cage with such force that he draws blood. At the risk of anthropomorphizing, it seems that Pinky's lost it. One day, Pinky bites Jenna. I forbid all interactions with him. The children are frightened and uncertain, but Jenna takes it well. She thinks it was an isolated incident. I'm unsure. Plus, as a teacher, I have to think about lawsuits. I take precautions. A lock goes on the cage and I've got the only key.

Soon, Pinky is dead. His bloody face and matted fur are too much for second graders to handle, so I put him in a shoebox and tell the kids I'm taking him to a pet cemetery. I toss him into a dumpster on the way home from work.

In the wake of Pinky's demise, the class is thrown into turmoil again, but this time it's worse. My popularity plummets. Ashley eats all of the blue crayons, Libby wets herself and Alexandra decides that she's a monkey. Eliza returns to her hunger strike with renewed vigor.

"Pinky," says Jenna as I apply more Neosporin to her wound, "wasn't just a hamster."

I'm not sure she understands the full weight of her words, but I can't disagree. She means, I think, that Pinky was also her friend, but I can't help but think Pinky was more than a friend. He was a symbol. Of what, I'm not sure.

George is unfazed. While the girls wail in mourning, George sits quietly with a book. Who does he think he is? Is he unaffected by this carnage? The girls look to George for support. He is their rock. I worry that their rock will turn out to be not so rock-like at all.

Then I realize that on the day Pinky got sick, it was George's turn to feed him. Coincidence? Probably. I think back to when I moved Pinky from his cage to his final resting place. His fur was bloody and matted, yes, but wasn't there also a slight stickiness? A gluey stickiness on his undercarriage? At first I chalked it up to moist blood but now, in retrospect, I wonder.

• • •

One day, a letter. This one is different from the others. It is alone, and addressed only to me. I find it in my cubbyhole covered in foreign-looking stamps with strange foreign curly-cued writing. I ask George to translate, but he claims he can't. I doubt it but I'm tired of arguing.

I don dishwashing gloves and shake the letter to check for anthrax spores. The address is also written sloppily in upper-case letters. The writer clearly doesn't speak English as a first language and that's a bad sign. I decide to open it anyway.

It's from Aidan.

The bad handwriting is a second grader's, it turns out, and that reflects poorly on me. I leave George and the girls to fend for themselves and rush into the teachers-only bathroom where I can be alone.

Aidan, it turns out, is doing just fine. His handwriting is poor, his diction and syntax worse, but the message is clear: he's happy with his decision to enlist. He's optimistic. He's proud. He doesn't miss any of the things he used to love: the Legos, the read aloud time, and least of all, the show and tell. In fact, he says (I'm paraphrasing) that war is kind of like show and tell on a grand scale. They show you an M16, and then they tell you how to use it. The only difference is, you then get to take your M16 back to your tent. When Eliza brought in her bunny, guess who took that home.

• • •

I'm cleaning out the fridge one day when I find Eliza's Lunchables. I stuck them in the fridge weeks ago but they're ageless. They look perfect in their packaging—uniform, clean, correct—and evoke some sort of pop culture ethos, like an edible Koons. I consider eating them but stop just before tearing off the cover. I return the Lunchables, untouched, to the fridge. Those Lunchables, I think, will outlive us all.

• • •

George is dealing glue. At least I think he is. One day, Rachel ducks into the coatroom just before naptime and emerges, minutes later, groggy and confused. Then Michelle does the same thing. George is nowhere to be found.

The hooks in the kids' coatroom are only about three feet off the ground. It would be impractical for someone my height to hang my coat on one of them so I've got no reason to investigate. I could pull rank but that would only exacerbate their distrust. But here's what I imagine:

George, white linen shirt rakishly unbuttoned, hair tousled just so, sprawled out like a Persian king on a pile of down jackets in the back of the coatroom like it's Medellin in '81 and he's Ochoa. I wouldn't be surprised if he were smoking a Cohiba or snorting coke off of Ashley's non-existent breasts.

He hands a paper bag filled with glue to his next customer. She's unsure what to do with it, but kids have a natural affinity for paste. He pushes her head into the bag and tells her to start huffing. After a few deep breaths, she pulls away, grinning stupidly. As she stumbles back into the classroom, our eyes meet, but there's not even a flicker of recognition. She pushes by me, and I retreat.

That's what I imagine. I give George an indefinite Time Out.

• • •

That afternoon I'm sitting at my desk long after the children are gone, wondering if I can be arrested for allowing a drug dealer to operate on school grounds. I'm pondering these options when I see my own jar of glue, sitting untouched on my desk. I think of Aidan in a ditch in the desert and I pick up the jar and inhale. I don't know what comes over me but I decide to put the jar into a paper bag and hyperventilate like it's a panic attack. I'm sorry, I'm sorry, I'm sorry, I huff into the bag, but I don't know if it's to myself or Aidan or someone else. But my troubles, George, Pinky, Aidan, they all get rolled up into a crinkled ball of blue construction paper and tossed away. There's a fuzzy throbbing in my head and ears but it feels warm and good, like being underwater as a tanker goes by a mile out to sea.

I take the finger paint from the cupboard. I take the red and mix in just a little bit of black. A drop of blue. Then I dip in my finger.

I know about Pinky, I write on a piece of wax paper.

Then I stick it into George's desk with a protractor and drive home with the windows down, eyes half closed, ears buzzing.

• • •

The next morning I come in late with a terrible hangover. It's not your run-of-the-mill alcohol hangover, it's worse. I can barely see/breathe/feel.

I walk to my classroom and see, through the little window in the door, that the principal is inside, speaking to George. The principal is gesticulating wildly and I can imagine what he's saying.

"Time out? Time out? What is this, the erstwhile Gitmo? There will be no time outs at this school as long as I'm principal, especially for someone of your, well, stature, George."

I turn away, head straight to my cubbyhole. It's quiet; everyone's in class. I peer into the dark and squint my eyes into focus. At first, I think it's empty but then I see something mashed up against the back wall. It's a letter from Aidan. I sit down right there next to the cubbyholes and tear it open.

I'm jealous of Aidan. He did what he wanted to do and is making a difference too. They say that youth is wasted on the young but I disagree. Aidan knows what he's doing better than I do.

Aidan's not happy, though. He doesn't know the words, but what he describes is manic depression. He's just plodding ahead, full steam, and then he's up and then he's down. The way he describes it, he's always on the precipice of something and always in a state of agitation. There's no middle ground. He wants middle ground. He doesn't come clean and say it, but what he wants is second grade.

What's he fighting for? he asks.

I want to take him in my arms and whisper, shh, shh, shh, I ask myself that everyday. But the next time I see Aidan, it will be at his funeral. I can feel it.

Ashley is coming up the hall so I rush into the boys' bathroom. I try to throw up but nothing comes. I can't stop shaking. I can taste iron. I tear up the note and go home sick.

• • •

The glue is addictive. I wander through the days looking out from behind a veil of lentil soup. As far as I can tell, the students aren't any better. But frankly, I'm not paying much attention. We go through the motions, a super slow-mo second grade, and for once it feels right. It feels drugged, but right. Or maybe I can't tell the difference.

There's no more turmoil among the students. Eliza hasn't gone back to her hunger strikes. In fact, she's put on weight. She eats constantly throughout the day—food, but also paste, crayons, etc. I allow it. They're all non-toxic, I'm pretty sure. I'm 50/50 sure. The students nap for three, sometimes four or five hours a day, without any prodding. Perhaps it's even more. It's hard to tell because usually I nap right along with them.

George is more industrious than ever. He cleans out the fish tank and buys a small shark that, he tells me, will grow to three feet long if fed properly. I ask what is proper and he says Christian babies. Maybe he said mice. He replaces Pinky with a chinchilla named Aristu. George says that Aristu is the softest thing in the world, softer than a cloud, but we are forbidden to hold him. He's delicate, says George. I write left-handed now, so George can't trace my handwriting back to the note I left on his desk. The snack fridge is full of foreign treats. Eliza's Lunchables have long since disappeared. I eat small semi-dried fruits all day. They look like little turds but they're delicious. I'm more regular than ever.

• • •

One day George says we should take a group picture and send it to the boys, in case they miss us. So we all stand behind the new shark tank with George in front, cupping Aristu in one hand and stroking him with the other. So soft, so soft, he mutters, and presses the animal to his lips. I set the digital camera on a ten-second timer and tell the students to say cheese. Some do, some don't. Flash.

I look at the photo. By a head count I know that we are all there, but we look fewer.

We're blurry. I delete it.

RESPECTS

RAMSEY CAMPBELL

By the time Dorothy finished hobbling downstairs, somebody had rung three times and knocked several more. Charmaine Bullough and some of her children were blocking the short garden path under a nondescript November sky. "What did you see?" Charmaine demanded at once.

"Why, nothing to bother about." Dorothy had glimpsed six-year-old Brad kicking the door, but tried to believe he'd simply wanted to help his mother. "Shouldn't you be at school?" she asked him.

Brad jerked a thumb at eight-year-old J-Bu. "She's not," he shouted.

Perhaps his absent siblings were, but not barely teenage Angelina, who was brandishing a bunch of flowers. "Are those for me?" Dorothy suggested out of pleasantness rather than because it seemed remotely likely, then saw the extent of her mistake. "Sorry," she murmured.

Half a dozen bouquets and as many wreaths were tied to the lamp-standard on the corner of the main road, beyond her gate. Charmaine's scowl seemed to tug the roots of her black hair paler. "What do you mean, it's not worth bothering about?"

"I didn't realise you meant last week," Dorothy said with the kind of patience she'd had to use on children and parents too when she was teaching.

"You saw the police drive our Keanu off the road, didn't you?"

"I'm afraid I can't say I did."

At once, despite their assortment of fathers, the children resembled their mother more than ever. Their aggressive defensiveness turned resentful in a moment, accentuating their features, which were already as sharp as smashed glass. "Can't or won't?" Charmaine said.

"I only heard the crash."

Dorothy had heard the cause as well—the wild screech of tyres as the fifteen-year-old had attempted to swerve the stolen Punto into her road apparently at eighty miles an hour, only to ram a van parked opposite her house—but she didn't want to upset the children, although Brad's attention seemed to have lapsed. "Wanna wee," he announced and made to push past her, the soles of his trainers lighting up at every step.

As Dorothy raised a hand to detain him, J-Bu shook a fist that set bracelets clacking on her thin arm. "Don't you touch my brother. We can get you put in prison."

"You shouldn't just walk into someone else's house," Dorothy said and did her best to smile. "You don't want to end up—"

"Like who?" Angelina interrupted, her eyes and the studs in her nose glinting. "Like Keanu? You saying he was in your house?"

Dorothy might have. The day before the crash she'd come home to find him gazing out of her front room. He hadn't moved until she managed to fumble her key into the lock, at which point he'd let himself out of the back door. Apart from her peace of mind he'd stolen only an old handbag that contained an empty purse, and so she hadn't hurried to report him to the overworked police. If she had, might they have given him no chance to steal the car? As Dorothy refrained from saying any of this, Charmaine dragged Brad back. "Come out of there. We don't want anyone else making trouble for us."

"I'm sorry not to be more help," Dorothy felt bound to say. "I do know how you feel."

Angelina peered so closely at her that Dorothy smelled some kind of smoke on the girl's breath. "How?"

"I lost my husband just about a year ago."

"Was he as old as you?" J-Bu said.

"Even older," said Dorothy, managing to laugh.

"Then it's not the same," Angelina objected. "It was time he went."

"Old people take the money we could have," said J-Bu.

"It's ours for all the things we need," Brad said.

"Never mind that now," said Charmaine and fixed Dorothy with her scowl. "So you're not going to be a witness."

"To what, forgive me?"

"To how they killed my son. I'll be taking them to court. The social worker says I'm entitled."

"They'll have to pay for Keanu," said Brad.

Dorothy took time over drawing a breath. "I don't think I've anything to offer except sympathy."

"That won't put shoes on their feet. Come on, all of you. Let's see Keanu has some fresh flowers. He deserves the best," Charmaine added louder still.

Brad ran to the streetlamp and snatched off a bouquet. About to throw them over Dorothy's wall, he saw her watching and flung them in the road. As Angelina substituted her flowers, Dorothy seemed to hear a noise closer to the house. She might have thought a rose was scratching at the window, but the flower was inches distant. In any case, the noise had sounded muffled by the glass. She picked up a beer can and a hamburger's polystyrene shell from her garden and carried them into the house.

When she and Harry had moved in she'd been able to run through it without pausing for breath. She could easily outdistance him to the bedroom, which had been part of their fun. Now she tried not to breathe, since the flimsy shell harboured the chewed remains of its contents. She hadn't reached the kitchen when she had to gasp, but any unwelcome smell was blotted out by the scents of flowers in vases in every downstairs room.

She dumped the rubbish in the backyard bin and locked the back door. The putty was still soft around the pane Mr. Thorpe had replaced. Though he'd assured her it was safe, she was testing the glass with her knuckles when something sprawled into the hall. It was the free weekly newspaper, and Keanu's death occupied the front page. **LOCAL TEENAGER DIES IN POLICE CHASE.**

She still had to decide whether to remember Harry in the paper. She took it into the dining-room, where a vaseful of chrysanthemums held up their dense yellow heads towards the false sun of a Chinese paper globe, and spread the obituary pages across the table. Keanu was in them too. Which of the remembrances were meant to be witty or even intended as a joke? "Kee brought excitement into everyone's life"? "He was a rogue like children are supposed to be"? "There wasn't a day he didn't come up with some new trick"? "He raced through life like he knew he had to take it while he could"? "Even us that was his family couldn't keep up with his speed"? Quite a few of them took it, Dorothy suspected, along with other drugs. "When he was little his feet lit up when he walked, now they do because he's God's new angel." She dabbed at her eyes, which had grown so blurred that the shadows of stalks drooping out of the vase appeared to grope at the newsprint. She could do with a walk herself.

She buttoned up her winter overcoat, which felt heavier than last year, and collected her library books from the front room. Trying to read herself to sleep only reminded her that she was alone in bed, but even downstairs she hadn't finished any of them—the deaths in the detective stories seemed insultingly trivial, and the comic novels left her cold now that she couldn't share the jokes. She lingered for a sniff at the multicoloured polyanthuses in the vase on her mother's old sideboard before loading her scruffiest handbag with the books. The sadder a bag looked, the less likely it was to be snatched.

The street was relatively quiet beneath the vague grey sky, with just a few houses pounding like nightclubs. The riots in Keanu's memory—children smashing shop windows and pelting police cars with bricks—had petered out, and in any case they hadn't started until nightfall. Most of the children weren't home from school or wherever else they were. Stringy teenagers were loitering near the house with the reinforced front door, presumably waiting for the owner of the silver Jaguar to deal with them. At the far end of the street from Dorothy's house the library was a long low blotchy concrete building, easily mistaken for a new church.

She was greeted by the clacking of computer keyboards. Some of the users had piled books on the tables, but only to hide the screens from the library staff. As she headed for the shelves Dorothy glimpsed instructions for making a bomb and caught sight of a film that might have shown an equestrian busy with the tackle of her horse if it had been wearing any. On an impulse Dorothy selected guides to various Mediterranean holiday resorts. Perhaps one or more of her widowed friends might like to join her next year. She couldn't imagine travelling by herself.

She had to slow before she reached her gate. A low glare of sunlight cast the shadow of a rosebush on the front window before being extinguished by clouds, leaving her the impression that a thin silhouette had reared up and then crouched out of sight beyond the glass. She rummaged nervously in her handbag and unlocked the door. It had moved just a few inches when it encountered an obstruction that scraped across the carpet. Someone had strewn Michaelmas daisies along the hall.

Were they from her garden? So far the vandals had left her flowers alone, no doubt from indifference. As her eyes adjusted to the dimness she saw that the plants were scattered the length of the hall, beyond which she could hear a succession of dull impacts as sluggish as a faltering heart. Water was dripping off the kitchen table from the overturned vase, where the trail of flowers ended. She flustered to the back door, but it was locked and intact, and there was no other sign of intrusion. She had to conclude that she'd knocked the vase over and, still without noticing unless she'd forgotten, tracked the flowers through the house.

The idea made her feel more alone and, in a new way, more nervous. She was also disconcerted by how dead the flowers were, though she'd picked them yesterday; the stalks were close to crumbling in her hands, and she had to sweep the withered petals into a dustpan. She binned it all and replenished the vase with Harry's cyclamen before sitting on the worn stairs while she rang Helena to confirm Wednesday lunch. They always met midweek, but she wanted to talk to someone. Once she realised that Helena's grandchildren were visiting she brought the call to an end.

The house was big enough for children, except that she and Harry couldn't have any, and now it kept feeling too big. Perhaps they should have moved, but she couldn't face doing so on her own. She cooked vegetables to accompany the rest of yesterday's casserole, and ate in the dining-room to the sound of superannuated pop songs on the radio, and leafed through her library books in the front room before watching a musical that would have made Harry restless. She could hear gangs roving the streets, and was afraid her lit window might attract them. Once she'd checked the doors and downstairs windows she plodded up to bed.

Girls were awaiting customers on the main road. As Dorothy left the curtains open a finger's width she saw Winona Bullough negotiate with a driver and climb into his car. Was the girl even sixteen? Dorothy was close to asking Harry, but it felt too much like talking to herself, not a habit she was anxious to acquire. She climbed into her side of the bed and hugged Harry's pillow as she reached with her free hand for the light-cord.

The night was a medley of shouts, some of which were merely conversations, and smashed glass. Eventually she slept, to be wakened by light in the room. As she blinked, the thin shaft coasted along the bedroom wall. She heard the taxi turn out of the road, leaving her unsure whether she had glimpsed a silhouette that reminded her of stalks. Perhaps the headlamps had sent a shadow from her garden, though wasn't the angle wrong? She stared at the dark and tried not to imagine that it was staring back at her. "There's nobody," she whispered, hugging the pillow.

She needed to be more active, that was all. She had to occupy her mind and tire her body out to woo a night's unbroken sleep. She spent as much of Saturday in weeding the front garden as the pangs of her spine would allow. By late afternoon she wasn't even half finished, and almost forgot to buy a wreath. She might have taken Harry some of his own flowers, but she liked to support the florist's on the main road, especially since it had been damaged by the riots. At least the window had been replaced. Though the florist was about to close, he offered Dorothy a cup of tea while his assistant plaited flowers in a ring. Some good folk hadn't been driven out yet, Dorothy told them both, sounding her age.

She draped the wreath over the phone in her hall and felt as if she was saying goodbye to any calls, an idea too silly to consider. After dinner she read about far places that might have changed since she and Harry had visited them, and watched a love story in tears that would have embarrassed him. She was in bed by the time the Saturday-night uproar began. Once she was wakened by a metallic clack that sounded closer than outside, but when she stumbled to the landing the hall was empty. Perhaps a wind had snapped the letterbox. As she huddled under the quilt she wondered if she ought to have noticed something about the hall, but the impression was too faint to keep her awake. It was on her mind when church bells roused her, and as soon as she reached the stairs she saw what was troubling her. There was no sign of the wreath.

She grabbed the banister so as not to fall. She was hastening to reassure herself that the flowers were under the hall table, but they weren't. Had she forgotten taking them somewhere? They were in none of the ground-floor rooms, nor the bathroom, her bedroom, the other one that could have been a nursery but had all too seldom even done duty as a guest room. She was returning downstairs when she saw a single flower on the carpet inches from the front door.

Could a thief have dragged the wreath through the letterbox? She'd heard that criminals used rods to fish property from inside houses. She heaved the bolts out of their sockets and flung the door open, but there was no evidence on the path. It didn't seem worth reporting the theft to the police. She would have to take Harry flowers from the garden. She dressed in her oldest clothes and brought tools from the shed, and was stooping to uproot a weed that appeared to have sprouted overnight when she happened to glance over the wall. She straightened up and gasped, not only with the twinge in her back. One of the tributes to Keanu looked far too familiar.

She clutched at her back as she hobbled to the streetlamp. There was the wreath she'd seen made up at the florist's. It was the only item to lack a written tag. "Earned yourself some wings, Kee" and "Give them hell up there" and "Get the angels singing along with your iPod" were among the messages. The wreath was hung on the corner of a bouquet's wrapping. Dorothy glared about as she retrieved it, daring anyone to object. As she slammed the front door she thought she heard small feet running away.

She had no reason to feel guilty, and was furious to find she did. She locked away the tools and changed into the dark suit that Harry used to like her to wear whenever they dined out. A bus from the shattered shelter on the main road took her to the churchyard, past houses twice the size of hers. All the trees in their gardens were bare now. She and Harry had been fond of telling each other that they would see them blossom next year. The trees in the graveyard were monotonously evergreen, but she never knew what that was meant to imply. She cleared last week's flowers away from Harry's stone and replaced them with the wreath, murmuring a few sentences that were starting to feel formulaic. She dropped the stale flowers in the wire bin outside the concrete wedge of a church on her way to the bus.

As it passed her road she saw the Bulloughs on her path. Charmaine and her offspring strode to meet her at the lamp. "Brad says you lifted our Keanu's flowers."

"Then I'm afraid he's mistaken. I'm afraid—"

"You should be," said Arnie, the biggest and presumably the eldest of the brood. "Don't talk to my mam like that, you old twat."

Dorothy had begun to shake—not visibly, she hoped—but stood her ground. "I don't think I'm being offensive."

"You're doing it now," Arnie said, and his face twisted with loathing. "Talking like a teacher."

"Leave it, Arn," his mother said more indulgently than reprovingly, and stared harder at Dorothy. "What were you doing touching Keanu's things?"

"As I was trying to explain, they weren't his. I'm not accusing anybody, but someone took a wreath I'd bought and put it here."

"Why didn't you?" demanded Angelina.

"Because they were for my husband."

"When are you going to get Kee some?" J-Bu said at once.

"She's not," Charmaine said, saving Dorothy the task of being more polite. "Where were these ones you took supposed to be?"

"They were in my house."

"Someone broke in, did they? Show us where."

"There's no sign of how they did it, but—"

"Know what I think? You're mad."

"Should be locked up," said Angelina.

"And never mind expecting us to pay for it," Arnie said.

"I'm warning you in front of witnesses," said their mother. "Don't you ever touch anything that belongs to this family again."

"You keep your dirty hands off," J-Bu translated.

"Mad old bitch," added Brad.

Dorothy still had her dignity, which she bore into the house without responding further. Once the door was closed she gave in to shivering. She stood in the hall until the bout was over, then peeked around the doorway of the front room. She didn't know how long she had to loiter before an angry glance showed that the pavement was deserted. "Go on, say I'm a coward," she murmured. "Maybe it isn't wise to be too brave when you're on your own."

Who was she talking to? She'd always found the notion that Harry might have stayed with her too delicate to put to any test. Perhaps she felt a little less alone for having spoken; certainly while weeding the garden she felt watched.

She had an intermittent sense of it during her meal, not that she had much appetite, and as she tried to read and to quell her thoughts with television. It followed her to bed, where she wakened in the middle of the night to see a gliding strip of light display part of a skinny silhouette. Or had the crouching shape as thin as twigs scuttled across the band of light? Blinking showed her only the light on the wall, and she let the scent of flowers lull her to sleep.

It took daylight to remind her there were no flowers in the room. There seemed to be more of a scent around her bed than the flowers in the house accounted for. Were her senses letting her down? She was glad of an excuse to go out. Now that they'd closed the post office around the corner the nearest was over a mile away, and she meant to enjoy the walk.

She had to step into the road to avoid vehicles parked on the pavement, which was also perilous with cyclists taking time off school. Before she reached the post office her aching skull felt brittle with the sirens of police cars and ambulances in a hurry to be elsewhere, not to mention the battering clatter of road drills. As she shuffled to the counter she was disconcerted by how much pleasure she took in complaining about all this to her fellow pensioners. Was she turning into just another old curmudgeon weighed down by weary grievances? Once she'd thanked the postmaster several times for her pension she headed for the bus stop. One walk was enough after all.

Although nobody was waiting outside her house, something was amiss. She stepped gingerly down from the bus and limped through gaps in the traffic. What had changed about her garden? She was at the corner of the road when she realised she couldn't see a single flower.

Every one had been trampled flat. Most of the stalks were snapped and the blossoms trodden into the earth, which displayed the prints of small trainers. Dorothy held onto the gatepost while she told herself that the flowers would grow again and she would live to see them, and then she walked stiff as a puppet into the house to call the police.

While it wasn't an emergency, she didn't expect to wait nearly four unsettled hours for a constable less than half her age to show up. By this time a downpour had practically erased the footprints, which he regarded as too common to be traceable. "Have you any idea who's responsible?" he hoped if not the opposite, and pushed his cap higher on his prematurely furrowed forehead.

"The family of the boy you were trying to catch last week."

"Did you see them?"

"I'm certain someone must have. Mrs. Thorpe opposite hardly ever leaves the house. Too worried that clan or someone like them will break in."

"I'll make enquiries." As Dorothy started to follow him he said "I'll let you know the outcome."

He was gone long enough to have visited several of her neighbours. She hurried to admit him when the doorbell rang, but he looked embarrassed, perhaps by her eagerness. "Unfortunately I haven't been able to take any statements."

"You mean nobody will say what they saw," Dorothy protested in disbelief.

"I'm not at liberty to report their comments."

As soon as he drove away she crossed the road. Mrs. Thorpe saw her coming and made to retreat from the window, then adopted a sympathetic wistful smile and spread her arms in a generalised embrace while shaking her head. Dorothy tried the next house, where the less elderly but equally frail of the unmarried sisters answered the door. "I'm sorry," she said, and Dorothy saw that she shouldn't expect any witness to risk more on her behalf. She was trudging home when she caught sight of an intruder in her front room.

Or was it a distorted reflection of Keanu's memorial, thinned by the glare of sunlight on the window? At first she thought she was seeing worse than unkempt hair above an erased face, and then she realised it was a tangle of flowers perched like a makeshift crown or halo on the head, even if they looked as though they were sprouting from a dismayingly misshapen cranium. As she ventured a faltering step the silhouette crouched before sidling out of view. She didn't think a reflection could do that, and she shook her keys at the house on her way to the door.

A scent of flowers greeted her in the hall. Perhaps her senses were on edge, but the smell was overpowering—sickly and thick. It reminded her how much perfume someone significantly older might wear to disguise the staleness of their flesh. Shadows hunched behind the furniture as she searched the rooms, clothes stirred in her wardrobe when she flung it open, hangers jangled at her pounce in the guest room, but she had already established that the back door and windows were locked. She halted on the stairs, waving her hands to waft away the relentless scent. "I saw you," she panted.

But had she? Dorothy kept having to glance around while she cooked her dinner and did her best to eat it, though the taste seemed to have been invaded by a floral scent, and later as she tried to read and then to watch television. She was distracted by fancying there was an extra shadow in the room, impossible to locate unless it was behind her. She almost said "Stay out of here" as she took refuge in bed. She mouthed the words at the dark and immediately regretted advertising her nervousness.

She had to imagine Harry would protect her before she was able to sleep. She dreamed he was stroking her face, and in the depths of the night she thought he was. Certainly something like a caress was tracing her upturned face. As she groped for the cord, the sensation slipped down her cheek. The light gave her time to glimpse the insect that had crawled off her face, waving its mocking antennae. It might have been a centipede or millipede—she had no chance to count its many legs as it scurried under the bed.

She spent the rest of the interminable night sitting against the headboard, the bedclothes wrapped tight around her drawn-up legs. She felt surrounded, not only by an oppressive blend of perfume that suggested somebody had brought her flowers—on what occasion, she preferred not to think. As soon as daylight paled Keanu's streetlamp she grabbed clothes and shook them above the stairs on her way to the bathroom.

She found a can of insect spray in the kitchen. When she made herself kneel, stiff with apprehension as much as with rheumatism, she saw dozens of flowers under her bed. They were from the garden—trampled, every one of them. Which was worse: that an intruder had hidden them in her room or that she'd unknowingly done so? She fetched a brush and dustpan and shuddered as she swept the debris up, but no insects were lurking. Once she'd emptied the dustpan and vacuumed the carpet she dressed for gardening. She wanted to clear up the mess out there, and not to think.

She was loading a second bin-liner with crushed muddy flowers when she heard Charmaine Bullough and her youngest children outdoing the traffic for noise on the main road. Dorothy managed not to speak while they lingered by the memorial, but Brad came to her gate to smirk at her labours. "I wonder who could have done this," she said.

"Don't you go saying it was them," Charmaine shouted. "That's defamation. We'll have you in court."

"I was simply wondering who would have had a motive."

"Never mind sounding like the police either. Why'd anybody need one?"

"Shouldn't have touched our Kee's flowers," J-Bu said.

Her mother aimed a vicious backhand swipe at her head, but a sojourn in the pub had diminished her skills. As Charmaine regained her balance Dorothy blurted "I don't think he would mind."

"Who says?" demanded Brad.

"Maybe he would if he could." Dorothy almost left it at that, but she'd been alone with the idea long enough. "I think he was in my house."

"You say one more word about him and you won't like what you get," Charmaine deafened her by promising. "He never went anywhere he wasn't wanted."

Then that should be Charmaine's house, Dorothy reflected, and at once she saw how to be rid of him. She didn't speak while the Bulloughs stared at her, although it looked as if she was heeding Charmaine's warning. When they straggled towards their house she packed away her tools and headed for the florist's. "Visiting again?" the assistant said, and it was easiest to tell her yes, though Dorothy had learned to stay clear of the churchyard during the week, when it tended to be occupied by drunks and other addicts. She wouldn't be sending a remembrance to the paper either. She didn't want to put Harry in the same place as Keanu, even if she wished she'd had the boy to teach.

Waiting for nightfall made her feel uncomfortably like a criminal. Of course that was silly, and tomorrow she could discuss next year's holiday with Helena over lunch. She could have imagined that her unjustified guilt was raising the scents of the wreath. It must be the smell of the house, though she had the notion that it masked some less welcome odour. At last the dwindling day released her, but witnesses were loitering on both sides of the road.

She would be committing no crime—more like the opposite. As she tried to believe they were too preoccupied with their needs to notice or at least to identify her, a police car cruised into the road. In seconds the pavements were deserted, and Dorothy followed the car, hoping for once that it wouldn't stop at the Bullough house.

It didn't, but she did. She limped up the garden path as swiftly as her legs would work, past a motor bicycle that the younger Bulloughs had tired of riding up and down the street, and posted the wreath through the massively brass-hinged mahogany door of the pebbledashed terrace house. She heard Charmaine and an indeterminate number of her children screaming at one another, and wondered whether they would sound any different if they had a more than unexpected visitor. "Go home to your mother," she murmured.

The police were out of sight. Customers were reappearing from the alleys between the houses. She did her best not to hurry, though she wasn't anxious to be nearby when any of the Bulloughs found the wreath. She was several houses distant from her own when she glimpsed movement outside her gate.

The flowers tied to the lamp-standard were soaked in orange light. Most of them were blackened by it, looking rotten. Though the concrete post was no wider than her hand, a shape was using it for cover. As she took a not entirely willing step a bunch of flowers nodded around the post and dodged back. She thought the skulker was using them to hide whatever was left of its face. She wouldn't be scared away from her own house. She stamped towards it, making all the noise she could, and the remnant of a body sidled around the post, keeping it between them. She avoided it as much as she was able on the way to her gate. As she unlocked the door she heard a scuttling of less than feet behind her. It was receding, and she managed not to look while it grew inaudible somewhere across the road.

The house still smelled rather too intensely floral. In the morning she could tone that down while she went for lunch. She made up for the dinner she'd found unappetising last night, and bookmarked pages in the travel guide to show Helena, and even found reasons to giggle at a comedy on television. After all that and the rest of the day she felt ready for bed.

She stooped to peer under it, but the carpet was bare, though a faint scent lingered in the room. It seemed unthreatening as she lay in bed. Could the flowers have been intended as some kind of peace offering? In a way she'd been the last person to speak to Keanu. The idea fell short of keeping her awake, but the smell of flowers roused her. It was stronger and more suggestive of rot, and most of all it was closer. The flowers were in bed with her. There were insects as well, which didn't entirely explain the jerky movements of the mass of stalks that nestled against her. She was able to believe they were only stalks until their head, decorated or masked or overgrown with shrivelled flowers, lolled against her face.

MELANIE KLEIN SAID

ROBERT McVEY

The psychoanalyst Melanie Klein said that life itself is an aberration. Now that's going for it. I believe when she was a child, she was blamed for her brother's death by her parents, but, as always, I haven't looked into the matter. But do not one and one make two in this instance? On the whole, per Melanie Klein, there should be only rocks and not even lichen on them to achieve a true state of nature, and so maybe she did kill him, and then said to her parents, doubting Thomases heretofore of her precept, "There, see what I mean?" But this was not to be my way. I stood in front of the class at age nine with a crayon drawing of a burning house and put my forefinger through a crayoned second-story window and cried, "Help, help, help!," wiggling the finger wildly. The teacher had told us to do drawings for a little girl named Anita, who had been burned out of her home last week in Philadelphia. It had been in the papers. She would be sent the drawings. Mine was a lively art, not like Melanie's demonstration. But what would it be like if any children were able to say at such a juncture, "What in God's name are crayon drawings made by strangers going to do for a homeless child? Do you think Anita wants to reflect on twenty-eight versions of the inferno from which she somehow escaped with her life? Is your intention to traumatize and retraumatize this child twenty-eight-fold, courtesy of Crayola? Or does it go deeper than that, are you demonstrating for Anita your belief in Freud's concept of the death instinct, Miss Neary? Are you attempting via artwork to induce in this child a regret that she ignored her unconscious urge to run back into the flames? In this attempt, are you using us as your cat's paw? Did you know Melanie Klein said life itself is an aberration?" One by one we all got in front of the class and showed our drawings. Mine was the only one which had a body part bursting out a window. Maybe from that I could have gone on to become a full-blooded male, a Jackson Pollack type, or, if not an artist, a hard-ass prosecutor type, or a soldier-of-fortune reporter type drunkenly heckling photo-op politicos in a war zone. But this as it happened was my high tide. I think it was Anita's, too. I think Anita burned her own house down, and I hope she did. No school for her the next day. No fish on Friday. Daddy's filthy porn an ash. Not only living things can be destroyed, Melanie. Everything can go, and people can live free, Miss Neary: Anita's Law.

GASLIGHT

JEFFREY FORD

We first heard about the child one evening at the Monday Afternoon Club from old Matterson, last heir to an empire of sweatshops. We'd been going round in a circle offering up stories of the supernatural to pass a dreary winter's eve. The ones we'd come out with so far were of a pedestrian nature—the haunted governess, the young woman who sees her father in an art museum in Italy at the moment of his death three continents away, the romance of certain old shoes—but then it was Matterson's turn, and the poor codger seemed to be experiencing some bout of internal distress. Well into his fourth whiskey and passing wind like a bellows in Hell, he came out with it, and when he did, he gave an unfeigned shiver, as did we all.

The tale held us captive in the face of its teller's overripe departures from decorum. Mr. Steel pinched his nostrils with thumb and pointer and begged a jot more speed in the telling. Matterson was not to be hurried, though. "All in due course," he said, and paused to run his fingers through his prodigious sideburns, like a pair of kittens, while from his southern hemisphere there issued a long slow ripping noise, proof that his trousers had seen their last. It was at this point that my man, Hubert, reached for a handkerchief. I'll admit, I was also rather faint, but the lure of the harrowing saga won out over self-preservation, and I dare say we all, Steel, Hubert, Mr. Cipus, and myself, tears forming in the corners of our eyes, forfeited no mean parcel of our respective life spans to hear it.

Matterson gave ample evidence of his own proximity to doom, and yet some infernal genius still burned and burnished his descriptions of the evil child, the manner in which the scamp emerged from the mist, his dripping paleness, the sharp teeth. And the setting, with its glistening gas-lit cobblestones and shadowed alleys gave the thing a ring of the genuine. His technique abolished all disbelief, even when we learned that the boy curled himself up, small as a squirrel, in a woman's handbag outside the opera one evening and was ferried, unknowingly, to her apartment. We accepted this strangeness gratefully as if it were fresh air. Even after the woman had gone to bed, and the sickly little phantom let himself out of her bag and crept to her side, we had no care for why or how, but wished only to know what was next to happen. Matterson took great pains with the scene of the woman's disemboweling. Every grim detail was gilded with adjectives as the boy clawed his way into her womb. "Ungodly," said Mr. Cipus, in his unfailing ability to state the obvious, and if I'm not mistaken, my good stoic, Hubert's, hands trembled slightly. I'd heard few things more ghastly, but this outlandishness was exceeded soon after when Matterson revealed the number of victims and recounted the specifics of their bloody deaths, punctuating each episode with a sulfurous staccato note reminiscent of the piccolo.

"Too much," cried Steel.

"There is ever more," replied Matterson, and with a volley of thunder, and a cruel smile upon his lips, he launched into the biography of the spirit. "Tommy Tim was the lad's name." He told us that in the neighborhoods around Wessel Street, a ditty was sung about the specter. I prayed he would not sing it, but he did, in a mock child's voice, accompanying himself with a complicated score like some mad Bach of the posterior.

> *Tommy Tim, Tommy Tim*
> *Look below, it is him*
> *Climbing up your lady's leg*
> *Climbing for your lady's egg*
> *Rip, rip, rip, and then*
> *Tommy Tim is home again.*

Most disturbing. And yet not the last word, for Matterson went on, dispensing horror from both ends, relaying the dismal life of the boy who would rise from a lonely, unmarked grave to wreak fear upon the living with his desire to be born again and seek that love which had been absent in his first go round. By this point I'd broken into a full sweat and had grown dizzy amidst the barrage of the storyteller's fromage. It was in that staggered condition, my thoughts verily whirling like a pinwheel, that I learned that only minutes after birth the lad had been trundled in a dirty blanket and left upon a doorstep—not a lucky one. He was raised in a drab orphanage where he was regularly beaten. Upon reaching the age of eight, he was sent to labor at the Gas Works. Although I swooned in and out of consciousness, I saw it all in my mind's eyes, a tapestry of destitution, depravity, and sodden depression. When, in Matterson's recounting, poor Tommy Tim, weak from incipient starvation, slips on the ledge above the putrefaction vat at work and plunges headlong into the boiling slurry of detritus, I, unable to draw a decent breath, also fell forward. I could feel Hubert catch me and heard his voice, "Bring the smelling salts . . . and for God's sake, a fan." Overcome by Matterson's wicked craft, I went out cold.

Perhaps not even a minute later, I came to with a sweet breeze of brisk air laving my face. Hubert had dragged me bodily to the window at the opposite end of the parlor and opened it halfway. Steel, Mr. Cipus, myself and my trusty man, all crowded around the portal. Behind us, still belaboring the atmosphere with raucous indiscretions, Matterson retrieved a cigar from his jacket pocket. As he cut the tip and tamped the end, he laughed and said, "I've reserved the most disturbing part for last."

"I'm surprised you've got anything left," said Steel.

Matterson lifted one cheek off the chair and snarled angrily. He took out his box of matches and setting one against the flint, said, "Are you familiar with the cuckoo bird?"

We four remained silent.

"The cuckoo," he said, "invades the nest of another species of bird while the adults are out hunting, destroys the existing eggs and lays its own in their place before vanishing. In a similar way, Tommy Tim hoped to trick some woman into raising him, into loving him. In his ghostly child's mind he cannot comprehend how his brutal incursions into the wombs of the living, the strangling of the expected child, etc., negate his desires as he tries to fulfill them."

Matterson struck the match but it failed.

Mr. Cipus understood before the rest of us that a spark might be fatal. "Duck, gentlemen," he said.

We did just that as Matterson, expelling a parade of gurglers, struck another. This one lit and a heartbeat later he exploded in an impressive fireball that consumed his chair. He burned fiercely and we frantically summoned Emmonds, the club's retainer, to bring bottles of soda water with which we extinguished the blaze. In the billowing smoke that resulted, Tommy Tim's figure appeared briefly. We all saw it. He held his arms out to us and called, "Daddy." We all confessed to feeling a chill. Then he vanished with the smoke, and Matterson sifted down to a pile of ash.

ENDLESS ENCORE

WILL LUDWIGSEN

At least she still comes to see me, the little girl in the white and lavender dress—some people would have left me behind to get help.

Every day in what I assume is the late afternoon, when the sun is far enough to the horizon to cast the edge of the well in shadow, she comes. All I can really see of her at first is her silhouette, the eclipse of her small head and dangling curls against the light. From so far down, she looks even smaller than she probably is, though her voice can somehow always find its way to me.

"Hello," she says every time. "Would you like a show?"

It doesn't do any good to say yes or to say no or to say, "Can you please go for help? I think my leg is broken." She doesn't seem to care much about how I fell down here or why I haven't left.

Whether I say yes or I say no, the puppets descend on their long strings. They're the old-fashioned wooden kind with patches of cloth and hair pasted on their flat surfaces. One seems to be a man dressed in Edwardian style with a brown-gray woolen suit and hat, and the other seems to be a little girl dressed in a white and lavender dress with blonde curls. Both wear paper fairy wings on their backs.

I know the story by heart now.

"Hello, little Lizabeth," says the man in the brown-gray suit.

"Hello, Duncan," says the girl in the lavender dress.

"Will you come walk with me?" says the man.

"May I take my puppets?" says the girl.

"Of course," he replies. "Maybe we can make a show."

The puppets' legs jerk and their arms swing, the little joints squeaking as they walk and walk. This part always strikes me as tedious for a puppet show, and I've wondered if the little girl is performing a literal time or distance. If she is, I have no idea how far or how long because neither has much meaning here in the well.

170

"Will you come sit with me?" says the man.

"Where?" asks the girl.

"Over here," says the man. "On my lap."

Both pairs of legs draw up and the puppets dangle a moment, maybe thinking, maybe admiring the willows together. To me, they're staring at wet stone walls furred over with moss.

"You're going to miss your sister, aren't you, Lizabeth?" asks the man.

"Very much, Duncan."

"Am I wrong to suspect that you're going to miss me, too?"

"Even more, Duncan."

"We won't be far, you know. Down the road a few miles in our own home, a place you're always welcome, with all the woods you could want."

"But who will come to my puppet shows? Father hasn't the time, and Mother doesn't like them."

"Lizabeth, we'll build you your own theater at Barrowgrange. A grand one, with enough room for you and all your marionettes."

The girl puppet hangs her arms and head, swinging quietly in the stale air above me. "What about you? Won't you be playing with me anymore?"

"Oh, Lizabeth!" The puppet reaches for her and she tugs away. "We can't stage plays for fairies in the well forever, you know. I wish we could. I'll miss those plays, truly. But when people get older, they stop climbing around dry wells and imagining fairy audiences at the bottom. Someday soon, you'll understand."

"Understand what?"

The puppet in the brown suit shakes its head slowly. "That people grow up. Me, your sister . . . even you. And grown ups play in different ways. You won't want to play with puppets someday, just as Mary and I don't."

"I'm going to play forever." The girl puppet's arms came together as though they were folded. "I want to do one more puppet show."

"Lizabeth—"

"I want to."

"I shouldn't even be here. The preparations for the wedding—"

"You be the prince and I'll be the princess." Then, in a slightly different voice accented with a stereotypical aristocracy, she says, "'Prince Duncan, Prince Duncan, whither are you going on the day of our wedding?'"

The other puppet hangs there, doing nothing.

"'Today was the day you swore to marry me,'" says the girl's voice.

"Is that what this is about, Lizabeth? Something I said when I was a boy, something to please your heart when you were sad?" The puppet reached and this time rested his wooden hand on the other's shoulder. "Oh, Lizabeth. You're still so young. Mary and I, we—"

The girl puppet whirls on its strings and reaches for him with her woodblock arms. "Mary and you! Mary and you! Mary and you!"

The puppets tangle now, the limbs clopping together. Their strings twist and twine into one cord. They clatter on one wall and then the other before dropping into the mud beside me. The head of the man puppet seems bent back at a horrible angle, and the girl puppet rests hers on his chest.

"And they lived happily ever after among the fairies," the girl at the top of the well says. "The end."

Today's performance ends.

"Wait," I'll say, a little weaker each time, but she doesn't reply. She never replies. She only pulls away, leaving me for another night and another day with nothing for company but these rotten wooden block bones, plus two sets of human ones.

COCKROACH

DALE BAILEY

After the examination, they gathered in the office of the physician, an obstetrician named Exavious that a friend of Sara's had recommended. Dr. Exavious specialized in what Sara termed "high-risk pregnancies," which Gerald Hartshorn took to mean that his wife, at thirty-seven, was too old to be having babies. Secretly, Gerald thought of his wife's . . . condition . . . not as a natural biological process, but as a disease: as fearsome and intractable, and perhaps—though he didn't wish to think of it—as fatal.

During the last weeks, a seed of fear Gerald had buried almost ten years ago—buried and *forgotten*, he had believed—had at last begun to germinate, to spread hungry tendrils in the rich loam of his heart, to feed.

And now, such thoughts so preoccupied him that Gerald only half-listened as Dr. Exavious reassured Sara. "We have made great strides in bringing to term women of your age," he was saying, "especially women in such superb condition as I have found you to be . . ."

These words, spoken in the obscurely accented English which communicated an aura of medical expertise to men of Gerald's class (white, affluent, conservative, and, above all, coddled by a network of expensive specialists)— these words should have comforted him.

They did not. Specialist or not, the fact remained that Gerald didn't like Exavious, slim and Arabic, with febrile eyes and a mustache like a narrow charcoal slash in his hazel flesh. In fact, Gerald didn't like much of anything about this . . . situation. Most of all, he didn't like being left alone with the doctor when Sara excused herself at the end of the meeting. He laced his fingers in his lap and gazed off into a corner, uncertain how to proceed.

"These times can be difficult for a woman," Exavious said. "There are many pressures, you understand, not least on the kidneys."

Gerald allowed himself a polite smile: recognition of the intended humor, nothing more. He studied the office—immaculate carpet, desk of dark expensive wood, diplomas mounted neatly on one wall—but saw no clock. Beyond tinted windows, the parking lot shimmered with mid-summer heat. Julian would be nuts at the office. But he didn't see how he could steal a glance at his watch without being rude.

Exavious leaned forward and said, "So you are to be a father. You must be very happy, Mr. Hartshorn."

Gerald folded and unfolded his arms. "Oh . . . I guess. Sure."

"If you have further questions, questions I haven't answered, I'd be happy to . . . " He let the rest of the sentence hang, unspoken, in the air. "I know this can be a trying experience for some men."

"I'm just a bit nervous, that's all."

"Ah. And why is that?"

"Well, her history, you know."

Exavious smiled. He waved a hand dismissively. "Such incidents are not uncommon, Mr. Hartshorn, as I'm sure you know. Your wife is quite healthy. Physiologically, she is twenty-five. You have nothing to fear."

Exavious sighed; he toyed with a lucite pyramid in which a vaguely alien-looking model of a fetus had been embedded. The name of a drug company had been imprinted in black around its base. "There is one thing, however."

Gerald swallowed. A slight pressure constricted his lungs. "What's that?"

"Your wife has her own fears and anxieties because of the history you mentioned. She indicated these during the examination—that's why she came to me in the first place. Emotional states can have unforeseen physiological effects. They can heighten the difficulty of a pregnancy. Most doctors don't like to admit it, but the fact is we understand very little about the mind-body relationship. However, one thing is clear: your wife's emotional condition is every bit as important as her physical state." Exavious paused. Some vagary of the air-conditioning swirled to Gerald's nostrils a hint of his after-shave lotion.

"I guess I don't really understand," Gerald said.

"I'm just trying to emphasize that your wife will need your support, Mr. Hartshorn. That's all."

"Are you suggesting that I wouldn't be supportive?"

"Of course not. I merely noticed that—"

"I don't know what you noticed, but it sounds to me—"

"Mr. Hartshorn, please."

"—like you think I'm going to make things difficult for her. You bet I'm nervous. Anyone in my circumstances would be. But that doesn't mean I won't be supportive." In the midst of this speech, Gerald found himself on his feet, a hot blush rising under his collar. "I don't know what you're suggesting—" he continued, and then, when Exavious winced and lifted his hands palms outward, he consciously lowered his voice. "I don't know what you're suggesting—"

"Mr. Hartshorn, please. My intent was not to offend. I understand that you are fearful for your wife. I am simply trying to tell you that she must not be allowed to perceive that you too are afraid."

Gerald drew in a long breath. He sat, feeling sheepish. "I'm sorry, it's . . . I've been under a lot of pressure at work lately. I don't know what came over me."

Exavious inclined his head. "Mr. Hartshorn, I know you are busy. But might I ask you a small favor—for your sake and for your wife's?"

"Sure, please."

"Just this: take some time, Mr. Hartshorn, take some time and think. Are you fearful for your wife's welfare, or are you fearful for your own?"

Just then, before Gerald could reply, the door from the corridor opened and Sara came in, her long body as yet unblemished by the child within. She brushed back a wisp of blonde hair as Gerald turned to face her. "Gerald, are you okay? I thought I heard your—"

"Please, Mrs. Hartshorn, there was nothing," the doctor said warmly. "Is that not correct, Mr. Hartshorn? Nothing, nothing at all."

And somehow Gerald recovered himself enough to accede to this simple deception as the doctor ushered them into the corridor. Outside, while Sara spoke with the receptionist, he turned at a feathery touch on his shoulder. Dr. Exavious enveloped his hand and gazed into his eyes for a long and obscurely terrible moment; and then Gerald wrenched himself away, feeling naked and exposed, as if those febrile eyes had illuminated the hollows of his soul, as if he too had been subjected to an examination and had been found wanting.

• • •

"I don't know," Gerald said as he guided the Lexus out of the clinic lot. "I don't like him much. I liked Schwartz better."

He glanced over at Sara, her long hand curved beneath her chin, but she wouldn't meet his eyes.

Rush hour traffic thickened around them. He should call Julian; there wasn't much point in trying to make it back to the office now. He had started to reach for the phone when Sara said, "He's a specialist."

"You heard him: you're in great shape. You don't need a specialist."

"I'd feel more comfortable with him."

Gerald shrugged. "I just didn't think he was very personable, that's all."

"Since when do we choose our doctors because they're personable, Gerald?" She drummed her fingers against the dash. "Besides, Schwartz wasn't especially charming." She paused; then, with a chill hint of emotion, she added, "Not to mention competent."

Like stepping suddenly into icy water, this—was it grief, after all these years? Or was it anger?

He extended a hand to her, saying, "Now come on, Sara—"

"Drop it, Gerald."

"Fine."

An oppressive silence filled the car. No noise from without penetrated the interior, and the concentrated purr of the engine was so muted that it seemed rather a negation of sound. A disquieting notion possessed him: perhaps there never had been sound in the world.

A fractured series of images pierced him: rain-slicked barren trees, black trunks whipped to frenzy by a voiceless wind; lane upon lane of stalled, silent cars, pouring fumes into the leaden sky; and Sara—Sara, her lips moving like the lips of a silent movie heroine, shaping words that could not reach him through the changeless air.

Gerald shook his head.

"Are you ready to go home or do you need to stop by the library?" he asked.

"Home. We need to talk about the library."

"Oh?"

"I'm thinking of quitting," she said.

"Quitting?"

"I need some time, Gerald. We have to be careful. I don't want to lose this baby."

"Well, sure," he said. "But quitting."

Sara swallowed. "Besides, I think the baby should be raised at home, don't you?"

Gerald slowed for a two-way stop, glanced into the intersection, and plunged recklessly into traffic, slotting the Lexus into a narrow space before a looming brown UPS truck. Sara uttered a brief, piercing shriek.

"I hadn't really thought about it," Gerald said.

And in fact he hadn't—hadn't thought about that, or dirty diapers, or pediatricians, or car seats, or teething, or a thousand other things, all of which now pressed in upon him in an insensate rush. For the first time he thought of the baby not as a spectral possibility, but as an imminent presence, palpable, new, central to their lives. He was too old for this.

But all he said was: "Quitting seems a little drastic. After all, it's only part-time."

Sara didn't answer.

"Why don't we think about it?"

"Too late," Sara said quietly.

"You quit?"

Gerald glanced over at her, saw a wry smile touch her lips, saw in her eyes that she didn't really think it funny.

"You quit?"

"Oh, Gerald," she said. "I'm sorry, I really am."

But he didn't know why she was apologizing, and he had a feeling that she didn't know why either. He reached out and touched her hand, and then they were at a stoplight. Gerald reached for the phone. "I've got to call Julian," he said.

• • •

The instrument of Gerald Hartshorn's ascension at the advertising firm of MacGregor, MacGregor, & Turn had been a six-foot-tall cockroach named Fenton, whom Gerald had caused to be variously flayed, decapitated, delimbed, and otherwise dispatched in a series of t.v. spots for a local exterminator who thereafter had surpassed even his nationally advertised competitors in a tight market. Now, a decade later, Gerald could recall with absolute clarity the moment of this singular inspiration: an early morning trip to the kitchen to get Sara a glass of grapefruit juice.

That had been shortly after Sara's first pregnancy, the abrupt, unforgettable miscarriage that for months afterwards had haunted her dreams. Waking in moans or screams or a cold accusatory silence that for Gerald had been unutterably more terrible, she would weep inconsolably as he tried to comfort her, and afterwards through the broken weary house they had leased in those impoverished days, she would send him for a bowl of ice cream or a cup of warm milk or, in this case, a glass of grapefruit juice. Without complaint, he had gone, flipping on lights and rubbing at his bleary eyes and lugging the heavy burden of his heart like a stone in the center of his breast.

He remembered very little of those days besides the black funnel of conflicting emotion which had swept him up: a storm of anger more deleterious than any he had ever known; a fierce blast of grief for a child he had not and could not ever know; and, sweeping all before it, a tempest of relief still more fierce, relief that he had not lost Sara. There had been a close moment, but she at least remained for him.

And, of course, he remembered the genesis of Fenton the cockroach.

Remembered how, that night, as his finger brushed the switch that flooded the cramped kitchen with its pitiless glare, he had chanced to glimpse a dark anomaly flee pell-mell to safety across the stained counter. Remembered the inspiration that rained down on him like a gift as he watched the loathsome creature wedge its narrow body into a crevice and disappear.

The Porter account, he had thought. Imagine:

Fade in with thunder on a screaming housewife, her hands clasped to her face, her expression stricken. Pan recklessly about the darkened kitchen, fulgurant with lightning beyond a rain-streaked window. Jumpcut through a series of angles on a form menacing and enormous, insectoid features more hidden than revealed by the storm's fury. Music as the tension builds. At last the armored figure of the exterminator to the rescue. Fade to red letters on a black background:

Porter Exterminators. Depend On Us.

But the piece had to be done straight. It could not be played for laughs. It had to be terrifying.

And though the ads had gradually softened during the decade since—though the cockroach had acquired a name and had been reduced to a cartoon spokesman who died comically at the end of every spot (*Please, please don't call Porter!*)—that first commercial had turned out very much as Gerald had imagined it: terrifying. And effective.

And that was the way Gerald thought of Fenton the giant cockroach even now. Not in his present animated incarnation, but in his original form, blackly horrifying, looming enraged from some shadowy corner, and always, always obscurely linked in his mind to the dark episode of his lost child and the wife he also had nearly lost.

But despite these connections, the Porter account had remained Gerald's single greatest success. Other accounts had been granted him; and though Fenton was now years in the past, promotions followed. So he drove a Lexus, lived in one of the better neighborhoods, and his wife worked part-time as an aide in the children's library not because she had to, but because she wanted to.

All things considered, he should have been content. So why, when he picked up the phone to call Julian MacGregor, should the conversation which followed so dishearten him?

"I can't make it back in today," he said. "Can the Dainty Wipe thing wait until Monday?"

And Julian, his boss for twelve years, replied with just a touch of . . . what? Exasperation?

Julian said: "Don't worry about that, I'm going to put Lake Conley on it instead."

Lake Conley, who was a friend.

Why should that bother him?

• • •

Gerald came to think of the pregnancy as a long, arduous ordeal: a military campaign, perhaps, conducted in bleak territory, beneath a bitter sky. He thought of Napoleon, bogged down in the snow outside of Moscow, and he despaired.

Not that the pregnancy was without beneficial effects. In the weeks after that first visit to Dr. Exavious—at two months—Gerald saw his Sara's few wrinkles begin to soften, her breasts to grow fuller. But mostly the changes were less pleasant. Nausea continued to plague her, in defiance of Exavious's predictions. They argued over names and made love with distressing infrequency.

Just when Gerald grudgingly acquiesced in repainting a bedroom (a neutral blue, Sara had decided, neither masculine nor feminine), he was granted a momentary reprieve when Sara decided to visit her mother, two hours away in another city.

"I'll see you tomorrow," she told him in the flat heat promised by the August dawn.

Gerald stepped close to her with sudden violent longing; he inhaled her warm powdered odor. "Love you."

"Me too." She flung an arm around him in a perfunctory embrace, and then the small mound of her abdomen interposed itself between them.

And then she was gone.

Work that day dragged through a series of ponderous crises that defied resolution, and it was with relief that Gerald looked up to see Lake Conley standing in the door.

"So Sara's out of town," Lake said.

"That's right."

"Let's have a drink. We should talk."

They found a quiet bar on Magnolia. There, in the cool dim, with the windows on the street like bright hot panes of molten light, Gerald studied Lake Conley, eleven years his junior and handsome seemingly by force of will. Lake combed his long hair with calculated informality, and his suit, half as expensive as Gerald's, fit him with unnatural elegance.

"Then Julian said, 'Frankly, Sue, I don't see the humor in this.' I swear, she nearly died." Lake laughed. "You should have seen it, Gerald."

Gerald chuckled politely and watched as Lake took a pull at his Dos Equis. He watched him place the beer on the bar and dig with slender fingers in a basket of peanuts. Weekly sessions in the gym had shown Gerald that the other man's slight frame was deceptive. Lake was savagely competitive in racquetball, and while it did not bother Gerald that he usually lost, it *did* bother him that when he won, he felt that Lake had permitted him to do so. It bothered him still more that he preferred these soulless victories to an endless series of humiliations.

Often he felt bearish and graceless beside the younger man. Today he just felt tired.

"Just as well I wasn't there," he said. "I'm sure Julian would have lit into me, too."

"Julian giving you a rough time?"

Gerald shrugged.

Lake gazed thoughtfully at him for a moment, then turned to the flickering television that played soundlessly over the bar. "Well," he said with forced cheer. "Sara doing okay? She big as a house yet?"

"Not yet." Gerald finished his drink and signaled for another. "Thank God for gin," he said.

"There's a good sign."

Gerald sipped at the new drink. "Been a while. We're not drinking much at home lately."

"What's the problem, Gerald?"

"She could have told me she stopped taking the pill."

"Sure."

"Or that she was quitting her job."

"Absolutely."

Gerald didn't say anything. A waitress backed through a swinging door by the bar, and tinny rock music blasted out of the kitchen. The sour odor of grease came to him, and then the door swung shut, and into the silence, Lake Conley said:

"You're not too happy about this."

"It's not just that she hasn't been telling me things. She's always been a little self-contained. And she's sorry, I know that."

"Then what is it?"

Gerald sighed. He dipped a finger in his drink and began to trace desultory patterns on the bar. "Our first baby," he said at last. "The miscarriage. It was a close call for Sara. It was scary then and it's even scarier now. She's all I have." Bitter laughter escaped him. "Her and Julian MacGregor."

"Don't forget Fenton."

"Ah yes, the cockroach." Gerald finished his drink, and this time the bartender had another waiting.

"Is that it?"

"No." He paused. "Let me ask you this: you ever feel . . . I don't know . . . weird about anything when Kaye was pregnant?"

Lake laughed. "Let me guess. You're afraid the baby's not yours." And then, when Gerald shook his head, he continued, "How about this? You're afraid the baby is going to be retarded or horrifically deformed, some kind of freak."

"I take it you did."

Lake scooped a handful of peanuts onto the bar and began to arrange them in a neat circle. Gerald looked on in bleary fascination.

Another drink had been placed before him. He tilted the glass to his lips.

"It's entirely normal," Lake was saying. "Listen, I was so freaked out that I talked to Kaye's obstetrician about it. You know what she said? It's a normal by-product of your anxiety, that's all. That's the first baby. Second baby? It's a breeze."

"That so?"

"Sure. Trust me, this is the best thing that's ever happened to you. This is going to be the best experience of your life."

Gerald slouched in his stool, vastly—

—and *illogically*, some fragment of his mind insisted—

—relieved.

"Another drink?" Lake asked.

Gerald nodded. The conversation strayed listlessly for a while, and then he looked up to see that daylight had faded beyond the large windows facing the street. A steady buzz of conversation filled the room. He had a sense of pressure created by many people, hovering just beyond the limits of his peripheral vision. He felt ill, and thrust half an ice-melted drink away from him.

Lake's face drifted in front of him, his voice came from far away: "Listen, Gerald, I'm driving you home, okay?"

Opening his eyes in Lake's car, he saw the shimmering constellation of the city beyond a breath-frosted window, cool against his cheek. Lake was saying something. What?

"You okay? You're not going to be sick are you?"

Gerald lifted a hand weakly. Fine, fine.

They were parked in the street outside Gerald's darkened house. Black dread seized him. The house, empty, Sara away. A thin, ugly voice spoke in his mind—the voice of the cockroach, he thought with sudden lucidity. And it said:

This is how it will look when she's gone. This is how it will look when she's dead.

She won't die. She won't die.

Lake was saying, "Gerald, you have to listen to me."

Clarity gripped him. "Okay. What is it?"

A passing car chased shadow across Lake's handsome features. "I asked you out tonight for a reason, Gerald."

"What's that?"

Lake wrapped his fingers around the steering wheel, took in a slow breath. "Julian talked to me today. He's giving me the Heather Drug campaign. I wanted to tell you. I told him you were depending on it, but . . . " Lake shrugged.

Gerald thought: *You son of a bitch. I ought to puke in your car.*

But he said: "Not your fault." He opened the door and stood up. Night air, leavened with the day's heat, embraced him. "Later."

And then somehow up the drive to the porch, where he spent long moments fitting the key into the door. Success at last, the door swinging open. Interior darkness leaked into the night.

He stumbled to the stairs, paused there to knot his tie around the newel post, which for some reason struck him as enormously funny. And then the long haul up the flight, abandoning one shoe halfway up and another on the landing, where the risers twisted to meet the gallery which opened over shining banisters into the foyer below.

Cathedral ceilings, he thought. The legacy of Fenton the cockroach. And with a twist like steel in his guts, the memory of that nasty internal voice came back to him. Not his voice. The voice of the cockroach:

This is how it will be when she's dead.

And then the bedroom. The sheets, and Sara's smell upon them. The long fall into oblivion.

• • •

He woke abruptly, clawing away a web of nightmare. He had been trapped in suffocating dark, while something—

—the cockroach—

—gnawed hungrily at his guts.

He sat up, breathing hard.

Sara stood at the foot of the bed, his shoes dangling in her upraised hand. She said, "You son of a bitch."

Gerald squinted at the clock-radio. Dull red numbers transformed themselves as he watched. 11:03. Sunlight lashed through the blinds. The room swam with the stink of sleep and alcohol.

"Sara . . . " He dug at his eyes.

"You son of a bitch," she said.

She flung the shoes hard into his stomach as, gasping, he stumbled from the bed. "Sara—"

But she had turned away. He glimpsed her in profile at the door, her stomach slightly domed beneath her drop-waist dress, and then she was gone.

Gerald, swallowing—how dry his throat was!—followed. He caught her at the steps, and took her elbow.

"Sara, it was only a few drinks. Lake and I—"

She turned on him, a fierce light in her eyes. Her fury propelled him back a step. She reminded him of a feral dog, driving an intruder from her pups.

"It's not that, Gerald," she said.

And then—

—goddamn it, I won't be treated like that!—

he stepped toward her, clasping her elbows. Wrenching her arm loose, she drew back her hand. The slap took them both by surprise; he could see the shock of it in her eyes, softening the anger.

His anger, too, dissipated, subsumed in a rising tide of grief and memory.

An uneasy stillness descended. She exhaled and turned away, stared over the railing into the void below, where the sun fell in bright patches against the parquet. Gerald lifted a hand to his cheek, and Sara turned now to face him, her eyes lifted to him, her hand following his to his face. He felt her touch him through the burning.

"I'm sorry," they said simultaneously.

Bright sheepish laughter at this synchronicity convulsed them, and Gerald, embracing her, saw with horror how close she stood to the stairs. Unbidden, an image possessed him: Sara, teetering on the edge of balance. In a series of strobic flashes, he saw it as it might have been. Saw her fall away from him, her arms outstretched for his grasping fingers. Saw her crash backwards to the landing, tumble down the long flight to the foyer. Saw the blood—

—*so little blood. My God, who would have thought? So little blood!*

"I'm sorry," he said again.

She dug her fingers into his back. "It's not that."

"Then what?"

She pulled away and fixed him with her stare. "Your shoes, Gerald. You left them on the stairs." Her hand stole over the tiny mound of her stomach. "I could have fallen."

"I'm sorry," he said, and drew her to him.

Her voice tight with controlled emotion, she spoke again, barely perceptible, punctuating her words with small blows against his shoulder. "Not again," she whispered.

Clasping her even tighter, Gerald drew in a faint breath of her floral-scented shampoo and gazed over her head at the stairs which fell infinitely away behind her.

"Not again," he said.

• • •

Gerald watched apprehensively as Dr. Exavious dragged the ultrasound transducer over Sara's belly, round as a small pumpkin and glistening with clear, odorless gel. The small screen flickered with a shifting pattern of gray and black, grainy and irresolute as the swirling path of a thunderstorm on a television meteorologist's radar.

Sara looked on with a clear light in her face. It was an expression Gerald saw with increasing frequency these days. A sort of tranquil beauty had come into her features, a still internal repose not unlike that he sometimes glimpsed when she moved over him in private rhythm, outward token of a concentration even then wholly private and remote.

But never, never so lost to him as now.

"There now," Exavious said softly. He pointed at the screen. "There is the heart, do you see it?"

Gerald leaned forward, staring. The room, cool, faintly redolent of antiseptic, was silent but for Sara's small coos of delight, and the muted whir of the VCR racked below the ultrasound scanner. Gerald drew a slow breath as the grayish knot Exavious had indicated drew in upon itself and expanded in a pulse of ceaseless, mindless syncopation.

"Good strong heart," Exavious said.

Slowly then, he began to move the transducer again. A feeling of unreality possessed Gerald as he watched the structure of his child unfold across the screen in changeable swaths of light. Here the kidneys—"Good, very good," Exavious commented—and there the spine, knotted, serpentine. The budding arms and legs—Exavious pausing here to trace lambent measurements on the screen with a wand, nodding to himself. And something else, which Exavious didn't comment on, but which Gerald thought to be the hint of a vestigial tail curling between the crooked lines of the legs. He had heard of children born with tails, anomalous throwbacks from the long evolutionary rise out of the jungle.

Sara said, "Can you get an image of the whole baby?"

Exavious adjusted the transducer once more. The screen flickered, settled, grew still at the touch of a button. "Not the whole baby. The beam is too narrow, but this is close."

Gerald studied the image, the thing hunched upon itself in a swirl of viscous fluid, spine twisted, misshapen head fractured by atavistic features: blind pits he took for eyes, black slits for nostrils, the thin slash of the mouth, like a snake's mouth, as lipless and implacable. He saw at the end of an outflung limb the curled talon of a hand. Gerald could not quell the feeling of revulsion which welled up inside him. It looked not like a child, he thought, but like some primitive reptile, a throwback to the numb, idiot fecundity of the primordial slime.

He and Sara spoke at the same time:

"It's beautiful."

"My God, it doesn't even look human."

He said this without thought, and only in the shocked silence that followed did he see how it must have sounded.

"I mean—" he said, but it was pointless. Sara would not meet his eyes.

Dr. Exavious said, "In fact, you are both correct. It is beautiful indeed, but it hardly looks human. Not yet. It will, though." He patted Sara's hand. "Mr. Hartshorn's reaction is not atypical."

"But not typical either, I'm guessing."

Exavious shrugged. "Perhaps." He touched a button and the image on the screen disappeared. He cleaned and racked the transducer, halted the VCR.

"I was just thinking it looks . . . like something very ancient," Gerald said. "Evolution, you know."

"Haeckel's law. Ontogeny recapitulates phylogeny."

"I'm sorry?"

"A very old idea, Mr. Hartshorn. The development of the individual recapitulates the development of the species."

"Is that true?" Sara asked.

"Not literally. In some metaphorical sense, I suppose." Bending, the doctor ejected the tape from the VCR and handed it to Gerald. "But let me assure you, your baby is fine. It is going to be a beautiful child."

At this, Gerald caught Sara's eye: I'm sorry, this look was meant to say, but she would not yield. Later though, in the car, she forgave him, saying: "Did you hear what he said, Gerald? A beautiful child." She laughed and squeezed his hand and said it again: "Our beautiful, beautiful baby."

Gerald forced a smile. "That's right," he told her.

But in his heart another voice was speaking, a thin ugly voice he knew. *Ontogeny recapitulates phylogeny,* it said, and Gerald gripped the steering wheel until the flesh at his knuckles went bloodless; he smiled at Sara, and tried to wall that voice away, and perhaps he thought he succeeded. But in the secret chambers of his heart it resonated still. And he could not help but listen.

• • •

Three weeks later, Indian summer began to die away into fall, and Sara reported that the baby had begun moving within her. Time and again over the next few weeks, Gerald cupped his hand over the growing mound of her belly, alert to even the tiniest shift, but he could feel nothing, nothing at all.

"There," Sara said. Breathlessly: "Can you feel it?"

Gerald shook his head, feeling, for no reason he could quite articulate, vaguely relieved.

Sara continued to put on weight, complaining gamely as her abdomen expanded and her breasts grew sensitive. Gerald sometimes came upon her unawares in the bedroom, standing in her robe and gazing ruefully at the mirror, or sitting on the bed, staring thoughtfully into a closet crowded with unworn clothes and shoes that cramped her swollen feet. A thin dark line extended to her naval (the rectus muscle, Exavious told them, never fear); she claimed she could do nothing with her hair. At night, waking beside her in the darkness, Gerald found his hands stealing over her in numb bewilderment. What had happened to Sara, long-known, much-loved? The clean, angular lines he had known for years vanished, her long bones hidden in this figure gently rounded and soft. Who was this strange woman sleeping in his bed?

And yet, despite all, her beauty seemed to Gerald only more pronounced. She moved easy in this new body, at home and graceful. That clear light he had glimpsed sporadically in her face gradually grew brighter, omnipresent, radiating out of her with a chill calm. For the first time in his life, Gerald believed that old description he had so often read: Sara's eyes indeed *did* sparkle. They danced, they *shone* with a brilliance that reflected his stare—hermetic, enigmatic, defying interpretation. Her gaze pierced through him, into a world or future he could not see or share. Her hands seemed unconsciously to be drawn to her swollen belly; they crept over it constantly, they caressed it.

Her gums swelled. She complained of heartburn, but she would not use the antacid tablets Exavious prescribed, would not touch aspirin or ibuprofen. In October, she could no longer sleep eight hours undisturbed. Once, twice, three times a night, Gerald woke to feel the mattress relinquish her weight with a long sigh. He listened as she moved through the heavy dark to the bathroom, no lights, ever considerate. He listened to the secret flow of urine, the flushing toilet's throaty rush. He woke up, sore-eyed, yawning, and Dr. Exavious's words—*there are many pressures, you understand, not least on the kidneys*—began to seem less like a joke, more like a curse.

In November, they began attending the childbirth classes the doctor had recommended. Twice a week, on Tuesday and Thursday afternoons, Gerald crept out of the office early, uncomfortably aware of Julian MacGregor's baleful gaze; at such moments, he could not help but think of Lake Conley and the Heather Drug campaign. As he retrieved the Lexus from the garage under the building and drove to the rambling old Baptist church where the classes met, his thoughts turned to his exhaustion-stitched eyes and his increasingly tardy appearances at the office every morning. Uneasy snakes of anxiety coiled through his guts.

One afternoon, he sneaked away half an hour early and stopped by the bar on Magnolia for two quick drinks. Calmer then, he drove to the church and parked, letting himself in through the side door of the classroom a few minutes early. Pregnant women thronged the room, luminous and beautiful and infinitely remote; those few men like himself already present stood removed, on the fringes, banished from this mysterious communion.

For a long terrible moment, he stood in the doorway and searched for Sara, nowhere visible. Just the room crowded with these women, their bellies stirring with a biological imperative neither he nor any man could know or comprehend, that same strange light shining in their inscrutable eyes. *They are in league against us,* whispered a voice unbidden in his mind. *They are in league against us.*

Was that the cockroach's voice? Or was it his own?

Then the crowd shifted, Sara slipped into sight. She came toward him, smiling, and he stepped forward to meet her, this question unresolved.

• • •

But the incident—and the question it inspired—lingered in his mind. When he woke from restless dreams, it attended him, nagging, resonant: that intimate communion of women he had seen, linked by fleshly sympathies he could not hope to understand. Their eyes shining with a passion that surpassed any passion he had known. The way they had—that Sara had—of cradling their swollen bellies, as if to caress the—

—*Christ, was it monstrous that came to mind?*—

—growths within.

He sat up sweating, sheets pooled in his lap. Far down in the depths of the house the furnace kicked on; overheated air, smelling musty and dry, wafted by his face. Winter folded the house in chill intimacy, but in here . . . hot, hot. His heart pounded. He wiped a hand over his forehead, dragged in a long breath.

Some watchful quality to the silence, the uneven note of her respiration, told him that Sara, too, was awake. In the darkness. Thinking.

She said, "You okay?"

"I don't know," he said. "I don't know."

And this was sufficient for her. She asked nothing more of him than this simple admission of weakness, she never had. She touched him now, her long hand cool against his back. She drew him to the softness at her breast, where he rested his head now, breath ragged, a panic he could not contain rising like wind in the desert places inside him. Heavy dry sobs wracked him.

"Shhh, now," she said, not asking, just rocking him gently. Her hands moved through his hair.

"Shhh," she whispered.

And slowly, by degrees imperceptible, the agony that had possessed him, she soothed away. Nothing, he thought. Of course, it had been nothing—anxieties, Lake Conley had said.

"You okay?" she asked again.

"I'm fine."

She pulled him closer. His hand came to her thigh, and without conscious intention, he found himself opening her gown, kissing her, her breasts, fuller now than he had ever known them. Her back arched. Her fingers were in his hair.

She whispered, "Gerald, that feels nice."

He continued to kiss her, his interest rising. The room was dark, but he could see her very clearly in his mind: the Sara he had known, lithe and supple; this new Sara, this strange woman who shared his bed, her beauty rising out of some deep reservoir of calm and peace. He traced the slope of her breasts and belly. Here. And here. He guided her, rolling her to her side, her back to him, rump out-thrust as Exavious had recommended during a particularly awkward and unforgettable consultation—

"No, Gerald," she said. She said, "No."

Gerald paused, breathing heavily. Below, in the depths of the darkened house, the furnace shut off, and into the immense silence that followed, he said, "Sara—"

"No," she said. "No, no."

Gerald rolled over on his back. He tried to throttle back the frustration rising once more within him, not gone after all, not dissipated, merely . . . pushed away.

Sara turned to him, she came against him. He could feel the bulk of her belly interposed between them.

"I'm afraid, Gerald. I'm afraid it'll hurt the baby."

Her fingers were on his thigh.

"It won't hurt the baby. Exavious said it won't hurt the baby. The books said it won't hurt the baby. Everyone says it won't hurt the baby."

Her voice in the darkness: "But what if it does? I'm afraid, Gerald."

Gerald took a deep breath. He forced himself to speak calmly. "Sara, it won't hurt the baby. Please."

She kissed him, her breath hot in his ear. Her fingers worked at him. She whispered, "See? We can do something else." Pleading now. "We can be close, I want that."

But Gerald, the anger and frustration boiling out of him in a way he didn't like, a way he couldn't control—it scared him—threw back the covers. Stood, and reached for his robe, thinking: *Hot. It's too hot. I've got to get out of here.* But he could not contain himself. He paused, fingers shaking as he belted the robe, to fling back these words: "I'm not so sure I want to be close, Sara. I'm not at all sure *what* I want anymore."

And then, in three quick strides, he was out the door and into the hall, hearing the words she cried after him—"Gerald, *please*"—but not pausing to listen.

• • •

The flagstone floor in the den, chill against his bare feet, cooled him. Standing behind the bar in the airy many-windowed room, he mixed himself a gin and tonic with more gin than tonic and savored the almost physical sense of heat, real and emotional, draining along his tension-knotted spine, through the tight muscles of his legs and feet, into the placid stones beneath.

He took a calming swallow of gin and touched the remote on the bar. The television blared to life in a far corner and he cycled through the channels as he finished his drink. Disjointed, half-glimpsed images flooded the darkened room: thuggish young men entranced by the sinister beat of the city, tanks jolting over desert landscape, the gang at Cheers laughing it up at Cliff's expense. Poor Cliff. You weren't supposed to identify with him, but Gerald couldn't help it. Poor Cliff was just muddling through like anyone—

—*Like you,* whispered that nasty voice, the voice he could not help but think of as the cockroach.

Gerald shuddered.

On principle, he hated the remote—the worst thing ever to happen to advertising—but now he fingered it again, moved past Letterman's arrogant smirk. He fished more ice from the freezer, splashed clean-smelling gin in his glass, chased it with tonic. Then, half-empty bottle of liquor and a jug of tonic clutched in one hand, drink and television remote in the other, Gerald crossed the room and lowered himself into the recliner.

His anger had evaporated—quick to come, quick to go, it always had been—but an uneasy tension lingered in its wake. He should go upstairs, apologize—he owed it to Sara—but he could not bring himself to move. A terrific inertia shackled him. He had no desire except to drink gin and thumb through the channels, pausing now and again when something caught his eye, half-clad dancers on MTV, a news story about the unknown cannibal killer in L.A., once the tail-end of a commercial featuring none other than Fenton the giant cockroach himself.

Christ.

Three or four drinks thereafter he must have dozed, for he came to himself suddenly and unpleasantly when a nightmare jolted him awake. He sat up abruptly, his empty glass crashing to the floor. He had a blurred impression of it as it shattered, sending sharp scintillas of brilliance skating across the flagstones as he doubled over, sharp ghosts of pain shooting through him, as something, Christ—

—the cockroach—

—gnawed ravenously at his swollen guts.

He gasped, head reeling with gin. The house brooded over him. Then he felt nothing, the dream pain gone, and when, with reluctant horror, he lifted his clutching hands from his belly, he saw only pale skin between the loosely belted flaps of robe, not the gory mess he had irrationally expected, not the blood—

—so little blood, who would have thought? So little blood and such a little—

No. He wouldn't think of that now, he wouldn't think of that at all.

He touched the lever on the recliner, lifting his feet, and reached for the bottle of gin beside the chair. He gazed at the shattered glass and then studied the finger or two of liquor remaining in the bottle; after a moment, he spun loose the cap and tilted the bottle to his lips. Gasoline-harsh gin flooded his mouth. Drunk now, dead drunk, he could feel it and he didn't care, Gerald stared at the television.

A nature program flickered by, the camera closing on a brown grasshopper making its way through lush undergrowth. He sipped at the gin, searched densely for the remote. Must have slipped into the cushions. He felt around for it, but it became too much of an effort. Hell with it.

The grasshopper continued to progress in disjointed leaps, the camera tracking expertly, and this alone exerted over him a bizarre fascination. How the hell did they film these things anyway? He had a quick amusing image: a near-sighted entomologist and his cameraman tramping through some benighted wilderness, slapping away insects and suffering the indignities of crotch-rot. Ha-ha. He touched the lever again, dropping the footrest, and placed his bare feet on the cool flagstones, mindful in a meticulously drunken way of the broken glass.

Through a background of exotic bird-calls, and the swish of antediluvian vegetation, a cultured masculine voice began to speak: "Less common than in the insect world, biological mimicry, developed by predators and prey through millennia of natural selection is still . . . "

Gerald leaned forward, propping his elbows on his knees. A faraway voice whispered in his mind. Natural selection. Sophomore biology had been long ago, but he recognized the term as an element of evolutionary theory. What had Exavious said?

That nasty voice whispering away . . .

He had a brief flash of the ultrasound video, which Sara had watched again only that evening: the fetus, reptilian, primitive, an eerie wakeful quality to its amniotic slumber.

On the screen, the grasshopper took another leap. Music came up on the soundtrack, slow, minatory, almost subliminal. " . . . less commonly used by predators," the voiceover said, "biological mimicry can be dramatically effective when it is . . . " The grasshopper took another leap and plummeted toward a clump of yellow and white flowers. Too fast for Gerald really to see, the flowers exploded into motion. He sat abruptly upright, his heart racing, as prehensile claws flashed out, grasped the stunned insect, and dragged it down. "Take the orchid mantis of the Malaysian rainforest," the voiceover continued. "Evolution has disguised few predators so completely. Watch again as . . . " And now the image began to replay, this time in slow motion, so that Gerald could see in agonizing detail the grasshopper's slow descent, the flower-colored mantis unfolding with deadly and inevitable grace from the heart of the blossom, grasping claws extended. Again. And again. Each time the camera moved in tighter, tighter, until the mantis seemed to fill the screen with an urgency dreadful and inexorable and wholly merciless.

Gerald grasped the bottle of gin and sat back as the narrator continued, speaking now of aphid-farming ants and the lacewing larva. But he had ceased to listen. He tilted the bottle to his lips, thinking again of that reptilian fetus, awash in the womb of the woman he loved and did not want to lose. And now that faraway voice in his mind sounded closer, more distinct. It was the voice of the cockroach, but the words it spoke were those of Dr. Exavious.

Ontogeny recapitulates phylogeny.

Gerald took a last pull of the bottle of gin. Now what exactly did that mean?

• • •

The ball whizzed past in a blur as Gerald stepped up to meet it, his racquet sweeping around too late. He spun and lunged past Lake Conley to catch the ricochet off the back wall, but the ball slipped past, bouncing twice, and slowed to a momentum draining roll.

"Goddamn it!" Gerald flung his racquet hard after the ball and collapsed against the back wall. He drew up his legs and draped his forearms over his knees.

"Game," Lake said.

"Go to hell." Gerald closed his eyes, tilted his head against the wall and tried to catch his breath. He could smell his own sweat, tinged with the sour odor of gin. He didn't open his eyes when Lake slid down beside him.

"Kind of an excessive reaction even for you," Lake said.

"Stress."

"Work?"

"That, too." Gerald gazed at Lake through slitted eyes.

"Ahh."

They sat quietly, listening to a distant radio blare from the weight-room. From adjoining courts, the squeak of rubber-soled shoes and the intermittent smack of balls came to them, barely audible. Gerald watched, exhaustion settling over him like a gray blanket, while Lake traced invisible patterns on the floor with the edge of his racquet.

"Least I don't have to worry about the Heather Drug campaign," Gerald said. Almost immediately, he wished he could pull the words back. Unsay them.

For a long time, Lake didn't answer. When he did, he said only, "You have a right to be pissed off about that."

"Not really. Long time since I put a decent campaign together. Julian knows what he's doing."

Lake shrugged.

Again, Gerald tilted his head against the wall, closing his eyes. There it was, there it always was anymore, that image swimming in his internal darkness: the baby, blind and primitive and preternaturally aware. He saw it in his dreams; sometimes when he woke he had vague memories of a red fury clawing free of his guts. And sometimes it wasn't this dream he remembered, but another: looking on, helpless, horrified, while something terrible exploded out of Sara's smoothly rounded belly.

That one was worse.

That one spoke with the voice of the cockroach. That one said: *You're going to lose her.*

Lake was saying, "Not to put too fine a point on it, Gerald, but you look like hell. You come to work smelling like booze half the time, I don't know what you expect."

Expect? What did he expect exactly? And what would Lake say if he told him?

Instead, he said, "I'm not sleeping much. Sara doesn't sleep well. She gets up two, three times a night."

"So you're just sucking down a few drinks so you can sleep at night, that right?"

Gerald didn't answer.

"What's up with you anyway, Gerald?"

Gerald stared into the darkness behind his closed eyes, the world around him wheeling and vertiginous. He flattened his palms against the cool wooden floor, seeking a tangible link to the world he had known before, the world he had known and lost, he did not know where or how. Seeking to anchor himself to an earth that seemed to be sliding away beneath him. Seeking solace.

"Gerald?"

In his mind, he saw the mantis orchid; on the screen of his eyelids, he watched it unfold with deadly grace and drag down the hapless grasshopper.

He said: "I watch the sonogram tape, you know? I watch it at night when Sara's sleeping. It doesn't look like a baby, Lake. It doesn't look like anything human at all. And I think I'm going to lose her. I think I'm going to lose her, it's killing her, it's some kind of . . . something . . . I don't know . . . it's going to take her away."

"Gerald—"

"No. Listen. When I first met Sara, I remember the thing I liked about her—one of the things I liked about her anyway, I liked so much about her, everything—but the thing I remember most was this day when I first met her family. I went home with her from school for a weekend and her whole family—her little sister, her mom, her dad—they were all waiting. They had prepared this elaborate meal and we ate in the dining room, and you knew that they were a family. It was just this quality they had, and it didn't mean they even liked each other all the time, but they were there for each other. You could feel it, you could breathe it in, like oxygen. That's what I wanted. That's what we have together, that's what I'm afraid of losing. I'm afraid of losing her."

He was afraid to open his eyes. He could feel tears there. He was afraid to look at Lake, to share his weakness, which he had never shared with anyone but Sara.

Lake said, "But don't you see, the baby will just draw you closer. Make you even more of a family than you ever were. You're afraid, Gerald, but it's just normal anxiety."

"I don't think so."

"The sonogram?" Lake said. "Your crazy thoughts about the sonogram? Everybody thinks that. But everything changes when the baby comes, Gerald. Everything."

"That's what I'm afraid of," Gerald said.

• • •

After the gym, Gerald drove for hours without conscious purpose, trusting mindless reflexes to take him where they would. Around him sprawled the city, senseless, stunned like a patient on a table, etherized by winter.

By the time he pulled the Lexus to the broken curb in a residential neighborhood that had been poor two decades past, a few flakes of snow had begun to swirl through the expanding cones of his headlights. Dusk fell out of the December sky. Gerald cracked his window, inhaled cold smoke-stained air, and gazed diagonally across the abandoned street.

Still there. My God, still there after these ten years. A thought recurred to him, an image he had not thought of in all the long months—ages, they felt like—since that first visit to Dr. Exavious: like stepping into icy water, this stepping into the past.

No one lived there anymore. He could see that from the dilapidated state of the house, yard gone to seed, windows broken, paint that had been robin's egg blue a decade ago weathered now to the dingy shade of mop water. Out front, the wind creaked a realtor's sign long since scabbed over with rust. The skeletal swing-set remained in the barren yard, and it occurred to him now that his child—his and Sara's child—might have played there if only . . .

If only.

Always and forever if only.

The sidewalk, broken and weedy, still wound lazily from the street. The concrete stoop still extruded from the front door like a grotesquely foreshortened tongue. Three stairs still mounted to the door, the railing— Dear God—shattered and dragged away years since.

So short. Three short stairs. So little blood. Who could have known?

He thought of the gym, Lake Conley, the story he had wanted to tell but had not. He had not told anyone. And why should he? No great trauma, there; no abuse or hatred, no fodder for the morning talk shows; just the subtle cruelties, the little twists of steel that made up life.

But always there somehow. Never forgotten. Memories not of this house, though this house had its share, God knows, but of a house very much like this one, in a neighborhood pretty much the same, in another city, in another state, a hundred years in the past or so it seemed. Another lifetime.

But unforgettable all the same.

Gerald had never known his father, had never seen him except in a single photograph: a merchant mariner, broad-shouldered and handsome, his wind-burned face creased by a broad incongruous smile. Gerald had been born in a different age, before such children became common, in a different world where little boys without fathers were never allowed to forget their absences and loss. His mother, he supposed, had been a good woman in her way—had tried, he knew, and now, looking back with the discerning eye of an adult, he could see how it must have been for her: the thousand slights she had endured, the cruelties visited upon a small-town girl and the bastard son she had gotten in what her innocence mistook for love. Yes. He understood her flight to the city and its anonymity; he understood the countless lovers; now, at last, he understood the drinking when it began in earnest, when her looks had begun to go. Now he saw what she had been seeking. Solace. Only solace.

But forgive?

Now, sitting in his car across the street from the house where his first child had been miscarried, where he had almost lost forever the one woman who had thought him worthy of her love, Gerald remembered.

The little twists of steel, spoken without thought or heat, that made up life.

How old had he been then? Twelve? Thirteen?

Old enough to know, anyway. Old enough to creep into the living room and crouch over his mother as she lay there sobbing, drunken, bruised, a cold wind blowing through the open house where the man, whoever he had been, had left the door to swing open on its hinges after he had beaten her. Old enough to scream into his mother's whiskey-shattered face: *I hate you! I hate you! I hate you!*

Old enough to remember her reply: *If it wasn't for you, you little bastard, he never would have left. If it wasn't for you, he never would have left me.*

Old enough to remember, sure.

But old enough to forgive? Not then, Gerald knew. Not now. And maybe never.

• • •

They did not go to bed together. Sara came to him in the den, where he sat in the recliner, drinking gin and numbly watching television. He saw her in the doorway that framed the formal living room they never used, and beyond that, in diminishing perspective, the broad open foyer: but Sara foremost, foregrounded and unavoidable.

She said, "I'm going to bed. Are you coming?"

"I thought I'd stay up for a bit."

She crossed the flagstone floor to him in stocking feet, soundlessly, like a grotesquely misshapen apparition—her belly preceding her. He wondered if the long lines of the body he used to know were in there somewhere. She was still beautiful, still graceful, to be sure. But she possessed now a grace and beauty unlike any he had known, ponderous and alien, wholly different from that she had possessed the first time he had seen her all those years ago— ghost-like then as well, an apparition from a world stable and dependable, a world of family, glimpsed in heart-wrenching profile through the clamorous throng of the University Center cafeteria.

She knelt by him. "Please come to bed."

He swished his drink. Ice bobbed and clinked. "I need to unwind."

"Gerald . . . "

"No really, I'm not sleepy, okay?" He smiled, and he could feel the falseness of the smile, but it satisfied her.

She leaned toward him, her lips brushed his cheek with a pressure barely present—the merest papery rush of moth wings in a darkened room. And then she was gone.

Gerald drank: stared into the television's poison glow and drank gin and tonic, nectar and ambrosia. *Tastes like a Christmas tree,* Sara had told him the first night they were together, really together. He had loved her, he thought. He touched the remote, cycled past a fragmentary highlight of an NFL football game; past the dependable hysteria over the LA cannibal killer, identity unknown; past the long face of Mr. Ed. Drank gin and cycled through and through the channels, fragmentary windows on a broken world. Oh, he had loved her.

Later, how much later he didn't know and didn't care, Gerald found his way to the bedroom. Without undressing, he lay supine on the bed and stared sightlessly at the ceiling, Sara beside him, sleeping the hard sleep of exhaustion for now, though Gerald knew it would not last. Before the night was out, the relentless demands of the child within her would prod her into wakefulness. Lying there, his eyes gradually adjusting to the dark until the features of the room appeared to stand out, blacker still against the blackness, something, some whim, some impulse he could not contain, compelled him to steal his hand beneath the covers: stealthy now, through the folds of the sheet; past the hem of her gown, rucked up below her breasts; at last flattening his palm along the arc of her distended belly. Sara took in a heavy breath, kicked at the covers restlessly, subsided.

Silence all through the house, even the furnace silent in its basement lair: just Sara's steady respiration, and Gerald with her in the weighty dark, daring hardly to breath, aware now of a cold sobriety in the pressure of the air.

The child moved.

For the first time, he felt it. He felt it move. An icy needle of emotion pierced him. It moved, moved again, the faintest shift in its embryonic slumber, bare adjustment of some internal gravity.

Just a month, he thought. *Only a month.*

The child moved, *really* moved now, palpable against his outstretched palm. Gerald threw back the covers, sitting upright, the room wheeling about him so swiftly that he had to swallow hard against an obstruction rising in his throat. Sara kicked in her sleep, and then was still.

Gerald looked down at her, supine, one long hand curled at her chin, eyes closed, mouth parted, great mound of belly half-visible below the hem of her up-turned gown. Now again, slowly, he lay a hand against her warm stomach, and yes, just as he had feared, it happened again: the baby moved, a long slow pressure against his palm.

Ontogeny recapitulates phylogeny, hissed the thin nasty voice of the cockroach. But what exactly did that mean?

He moved his palm along her taut belly, pausing as Sara sighed in her sleep, and here too, like the slow pressure of some creature of the unknown deep, boiling through the placid waters, came that patient and insistent pressure. And then something more, not mere pressure, not gentle: a sudden, powerful blow. Sara moaned and arched her back, but the blow came again, as though the creature within her had hurled itself against the wall of the imprisoning womb. *Why didn't she wake up?* Gerald drew his hand away. Blow wasn't really the right word, was it?

What was?

His heart hammered at his ribcage; transfixed, Gerald moved his hand back toward Sara's belly. No longer daring to touch her, he skated his hand over the long curve on an inch-thin cushion of air. My God, he thought. My God. For he could see it now, he could *see* it: an outward bulge of the taut flesh with each repeated blow, as though a fist had punched her from within. He moved his hand, paused, and it happened again, sudden and sure, an outward protrusion that swelled and sank and swelled again. In a kind of panic—

—*what the hell was going on here*—

—Gerald moved his hand, paused, moved it again, tracing the curve of Sara's belly in a series of jerks and starts. And it *followed* him. Even though he was no longer touching her, it followed him, that sudden outward protrusion, the thing within somehow aware of his presence and trying to get at him. The blows quickened even as he watched, until they began to appear and disappear with savage, violent speed.

And still she did not wake up.

Not a blow, he thought. A strike.

Like the swift, certain strike of a cobra. An image unfolded with deadly urgency in Gerald's mind: the image of the orchid-colored mantis exploding outward from its flowery hole to drag down the helpless grasshopper and devour it.

Gerald jerked his hand away as if stung.

Sara's abdomen was still and pale as a tract of mountain snow. Nothing moved there. He reached the covers across her and lay back. A terrific weight settled over him; his chest constricted with panic; he could barely draw breath.

The terrible logic of the thing revealed itself to him at last. Ontogeny recapitulates phylogeny, Exavious had told him. And what if it was true? What if each child reflected in its own development the evolutionary history of the entire species?

Imagine:

Somewhere, far far back in the evolutionary past—who could say how far?—but somewhere, it began. A mutation that should have died, but didn't, a creature born of man and woman that survived to feed . . . and reproduce. Imagine a recessive gene so rare that it appeared in only one of every ten thousand individuals—one of every hundred thousand even. For that would be sufficient, wouldn't it? Gerald couldn't calculate the odds, but he knew that it would be sufficient, that occasionally, three or four times in a generation, two carriers of such a gene would come together and produce . . . What? A child that was not what it appeared to be. A child that was not human. A monster clothed in human flesh.

Beside him, Sara moaned in her sleep. Gerald did not move.

He shut his eyes and saw against the dark screens of his eyelids, the flower-colored mantis, hidden in its perfumed lair; saw its deadly graceful assault, its pincers as they closed around the helpless grasshopper and dragged it down. The words of the narrator came back to him as well: natural selection favors the most efficient predator. And the most efficient predator is the monster that walks unseen among its chosen prey.

Terror gripped him as at last he understood how it must have been through all the long span of human history: Jack the Ripper, the Zodiac, the cannibal killer loose even now in the diseased bowels of Los Angeles.

We are hunted, he thought. We are hunted.

He stumbled clumsily from the bed and made his way into the adjoining bathroom, where for a long time he knelt over the toilet and was violently, violently sick.

• • •

Sanity returned to him in perceptual shards: watery light through the slatted blinds, the mattress rolling under him like a ship in rough waters, a jagged sob of fear and pain that pierced him through. Sara.

Gerald sat upright, swallowing bile. He took in the room with a wild glance.

Sara: in the doorway to the bathroom, long legs twisted beneath her, hands clutched in agony at her bloated abdomen. And blood—

—*my God, how could you have*—

—so much blood, a crimson gout against the pale carpet, a pool spreading over the tiled floor of the bathroom.

Gerald reached for the phone, dialed 911. And then he went to her, took her in his arms, comforted her.

• • •

Swarming masses of interns and nurses in white smocks swept her away from him at the hospital. Later, during the long gray hours in the waiting room— hours spent staring at the mindless flicker of television or gazing through

203

dirty windows that commanded a view of the parking lot, cup after cup of sour vending-machine coffee clutched in hands that would not warm—Gerald could not recall how they had spirited her away. In his last clear memory he saw himself step out of the ambulance into an icy blood-washed dawn, walking fast beside the gurney, Sara's cold hand clutched in his as the automatic doors slipped open on the chill impersonal reaches of the emergency room.

Somehow he had been shunted aside, diverted without the solace of a last endearment, without even a backwards glance. Instead he found himself wrestling with a severe gray-headed woman about insurance policies and admission requirements, a kind of low-wattage bureaucratic hell he hated every minute of, but missed immediately when it ended and left him to his thoughts.

Occasionally he gazed at the pay phones along the far wall, knowing he should call Sara's mother but somehow unable to gather sufficient strength to do so. Later, he glimpsed Exavious in an adjacent corridor, but the doctor barely broke stride. He merely cast at Gerald a speculative glance—

—he knows, he knows—

—and passed on, uttering over his shoulder these words in his obscurely accented English: "We are doing everything in our power, Mr. Hartshorn. I will let you know as soon as I have news."

Alone again. Alone with bitter coffee, recriminations, the voice of the cockroach.

An hour passed. At eleven o'clock, Exavious returned. "It is not good, I'm afraid," he said. "We need to perform a caesarean section, risky under the circumstances, but we have little choice if the baby is to survive."

"And Sara?"

"We cannot know, Mr. Hartshorn." Exavious licked his lips, met Gerald's gaze. "Guarded optimism, shall we say. The fall . . . " He lifted his hand. "Your wife is feverish, irrational. We need you to sign some forms."

And afterwards, after the forms were signed, he fixed Gerald for a long moment with that same speculative stare and then he turned away. "I'll be in touch."

Gerald glared at the clock as if he could by force of will speed time's passage. At last he stood, crossed once more to the vending machines, and for the first time in seven years purchased a pack of cigarettes and a lighter. After a word with the receptionist, he stepped into the bitterly cold December morning to smoke.

A few flakes of snow had begun to drift aimlessly about in the wind. Gerald stood under the E.R. awning, beneath the bruised and sullen sky, the familiar stink of cigarette smoke somehow comforting in his nostrils. He gazed out over the crowded parking lot, his eyes watering. Like stepping into icy water, he thought, this stepping into the past: for what he saw was not the endless rows of cars, but the house he had visited for the first time in a decade only a day ago. And the voice he heard in his head was neither the voice of the hospital p.a. system or the voice of the wind. It was the voice of the cockroach, saying words he did not want to hear.

• • •

You, the cockroach told him. *You are responsible.*

Gerald flipped his cigarette, still burning, into the gutter and wrapped his arms close about his shoulders. But the cold he felt was colder than mere weather.

Responsible.

He supposed he had been. Even now, he could not forget the isolation they had endured during the first years of their marriage. The fear. It hadn't been easy for either of them—not for Gerald, sharing for the first time the bitter legacy of a life he had still to come to terms with; not for Sara, smiling patrician Sara, banished from a family who would not accept the impoverished marriage she had made. To this day Gerald had not forgiven his in-laws for the wedding: the thin-lipped grimace that passed for his mother-in-law's smile; the encounter with his father-in-law in the spotless restroom of the Marriott, when the stout old dentist turned from a urinal to wag a finger in Gerald's face. "Don't ever ask me for a dime, Gerald," he had said. "Sara's made her choice and she'll have to abide by it."

No wonder we were proud, he thought. Sara had taken an evening job as a cashier at a supermarket. Gerald continued at the ad agency, a poorly paid associate, returning nightly to the abandoned rental house where he sat blankly in front of the television and awaited the sound of Sara's key in the lock. God knows they hadn't needed a baby.

But there it was. There it was.

And so the pressure began to tell, the endless pressure to stretch each check just a little further. Gerald could not remember when or why—money he supposed—but gradually the arguments had begun. And he had started drinking. And one night . . .

One night. Well.

Gerald slipped another cigarette free of the pack and brought it to his lips. Cupping his hands against the wind, he set the cigarette alight, and drew deeply.

One night, she was late from work and, worried, Gerald met her at the door. He stepped out onto the concrete stoop to greet her, his hand curled about the graying wooden rail. When Sara looked up at him, her features taut with worry in the jaundiced corona of the porch light, he had just for a moment glimpsed a vision of himself as she must have seen him: bearish, slovenly, stinking of drink. And poor. Just another poor fucking bastard, only she had married this one.

He opened his arms to her, needing her to deny the truth he had seen reflected in her eyes. But she fended him off, a tight-lipped little moue of distaste crossing her features—he knew that expression, he had seen it on her mother's face.

Her voice was weary when she spoke. Her words stung him like a lash. "Drinking again, Gerald?" And then, as she started to push her way past him: "Christ, sometimes I think Mom was right about you."

And he had struck her.

For the first and only time in all the years they had been married, he had struck her—without thought or even heat, the impulse arising out of some deep poisoned well-spring of his being, regretted even as he lifted his hand.

Sara stumbled. Gerald moved forward to steady her, his heart racing. She fell away from him forever, and in that timeless interval Gerald had a grotesquely heightened sense of his surroundings: the walk, broken and weedy; the dim shadow of a moth battering himself tirelessly against the porch light; in the sky a thousand thousand stars. Abruptly, the world shifted into motion again;

in confusion, Gerald watched an almost comically broad expression of relief spread over Sara's face. The railing. The railing had caught her.

"Jesus, Sara, I'm sorr—" he began to say, but a wild gale of hilarity had risen up inside her.

She hadn't begun to realize the consequences of this simple action, Gerald saw. She did not yet see that with a single blow he had altered forever the tenor of their relationship. But the laughter was catching, and he stepped down now, laughing himself, laughing hysterically in a way that was not funny, to soothe away her fears before she saw the damage he had done. Maybe she would never see it.

But just at that moment, the railing snapped with a sound like a gunshot. Sara fell hard, three steps to the ground, breath exploding from her lungs.

But again, she was okay. Just shaken up.

Only later, in the night, would Gerald realize what he had done. Only when the contractions took her would he begin to fear. Only when he tore back the blankets of the bed and saw the blood—

—*so little blood*—

—would he understand.

Gerald snapped away his cigarette in disgust. They had lost the child. Sara, too, had almost died. And yet she had forgiven him. She had forgiven him.

He shivered and looked back through the cold-fogged windows at the waiting room, but he couldn't tolerate the idea of another moment in there. He turned back to the parking lot, exhaled into his cupped hands. He thought of Dr. Exavious, those febrile eyes, the way he had of seeming to gaze into the secret regions of your heart. Probing you. Judging you. Finding you wanting.

There was something else.

Last night.

With this thought, Gerald experienced bleak depths of self-knowledge he had never plumbed before. He saw again the smooth expanse of his wife's belly as he had seen it last night, hideously aswarm with the vicious assaults of the creature within. Now he recognized this vision as a fevered hallucination, nothing more. But last night, last night he had believed. And after his feverish dream, after he had been sick, he had done something else, hadn't he? Something so monstrous and so simple that until this moment he had successfully avoided thinking of it.

He had stood up from the toilet, and there, in the doorway between the bedroom and the bathroom, he had kicked off his shoes, deliberately arranging them heel up on the floor. Knowing she would wake to go to the john two, maybe three times in the night. Knowing she would not turn on the light. Knowing she might fall.

Hoping.

You are responsible.

Oh yes, he thought, you are responsible, my friend. You are guilty.

Just at that moment, Gerald felt a hand on his shoulder. Startled, he turned too fast, feeling the horror rise into his face and announce his guilt to anyone who cared to see. Exavious stood behind him. "Mr. Hartshorn," he said.

• • •

Gerald followed the doctor through the waiting room and down a crowded corridor that smelled of ammonia. Exavious did not speak; his lips pressed into a narrow line beneath his mustache. He led Gerald through a set of swinging doors into a cavernous chamber lined with pallets of supplies and soiled linen heaped in laundry baskets. Dusty light-bulbs in metal cages cast a fitful glow over the concrete floor.

"What's going on?" Gerald asked. "How's Sara?"

Exavious did not reply. He stopped by a broad door of corrugated metal that opened on a loading dock, and thumbed the button of the freight elevator.

"One moment, please, Mr. Hartshorn," he said.

They waited silently as the doors slid aside. Exavious gestured Gerald in, and pressed the button for six. With a metallic clunk of gears, they lurched into motion. Gerald stared impassively at the numbers over the door, trying to conceal the panic that had begun to hammer against his ribs. The noisy progress of the elevator seemed almost to speak to him; if he listened closely, he could hear the voice of the cockroach, half-hidden in the rattle of machinery:

She's dead, Gerald. She's dead and you're responsible.

Exavious knew. Gerald could see that clearly now. He wasn't even surprised when Exavious reached out and stopped the lift between the fifth and sixth floors. Just sickened, physically sickened by a sour twist of nausea that doubled him over as the elevator ground to a halt with a screech of overtaxed metal. Gerald sagged against the wall as a wave of vertigo passed through him. Sara. Lost. Irrevocably lost. He swallowed hard against the metallic taste in his mouth and closed his eyes.

They hung suspended in the shaft, in the center of an enormous void that seemed to pour in at Gerald's eyes and ears, at every aperture of his body. He drew it in with his breath, he was drowning in it.

Exavious said: "This conversation never occurred, Mr. Hartshorn. I will deny it if you say it did."

Gerald said nothing. He opened his eyes, but he could see only the dull sheen of the elevator car's walls, scarred here and there by careless employees. Only the walls, like the walls of a prison. He saw now that he would not ever really leave this prison he had made for himself. Everything that had ever been important to him he had destroyed—his dignity, his self-respect, his honor and his love. And Sara. Sara most of all.

Exavious said: "I have spoken with Dr. Schwartz. I should have done so sooner." He licked his lips. "When I examined your wife I found no evidence to suggest that she could not carry a child to term. Even late-term miscarriages are not uncommon in first pregnancies. I saw no reason to delve into her history."

He said all this without looking at Gerald. He did not raise his voice or otherwise modify his tone. He stared forward with utter concentration, his eyes like hard pebbles.

"I should have seen the signs. They were present even in your first office visit. I was looking at your wife, Mr. Hartshorn. I should have been looking at you."

Gerald's voice cracked when he spoke. "Schwartz—what did Schwartz say?"

"Dr. Schwartz was hesitant to say anything at all. He is quite generous: he wished to give you the benefit of the doubt. When pressed, however, he admitted that there had been evidence—a bruise on your wife's face, certain statements she made under anesthesia—that the miscarriage had resulted from an altercation, a physical blow. But you both seemed very sorrowful, so he did not pursue the matter."

Exavious turned to look at Gerald, turned on him the terrific illumination of his gaze, his darkly refulgent eyes exposing everything that Gerald had sought so long to hide. "A woman in your wife's superb physical condition does not often have two late-term miscarriages, Mr. Hartshorn. Yet Mrs. Hartshorn claims that her fall was accidental, that she tripped over a pair of shoes. Needless to say, I do not believe her, though I am powerless to act on my belief. But I had to speak, Mr. Hartshorn—not for you, but for myself."

He punched a button. The elevator jerked into motion once more.

"You are a very lucky man, Mr. Hartshorn. Your wife is awake and doing well. She is recovering from the epidural." He turned once more and fixed Gerald in his gaze. "The baby survived. A boy. You are the father of a healthy baby boy."

The elevator stopped and the doors opened onto a busy floor. "It is more than you deserve."

• • •

Sara, then.

Sara at last, flat on her back in a private room on the sixth floor. At the sight of her through the wire-reinforced window in the door, Gerald felt a bottomless relief well up within him.

He brushed past Dr. Exavious without speaking. The door opened so silently on its oiled hinges that she did not hear him enter. For a long moment, he stood there in the doorway, just looking at her—allowing the simple vision of her beauty and her joy to flow through him, to fill up the void that had opened in his heart.

He moved forward, his step a whisper against the tile. Sara turned to look at him. She smiled, lifted a silencing finger to her lips, and then nodded, her eyes returning to her breast and the child that nursed there, wizened and red and patiently sucking.

Just a baby. A child like any other. But different, Gerald knew, different and special in no way he could ever explain, for this child was his own. A feeling like none he had ever experienced—an outpouring of warmth and affection so strong that it was almost frightening—swept over him as he came to the bedside.

Everything Lake Conley had told him was true.

What happened next happened so quickly that Gerald for a moment believed it to be an hallucination. The baby, not yet twelve hours old, pulled away from Sara's breast, pulled away and turned, turned to look at him. For a single terrifying moment Gerald glimpsed not the wrinkled child he had beheld when first he entered the room, but . . . something else.

Something quicksilver and deadly, rippling with the sleek, purposeful musculature of a predator. A fleeting impression of oily hide possessed him—of a bullet-shaped skull from which glared narrow-pupiled eyes ashine with chill intelligence. Eyes like a snake's eyes, as implacable and smugly knowing.

Mocking me, Gerald thought. Showing itself not because it has to, but because it wants to. Because it can.

And then his old friend the cockroach: *Your child. Yours.*

Gerald extended his hands to Sara. "Can I?" he asked.

And then he drew it to his breast, blood of his blood, flesh of his flesh, this creature that was undeniably and irrevocably his own child.

BY THE MARK
GEMMA FILES

All naming is already murder.
—Lacan

Hepzibah, she called herself, mouthing the syllables whenever she thought no one else was looking. *Hep-zi-bah.* A powerful name, with strength in every note of it; a witch's name. She whispered it in each night's darkness, dreaming of poisons.

Outside, across the great divide between schoolyard and backyard, she knew her garden lay empty, sere and withered, topsoil still bleak with frost. Snow festered, greying, on top of the trumpet-vine's dead tangle. Behind that, the fence; further, a sloping away. Down past graffiti in full seasonal bloom, down into the mud at the base of the bridge, into the shadows under the pass, where the "normal" kids fought and kissed and loudly threatened suicide.

Into the Ravine.

One month more until spring. Then the nightshade bushes on either side of the property line would be green, each leaf bitter with possibilities. But here she sat in Wang's homeroom class, textbooks laid open on the desktop in front of her: Fifth Grade English like an endless boring string of Happiness-Is-To-Me, When-I-Grow-Up-I, My-Favorite-Whatever Journal exercises, Fifth Grade math like hieroglyphics in Martian. Real reading matter poking out from underneath, just barely visible whenever she squinted hard enough—*Perennials and Parasites, A City Garden Almanac*; roots and shoots, pale green print on pale cream paper, a leftover swatch of glue from where she'd ripped the school library slip off the inside back cover still sticking its back pages together. She sat there scanning entries while Mr. Wang reeled off roll-call behind her, desperately searching for something, anything she could recognize from that all-too-familiar tangle of weeds along the winding path she usually took home, wasting as much time as possible until Ravine finally turned to driveway and the house—

—"her" house—

—that place where she lived, on Janice and Doug's sufferance, reared itself up against the sky like a tumor, a purse-lipped mouth poised to pop open and swallow her whole.

"Diamond, Jennifer," Wang droned, meanwhile, back in the world nine people out of ten seemed to agree was real. "Edgecomb, Caroline. Garza, Shelby. Gilford, Darien. Goshawk . . . "

Daffodil (Narcissus pseudonarcissus); Looks like: Star-shaped bright yellow corona of petals around a bonnet-shaped bell, with long, tulip-like stem and leaves. Toxic part: Bulbs, which are often mistaken for onions. Symptoms: Nausea, gastroenteritis, vomiting, persistent emesis, diarrhoea, and convulsive trembling which may lead to fatality.

"Often mistaken for onions . . . " like the kind Doug insisted on in his micro-organic salad, maybe. So no one'd be likely to question her having them, even away from the kitchen. Even hidden somewhere in her room . . .

She frowned, tapping the textbook's covering page. "May lead," though; not good enough. Not nearly good enough, for what she had in mind.

"Herod, Kevin. Hu, Darlanne. Isaak, Stephanie."

Oleander (Nerium oleander); Looks like: Smallish, wide-spread pansy-like blooms on thin, tough stems with floppy leaves. Toxic part: Entire plant, green or dried—when a branch of an oleander plant is used to skewer meat at a barbecue, the poison is transferred to the meat. Symptoms: Nausea, depression, lowered and irregular pulse, bloody diarrhoea, paralysis and possibly death.

Nausea, depression—nothing new there, she thought, with a black little lick of humor. But Jesus, wasn't there anything in here that didn't come naturally (ha, ha) attached to having to roll on the floor and shit yourself to death? Anything that just made you . . . God, she didn't know . . . fall asleep, sink into peaceful darkness, just drift off and never wake up?

Aside from those pills in Janice's cupboard, the ones she'd probably miss before you even could swallow 'em? a little voice asked, at the back of her mind. *No, probably not. 'Cause that'd be way too easy.*

And if she wanted easy, then why play around with plants and leaves and tubers at all? Why not just straddle the rough stones of the St. Clair East bridge, shut her eyes and let go, like any normal person? Choose her spot, avoid the trees, and there wouldn't be anything to break her fall but gravity. A mercifully short plunge, brief downward rush of wind and queasy freedom, with maybe one short, sharp shock as her head met the rocks below—

"Jenkins, Jason. Jowaczyk, William. Lien, Elvis."

Deadly Nightshade (Atropa belladonna); Looks like: Drooping white bloom over broad, veiny leaves, berries couched in beds of wispy leaflets. Toxic part: Entire plant, especially bright black berries. Symptoms: Dry mouth and difficulty in swallowing and speaking, flushed dry skin, rapid heartbeat, dilated pupils and blurred vision, neurological disturbances including excitement, giddiness, delirium, headache, confusion, and hallucinations. Repeated ingestion can lead to dependency and glaucoma.

Not exactly *deadly*, then, is it? She thought, annoyed—and raised her head right at the same time that Wang raised his voice, all eyes already skittering to check her reaction: "Heather Millstone."

(You mean *Hepzibah*. Don't you?)

"Present."

Name after name after name, a whole limping alphabet of them—the roster of her "peers." She watched Wang's chin wag through the remaining call-and-response, counting freckles: Two faint ones near the corner of his mouth, one closer to the centre—a lopsided, tri-eyed face. From upside-down, it almost looked like he was smiling.

Mr. Wang paused, apparently out of breath; sweat rose off him in every direction—a stinky heat haze, like asphalt in summer. He wore the same pale blue pin-striped shirts every day, and you could usually mark what time it was by how far the matching yellow circle at either armpit had spread. Whenever he gestured, waves of cologne and old grease spread in the direction of his ire. She was vaguely aware of having spent the last few minutes experimenting with his voice, even as her conscious mind turned lightly to thoughts of suicide—turning it up, turning it down, letting the words stretch sideways like notes of music. Shrinking it to a breath, a hum . . .

" . . . Heather?"

Aware of his attention, finally, she looked up, met his eyes. And: "Yes," she replied, reflexively—knowing that usually worked, even though she hadn't been listening well enough to really know what she was agreeing to.

"Yes, what?"

"Yes—Mr. Wang?"

An audible giggle, two desks to the right: Jenny Diamond, self-elected Queen of Normal, Ontario. They'd been friends, once upon a time—or maybe Jenny had just tolerated her, letting her run to keep up with the rest of the clique while simultaneously making sure she stayed pathetically unaware how precarious her status as token Jenny wannabe really was. The last to know, as ever.

"I said, you're up. Yesterday's journal entry?" Another pause. "Sometime this week might be nice, especially for the rest of the class."

Oh, I'm sure. *Especially* for them.

The particularly funny thing being, of course, that she actually had done the work in question (for once). Poem, any subject, any length. She could just see the corner of it poking from her binder, if she strained—an uneven totem-pole of assonant paragraphs, neat black pen rows on pale blue-lined sheets, whose first lines went like so:

Always a shut door between us
Yet I clung fast
out here on the volcano's rim
For five more years or a hundred,
Whichever came last;
How tall this pain has grown.
wavering, taking root
At the split mouth of bone.
Your love like lava, sealing my throat.
Words, piling up like bones . . .

"Well, Heather? You know the drill. Stand up, and let's get started."

Students normally stood to read, displaying themselves; the class listened, kept the snickers to a minimum, clapped when you were done. Big flourish. Good mark. Centre of attention, all that—

But. But, but, but.

Staring down at her own lap, caught short like some idiot fish half-hooked through the cornea. Staring at her poem, the binder's edge, one blue-jeaned leg, the other. The edge of her peasant shirt, only barely hiding the area between, where well-worn fabric slid first to blue, then pale, then white along the seam. Normally, that is.

Tomato-red flower blooming at the juncture now, spreading pinky-gross back along the track of her hidden zipper, her crotch's bleached denim ridge. Evidence that she had yet once more left the house at that particular time of the month unsupplied, probably because her mind was frankly elsewhere: Choking on the thought of how unexpectedly soon Doug might return home from his latest "buying trip," maybe. Spitting it out like an unchewed cud of cereal into her napkin . . .

And: "8:30," Janice had said, grabbing her bowl; the chair, pulled out from under her, shrieked protest. "Up and at 'em, pie."

Muttered: "Whatever."

"What's that?"

"Nothing."

Janice had turned, abruptly—a bad move, considering how you didn't ever want her full attention on you, not more than you could help. Best just to stay background noise, an optical illusion: The amazing vanishing kid, briefly glimpsed from room to room. Because backtalk inevitably set Janice thinking of stove burners set on one, or pepper rubbed in the nostrils—enough to hurt, bad, yet too little to leave a (permanent) mark.

"Seems to me there's been a bit too much 'nothing' said around here, lately," Janice had said. "Seems to me, *somebody* might want to keep that in mind." Pause. "Well?"

"Yes."

"Yes, what?"

The exchange woke another surf-curl wave of memory, washing her right on back to the moment at hand—homeroom, Mr. Wang, her poem. The impossibility of movement, without flashing her shame to the room at large. Her breakfast placemat's pattern swum briefly before her eyes, just for a second: A laminated rose-garden under improbably blue skies. Here and there, wherever the lines blurred, faces peeped out—pale and wizened features, ginseng death-masks, leering back up at her like tubers left to dry.

Thinking: *Yes. Yes, Mr. Wang. Yes . . .*

. . . Mom.

Her tiny store of delaying tactics worn through at last, she swallowed hard and felt the vise inside her throat snap shut—tight, and hot, and dry. Jenny's clique were snickering openly now; the rest of the class just leaned forward, mouths slack in anticipation of tears. Nothing quite as amusing as a post-pubertal monster hemmed in by pre-teens, after all: Face stretched and straining, eyes aflutter while a grown man impatiently panned for public apologies.

And: *Oh yes, you're so right, I'm so sorry, sir.* Like anybody but him really gave a shit.

She stared down at her own feet, the one knee visible through a rip in her jeans, scabby from crouching in the back yard—head bent, intent, waiting for monk's-hood to flourish. Then looked up again to find herself suddenly risen, blood-spotted ass flapping free in the wind, face to surprised face with Wang himself.

"Ask *her*," she meant to say, giving a pert flip of the head towards Jenny—but the words came out in a scream, and took her desk with them.

A general flurry ensued: Much ducking, the desk hitting the nearest window dead centre, with a concussive thump. Cracks rayed.

By the time Wang had uncrouched himself, she was already gone.

• • •

So who knows?
It is well-fed.
And once it has tasted blood,
Who knows
What seeds this thing may sow?
But when the door closes this time,
I won't look back. Won't check
To see how little time it took

217

For me to be erased.
No longer plead my case
Or tear my hair,
That black engine behind your stare
Pulling me away into darkness:
I'm nothing now but air.
Not even fit to disappear.

Two rats stuck together at the sewer-grate's mouth: Carcinogens sprayed right and left as they thrashed together, squealing. She sat watching on the far bank, her fresh-washed jeans clammy against her thighs, burning with pollution. A stream of waste cut the Ravine's heart in two uneven halves, like a diseased aorta; here it shrank to a mere grey trickle over stones. A doll's face stared up at her from the nearest tangle of weeds—one eye gone, the other washed blind by the current.

God, please, please, God.

Not, of course, that she really put too much faith in that particular fable, any more than she truly "believed" any of the other mildly comforting stories she'd told herself over the years. Or maybe she did—but only at moments like these. Only when the stakes were high, and all other avenues of escape closed.

Make Wang not tell. Make Janice not be home when the school calls.

A bird sang suddenly, somewhere in the gathering dark.

Make Doug not come home. Not yet. Not ever.

It was cold.

Yeah, and why not ask for a smaller rack while you're at it, reality sneered back at her, from every visible angle.

Rustling in the bushes, now, on either side. Snide whispers. Giggling.

"Hey, Hea-ther . . ."

Just two weeks before, Mrs. Diamond (Jenny's mother, the school nurse and that most contradictory of things, a nice adult) had maintained cheerily that all these girls would be jealous of her in a year—even, improbably enough, Jenny herself. In a year, they'd be desperate to have what she had, to be what they thought she was. The same Jenny who'd already decided it was real good fun to make sure an open box of Tampax somehow snuck onto her desk during recess, or rifle through her bag at lunch and then leave one of her pads—oh so artistically arranged—where everybody could see it, snicker, make comments. A white-winged hunk of cotton squatting in the homeroom doorway like some flattened mouse: *Ooh, hey, guys. What'cha think this is, huh?*

(Well, we know who it prob'ly belongs to, at least . . .)

Snicker, snicker, snicker.

Dropping squashed packages of McDonald's ketchup in her binder, knowing they'd smear and dry like brown Krazy Glue all across her journal, her poems. *Just looked like the kinda thing you'd like, Heyyy-ther. Soh-REE.*

Didn't matter how many words she strung together, or how well—how many plants she could raise, catalogue, research or harvest, to what mysterious and potentially fatal purposes. In the world outside her own freakishly pubescent body, it was the Jenny Diamonds who had the real power, always. Always.

But: Poor Mrs. Diamond, bound and determined to put the best possible face on everything, however bleak. While she just sat there, thinking—

Yeah, well. In a year, a thousand different things could happen. I could be dead in a year.

Or rather: *Christ, I hope so.*

"Yo, Heyyyy-ther . . . "

She levered up, made the stream's far side in one long-legged jump. Heard yelps rise behind her at the flicker of movement (*there she is, there she IS!*), and ducked headlong into the underbrush without a backwards glance, heading directly up: Up through the poison oak, up under the shifting grey-green shadows of trees, up where the hiking trail's woodchip-lined trail turned to mud and mush. Remembered the last time the clique had chased her down here, running her through the blackberry bushes till she was breathless with stinging scratches. Like she'd accidentally grabbed the Black Spot and just not known it; like she was marked with fluorescent paint, invisible to everyone but them. Like she was some kind of, what was that word—scapegoat?

Chosen ahead of time, like around kindergarten, to sink and drown under a steady tide of bullying, or picked on simply because she'd been unlucky enough to have grown boobs a year earlier than everybody else—to have them when they were still age-inappropriate enough to be weird instead of jealousy-bait, before they were prized collateral on instant cool. On top of every other unlucky goddamn thing.

And then that older guy Paul—fifteen at least, a kept-back retard hanging with the Fives and playing Master Of The Universe 'cause everybody else didn't know any better—had caught up to her at last, shot out in front of everybody else to grab her by the sleeve and wrench, so the two of them went down in a heap together with her hair in the mud, and him on top. Grinning a wet, dumb smile as he stuck his hand down her shirt, like he was fishing for some kind of surprise gift-bag through a carny peep-hole.

"Heather, baby—man, that set feels nice. Just like a couple a' water-balloons."

"Get *off*—"

"Aw, you know you *want* it. Just be cool and go 'long, baby, everybody knows you're fifty pounds of slut in a five-pound bag . . ."

(They can, y'know—just *smell* it on you.)

She felt poison well in her heart, a cold black spurt; rolled and got on top of him all in one crazy lurch, using both fists to hammer his head down hard against the nearest hard thing: A root, a rock.

"Crazy mother b—"

He jumped back, bleeding, and the fear on his face was the most beautiful thing she'd ever seen. But the rush of it drained away, so fast.

• • •

If this was a movie, it only occurred to her now (as she pulled herself ever further upwards through the mucky treeline, her boots sopping-slippery with mud), then Jenny and her gang would later turn out to have cut the first girl to menstruate from the school herd every year. There'd be some conspiracy. These girls would disappear, never to be seen again—bleached bones under a swatch of weeds somewhere in the Ravine, after a terrifying midnight hunt . . .

But it wasn't a movie: Just life, nothing more or less. Considerably less interesting. Considerably more hurtful.

Further up the hill, the house's porch-light had come on. A car was pulling up outside—driver's side door painted with a coal-bright tiger, crouched and ready to pounce. The other was hidden from this angle; a voluptuous woman, censored by flowers.

God, you bastard.

The tiger opened. So did the front door.

She straightened, suddenly composed.

Tell you what, she thought. *Make you a deal. You don't really have to make anything happen, okay? Just make me not care, when it does.*

That's all.

A heartfelt prayer. Yet God, as usual, stayed silent.

And oh but she knew, so very very well, that her whole stupid life was an Afterschool Special cliché from top to bottom—her problems clichés too, each and every one of them. Plot twists so stale they all but gave off dust. Ludicrous. Laughable. Lame.

None of which made the pain any easier to take, however, if and—

(no, just when)

—it came.

The rats, sated, had long since gone their ways. Janice was heading down the yard, already almost to the Ravine's lip. Beside her was a shadow in embroidered jeans, sizeable hand on equally sizeable hip. No visible means of escape.

Before her parents could start to call, therefore, she stood up. And waved.

• • •

"You decent?" Doug asked, pushing the door open; luckily, she was. This time.

She stood in front of the mirror, flossing carefully. One side, then the other, each tooth in turn. Wrap and pull. Up, down and all around, like a see-saw.

The dentist was a luxury. If she'd left it up to them, she wouldn't have a tooth left in her head.

Go away.

"Missed you at dinner, pie."

Right hand on her shoulder, heavy as a full vacuum-cleaner bag. The warped mirror bent his fingers back, blurring them together: One strange flipper.

"Ah elt ick," she said, mid-wrap.

"Put that down, babe. Let me look at you a while."

That's an order, she thought, bracing herself. Floss to the garbage, with a flick. She turned, eyes shaded, as if to some erratic light-source more apt to blind than to illuminate. He grinned back, eyes glued to her chest, watching it bounce with the movement.

"Jan told me you did some more growing up while I was gone this time," he said. "And I thought she was joking. My oh my."

A whiff of dope from down the hall; Van Morrison on the stereo. She could almost hear him now, soft and infinitely plausible, at least to a woman kite-high on Doug's own no-name brand of weed: *Just leave us two alone to get reacquainted a while, Jan—play Daddy, y'know. All that good crap.*

"'Course, I already saw you when I got back."

The cap was off the toothpaste. "Driving up, you mean."

Big grin. "Naaah, I mean last night. I was just off shopping, that's why I wasn't there at breakfast. But I saw you, all right. Was about three, so you were fast asleep, cute as a button, lyin' there in that big t-shirt . . . you sure you don't remember?"

She swallowed; the vise was back again. "No."

"Well, here I was watching you—and it being so long and all, I decided I'd give you a kiss. So I bend down, put my hand up to touch your face, and you know what you did?" Pause for reaction. None forthcoming, so: "Latched onto my fingers, and then you start—licking 'em, right? Like each one was some old lollipop. Licking and licking." Still nothing. "Isn't that just the sweetest?"

"I'd never."

A shrug. "'Cept you did."

She finally spotted the cap, a red smudge wedged between divisions, halfway down the drain. Have to use the tweezers on that. "You're lying," she said, not looking up.

"Now, would I lie?"

Only every day of my life.

"I gotta go to bed. School."

But he caught her in mid-stride, backing the door shut; licorice on his breath, rank with time. Pinning both her hands as he reached high over her head for the nearest bottle of moisturizer.

"Dad, please don't," she whispered. "Not anymore. Please, it hurts."

"But sweetie," he said, almost genuinely shocked. "You know I only do this for *you*, right? All part'a growing up."

Don't break you in now, it just hurts that much worse, later on . . .

And then they were down on the floor, the tiles cold on her face. *Let me not care, let me not care.* His hands. Grunting. Distant shapes in the mirror, blurred and distorted beyond recognition.

Plus God, somewhere, laughing his nonexistent ass off.

• • •

She dreamed, later—for the first time since she was seven or so, that she could recall. The year it either all started going to hell or she started noticing how bad it already was, whichever came first.

In the dream, she was wearing her long black dress—the one with the stiff Afghani embroidery, red and yellow with little round bits of mirror sewn across the bodice and down the front. A witch's dress. In real life, it didn't fit anymore; she slept with it tucked inside her pillow-case, rough against her cheek in darkness.

Hepzibah, a voice called. *Hep-zi-bah.*

She brushed red hair from her eyes—thigh-long, bloody with a power that crackled through her fingers. The voice seemed to be coming from outside, in the backyard, or further: Yes, from the Ravine. She knelt down from the trumpet-vine's main knot, awaiting further instructions.

What do you want? The voice asked, finally.

Janice and Doug gone. And Wang. And Jenny Diamond. I don't want to have to go to school. I want people to leave me alone, or die.

As quick as she said it, the words bred and splintered. A thousand thousand shades of grey, but one true meaning: *I want them all to be as much afraid of me as I am, of them.*

And it came to her, sitting there in the cool, impossible dirt of her impossible garden—all her carefully-tended poisons abloom at last, ripe

223

and lush for plucking—that there might still be a way to unpick the thread between her and the world around her, even now. To give up all hope of love. To give up pain. To be free, free, free at last.

She felt it all collect, hard and hot, in a lump just below her sternum—a smooth black egg, finally about to hatch.

And: *This is the gift,* came that same whisper again—from inside, outside or maybe just everywhere, at once. *This is what you were marked for. To* live.

Confirmation, finally, that the fantasy which had sustained her so far might actually be meant to be . . . more. Truth, or truth-to-be.

Foreshadowing.

To OUT-live, Hepzibah. Everyone.

Repeating the words, tasting every inch of them, and wondering at the welcome, impossible weight of them.

(*everyone*)

After all, what did she owe anyone still left inside this shell she called her life? Really?

I always knew it, she thought, amazed at her own perceptiveness. *That if I only didn't have to feel—then nobody could hurt me. Because when you feel nothing, you can do . . .*

. . . anything.

• • •

Later that night, after Doug and Janice had smoked and screwed themselves to sleep, she found their stash, their money, Doug's ridiculously "high-class" straight-razor. Turned it in her hands thoughtfully, thinking about what if this was America, what if the razor were a gun. Standing over them in the dark, watching them breathe and grumble until the weight of her shadow brought Doug up from sleep.

"Pie—" he'd begin. And: "My name is Hepzibah," she'd answer. Then shoot him in the face.

Janice might even have time to scream, once.

Resurfacing in darkness, turning away. Musing how in a perfect world, a *movie* world, this ultimate revelation would have come to her just in time for the nightshade harvest, so she'd have already had time to gather and dry enough atropine-laced leaves to cut her parents' brownie-hash with dementia and blindness. But you couldn't always get what you wanted, as she knew all too well; daffodil bulbs stolen from the corner flower-shop and added to tomorrow's left-out salad-makings would simply have to do, in terms of a stop-gap. Not that she suspected either Doug or Janice would be in any ultra-big hurry to call the cops, anyway, especially over something like the famous disappearing kid having finally just, well—disappeared. For good.

Hepzibah slipped the razor in her jeans pocket and the pre-baggie'd weed down the back of her waistband, pulling her sweatshirt down to cover it. She paused by the hall closet to "choose" between her usual thin coat and Doug's thick sheepskin jacket, then paused again by the front door to dredge a single, marvelously unfamiliar word up from the very bottom of herself, a new mantra, well worth saying over and over and over.

"*No*," she whispered, into the newfound night—an ornate and intact sound, utterly crackless. It pleased her so much that she made it again and again, in time with her own footsteps: Down the stairs, onto the pavement, 'round the corner.

Gone.

A new poem growing, unstoppable, in every fresh beat of her tread.

But beyond their art still lies my heart
Which no one knows, or owns.
A porcelain frame for my secret name;
An eggshell, crammed with broken bones.

• • •

It would be thirteen more years and too many dreams of murder to count—fulfilled, unfulfilled, otherwise—before she finally made her first mistake.

THE DISAPPEARANCE OF JAMES H___

HAL DUNCAN

1. The New Boy

There is a new boy at the school. He sits at the desk where Brown once sat, and carved his name in the wood with a pocketknife's point, and was caned for it; but he is not Brown. He is green. His eyes flash emerald and jade, the colour of gemstones and jungles, foreign seas and forest serpents. He sits where Brown once sat but the master does not notice, nor order him to read from Homer, nor snap his name as he gazes out the window. As he turns to look at me, languid, smiling in his sly silence.

2. A Fob Watch

We watch the fifth formers in the cloisters, all tall enough to wear tailcoats, dandies in top hats, thin cigars in their mouths. I have studied the way they stand, perfected the slouch—both knees bent a little, one shoulder slightly higher than the other, one hand jammed into a pocket. But I still need my fob watch to strike that pose, to be *fetching it out to check the time,* not simply, self-assuredly louche. So Scottish in my reserve.

—Why do you want to be like them? he says.

—I do not want to be like Brown, I say.

3. In the Dormitory

He takes off the starched collar and the bum-freezer jacket, unbuttons his shirt. In his white breeches and shirt open to the waist but still tucked in, he looks like some prince kidnapped by pirates to serve as cabin boy, or some pauper taken in by a kind doctor, scrubbed clean to wear a lost son's clothes. Half-dressed, he seems half-costumed. An actor changing between scenes.

226

His nightshirt lies on the bed, long flowing white as if he is to play Juliet. But it is my cheeks that are blushed and virginal. He removes his shirt. His breeches. His drawers.

4. Never Never

—Shall I play the pipes for you, James? he asks. Shall I play a hornpipe that'll make you jig?

The others lie asleep in their dormitory beds while I sit on the edge of mine, watching him in the moonlight, the way it throws the shadow of his cock's-comb shock of hair on the wall behind him, spikes on either side like horns. In the shadow his peter rises to his jutting chin, cocky with his cocked head, cocked hip.

—Come with me, he says quietly.

—I can't, I say.

A whisper:

—Come with me.

—Never, I say. Never never.

5. A Roasting

—What happened to Brown? he asks.

I look at the empty bed where Brown lay sobbing from the pain and humiliation after Flashman was done.

—Flashman gave him a roasting, I say.

I picture them holding Brown to the roaring fire, turning him, laughing. But that is not how it happened, not how it happened to me. I picture them stripping him, spit-roasting him between them, fingers twisted in his hair, holding his head down, fingernails digging into his hips. That is what the fifth form do here, why Flashman left in disgrace.

—How savage, he says. How truly beastly.

6. A Crocodile Tear

He lies on top of the bed, on top of the empty nightshirt, knees curled up to his chin, arms wrapped around them. His eyes glint green even in the moonlight. He does not sleep, does not close his eyes and sleep, only bats his lashes slowly closed and open again, once, twice. It seems a considered, reptilian action, as inscrutable as the tear that trickles down his cheek. A crocodile tear.

His shadow rises on the wall behind him, pads across the floor to my bed. I pull the covers back, and the darkness climbs in to my embrace.

7. Morning Will Not Find Us

—Let me help you sleep, the shadow says. It is only when you sleep that we can disappear into your dreams.

His shadow curls to fit my form. I feel its breath warm on the back of my neck, its arms wrapped round my ribs, one hand over my heart, the other sliding down into black, curly hair. I feel safe with his shadow as my cloak, so close, so tight it seems within rather than around me. To disappear. . . .

—But in the morning . . . , I say.

—Morning will not find us here, it says. We must go looking for it.

8. Lush Green Vines

We sail on oceans uncharted, gliding through the night by constellations we invent. We hunt the morning, the rising sun, but for him it is the morning of yesterday, I think, for me the morning of tomorrow . . . *tomorrow*. We hunt it as something we desire and fear, and the dawn we find is a beach of azure sky above, golden sand beneath us, flesh hard between us, edged by lush green vines and veins. I kiss—

—I'm not like that, he says. I'm not a . . .

Fairy?

—Every time you say that, I whisper, a little part of you will die.

9. Lions and Tigers and Bears

Adventurers on this island, we explore its reaches and its recesses. We glimpse beasts in the forest and in ourselves—the pride of lions, the camouflage of hidden tigers, and the vicious, swinging hook of a bear claw—but he laughs at them all. I strut in the frock coat and tricorn hat that is his shadow. He crows like a cockerel in the green rags of my lust, legs spread wide, hands on his hips, up on a rock. A statue on a pedestal. He darts from my grasp, teasing.

I brood. Will he play games with me forever?

• • •

10. The Lost Boys

　—Come with me, I say.

My hand reaches out for him, to wipe the tear that is always on his cheek but that only I ever see, to grasp the smooth skin of his shoulder with gentle strength. To hold him so he knows that we are both lost, with each other. To touch. To do unspeakable things to his flesh.

　—Never, he screams. Never never.

His blade flashes a wide, panicked arc through air, through skin and bone. I fall to my knees, clutching a bloody stump.

　It is the hook in my heart, however, which hurts the most.

I WAS A TEENAGE SLASHER VICTIM

STEPHEN GRAHAM JONES

You're riding in the car with your mom when she kind of shudders in a way you think you're not supposed to see, grips the wheel harder, and adjusts the rearview mirror away from you.

It's night, late, maybe even midnight. You can't see the clock from your seatbelt.

Once before you've stayed up past midnight, but that was when your Uncle Dani wrecked her motorcycle and you had to eat dinner from a dollar-machine in the hall and everybody was crying.

You're ten, say.

It's a Friday, almost Halloween.

Where your mom's driving you is the long way to your dad's new house. It's supposed to be a surprise visit, an early trick 'r treat.

But now she's crying.

"Mom?" you say, leaning forward as far as you can without breaking the seatbelt rule.

She shakes her head no, nothing.

A few roads later she adjusts the mirror back to you.

"What is it?" you ask, and can hear it in your voice, that her crying is trying to spread to you.

She can hear it too.

"I was—I was just thinking about when I was . . . a long time ago. I don't know why."

"When you were my age?"

"When I met your father."

"High school," you say, because you know the story of where they met: summer camp at the lake with the complicated name.

She nods too fast. Rubs her nose with the back of her hand.

"Tell me again," you say.

It's comfortable, this story. It's canoes and sloppy joes in a pot big enough to hold a dog (that's the joke every year), and it's sneaking out at night to swim, which you're never supposed to do but everybody does.

Your mom clicks her headlights to bright—there hasn't been another car for longer than it usually takes to even *get* to your dad's—and nods her head like okay. Like this is good. Like she can do this.

It's the same kind of nod you do in your room when you've built cities of blocks and are about to walk through them slow, so you can watch each building crash into the next building, and do the sounds with your mouth. It's from the monster movies your dad watches with you on Saturday mornings. But he never understands them right, he always thinks the monsters are from bombs or from the ocean or from some scientist.

You know, though. The reason they're so strong is they've got future muscles. *Every*body where they come from can breathe fire.

How else could it be?

As for why the big split between her and your dad, it's pretty much the usual mystery, except one fight you heard the end of was something about a door being closed. How she should have known right then and right there. And your dad saying no, that he was sorry, that he could fix it, he could make it up. That he would do it right now if she wanted, he would walk right in there with the axe or a bowling ball or whatever and he would—

After that, at night, you checked all the doors in the house, with everybody sleeping. That's what the fight had been about.

They all worked perfectly. Except maybe your mom and dad's, but that one was locked like always. Like they're scientists in there, trying to cook up a monster but embarrassed about it.

Your friend Trace says that when his parents fight, one of them always sleeps on the couch.

Not at your house.

"We were seventeen," your mom says from the front seat, and you close your eyes, are there with her again, seeing summer camp through her eyes.

Except this time there's more.

• • •

Your mom's so young, and she looks at her knees a lot.

She's a counselor. Her and your dad, in his short shorts with the two stripes on the side like a green racetrack.

Don't laugh.

They don't know each other yet, even.

The game your dad used to play with you in your room—it's nothing bad—it was for the two of you to dress up from the costume box (clowns, pirates, alligator heads) to look at their old pictures from the album. But to see them right you had to look through the frame of the mirror from the hall you'd accidentally broke, that had all the mirror gone now, and the back part as well. Your dad would lean the brown frame up against the wall and then put the picture album down under it, and always be careful to reach around to turn the pages. He said this was how you looked into the past.

So, when you close your eyes to see him and your mom at camp, the sky all golden and dusty every day, it's like your dad's sitting there beside you with a pirate patch over his eye.

Looking at the old pictures started when your dog Philip (you chose the name) had to go live with people in the country, so he could run and be free and have a better life.

It was like trading Philip for summer camp. And it was a good trade.

Your mom and dad didn't take pictures of everything, though.

Because your mom knows you know all the normal parts, she doesn't go through them this time. They've told you all about the archery, about the tire swing into the lake. About how the moose head in the cafeteria was supposed to be haunted, and about how, the last night there was bonfire night, and that that was when your dad first put his arm around your mom, with all those sparks leaking up into the sky, never coming down.

Those are the parts you want, but now there's more parts.

This time there's the accident with the arrow. That's what your mom calls it from the front seat.

Through her eyes or her words, you can't tell anymore, you see it: the newest counselor, the one who just walked up, hasn't even checked in yet. He's behind the big hay targets. Not accidentally shot once, maybe in the eye because that would be deadliest, but shot twelve times, all in the face. From somebody who had to have been standing right over him. Standing on his arms probably.

"His head was a—it was a *pincushion*," your mom says all at once, the crying back in her voice. And she tried to lift him up but couldn't, because he was stuck by the head to the ground.

By the time she pulled everybody back to the archery range, the dead counselor was gone gone gone. Not even any blood.

They counted the arrows and there was one quiverful missing, but nobody took your mom's screaming seriously. Not even your dad.

Then, next, two counselors who had been kissing in the shut-down showers—all your mom can get out before her voice breaks down, it's blood, swirling around the super-rusted drain. Then clumping. And there was hair on the wall, maybe. Hair that wasn't attached anymore.

And—this makes her lose the car's direction, scatter gravel up from the ditch—this time she saw someone running off. Or she heard them, fast feet, and built a shadow up from there.

But how tall? What kind of hair? Did it look back at her while it was running away?

And then the girl who had been killed in the shower, had had things done to her chest area, had her hair already smeared on the wall, she grabbed her hand onto your mom's ankle.

Your mom screamed, kicked away.

"It was . . . it's—it's," the girl managed to say, then conked, something black like coffee pouring out one side of her mouth.

Before your mom could get your dad back to those shut-down restrooms (he'd been fiberglassing the slow canoe for the next day), the shut-down restrooms suddenly burned down like they were made of hay bales and gasoline.

It was like bonfire night, too early.

The owners of the camp sprayed it with water, then, in the morning, put yellow tape all around it, because the place was dangerous. They said the two dead counselors had really just left to go home, and the fire, it was probably campers smoking cigarettes. Or smoking something.

When they said that "something," your dad's hand squeezed your mom's harder, like he was scared.

Meaning they lied, about him putting his arm around her for the first time on that last night.

This is the real story, the secret story.

You're almost holding your breath.

• • •

The next day was normal, just the usual canoe races, the counselor hiding with snorkel tubes after the finish line, to dump everybody over, winners and all.

Except one of those campers, when she came back up, it was with a dead body draped over her like moss.

It was one of the owners, the wife. Her eyes had been sewed shut, her mouth cut too wide, all the skin and meat cut from her fingerbones.

Then the owner who was the husband floated up, floating like a log with eyes.

After getting everybody to shore and turning their screaming into whimpering, your dad tried to start all the cars but none of them had any battery. And the telephones were all dead.

Your mom and dad did important eyes to each other about all of this. Scared eyes.

Everybody camped in the cafeteria, even though all the walls were windows. They kept all the lights on. They watched the moose in shifts.

Two more nights, then the purple bus would show back up.

In the front seat, your mom's not trying not to cry anymore.

"You were so brave," you tell her.

This makes her cry harder.

"We didn't know who it was!" she says, hitting her hand onto the steering wheel. "We thought it had to be one of us, though. Right? Right?"

You nod, are liking this story. The past is an interesting place.

That night, most of the littler kids asleep, your dad outside so he can smoke one of his cigarettes, all the lights suddenly suck back into their light bulbs, and won't turn back on.

In the darkness, a small hand takes your mom's hand.

She screams, shakes the hand off.

When they finally get some candles going, it turns out the hand she shook off was one of the littler kids', the one who's always been scared the whole time, even before the dead bodies. He's crying in the corner, asking for his mom, and the way he's scared of your dad means he's scared of his own dad too.

It makes your mom from back then cry, and she's crying when she's talking about crying, too. How much she hated herself. How mad it made her, that a kid's dad would hurt him. And that now she was like that dad, hurting the kid too.

So they decided to do something about this.

The next morning, instead of hiding, they tried to do the usual camp stuff, just always staying with a buddy.

Only, what whoever was doing this didn't know—unless it was one of them—was that each counselor had a weapon hidden in their shirt or their pants.

Your dad had a fireplace poker. Your mom had one of the knives from the high shelf.

Their idea was to lure this person out, then do something to him.

"But it only happens at night, right?" you say.

Your mom doesn't answer.

The kids all line up for the tire swing, your dad shimmying (he's so *skinny*) out onto the big branch, to make sure there's nothing wrong with the rope, or the limb.

It's all just normal.

He nods and one of the other counselors secretly hands his little baseball bat to the other counselor and rears back on the tire swing, holding it the way the old kids get to, and runs for the water with it.

He goes out high, higher, then lets go at the perfect time, reaching up for the sky with his feet like upside-down diving.

But your dad didn't check the lake.

Bobbing right there under this counselor is one of the triangle buoys, its orange and white stripes painted over, just a blue kind of black.

The counselor sees the top of that upside-down ice-cream cone coming for him, and he flaps and twists and screams.

It doesn't matter.

It goes in through his stomach, splashes up through his back.

On shore, kids and counselors scatter everywhere.

The only two counselors now are your mom and your dad.

And, "And we didn't think it was a *kid* doing it," your mom says, her eyes in the mirror so red by now.

You're peeking.

Don't.

But you see it anyway, on the side of the road.

It's a man, tall like your dad. Like he's asking for a ride.

Your mom takes her foot off the gas so the car's coasting, so quiet, and, just when the headlights are about to touch the man, show who he is, she clicks the headlights off.

You twist around, see his shape in the brake lights anyway, when your mom's still thinking about stopping.

He's got a fireplace poker.

• • •

"I don't even know where all the kids *went*," your mom says, lighting the road back up.

"Is Philip out here?" you say to her, because this can't be the way to your dad's house, and she laughs and cries at the same time, like a cough that hurts.

Because some of the kids go back to their assigned bunkhouses to hide in their beds, under the covers, your mom and dad go there too.

They have their weapons out in the open now.

And, that one little kid who the whole time at camp has been trying to tell your mom about a ghost he's been seeing at night, the one who tried to hold your mom's hand in the cafeteria when the lights went out, he shows her the pictures he's been drawing.

They're mostly about the mouth. Red and evil. Teeth like little gravestones.

Your mom holds that kid close, sees her own face reflected in the trembly blade of her knife.

That night, instead of candles, they do the bonfire. Right on schedule.

Everybody sits close enough to it (your dad holding your mom close, your mom leaning into him) that they don't see the big shadowy person standing behind them, just watching.

Whoever it is shines his light from face to face, everybody screaming inside, too scared to run.

It's just the sheriff, though.

The kids pile onto his legs like puppies, and he lets them.

Finally he settles his flashlight on your mom and dad. His light bright on your mom's knife.

"What's going on here?" he says.

Your mom swallows, the sound loud in her ears.

Why the sheriff's there is that one of the kids' cousins was getting called to the army, so that kid needed to go home, say bye in case that was the last time to say it.

But he never expected this.

"Where's Ralph and Laurie?" he says, his light up on your mom's face now.

Your dad hooks his head out to the lake like he's sorry and the sheriff steps over there as best he can, with kids all over him, and shines his light on the three bodies in the lake: the owners at the edge, the counselor on the buoy.

He wades through the kids, back to his car.

Only, when he starts to scream something into his radio, a hand pulls his forehead back against his seat, and another hand, from the other side, drags a shiny knife across his throat like just drawing a line in Jell-o.

His blood burbles out onto his light brown shirt, and, when he falls forward, he pushes the sirens on.

The kids scream, everybody's screaming, running through the red lights flashing everywhere, and your mom runs for the Chestnuts bunkhouse because it's closest, but your dad's already there, pulling the door shut behind him and pushing the wooden peg in to lock it.

She beats on it with her fists and stabs it with her knife but your dad's in the bathroom already, hiding in the bathtub. Except the bathtub's where that one artist kid has been leaving all his paintings, so it's like the killer or the ghost is in there with him already.

Your mom finally crawls in through the window right over him, falls down

237

onto him even though he locked her out, and somehow he doesn't stab her with his poker and she doesn't cut him with her knife, and they hide like that until the bus shows up, and then get married and love each other and have you someday.

But: "Who was it?" you ask.

"The—the artist kid's dad," your mom says.

They found him trapped in a complicated trap at the edge of the woods. It was a hole with broken paddles on the bottom, splinter-side-up. He had blood all over them, and his mouth was painted red just like his son had been drawing. Because the dad was a clown for parties.

"He got caught in one of his own things," your mom said, looking to you like you're supposed to nod.

You don't, though.

• • •

What you're trying to think is how could your dad know about the Sheriff getting cut like that across the throat if he was already in the Chestnuts bunkhouse?

But your mom must have seen it, told him.

Right?

But now your mom's all over the road, and there are no lights at all out here.

"Was that Dad back there?" you ask.

"*It's too late!*" she screams about your question, and spills her purse onto the seat beside her, isn't even driving anymore, is just scratching for something.

She pushes it back to you.

You uncrumple it—it's old paper—and you kind of have to smile.

It's one of the artist kid's drawing. She must have saved it all this time.

"We're going to see Philip, yes," she says, and hunches over the wheel like somebody just hit her in the stomach. "You'll like it there, it'll be . . . right."

You see her eyes in the mirror for a moment but she pulls them away. Like she's scared.

Clowns.

It's what the kid was drawing.

Only—only it's not a dad at all.

When you were dressed like this, your dad was wearing a pirate patch on his eye.

Not you.

You always liked the big wig, the funny nose, the red mouth. That scratchy collar that was like paper folded over and over. The floppy shoes that made that sound when you ran.

Maybe that's how your mom figured it out.

Maybe she heard you running in the hall. And remembered.

But it's not your fault, even. Some days your dad, he forgets to put the mirror frame up, doesn't he? Just leaves it leaning there. And, without him to tell you not to, instead of reaching around like he taught, you can reach right through for that perfect magic summer camp. You're even small enough to *step* through. To be there with them in the album. To watch them from the edges of the woods. From the dock, at night.

And you were right about future muscles.

"It's you," your mom says, her body all-the-way pressed to the door, like she wants to be as far away as possible.

You lean over so you can see her in the mirror again.

She's trying to hide.

You smile, feel the paint crackle around your mouth.

It's how she found you earlier, in your room. Already dressed up.

Paint on your hands too, but that's not paint.

"I was just playing," you tell her. "Are we really going to see Philip?"

She nods yes, yes yes yes, that's *right* where you're going, and you nod, look out the side window at the shadows of fence posts blurring together.

But there's something in the floorboard, too.

It's peeking out from under the seat, where you hid it.

The thick black blade from your dad's lawnmower. The one he threw away.

You nod, look out the side window again.

Your heart's thumping like a rabbit now.

Go ahead, lift the blade with your toe so it meets your hand, know that your dad won't catch up this far for ten or thirty minutes.

It'll be just like camp. The best one ever.

You smile, lean forward, breaking the seatbelt rule but the seatbelt rule doesn't matter anymore.

Your mom, though. She's been through all this before, hasn't she? She doesn't just remember the bad parts, she remembers how to live, too. She opens her door, rolls out into the darkness, and, one hand on the back of the front seat, you see the road about to turn in front of you, but there's nobody to turn the wheel anymore. To keep up with the road.

"Philip," you say, right at the end.

It was the artist kid's name. The one who wouldn't ever go to sleep. The one who would never come out into the woods to play.

When the car hits whatever it hits, you launch over the front seat, and it's just like letting go of a tire swing at the exact perfect right time. Especially when you see that the window's already breaking. The glass is going away, getting ready for you.

Leaving only the frame it was in.

You're just small enough to slip through it without touching it, even with the back of your clown shoe. Just small enough to crash into the water of the past, like always.

You stand from it, the water dripping off the lawnmower blade you still have.

Right now the camp's empty, deserted, lonely.

But it won't always be.

BLUE ROSE

PETER STRAUB

(for Rosemary Clooney)

1.

On a stifling summer day the youngest of the five Beevers children, Harry and Little Eddie, were sitting on cane-backed chairs in the attic of their house on South Sixth Street in Palmyra, New York. Their father called it "the upstairs junk room," as this large irregular space was reserved for the boxes of table-cloths, stacks of diminishingly sized girl's winter coats, and musty old dresses Maryrose Beevers had mummified as testimony to the superiority of her past to her present.

A tall mirror that could be tilted in its frame, an artifact of their mother's onetime glory, now revealed to Harry the rear of Little Eddie's head. This object, looking more malleable than a head should be, an elongated wad of Play-Doh covered with straggling feathers, was just peeking above the back of the chair. Even the back of Little Eddie's head looked tense to Harry.

"Listen to me," Harry said. Little Eddie squirmed in his chair, and the wobbly chair squirmed with him. "You think I'm kidding you? I had her last year."

"Well, she didn't kill *you*," Little Eddie said.

"Course not, she liked me, you little dummy. She only hit me a couple of times. She hit some of those kids every single day."

"But teachers can't *kill* people," Little Eddie said.

At nine, Little Eddie was only a year younger than he, but Harry knew that his undersized fretful brother saw him as much a part of the world of big people as their older brothers.

"Most teachers can't," Harry said. "But what if they live right in the same building as the principal? What if they won *teaching awards,* hey, and what if

241

every other teacher in the place is scared stiff of them? Don't you think they can get away with murder? Do you think anybody really misses a snot-faced little brat—a little brat like you? Mrs. Franken took this kid, this runty little Tommy Golz, into the cloakroom, and she killed him right there. I heard him scream. At the end, it sounded just like bubbles. He was trying to yell, but there was too much blood in his throat. He never came back, and nobody ever said boo about it. She killed him, and next year she's going to be your teacher. I hope you're afraid, Little Eddie, because you ought to be." Harry leaned forward. "Tommy Golz even looked sort of like you, Little Eddie."

Little Eddie's entire face twitched as if a lightning bolt had crossed it.

In fact, the young Golz boy had suffered an epileptic fit and been removed from school, as Harry knew.

"Mrs. Franken especially hates selfish little brats that don't share their toys."

"I do share my toys," Little Eddie wailed, tears beginning to run down through the delicate smears of dust on his cheeks. "Everybody *takes* my toys, that's why."

"So give me your Ultraglide Roadster," Harry said. This had been Little Eddie's birthday present, given three days previous by a beaming father and a scowling mother. "Or I'll tell Mrs. Franken as soon as I get inside that school, this fall."

Under its layer of grime, Little Eddie's face went nearly the same white-gray shade as his hair.

An ominous slamming sound came up the stairs.

"Children? Are you messing around up there in the attic? Get down here!"

"We're just sitting the chairs, Mom," Harry called out.

"Don't you bust those chairs! Get down here this minute!"

Little Eddie slid out of his chair and prepared to bolt.

"I want that car," Harry whispered. "And if you don't give it to me, I'll tell Mom you were foolin' around with her old clothes."

"I didn't do nothin'!" Little Eddie wailed, and broke for the stairs.

"Hey, Mom, we didn't break any stuff, honest!" Harry yelled. He bought a few minutes more by adding, "I'm coming right now," and stood up and went toward a cardboard box filled with interesting books he had noticed the day before his brother's birthday, and which had been his goal before he had remembered the Roadster and coaxed Little Eddie upstairs.

When, a short time later, Harry came through the door to the attic steps, he was carrying a tattered paperback book. Little Eddie stood quivering with misery and rage just outside the bedroom the two boys shared with their older brother Albert. He held out a small blue metal car, which Harry instantly took and eased into a front pocket of his jeans.

"When do I get it back?" Little Eddie asked.

"Never," Harry said. "Only selfish people want to get presents back. Don't you know anything at all?" When Eddie pursed his face up to wail, Harry tapped the book in his hands and said, "I got something here that's going to help you with Mrs. Franken, so don't complain."

• • •

His mother intercepted him as he came down the stairs to the main floor of the little house—here were the kitchen and living room, both floored with faded linoleum, the actual "junk room" separated by a stiff brown woolen curtain from the little makeshift room where Edgar Beevers slept, and the larger bedroom reserved for Maryrose. Children were never permitted more than a few steps within this awful chamber, for they might disarrange Maryrose's mysterious "papers" or interfere with the rows of antique dolls on the window seat, which was the sole, much-revered architectural distinction of the Beevers house.

Maryrose Beevers stood at the bottom of the stairs, glaring suspiciously up at her fourth son. She did not ever look like a woman who played with dolls, and she did not look that way now. Her hair was twisted into a knot at the back of her head. Smoke from her cigarette curled up past the big glasses like bird's wings which magnified her eyes.

Harry thrust his hand into his pocket and curled his fingers protectively around the Ultraglide Roadster.

"Those things up there are the possessions of my family," she said. "Show me what you took."

Harry shrugged and held out the paperback as he came down within striking range.

His mother snatched it from him, and tilted her head to see its cover through the cigarette smoke. "Oh. This is from that little box of books up there? Your father used to pretend to read books." She squinted at the print on the cover "*Hypnosis Made Easy*. Some drugstore trash. You want to read this?"

Harry nodded.

"I don't suppose it can hurt you much." She negligently passed the book back to him. "People in society read books, you know—I used to read a lot, back before I got stuck here with a bunch of dummies. *My* father had a lot of books."

Maryrose nearly touched the top of Harry's head, then snatched back her hand. "You're my scholar, Harry. You're the one who's going places."

"I'm gonna do good in school next year," he said.

"*Well*. You're going to do well. As long as you don't ruin every chance you have by speaking like your father."

Harry felt that particular pain composed of scorn, shame, and terror that filled him when Maryrose spoke of his father in this way. He mumbled something that sounded like acquiescence, and moved a few steps sideways and around her.

2.

The porch of the Beevers house extended six feet on either side of the front door, and was the repository for furniture either too large to be crammed into the junk room or too humble to be enshrined in the attic. A sagging porch swing sat beneath the living-room window, to the left of an ancient couch whose imitation green leather had been repaired with black duct tape; on the other side of the front door, through which Harry Beevers now emerged, stood a useless icebox dating from the earliest days of the Beeverses' marriage and two unsteady camp chairs Edgar Beevers had won in a card game. These had never been allowed into the house. Unofficially, this side of the porch was Harry's father's, and thereby had an entirely different atmosphere, defeated, lawless, and shameful, from the side with the swing and couch.

Henry knelt down in neutral territory directly before the front door and fished the Ultraglide Roadster from his pocket. He placed the hypnotism book on the porch and rolled the little metal car across its top. Then he gave the car a hard shove and watched it clunk nose-down onto the wood. He repeated this several times before moving the book aside, flattening himself out on his stomach, and giving the little car a decisive push toward the swing and the couch.

The Roadster rolled a few feet before an irregular board tilted it over on its side and stopped it.

"You dumb car," Harry said, and retrieved it. He gave it another push deeper into his mother's realm. A stiff, brittle section of paint which had separated from its board cracked in half and rested atop the stalled Roadster like a miniature mattress.

Harry knocked off the chip of paint and sent the car backwards down the porch, where it flipped over again and skidded into the side of the icebox. The boy ran down the porch and this time simply hurled the little car back in the direction of the swing. It bounced off the swing's padding and fell heavily to the wood. Harry knelt before the icebox, panting.

His whole head felt funny, as if wet hot towels had been stuffed inside it. Harry picked himself up and walked across to where the car lay before the swing. He hated the way it looked, small and helpless. He experimentally stepped on the car and felt it pressing into the undersole of his moccasin. Harry raised his other foot and stood on the car, but nothing happened. He jumped on the car, but the moccasin was not better than his bare foot. Harry bent down to pick up the Roadster.

"You dumb little car," he said. "You're no good anyhow, you low-class little jerky thing." He turned it over in his hands. Then he inserted his thumbs between the frame and the little tires. When he pushed, the tire moved. His face heated. He mashed his thumbs against the tire, and the little black donut popped into the tall thick weeds before the porch. Breathing hard more from emotion than exertion, Harry popped the other front tire into the weeds. Harry whirled around, and ground the car into the wall beside his father's bedroom window. Long deep scratches appeared in the paint. When Harry peered at the top of the car, it too was scratched. He found a nailhead which protruded a quarter of an inch out from the front of the house, and scraped a long paring of blue paint off the driver's side of the Roadster. Gray metal shone through. Harry slammed the car several times against the edge of the nailhead, chipping off small quantities of paint. Panting, he popped off the two small rear tires and put them in his pocket because he liked the way they looked.

Without tires, well scratched and dented, the Ultraglide Roadster had lost most of its power. Harry looked it over with a bitter, deep satisfaction and walked across the porch and shoved it far into the nest of weeds. Gray metal and blue paint shone at him from within the stalks and leaves. Harry thrust his hands into their midst and swept his arms back and forth. The car tumbled away and fell into invisibility.

When Maryrose appeared scowling on the porch, Harry was seated serenely on the squeaking swing, looking at the first few pages of the paperback book.

"What are you doing? What was all that banging?"

"I'm just reading, I didn't hear anything," Harry said.

3.

"Well, if it isn't the shitbird," Albert said, jumping up on the porch steps thirty minutes later. His face and T-shirt bore broad black stripes of grease. Short, muscular, and thirteen, Albert spent every possible minute hanging around the gas station two blocks from their house. Harry knew that Albert despised him. Albert raised a fist and make a jerky, threatening motion toward Harry, who flinched. Albert had often beaten him bloody, as had their two older brothers, Sonny and George, now at army bases in Oklahoma and Germany. Like Albert, his two oldest brothers had seriously disappointed their mother.

Albert laughed, and this time swung his fist within a couple of inches of Harry's face. On the backswing he knocked the book from Harry's hands.

"Thanks," Harry said.

Albert smirked and disappeared around the front door. Almost immediately Harry could hear his mother beginning to shout about the grease on Albert's face and clothes. Albert thumped up the stairs.

Harry opened his clenched fingers and spread them wide, closed his hands into fists, then spread them wide again. When he heard the bedroom door slam shut upstairs, he was able to get off the swing and pick up the book.

Being around Albert made him feel like a spring coiled up in a box. From the upper rear of the house, Little Eddie emitted a ghostly wail. Maryrose screamed that she was going to start smacking him if he didn't shut up, and that was that. The three unhappy lives within the house fell back into silence. Harry sat down, found his page, and began reading again.

A man named Dr. Roland Mentaine had written *Hypnosis Made Easy*, and his vocabulary was much larger than Harry's. Dr. Mentaine used words like "orchestrate" and "ineffable" and "enhance," and some of his sentences wound their way through so many subordinate clauses that Harry lost his way. Yet Harry, who had begun the book only half expecting that he would comprehend anything in it at all, found it a wonderful book. He had made it most of the way through the chapter called "Mind Power."

Harry though it was neat that hypnosis could cure smoking, stuttering, and bedwetting. (He himself had wet the bed almost nightly until months after his ninth birthday. The bedwetting stopped the night a certain lovely dream came to Harry. In the dream he had to urinate terribly, and was hurrying down a stony castle corridor past suits of armor and torches guttering on the walls. At last Harry reached an open door, through which he saw the most splendid bathroom of his life. The floors were of polished marble, the walls white-tiled. As soon as he entered the gleaming bathroom, a uniformed butler waved him toward the rank of urinals. Harry began pulling down his zipper, fumbled with himself, and got his penis out of his underpants just in time. As the dream-urine gushed out of him, Harry had blessedly awakened.) Hypnotism could get you right inside someone's mind and let you do things there. You could make a person speak in any foreign language they'd ever heard, even if they'd only heard it once, and you could make them act like a baby. Harry considered how pleasurable it would be to make his brother Albert lie squalling and red-faced on the floor, unable to walk or speak as he pissed all over himself.

Also, and this was a new thought to Harry, you could take a person back to a whole row of lives they had led before they were born as the person they were now. This process of rebirth was called reincarnation. Some of Dr. Mentaine's patients had been kings in Egypt and pirates in the Caribbean, some had been murderers, novelists, and artists. They remembered the houses they'd lived in, the names of their mothers and servants and children, the locations of shops where they'd bought cake and wine. Neat stuff, Harry thought. He wondered if someone who had been a famous murderer a long time ago could remember pushing in the knife or bringing down the hammer. A lot of the books remaining in the little cardboard box upstairs, Harry had noticed, seemed to be about murderers. If would not be any use to take Albert back to a previous life, however. If Albert had any previous lives, he had spent them as inanimate objects on the order of boulders and anvils.

Maybe in another life Albert was a murder weapon, Harry thought.

"Hey, college boy! Joe College!"

Harry looked toward the sidewalk and saw the baseball cap and T-shirted gut of Mr. Petrosian, who lived in a tiny house next to the tavern on the corner of South Sixth and Livermore Street. Mr. Petrosian was always shouting genial things at kids, but Maryrose wouldn't let Harry or Little Eddie talk to him. She said Mr. Petrosian was common as dirt. He worked as a janitor in the telephone building and drank a case of beer every night while he sat on his porch.

"Me?" Harry said.

"Yeah! Keep reading books, and you could go to college, right?"

Harry smiled noncommittally. Mr. Petrosian lifted a wide arm and continued to toil down the street toward his house next to the Idle Hour.

In seconds Maryrose burst through the door, folding an old white dish towel in her hands. "Who was that? I heard a man's voice."

"Him," Harry said, pointing at the substantial back of Mr. Petrosian, now half of the way home.

"What did he say? As if it could be possibly interesting, coming from an Armenian janitor."

"He called me Joe College."

Maryrose startled him by smiling.

"Albert says he wants to go back to the station tonight, and I have to go to work soon." Maryrose worked the night shift as a secretary at St. Joseph's Hospital. "God knows when your father'll show up. Get something to eat for Little Eddie and yourself, will you, Harry? I've just got too many things to take care of, as usual."

"I'll get something at Big John's." This was a hamburger stand, a magical place to Harry, erected the summer before in a vacant lot on Livermore Street two blocks down from the Idle Hour.

His mother handed him two carefully folded dollar bills, and he pushed them into his pocket. "Don't let Little Eddie stay in the house alone," his mother said before going back inside. "Take him with you. You know how scared he gets."

"Sure," Harry said, and went back to his book. He finished the chapter on "Mind Power" while first Maryrose left to stand up at the bus stop on the corner and then Albert nosily departed. Little Eddie sat frozen before his soap operas in the living room. Harry turned a page and started reading "Techniques of Hypnosis."

4.

At eight-thirty that night the two boys sat alone in the kitchen, on opposite sides of the table covered in yellow bamboo Formica. From the living room came the sound of Sid Caesar babbling in fake German to Imogene Coca on *Your Show of Shows*. Little Eddie claimed to be scared of Sid Caesar, but when Harry had returned from the hamburger stand with a Big Johnburger (with "the works") for himself and a Mama Marydog for Eddie, double fries, and two chocolate shakes, he had been sitting in front of the television, his face moist with tears of moral outrage. Eddie usually liked Mama Marydogs, but he had taken only a couple of meager bites from the one before him now, and was disconsolately pushing a French fry through a blob of ketchup. Every now and then he wiped at his eyes, leaving nearly symmetrical smears of ketchup to dry on his cheeks.

"Mom *said* not to leave me alone in the house," said Little Eddie. "I heard. It was during *The Edge of Night* and you were on the porch. I think I'm gonna tell on you." He peeped across at Harry, then quickly looked back at the French fry and drew it out of the puddle of ketchup. "I'm ascared to be alone in the house." Sometimes Eddie's voice was like a queer speeded-up mechanical version of Maryrose's.

"Don't be so dumb," Harry said, almost kindly. "How can you be scared in your own house? You live here, don't you?"

"I'm ascared of the attic," Eddie said. He held the dripping French fry before his mouth and pushed it in. "The attic makes noise." A little squirm of red appeared at the corner of his mouth. "You were supposed to take me with you."

"Oh jeez, Eddie, you slow everything down. I wanted to just get the food and come back. I got you your dinner, didn't I? Didn't I get you what you like?"

In truth, Harry liked hanging around Big John's by himself because then he could talk to Big John and listen to his theories. Big John called himself a "renegade Papist" and considered Hitler the greatest man of the twentieth century, followed closely by Paul VI, Padre Pio who bled from the palms of his hands, and Elvis Presley.

All these events occurred in what is usually but wrongly called a simpler time, before Kennedy and feminism and ecology, before the Nixon presidency and Watergate, and before American soldiers, among them a twenty-one-year-old Harry Beevers, journeyed to Vietnam.

"I'm still going to tell," said Little Eddie. He pushed another French fry into the puddle of ketchup. "And that car was my birthday present." He began to snuffle. "Albert hit me, and you stole my car, and you left me alone, and I was scared. And I don't wanna have Mrs. Franken next year, cuz I think she's gonna hurt me."

Harry had nearly forgotten telling his brother about Mrs. Franken and Tommy Golz, and this reminder brought back very sharply the memory of destroying Eddie's birthday present.

Eddie twisted his head sideways and dared another quick look at his brother. "Can I have my Ultraglide Roadster back, Harry? You're going to give it back to me aren'cha? I won't tell Mom you left me alone if you give it back."

"Your car is okay," Harry said. "It's in a sort of secret place I know."

"You hurt my car!" Eddie squalled. "You did!"

"Shut up!" Harry shouted, and Little Eddie flinched. "You're driving me crazy!" Harry yelled. He realized he was leaning over the table, and that Little Eddie was getting ready to cry again. He sat down. "Just don't scream at me like that, Eddie."

"You did something to my car," Eddie said with a stunned certainty. "I knew it."

"Look, I'll prove your car is okay," Harry said, and took the two rear tires from his pocket and displayed them on his palm.

Little Eddie stared. He blinked, then reached out tentatively for the tires.

Harry closed his fist around them. "Do they look like I did anything to them?"

"You took them *off!*"

"But don't they look okay, don't they look fine?" Harry opened his fist, closed it again, and returned the tires to his pocket. "I didn't want to show you the whole car, Eddie, because you'd get all worked up, and you gave it to me. Remember? I wanted to show you the tires so you'd see everything was all right. Okay? Got it?"

Eddie miserably shook his head.

"Anyway, I'm going to help you, just like I said."

"With Mrs. Franken?" A fraction of his misery left Little Eddie's smeary face.

"Sure. You ever hear of something called hypnotism?"

"I heard a hypmotism." Little Eddie was sulking. "Everybody in the whole world heard a that."

"Hypnotism, stupid, not hypmotism."

"Sure, hypmotism. I saw it on the TV. They did it on *As the World Turns*. A man made a lady go to sleep and think she was going to have a baby."

Harry smiled. "That's just TV, Little Eddie. Real hypnotism is a lot better than that. I read all about it in one of the books from the attic."

Little Eddie was still sulky because of the car. "So what makes it better?"

"Because it lets you do amazing things," Harry said. He called on Dr. Mentaine. "Hypnosis unlocks your mind and lets you use all the power you really have. If you start now, you'll really knock those books when school starts again. You'll pass every test Mrs. Franken gives you, just like the way I did." He reached across the table and grasped Little Eddie's wrist, stalling a fat brown French fry on its way to the puddle. "But it won't just make you good in school. If you let me try it on you, I'm pretty sure I can show you that you're a lot stronger than you think you are."

Eddie blinked.

"And I bet I can make you so you're not scared of anything anymore.

Hypnotism is real good for that. I read in this book, there was this guy who was afraid of bridges. Whenever he even *thought* about crossing a bridge he got all dizzy and sweaty. Terrible stuff happening to him, like he lost his job and once he just had to ride in a car across a bridge and he dumped a load in his pants. He went to see Dr. Mentaine, and Dr. Mentaine hypnotized him and said he would never be afraid of bridges again, and he wasn't."

Harry pulled the paperback from his hip pocket. He opened it flat on the table and bent over the pages. "Here. Listen to this. 'Benefits of the course of treatment were found in all areas of the patient's life, and results were obtained for which he would have paid any price.'" Harry read those words haltingly, but with complete understanding.

"Hypmotism can make me strong?" Little Eddie asked, evidently having saved this point in his head.

"Strong as a bull."

"Strong as Albert?"

"A lot stronger than Albert. A lot stronger than me, too."

"And I can beat up on big guys that hurt me?"

"You just have to learn how."

Eddie sprang up from the chair, yelling nonsense. He flexed his stringlike biceps and for some time twisted his body into a series of muscleman poses.

"You want to do it?" Harry finally asked.

Little Eddie popped into his chair and stared at Harry. His T-shirt's neckband sagged all the way to his breastbone without ever actually touching his chest. "I wanna start."

"Okay, Eddie, good man." Harry stood up and put his hand on the book. "Up to the attic."

"Only, I don't wanna go in the attic," Eddie said. He was still staring at Harry, but his head was tilted over like a weird little echo of Maryrose, and his eyes had filled with suspicion.

"I'm not gonna *take* anything from you, Little Eddie," Harry said. "It's just, we should be out of everybody's way. The attic's real quiet."

Little Eddie stuck his hand inside his T-shirt and let his arm dangle from the wrist.

"You turned your shirt into an armrest," Harry said.

Eddie jerked his hand out of its sling.

"Albert might come waltzing in and wreck everything if we do it in the bedroom."

"If you go up first and turn on the lights," Eddie said.

5.

Harry held the book open on his lap, and glanced from it to Little Eddie's tense smeary face. He had read these pages over many times while he sat on the porch. Hypnotism boiled down to a few simple steps, each of which led to the next. The first thing he had to do was to get his brother started right, "relaxed and receptive," according to Dr. Mentaine.

Little Eddie stirred in his cane-backed chair and kneaded his hands together. His shadow, cast by the bulb dangling overhead, imitated him like a black little chair-bound monkey. "I wanna get started, I wanna get strong," he said.

"Right here in this book it says you have to be relaxed," Harry said. "Just put your hands on top of your legs, nice and easy, with your fingers pointing forward. Then close your eyes and breathe in and out a couple of times. Think about being nice and tired and ready to go to sleep."

"I don't wanna go to sleep!"

"It's not really sleep, Little Eddie, it's just sort of like it. You'll still really be awake, but nice and relaxed. Or else it won't work. You have to do everything I tell you. Otherwise everybody'll still be able to beat up on you, like they do now. I want you to pay attention to everything I say."

"Okay." Little Eddie made a visible effort to relax. He placed his hands on his thighs and twice inhaled and exhaled.

"Now close your eyes."

Eddie closed his eyes.

Harry suddenly knew that it was going to work—if he did everything the book said, he would really be able to hypnotize his brother.

"Little Eddie, I want you just to listen to the sound of my voice," he said, forcing himself to be calm. "You are already getting nice and relaxed, as easy and peaceful as if you were lying in bed, and the more you listen to my voice, the more relaxed and tired you are going to get. Nothing can bother you. Everything bad is far away, and you're just sitting here, breathing in and out, getting nice and sleepy."

He checked his page to make sure he was doing it right, and then went on.

"It's like lying in bed, Eddie, and the more you hear my voice, the more tired and sleepy you're getting, a little more sleepy the more you hear me. Everything else is sort of fading away, and all you can hear is my voice. You feel tired but good, just like the way you do right before you fall asleep. Everything is fine, and you're drifting a little bit, drifting and drifting, and you're getting ready to raise your right hand."

He leaned over and very lightly stroked the back of Little Eddie's grimy right hand. Eddie sat slumped in the chair with his eyes closed, breathing shallowly. Harry spoke very slowly.

"I'm going to count backwards from ten, and every time I get to another number, your hand is going to get lighter and lighter. When I count, your right hand is going to get so light it floats up and finally touched your nose when you hear me say 'one.' And then you'll be in a deep sleep. Now I'm starting. Ten. Your hand is already feeling light. Nine. It wants to float up. Eight. Your hand really feels light now. It's going to start to go up now. Seven."

Little Eddie's hand obediently floated an inch up from his thigh.

"Six." The grimy little hand rose another few inches. "It's getting lighter and lighter now, and every time I say another number it gets closer and closer to your nose, and you get sleepier and sleepier. Five."

The hand ascended several inches nearer Eddie's face.

"Four."

The hand now dangled like a sleeping bird half of the way between Eddie's knee and his nose.

"Three."

It rose nearly to Eddie's chin.

"Two."

Eddie's hand hung a few inches from his mouth.

"One. You are going to fall asleep now."

The gently curved, ketchup-streaked forefinger delicately brushed the tip of Little Eddie's nose, and stayed there while Eddie sagged against the back of the chair.

Harry's heart beat so loudly that he feared the sound would bring Eddie out of his trance. Eddie remained motionless. Harry breathed quietly by himself for a moment. "Now you can lower your hand to your lap, Eddie. You are going deeper and deeper into sleep. Deeper and deeper and deeper."

Eddie's hand sank gracefully downward.

The attic seemed hot as the inside of a furnace to Harry. His fingers left blotches on the open pages of the book. He wiped his face on his sleeve and looked at his little brother. Little Eddie had slumped so far down in the chair that his head no longer visible in the tilting mirror. Perfectly still and quiet, the attic stretched out on all sides of them, waiting (or so it seemed to Harry) for what would happen next. Maryrose's trunks sat in rows under the eaves far behind the mirror, her old dresses hung silently within the dusty wardrobe. Harry rubbed his hands on his jeans to dry them, and flicked a page over with the neatness of an old scholar who had spent half his life in libraries.

"You're going to sit up straight in your chair," he said.

Eddie pulled himself upright.

"Now I want to show you that you're really hypnotized, Little Eddie. It's like a test. I want you to hold your right arm straight out before you. Make it as rigid as you can. This is going to show you how strong you can be."

Eddie's pale arm rose and straightened to the wrist, leaving his fingers dangling.

Harry stood up and said, "That's pretty good." He walked the two steps to Eddie's side and grasped his brother's arm and ran his fingers down the length of it, gently straightening Eddie's hand. "Now I want you to imagine that your arm is getting harder and harder. It's getting as hard and rigid as an iron bar. Your whole arm is an iron bar, and nobody on earth could bend it. Eddie, it's stronger than Superman's arm." He removed his hands and stepped back.

"Now. This arm is so strong and rigid that you can't bend it no matter how hard you try. It's an iron bar, and nobody on earth could bend it. Try. Try to bend it."

Eddie's face tightened up, and his arm rose perhaps two degrees. Eddie grunted with invisible efforts, unable to bend his arm.

"Okay, Eddie, you did real good. Now your arm is loosening up, and when I count backwards from ten, it's going to get looser and looser. When I get to *one*, your arm'll be normal again." He began counting and Eddie's fingers loosened and drooped, and finally the arm came to rest again on his leg.

Harry went back to his hair, sat down, and looked at Eddie with great satisfaction. Now he was certain that he would be able to do the next demonstration, which Dr. Mentaine called "The Chair Exercise."

"Now you know that this little stuff really works, Eddie, so we're going to do something a little harder. I want you to stand up in front of your chair."

Eddie obeyed. Harry stood up and moved his chair forward and to the side so that its cane seat faced Eddie, about four feet away.

"I want you to stretch out between these chairs, with your head on your chair and your feet on mine. And I want you to keep your hands at your sides."

Eddie hunkered down uncomplainingly and settled his head back on the seat of his chair. Supporting himself with his arms, he raised one leg and placed his foot on Harry's chair. Then he lifted the other foot. Difficulty immediately appeared in his face. He raised his arms and clamped then in so that he looked trussed.

"Now your whole body is slowly becoming as hard as iron, Eddie. Your entire body is one of the strongest things on earth. Nothing can make it bend. You could hold yourself there forever and never feel the slightest pain or discomfort. It's like you're lying on a mattress, you're so strong."

The expression of strain left Eddie's face. Slowly his arms extended and relaxed. He lay propped string-straight between the two chairs, so at ease that he did not even appear to be breathing.

"While I talk to you, you're getting stronger and stronger. You could hold up anything. You could hold up an elephant. I'm going to sit down on your stomach to prove it."

Cautiously, Harry seated himself down on his brother's midriff. He raised his legs. Nothing happened. After he counted slowly to fifteen, Harry lowered his legs and stood. "I'm going to take my shoes off now, Eddie, and stand on you."

He hurried over to a piano stool embroidered with fulsome roses and carried it back; then he slipped off his moccasins and stepped on top of the stool. As Harry stepped on top of Eddie's exposed thin belly, the chair supporting his brother's head wobbled. Harry stood stock-still a moment, but the chair held. He lifted the other foot from the stool. No movement from the chair. He set the other foot on his brother. Little Eddie effortlessly held him up.

Harry lifted himself experimentally up on his toes and came back down on his heels. Eddie seemed entirely unaffected. Then Harry jumped perhaps a half an inch into the air, and since Eddie did not even grunt when he landed, he kept jumping, five, six, seven, eight times, until he was breathing hard. "You're amazing, Little Eddie," he said, and stepped off onto the stool. "Now you can begin to relax. You can put your feet on the floor. Then I want you to sit back up in your chair. Your body doesn't feel stiff anymore."

Little Eddie had been rather tentatively lowering one foot, but as soon as Harry finished speaking, he buckled in the middle and thumped his bottom on the floor. Harry's chair (Maryrose's chair) sickeningly tipped over, but landed soundlessly on a neat woolen stack of layered winter coats.

Moving like a robot, Little Eddie slowly sat upright on the floor. His eyes were open but unfocused.

"You can stand up now and get back in your chair," Harry said. He did not remember leaving the stool, but he had left it. Sweat ran into his eyes. He pressed his face into his shirt sleeve. For a second, panic had brightly beckoned. Little Eddie was sleepwalking back to his chair. When he sat down, Harry said, "Close your eyes. You're going deeper and deeper into sleep. Deeper and deeper, Little Eddie."

Eddie settled into the chair as if nothing had happened, and Harry reverently set his own chair upright again. Then he picked up the book and opened it. The print swam before his eyes. Harry shook his head and looked again, but still the lines of print snaked across the page. (When Harry was a sophomore at Adelphi College he was asked to read several poems by Guillaume Apollinaire, and the appearance of the wavering lines on the page brought back this moment with a terrible precision.) Harry pressed the palms of his hands against his eyes, and red patterns exploded across his vision.

He removed his hands from his eyes, blinked, and found that although the lines of print were now behaving themselves, he no longer wanted to go on.

The attic was too hot, he was too tired, and the toppling of the chair had been too close a brush with actual disaster. But for a time he leafed purposefully through the book while Eddie tranced on, and then found the subheading "Post-Hypnotic Suggestion."

"Little Eddie, we're just going to do one more thing. If we ever do this again, it'll help us go faster." Harry shut the book. He knew exactly how this went; he would even use the same phrase Dr. Mentaine used with his patients. *Blue rose*—Harry did not quite know why, but he liked the sound of that.

"I'm going to tell you a phrase, Eddie, and from now on whenever you hear me say this phrase, you will instantly go back to sleep, and be hypnotized again. The phrase is 'blue rose.' 'Blue rose.' When you hear me say 'blue rose,' you will go right to sleep. Just the way you are now, and we can make you stronger again. 'Blue rose' is our secret, Eddie, because nobody else knows it. What is it?"

"Blue rose," Eddie said in a muffled voice.

"Okay, I'm going to count backward from ten, and when I get to 'one' you will be wide awake again. You will not remember anything we did, but you will feel happy and strong. Ten."

As Harry counted backwards, Little Eddie twitched and stirred, let his arms fall to his sides, thumped one foot carelessly on the floor, and at "one" opened his eyes.

"Did it work? What'd I do? Am I strong?"

"You're a bull," Harry said. "It's getting late, Eddie—time to go downstairs."

Harry's timing was accurate enough to be uncomfortable. As soon as the two boys closed the attic door behind them they heard the front door slide open in a cacophony of harsh coughs and subdued mutterings followed by the sound of unsteady footsteps proceeding to the bathroom. Edgar Beevers was home.

6.

Late that night the three homebound Beevers sons lay in their separate beds in the good-sized second-floor room next to the attic stairs. Directly above Maryrose's bedroom, its dimensions were nearly identical to it except that the boys' room, the "dorm," had no window seat and the attic stairs shaved a couple of feet from Harry's end. When the other two boys had lived at home, Harry and Little Eddie had slept together, Albert had slept in a bed with Sonny, and only George, who at the time of his induction into the army had been six feet tall and weighed two hundred and one pounds, had slept alone. In those days, Sonny had often managed to make Albert cry out in the middle of the night. The very idea of George could still make Harry's stomach freeze.

Though it was not very late, enough light from the street came in through the white net curtains to give complex shadows to the bunched muscles of Albert's upper arms as he lay stretched out atop his sheets. The voices of Maryrose and Edgar Beevers, one approximately sober and the other unmistakably drunk, came clearly up the stairs and through the open door.

"*Who* says I waste my time. I don't say that. I don't waste my time."

"I suppose you think you've done a good day's work when you spell a bartender for a couple of hours—and then drink up your wages! That's the story of your life, Edgar Beevers, and it's a sad sad story of w-a-s-t-e. If my father could have seen what would become of you . . . "

"I ain't so damn bad."

"You ain't so damn good, either."

"Albert," Eddie said softly from his bed between his two brothers.

As if galvanized by Little Eddie's voice, Albert suddenly sat up in bed, leaned forward, and reached out to try to smack Eddie with his fist.

"I didn't do nothin'!" Harry said, and moved to the edge of his mattress. The blow had been for him, he knew, not Eddie, except that Albert was too lazy to get up.

"I hate your lousy guts," Albert said. "If I wasn't too tired to get out of this-here bed, I'd pound your face in."

"Harry stole my birthday car, Albert," Eddie said. "Makum gimme it back."

"One day," Maryrose said from downstairs, "at the end of the summer when I was seventeen, late in the afternoon, my father said to my mother, 'Honey, I believe I'm going to take out our pretty little Maryrose and get her something special,' and he called up to me from the drawing room to make myself pretty and get set to go, and because my father was a gentleman and a Man of His Word, I got ready in two shakes. My father was wearing a very

handsome brown suit and a red bow tie and his boater. I remember just like
I can see it now. He stood at the bottom of the staircase, waiting for me, and
when I came down he took my arm and we just went out that front door
like a courting couple. Down the stone walk, which my father put in all by
himself even though he was a white-collar worker, down Majeski Street, arm
in arm, down to South Palmyra Avenue. In those days all the best people, all
the people who counted, did their shopping on South Palmyra Avenue."

"I'd like to knock your teeth down your throat," Albert said to Harry.

"Albert, he took my birthday car, he really did, and I want it back. I'm
ascared he busted it. I want it back so much I'm gonna die."

Albert propped himself up on an elbow and for the first time really looked
at Little Eddie. Eddie whimpered. "You're such a twerp," Albert said. "I wish
you *would* die, Eddie, I wish you'd just drop dead so we could stick you in the
ground and forget about you. I wouldn't even cry at your funeral. Prob'ly I
wouldn't even be able to remember your name. I'd just say, 'Oh yeah, he was
that little creepy kid used to hang around cryin' all the time, glad he's dead,
whatever his name was.'"

Eddie had turned his back on Albert and was weeping softly, his unwashed
face distorted by the shadows into an uncanny image of the mask of tragedy.

"You know, I really wouldn't mind if you dropped dead," Albert mused.
"You neither, shitbird."

" . . . realized he was taking me to Alouette's. I'm sure you used to look in
their windows when you were a little boy. You remember Alouette's, don't
you? There's never been anything so beautiful as that store. When I was a little
girl and lived in the big house, all the best people used to go there. My father
marched me right inside, with his arm around me, and took me up in the
elevator and we went straight to the lady who managed the dress department.
'Give my little girl the best,' he said. Price was no object. Quality was all he
cared about. 'Give my little girl the best.' *Are you listening to me, Edgar?*"

• • •

Albert snored face-down into his pillow; Little Eddie twitched and snuffled.
Harry lay awake for so long he thought he would never get to sleep. Before him

he kept seeing Little Eddie's face all slack and dopey under hypnosis—Little Eddie's face made him feel hot and uncomfortable. Now that Harry was lying down in bed, it seemed to him that everything he had done since returning from Big John's seemed really to have been done by someone else, or to have been done in a dream. Then he realized that he had to use the bathroom.

Harry slid out of bed, quietly crossed the room, went out onto the dark landing, and felt his way downstairs to the bathroom.

When he emerged, the bathroom light showed him the squat black shape of the telephone atop the Palmyra directory. Harry moved to the low telephone table beside the stairs. He lifted the phone from the directory and opened the book, the width of a Big 5 tablet, with his other hand. As he had done on many other nights when his bladder forced him downstairs, Harry leaned over the page and selected a number. He kept the number in his head as he closed the directory and replaced the telephone. He dialed. The number rang so often Harry lost count. At last a hoarse voice answered. Harry said, "I'm watching you, and you're a dead man." He softly replaced the receiver in the cradle.

7.

Harry caught up with his father the next afternoon just as Edgar Beevers had begun to move up South Sixth Street toward the corner of Livermore. His father wore his usual costume of baggy gray trousers cinched far above his waist by a belt with a double buckle, a red-and-white plaid shirt, and a brown felt hat stationed low over his eyes. His long fleshy nose swam before him, cut in half by the shadow of the hat brim.

"Dad!"

His father glanced incuriously at him, then put his hands back in his pockets. He turned sideways and kept walking down the street, though perhaps a shade more slowly. "What's up, kid? No school?"

"It's summer, there isn't any school. I just thought I'd come with you for a little."

"Well, I ain't doing much. Your ma asked me to pick up some hamburg on Livermore, and I thought I'd slip into the Idle Hour for a quick belt. You won't turn me in, will you?"

"No."

"You ain't a bad kid, Harry. Your ma's just got a lot of worries. I worry about Little Eddie too, sometimes."

"Sure."

"What's with the books? You read when you walk?"

"I was just sort of looking at them," Harry said.

His father insinuated his hand beneath Harry's left elbow and extracted two luridly jacketed paperback books. They were titled *Murder, Incorporated* and *Hitler's Death Camps.* Harry already loved both of these books. His father grunted and handed *Murder, Incorporated* back to him. He raised the other book nearly to the tip of his nose and peered at the cover, which depicted a naked woman pressing herself against a wall of barbed wire while a uniformed Nazi aimed a rifle at her back.

Looking up at his father, Harry saw that beneath the harsh line of shade cast by the hat brim his father's whiskers grew in different colors and patterns. Black and brown, red and orange, the glistening spikes swirled across his father's cheek.

"I bought this book, but it didn't look nothing like that," his father said, and returned the book.

"What didn't?"

"That place. Dachau. That death camp."

"How do you know?"

"I was there, wasn't I? You wasn't even born then. It didn't look anything like that picture on that book. It just looked like a piece of shit to me, like most of the places I saw when I was in the army."

This was the first time Harry had heard that his father had been in the service.

"You mean, you were in World War II?"

"Yeah, I was in the Big One. They made me a corporal over there. Had me a nickname too. 'Beans.' 'Beans' Beevers. And I got a Purple Heart from the time I got an infection."

"You saw Dachau with your own eyes?"

"Damn straight, I did." He bent down suddenly. "Hey—don't let your ma catch you readin' that book."

Secretly pleased, Harry shook his head. Now the book and the death camp were a bond between himself and his father.

"Did you ever kill anybody?"

His father wiped his mouth and both cheeks with one long hand. Harry saw a considering eye far back in the shadow of the brim.

"I killed a guy once."

A long pause.

"I shot him in the back."

His father wiped his mouth again, and then motioned forward with his head. He had to get to the bar, the butcher, and back again in a very carefully defined period of time. "You really want to hear this?"

Harry nodded. He swallowed.

"I guess you do, at that. Okay—we was sent into this camp, Dachau, at the end of the war to process the prisoners and arrest the guards and the commandant. Everything was all arranged. A bunch of brass hats from Division were going to come on an inspection, so we had to wait there a couple of days. We had these guards lined up, see, and these skinny old wrecks would come up and give 'em hell. We wasn't supposed to let 'em get too near."

They were passing Mr. Petrosian's little tar-paper house, and Harry felt a spasm of relief that Mr. Petrosian was not out on his tiny porch working on his case of beer. The Idle Hour was only a few paces ahead.

"Anyhow, one of these guards, one of the worst ones, suddenly decided he's going to run for it. He takes off, runnin' like crazy toward the woods. What do I do? I ask. Nobody knows what the hell to do. Shoot him, somebody says. So I shot him in the back. That was all she wrote."

Now they had reached the screen door which led into the Idle Hour, and the smells of malt and hops filled the air. "See you back at the house," his father said, and disappeared through the screen door like a magician.

8.

After Harry had read a hundred pages of *Murder, Incorporated,* his favorite murderers were Louis "Lepke" Buchalter and Abe "Kid Twist" Reles. They were dependable professionals. A kind of black light surrounded them and made them glitter. Lepke Buchalter and Abe Reles looked out at the world from the shadows of their hat brims. They lived in shadowy rooms and peered out through the curtains. They appeared on a dark corner before their terrified victim, did their work, and walked away, turning up their coat collars.

Suppose you had some kind of job that took you around the country, like a salesman's job, Harry thought as he read away the afternoon in the porch swing; suppose you had a job that took you from one town to another. Suppose you killed someone in each one of those towns, carefully and quietly, and hid the bodies so it would take people a long time to find them. Your work would never be done.

9.

"Blue rose," Harry said.

Little Eddie sagged openmouthed against the cane of his chair, his hands loose in his lap.

It had worked. Harry looked around as if he expected applause, and did feel that all the things in the attic looked back at him with warm approval. It was nine-thirty at night; he and Eddie, alone in the house, occupied the attic in perfect safety. Harry wanted to see if he could put other people under and make them do things, but for now, for tonight, he was content to experiment with Eddie.

"You're going deeper and deeper asleep, Eddie, deeper and deeper, and you're listening to every word I say. You're just sinking down and down, hearing my voice come to you, going deeper and deeper with every word, and now you are real deep asleep and ready to begin."

Little Eddie sat sprawled over Maryrose's cane-backed chair, his chin touching his chest and his little pink mouth drooling open. He looked like a slightly undersized seven-year-old, like a second-grader instead of the fourth-grader he would be when he joined Mrs. Franken's class in the fall. Suddenly he reminded Harry of the Ultraglide Roadster, scratched and dented and stripped of its tires.

"Tonight you're going to see how strong you really are. Sit up, Eddie."

Eddie pulled himself upright and closed his mouth, almost comically obedient.

Harry thought it would be fun to make Little Eddie believe he was a dog and trot around the attic on all fours, barking and lifting his leg. Then he saw Little Eddie staggering across the attic, his tongue bulging out of his mouth, his own hands squeezing and squeezing his throat. Maybe he would try that too, after he had done several other exercises he had discovered in Dr. Mentaine's book. He checked the underside of his collar for maybe the fifth time that evening, and felt the long thin shaft of the pearl-headed hatpin he had stopped reading *Murder, Incorporated* long enough to smuggle out of Maryrose's bedroom after she had left for work.

"Eddie," he said, "now you are very deeply asleep, and you will be able to do everything I say. I want you to hold your right arm straight out in front of you."

Eddie stuck his arm out like a poker.

"That's good, Eddie. Now I want you to notice that all the feeling is leaving that arm. It's getting number and number. It doesn't even feel like flesh and blood anymore. It feels like it's made out of steel or something. It's so numb that you can't feel anything there anymore. You can't even feel pain in it."

Harry stood up, went toward Eddie, and brushed his fingers along his arm. "You didn't feel anything, did you?"

"No," Eddie said in a slow gravel-filled voice.

"Do you feel anything now?" Harry pinched the underside of Eddie's forearm.

"No."

"Now?" Harry used his nails to pinch the side of Eddie's biceps, hard, and left purple dents in the skin.

"No," Eddie repeated.

"How about this?" He slapped his hand against Eddie's forearm as hard as he could. There was a sharp loud smacking sound, and his fingers tingled. If Little Eddie had not been hypnotized, he would have tried to screech down the walls.

"No," Eddie said.

Harry pulled the hatpin out of his collar and inspected his brother's arm. "You're doing great, Little Eddie. You're stronger than anybody in your whole class—you're stronger than the whole rest of school." He turned Eddie's arm

PETER STRAUB

so that the palm was up and the white forearm, lightly traced by small blue veins, faced him.

Harry delicately ran the point of the hatpin down Eddie's pale, veined forearm. The pinpoint left a narrow chalk-white scratch in its wake. For a moment Harry felt the floor of the attic sway beneath his feet; then he closed his eyes and jabbed the hatpin into Little Eddie's skin as hard as he could.

He opened his eyes. The floor was still swaying beneath him. From Little Eddie's lower arm protruded six inches of the eight-inch hatpin, the mother-of-pearl head glistening softly in the light from the overhead bulb. A drop of blood the size of a watermelon seed stood on Eddie's skin. Harry moved back to his chair and sat down heavily. "Do you feel anything?"

"No," Eddie said again in that surprisingly deep voice.

Harry stared at the hatpin embedded in Eddie's arm. The oval drop of blood lengthened itself out against the white skin and began slowly to ooze toward Eddie's wrist. Harry watched it advance across the pale underside of Eddie's forearm. Finally he stood up and returned to Eddie's side. The elongated drop of blood had ceased moving. Harry bent over and twanged the hatpin. Eddie could feel nothing. Harry put his thumb and forefinger on the glistening head of the pin. His face was so hot he might have been standing before an open fire. He pushed the pin a further half inch into Eddie's arm, and another small quantity of blood welled up from the base. The pin seemed to be moving in Harry's grasp, pulsing back and forth as if it were breathing.

"Okay," Harry said. "Okay."

He tightened his hold on the pin and pulled. It slipped easily from the wound. Harry held the hatpin before his face just as a doctor holds up a thermometer to read a temperature. He had imagined that the entire bottom section of the shaft would be painted with red, but saw that only a single winding glutinous streak of blood adhered to the pin. For a dizzy second he thought of slipping the end of the pin in his mouth and sucking it clean.

He thought: Maybe in another life I was Lepke Buchalter.

He pulled his handkerchief, a filthy square of red paisley, from his front pocket and wiped the streak of blood from the shaft of the pin. Then he leaned over and gently wiped the red smear from Little Eddie's underarm. Harry

266

refolded the handkerchief so the blood would not show, wiped sweat from his face, and shoved the grubby cloth back into his pocket.

"That was good, Eddie. Now we're going to do something a little bit different."

He knelt down beside his brother and lifted Eddie's nearly weightless, delicately veined arm. "You still can't feel a thing in this arm, Eddie, it's completely numb. It's sound asleep and it won't wake up until I tell it to." Harry repositioned himself in order to hold himself steady while he knelt, and put the point of the hatpin nearly flat against Eddie's arm. He pushed it foreword far enough to raise a wrinkle of flesh. The point of the hatpin dug into Eddie's skin but did not break it. Harry pushed harder, and the hatpin raised the little bulge of skin by a small but appreciable amount.

Skin was a lot tougher to break through than anyone imagined.

The pin was beginning to hurt his fingers, so Harry opened his hand and positioned the head against the base of his middle finger. Grimacing, he pushed his hand against the pin. The point of the pin popped through the raised wrinkle.

"Eddie, you're made out of beer cans," Harry said, and tugged the head of the pin backwards. The wrinkle flattened out. Now Harry could shove the pin forward again, sliding the shaft deeper and deeper under the surface of Little Eddie's skin. He could see the raised line of the hatpin marching down his brother's arm, looking as prominent as the damage done to a cartoon lawn by a cartoon rabbit. When the mother-of-pearl head was perhaps three inches from the entry hole, Harry pushed it down into Little Eddie's flesh, thus raising the point of the pin. He gave the head a sharp jab, and the point appeared at the end of the ridge in Eddie's skin, poking through a tiny smear of blood. Harry shoved the pin in further. Now it showed about an inch and a half of gray metal at either end.

"Feel anything?"

"Nothing."

Harry jiggled the head of the pin, and a bubble of blood walked out of the entry wound and began to slid down Eddie's arm. Harry sat down on the attic floor beside Eddie and regarded his work. His mind seemed pleasantly empty of thought, filled only with a variety of sensations. He *felt* but could not hear a buzzing in his head, and a blurry film seemed to cover his eyes. He breathed through his mouth. The long pin stuck through Little Eddie's arm looked monstrous seen one way; seen another, it was sheerly beautiful. Skin, blood, and metal. Harry had never seen anything like it before. He reached out and twisted the pin, causing another little blood-snail to crawl from the exit wound. Harry saw all this as if through smudgy glasses, but he did not mind. He knew the blurriness was only mental. He touched the head of the pin again and moved it from side to side. A little more blood leaked from both punctures. Then Harry shoved the pin in, partially withdrew it so that the point nearly disappeared back into Eddie's arm, moved it forward again, and went on like this, back and forth, back and forth as if he were sewing his brother up, for some time.

Finally he withdrew the pin from Eddie's arm. The two long streaks of blood had nearly reached his brother's wrist. Harry ground the heels of his hands into his eyes, blinked, and discovered that his vision had cleared.

He wondered how long he and Eddie had been in the attic. It could have been hours. He could not quite remember what had happened before he had slid the hatpin into Eddie's skin. Now his blurriness really was mental, not visual. A loud uncomfortable pulse beat in his temples. Again he wiped the blood from Eddie's arm. Then he stood on wobbling knees and returned to his chair.

"How's your arm feel, Eddie?"

"Numb," Eddie said in his gravelly sleepy voice.

"The numbness is going away now. Very, very slowly. You are beginning to feel your arm again, and it feels very good. There is no pain. It feels like the sun was shining on it all afternoon. It's strong and healthy. Feeling is coming back into your arm, and you can move your fingers and everything."

When he had finished speaking Harry leaned back against the chair and closed his eyes. He rubbed his forehead with his hand and wiped the moisture off on his shirt.

"How does your arm feel?" he said without opening his eyes.

"Good."

"That's great, Little Eddie." Harry flattened his palms against his flushed face, wiped his cheeks, and opened his eyes.

I can do this every night, he thought. I can bring Little Eddie up here every single night, at least until school starts.

"Eddie, you're getting strong and stronger every day. This is really helping you. And the more we do it, the stronger you'll get. Do you understand me?"

"I understand you," Eddie said.

"We're almost done for tonight. There's just one more thing I want to try. But you have to be really deep asleep for this to work. So I want you to go deeper and deeper, as deep as you can go. Relax, and now you are really deep asleep, deep deep, and relaxed and ready and feeling good."

Little Eddie sat sprawled in his chair with his head tilted back and his eyes closed. Two tiny dark spots of blood stood out like mosquito bites on his lower right forearm.

"When I talk to you, Eddie, you're slowly getting younger and younger, you're going back in time, so now you're not nine years old anymore, you're eight, it's last year and you're in the third grade, and now you're seven, and now you're six years old . . . and now you're five, Eddie, and it's the day of your fifth birthday. You're five years old today, Little Eddie. How old are you?"

"I'm five." To Harry's surprised pleasure, Little Eddie's voice actually seemed younger, as did his hunched posture in the chair.

"How do you feel?"

"Not good. I hate my present. It's terrible. Dad got it, and Mom says it should never be allowed in the house because it's just junk. I wish I couldn't ever have to have birthdays, they're so terrible. I'm gonna cry."

His face contracted. Harry tried to remember what Eddie had gotten for his fifth birthday, but could not—he caught only a dim memory of shame and disappointment. "What's your present, Eddie?"

In a teary voice, Eddie said, "A radio. But it's busted and Mom says it looks like it came from the junkyard. I don't want it anymore. I don't even wanna *see* it."

Yes, Harry thought, yes, yes, yes. He could remember. On Little Eddie's fifth birthday, Edgar Beevers had produced a yellow plastic radio which even Harry had seen was astoundingly ugly. The dial was cracked, and it was marked here and there with brown circular scablike marks where someone had mashed out cigarettes on it.

The radio had long since been buried in the junk room, where it now lay beneath several geological layers of trash.

"Okay, Eddie, you can forget the radio now, because you're going backwards again, you're getting younger, you're going backwards through being four years old, and now you're three."

He looked with interest at Little Eddie, whose entire demeanor had changed. From being tearfully unhappy, Eddie now demonstrated a self-sufficient good cheer Harry could not ever remember seeing in him. His arms were folded over his chest. He was smiling, and his eyes were bright and clear and childish.

"What do you see?" Harry asked.

"Mommy-ommy-om."

"What's she doing?"

"Mommy's at her desk. She's smoking and looking through her papers." Eddie giggled. "Mommy looks funny. It looks like smoke is coming out of the top of her head." Eddie ducked his chin and hid his smile behind a hand. "Mommy doesn't see me. I can see her, but she doesn't see me. Oh! Mommy works hard! She works hard at her desk!"

Eddie's smile abruptly left his face. His face froze for a second in a comic rubbery absence of expression; then his eyes widened in terror and his mouth went loose and wobbly.

"What happened?" Harry's mouth had gone dry.

"No, Mommy!" Harry wailed. "Don't, Mommy! I wasn't spying. I wasn't, I promise—" His words broke off into a screech. "NO, MOMMY! DON'T! DON'T, MOMMY!" Eddie jumped upward, sending his chair flying back, and ran blindly toward the rear of the attic. Harry's head rang with Eddie's screeches. He heard a sharp *crack!* of wood breaking, but only as a small part of all the noise Eddie was making as he charged around the attic. Eddie had run into a tangle of hanging dresses, spun around, enmeshing himself deeper in the dresses, and was now tearing himself away from the web of dresses, pulling some of them off the rack. A long-sleeved purple dress with an enormous lace collar had draped itself around Eddie like a ghostly dance partner, and another dress, this of dull velvet, snaked around his right leg. Eddie screamed and yanked himself away from the tangle. The entire rack of clothes wobbled and then went over in a mad jangle of sound.

"NO!" he screeched. "HELP!" Eddie ran straight into a big wooden beam marking off one of the eaves, bounced off, and came windmilling toward Harry. Harry knew his brother could not see him.

"Eddie, stop," he said, but Eddie was past hearing him. Harry tried to make Eddie stop by wrapping his arms around him, but Eddie slammed right into him, hitting Harry's chest with a shoulder and knocking his head painfully against Harry's chin; Harry's arms closed on nothing and his eyes lost focus, and Eddie went crashing into the tilting mirror. The mirror yawned over sideways. Harry saw it tilt with dreamlike slowness toward the floor, then in an eye blink drop and crash. Broken glass sprayed across the attic floor.

"STOP!" Harry yelled. "STAND STILL, EDDIE!"

Eddie came to rest. The ripped and dirty dress of dull red velvet still clung to his right leg. Blood oozed down his temple from an ugly cut above his eye. He was breathing hard, releasing air in little whimpering exhalations.

"Holy SHIT," Harry said, looking around the attic. In only a few seconds Eddie had managed to create what looked at first like absolute devastation. Maryrose's ancient dresses lay tangled in a heap of dusty fabrics from which wire hangers skeletally protruded; gray Eddie-sized footprints lay like a pattern over the muted explosions of colors the dresses now created. When the rack had gone over, it had knocked a section the size of a dinner plate out of a round wooden coffee table Maryrose had particularly prized for its being made from a single section of teak—"a single section of *teak*, the rarest wood in all the world, all the way from Ceylon!" The much-prized mirror lay in hundreds of glittering pieces across the attic floor. With growing horror, Harry saw that the wooden frame had cracked like a bone, showing a bone-pale, shockingly white fracture in the expanse of dark stain.

Harry's blood tipped within his body, nearly tipping him with it, like the mirror. "Oh God oh God oh God."

He turned slowly around. Eddie stood blinking two feet to his side, wiping ineffectually at the blood running from his forehead and now covering most of his left cheek. He looked like an Indian in war paint—a defeated, lost Indian, for his eyes were dim and his head turned aimlessly from side to side.

A few feet from Eddie lay the chair in which he had been sitting. One of its thin curved wooden arms lay beside it, crudely severed. It looked like an insect's leg, Harry thought, like a toy gun.

For a moment Harry thought that his face too was red with blood. He wiped his hand over his forehead and looked at his glistening palm. It was only sweat. His heart beat like a bell. Beside him Eddie said, "Aaah . . . what . . . ?" The injury to his head had brought him out of the trance.

The dresses were ruined, stepped on, tangled, torn. The mirror was broken. The table had been mutilated. Maryrose's chair lay on its side like a murder victim, its severed arm ending in a bristle of snapped ligaments.

"My head *hurts,*" Eddie said in a weak, trembling voice. "What happened? Ah! I'm all blood! I'm all blood, Harry!"

"You're all blood, you're all blood?" Harry shouted at him. "Everything's *all blood,* you dummy! Look around!" He did not recognize his own voice, which sounded high and tinny and seemed to be coming from somewhere else. Little Eddie took an aimless step away from him, and Harry wanted to fly at him, to pound his bloody head into a pancake, to destroy him, smash him . . .

Eddie held up his bloodstained palm and stared at it. He wiped it vaguely across the front of his T-shirt and took another wandering step. "I'm ascared, Harry," his tiny voice uttered.

"Look what you did!" Harry screamed. "You wrecked everything! Damn it! What do you think is going to happen to us?"

"What's Mom going to do?" Eddie asked in a voice only slightly above a whisper.

"You don't know?" Harry yelled. "You're dead!"

Eddie started to weep.

Harry bunched his hands into fists and clamped his eyes shut. They were both dead, that was the real truth. Harry opened his eyes, which felt hot and oddly heavy, and stared at his sobbing, red-smeared, useless little brother. "Blue rose," he said.

10.

Little Eddie's hands fell to his sides. His chin dropped, and his mouth fell open. Blood ran in a smooth wide band down the left side of his face, dipped under the line of his jaw, and continued down his neck and into his T-shirt. Pooled blood in his left eyebrow dripped steadily onto the floor, as if from a faucet.

"You are going deep *asleep*," Harry said. Where was the hatpin? He looked back to the single standing chair and saw the mother-of-pearl head glistening on the floor near it. "Your whole body is *numb*." He moved over to the pin, bent down, and picked it up. The metal shaft felt warm in his fingers. "You can feel no *pain*." He went back to Little Eddie. "Nothing can *hurt* you." Harry's breath seemed to be breathing itself, forcing itself into his throat in hot harsh shallow pants, then expelling itself out.

"Did you *hear* me, Little Eddie?"

In his gravelling, slow-moving hypnotized voice, Little Eddie said, "I heard you."

"And you can feel no *pain*?"

"I can feel no pain."

Harry drew his arm back, the point of the hatpin extended forward from his fist, and then jerked his hand forward as hard as he could and stuck the pin into Eddie's abdomen right through the blood-soaked T-shirt. He exhaled sharply, and tasted a sour misery on his breath.

"You don't feel a thing."

"I don't feel a thing."

Harry opened his right hand and drove his palm against the head of the pin, hammering it in another few inches. Little Eddie looked like a voodoo doll. A kind of sparkling light surrounded him. Harry gripped the head of the pin with his thumb and forefinger and yanked it out. He held it up and inspected it. Glittering light surrounded the pin too. The long shaft was painted with blood. Harry slipped the point into his mouth and closed his lips around the warm metal.

He saw himself, a man in another life, standing in a row with men like himself in a bleak gray landscape defined by barbed wire. Emaciated people in rags shuffled up toward them and spat on their clothes. The smells of dead flesh and of burning flesh hung in the air. Then the vision was gone, and Little Eddie stood before him again, surrounded by layers of glittering light.

Harry grimaced or grinned, he could not have told the difference, and drove his long spike deep into Eddie's stomach.

Eddie uttered a small *oof*.

"You don't feel anything, Eddie," Harry whispered. "You feel good all over. You never felt better in your life."

"Never felt better in my life."

Harry slowly pulled out the pin and cleaned it with his fingers.

He was about to remember every single thing anyone had ever told him about Tommy Golz.

"Now you're going to play a funny, funny game," he said. "This is called the Tommy Golz game because it's going to keep you safe from Mrs. Franken. Are you ready?" Harry carefully slid the pin into the fabric of his shirt collar, all the while watching Eddie's slack blood-streaked person. Vibrating bands of light beat rhythmically and steadily about Eddie's face.

"Ready," Eddie said.

"I'm going to give you your instructions now, Little Eddie. Pay attention to everything I say and it's all going to be okay. Everything's going to be okay—as long as you play the game exactly the way I tell you. You understand, don't you?"

"I understand."

"Tell me what I just said."

"Everything's gonna be okay as long as I play the game exactly the way you tell me." A dollop of blood slid off Eddie's eyebrow and splashed onto his already soaked T-shirt.

"Good, Eddie. Now the first thing you do is fall down—not now, when I tell you. I'm going to give you all the instructions, and then I'm going to count backwards from ten, and when I get to *one,* you'll start playing the game. Okay?"

"Okay."

"So first you fall down, Little Eddie. You fall down real hard. Then comes the fun part of the game. You bang your head on the floor. You start to go crazy. You twitch, and you bang your hands and feet on the floor. You do that for a long time. I guess you do that until you count to about a hundred. You foam at the mouth, you twist all over the place. You get real stiff, and then you get real loose, and then you get real stiff, and then real loose again, and all this time you're banging your head and your hands and feet on the floor, and you're twisting all over the place. Then when you finish counting to a hundred, in your head, you do the last thing. You swallow your tongue. And that's the game. When you swallow your tongue you're the winner. And then nothing bad can happen to you, and Mrs. Franken won't be able to hurt you ever ever ever."

Harry stopped talking. His hands were shaking. After a second he realized that his insides were shaking too. He raised his trembling fingers to his shirt collar and felt the hatpin.

"Tell me how you win the game, Little Eddie. What's the last thing you do?"

"I swallow my tongue."

"Right. And then Mrs. Franken and Mom will never be able to hurt you, because you won the game."

"Good," said Little Eddie. The glittering light shimmered about him.

"Okay, we'll start playing right now," Harry said. "Ten." He went toward the attic steps. "Nine." He reached the steps. "Eight."

He went down one step. "Seven." Harry descended another two steps. "Six." When he went down another two steps, he called up in a slightly louder voice, "Five."

Now his head was beneath the level of the attic floor, and he could not see Little Eddie anymore. All he could hear was the soft, occasional plop of liquid hitting the floor.

"Four."

"Three."

"Two." He was now at the door to the attic steps. Harry opened the door, stepped through it, breathed hard, and shouted "One!" up the stairs.

He heard a thud, and then quickly closed the door behind him.

Harry went across the hall and into the dormitory bedroom. There seemed to be a strange absence of light in the hallway. For a second he saw—was sure he saw—a line of dark trees across a wall of barbed wire. Harry closed this door behind him too, and went to his narrow bed and sat down. He could feel blood beating in his face; his eyes seemed oddly warm, as if they were heated by filaments. Harry slowly, almost reverently extracted the hatpin from his collar and set it on his pillow. "A hundred," he said. "Ninety-nine, ninety-eight, ninety-seven, ninety-six, ninety-five, ninety-four . . . "

When he had counted down to "one," he stood up and left the bedroom. He went quickly downstairs without looking at the door behind which lay the attic steps. On the ground floor he slipped into Maryrose's bedroom, crossed over to her desk, and slid open the bottom right-hand drawer. From the drawer he took a velvet-covered box. This he opened, and jabbed the hatpin into the ball of material, studded with pins of all sizes and descriptions, from which he had taken it. He replaced the box in the drawer, pushed the drawer into the desk, and quickly left the room and went upstairs.

Back in his own bedroom, Harry took off his clothes and climbed into his bed. His face still burned.

• • •

He must have fallen asleep very quickly, because the next thing he knew Albert was slamming his way into the bedroom and tossing his clothes and boots all over the place. "You asleep?" Albert asked. "You left the attic light on, you fuckin' dummies, but if you think I'm gonna save your fuckin' asses and go up and turn it off, you're even stupider than you look."

Harry was careful not to move a finger, not to move even a hair.

He held his breath while Albert threw himself onto his bed, and when Albert's breathing relaxed and slowed, Harry followed his big brother into sleep. He did not awaken again until he heard his father half screeching, half sobbing up in the attic, and that was very late at night.

11.

Sonny came from Fort Sill, George all the way from Germany. Between them, they held up a sodden Edgar Beevers at the gravesite while a minister Harry had never seen before read from a Bible as cracked and rubbed as an old brown shoe. Between his two older sons, Harry's father looked bent and ancient, a skinny old man only steps from the grave himself. Sonny and George despised their father, Harry saw—they held him up on sufferance, in part because they had chipped in thirty dollars apiece to buy him a suit and did not want to see it collapse with its owner inside into the lumpy clay of the graveyard. His whiskers glistened in the sun, and moisture shone beneath his eyes and at the corners of his mouth. He had been shaking too severely for either Sonny or George to shave him, and had been capable of moving in a straight line only after George let him take a couple of long swallows from a leather-covered flask he took out of his duffel bag.

The minister uttered a few sage words on the subject of epilepsy.

Sonny and George looked as solid as brick walls in their uniforms, like prison guards or actual prisons themselves. Next to them, Albert looked shrunken and unfinished. Albert wore the green plaid sport jacket in which he had graduated from the eighth grade, and his wrists hung prominent and red four inches below the bottoms of the sleeves. His motorcycle boots were visible beneath his light gray trousers, but, like the green jacket, had lost their flash. Like Albert, too. Ever since the discovery of Eddie's body, Albert had gone around the house looking as if he'd just bitten off the end of his tongue and was trying to decide whether or not to spit it out. He never looked anybody in the eye, and he rarely spoke. Albert acted as though a gigantic padlock had been fixed to the middle of his chest and *he* was damned if he'd ever take it off. He had not asked Sonny or George a single question about the Army. Every now and then he would utter a remark about the gas station so toneless that it suffocated any reply.

Harry looked at Albert standing beside their mother, kneading his hands together and keeping his eyes fixed as if by decree on the square foot of ground before him. Albert glanced over at Harry, knew he was being looked at, and did what to Harry was an extraordinary thing. Albert *froze.* All expression drained out of his face, and his hands locked immovably together. He looked as little able to see or hear as a statue. *He's that way because he told Little Eddie that he wished he would die,* Harry thought for the tenth or eleventh time since he had realized this, and with undiminished awe. Then he was lying?. Harry wondered. And if he really did wish that Little Eddie would drop dead, why isn't he happy now? Didn't he get what he wanted? Albert would never spit out that piece of his tongue, Harry thought, watching his brother blink slowly and sightlessly toward the ground.

Harry shifted his gaze uneasily to his father, still propped up between George and Sonny, heard that the minister was finally reaching the end of his speech, and took a fast look at his mother. Maryrose was standing very straight in a black dress and black sunglasses, holding the straps of her bag in front of her with both hands. Except for the color of her clothes, she could have been a spectator at a tennis match. Harry knew by the way she was holding her face that she was wishing she could smoke. Dying for a cigarette, he thought, ha-ha, the Monster Mash, it's a graveyard smash.

The minister finished speaking, and made a rhetorical gesture with his hands. The coffin sank on ropes into the rough earth. Harry's father began to weep loudly. First George, then Sonny, picked up large damp shovel-marked pieces of the clay and dropped them on the coffin. Edgar Beevers nearly fell in after his own tiny clod, but George contemptuously swung him back. Maryrose marched forward, bent and picked up a random piece of clay with thumb and forefinger as if using tweezers, dropped it, and turned away before it struck. Albert fixed his eyes on Harry—his own clod had split apart in his hand and crumbled away between his fingers. Harry shook his head *no*. He did not want to drop dirt on Eddie's coffin and make that noise. He did not want to look at Eddie's coffin again. There was enough dirt around to do the job without him hitting that metal box like he was trying to ring Eddie's doorbell. He stepped back.

"Mom says we have to get back to the house," Albert said.

Maryrose lit up as soon as they got into the single black car they had rented through the funeral parlor, and breathed out acrid smoke over everybody crowded into the back seat. The car backed into a narrow graveyard lane, and turned down the main road toward the front gates.

In the front seat, next to the driver, Edgar Beevers drooped sideways and leaned his head against the window, leaving a blurred streak on the glass.

"How in the name of hell could Little Eddie have epilepsy without anybody knowing it?" George asked.

Albert stiffened and stared out the window.

"Well, that's epilepsy," Maryrose said. "Eddie could have gone on for years without having an attack." That she worked in a hospital always gave her remarks of this sort a unique gravity, almost as if she were a doctor.

"Must have been some fit," Sonny said, squeezed into place between Harry and Albert.

"Grand mal," Maryrose said, and took another hungry drag on her cigarette.

"Poor little bastard," George said. "Sorry, Mom."

"I know you're in the armed forces, and armed forces people speak very freely, but I wish you would not use that kind of language."

Harry, jammed into Sonny's rock-hard side, felt his brother's body twitch with a hidden laugh, though Sonny's face did not alter.

"I said I was sorry, Mom," George said.

"Yes. Driver! Driver!" Maryrose was leaning forward, reaching one claw to tap the chauffeur's shoulder. "Livermore is the next right. Do you know South Sixth Street?"

"I'll get you there," the driver said.

This is not my family, Harry thought. I came from somewhere else and my rules are different from theirs.

• • •

His father mumbled something inaudible as soon as they got in the door and disappeared into his curtained-off cubicle. Maryrose put her sunglasses in her purse and marched into the kitchen to warm the coffee cake and the macaroni casserole, both made that morning, in the oven. Sonny and George wandered into the living room and sat down on opposite ends of the couch. They did not look at each other—George picked up a *Reader's Digest* from the table and began leading through it backward, and Sonny folded his hands in his lap and stared at his thumbs. Albert's footsteps plodded up the stairs, crossed the landing, and went into the dormitory bedroom.

"What's she in the kitchen for?" Sonny asked, speaking to his hands. "Nobody's going to come. Nobody ever comes here, because she never wanted them to."

"Albert's taking this kind of hard, Harry," George said. He propped the magazine against the stiff folds of his uniform and looked across the room at his little brother. Harry had seated himself beside the door, as out of the way as possible. George's attentions rather frightened him, though George behaved with consistent kindness ever since his arrival two days after Eddie's death. His crew cut still bristled and he could still break rocks with his chin, but some violent demon seemed to have left him. "You think he'll be okay?"

"Him? Sure." Harry titled his head, grimaced.

"He didn't see Little Eddie first, did he?"

"No, Dad did," Harry said. "He saw the light on in the attic when he came home, I guess. Albert went up there, though. I guess there was so much blood Dad thought somebody broke in and killed Eddie. But he just bumped his head, and that's where the blood came from."

"Head wounds bleed like bastards," Sonny said. "A guy hit me with a bottle once in Tokyo. I thought I was gonna bleed to death right there."

"And Mom's stuff got all messed up?" George asked quietly.

This time Sonny looked up.

"Pretty much, I guess. The dress rack got knocked down. Dad cleaned up what he could, the next day. One of the cane-back chairs got broke, and a hunk got knocked out of the teak table. And the mirror got broken into a million pieces."

Sonny shook his head and a made a soft whistling sound through his pursed lips.

"She's a tough old gal," George said. "I hear her coming, though, so we have to stop, Harry. But we can talk tonight."

Harry nodded.

12.

After dinner that night, when Maryrose had gone to bed—the hospital had given her two nights off—Harry sat across the kitchen table from a George who clearly had something to say. Sonny had polished off a six-pack by himself in front of the television and gone up to the dormitory bedroom by himself. Albert had disappeared shortly after dinner, and their father had never emerged from his cubicle beside the junk room.

"I'm glad Pete Petrosian came over," George said. "He's a good old boy. Ate two helpings too."

Harry was startled by George's use of their neighbor's first name—he was not even sure that he had ever heard it before.

Mr. Petrosian had been their only caller that afternoon. Harry had seen that his mother was grateful that someone had come, and despite her preparations wanted no more company after Mr. Petrosian had left.

"Think I'll get a beer, that is if Sonny didn't drink it all," George said, and stood up and opened the fridge. His uniform looked as if it had been painted on his body, and his muscles bulged and moved like a horse's. "Two left," he said. "Good thing you're underage." George popped the caps off both bottles and came back to the table. He winked at Harry, then tilted the first bottle to his lips and took a good swallow. "So what the devil was Little Eddie doing up there anyhow? Trying on dresses?"

"I don't know," Harry said. "I was asleep."

"Hell, I know I kind of lost touch with Little Eddie, but I got the impression he was scared of his own shadow. I'm surprised he had the nerve to go up there and mess around with Mom's precious stuff."

"Yeah," Harry said. "Me too."

"You didn't happen to go with him, did you?" George tilted the bottle to his mouth and winked at Harry again.

Harry just looked back. He could feel his face getting hot.

"I was just thinking maybe you saw it happen to Little Eddie, and got too scared to tell anybody. Nobody would be mad at you, Harry. Nobody would blame you for anything. You couldn't know how to help someone who's having an epileptic fit. Little Eddie swallowed his tongue. Even if you'd been standing next to him when he did it and had the presence of mind to call an ambulance, he would have died before it got here. Unless you knew what was wrong and how to correct it. Which nobody would expect you to know, not in a million years. Nobody'd blame you for anything, Harry, not even Mom."

"I was asleep," Harry said.

"Okay, okay. I just wanted you to know."

They sat in silence for a time, the both spoke at once.

"Did you know—"

"We had this—"

"Sorry," George said. "Go on."

"Did you know that Dad used to be in the Army? In World War II?"

"Yeah, I knew that. Of course I knew that."

"Did you know that he committed the perfect murder once?"

"*What?*"

"Dad committed the perfect murder. When he was at Dachau, that death camp."

"Oh Christ, is that what you're talking about? You got a funny way of seeing things, Harry. He shot an enemy who was trying to escape. That's not murder, it's war. There's one hell of a big difference."

"I'd like to see war someday," Harry said. "I'd like to be in the Army, like you and Dad."

"Hold your horses, hold your horses," George said, smiling now. "That's sort of one of the things I wanted to talk to you about." He set down the beer bottle, cradled his hands around it, and tilted his head to look at Harry. This was obviously going to be serious. "You know, I used to be crazy and stupid, that's the only way to put it. I used to look for fights. I had a chip on my shoulder the size of a house, and pounding some dipshit into a coma was my idea of a great time. The Army did me a lot of good. It made me grow up. But I don't think you need that, Harry. You're too smart for that—if you have to go, you go, but out of all of us, you're the one who could really amount to something in the world. You could be a doctor. Or a lawyer. You ought to get the best education you can, Harry. What you have to do is stay out of trouble and get to college."

"Oh, college," Harry said.

"Listen to me, Harry. I make pretty good money, and I got nothing to spend it on. I'm not going to get married and have kids, that's for sure. So I want to make you a proposition. If you keep your nose clean and make it through high school, I'll help you out with college. Maybe you can get a scholarship—I think you're smart enough, Harry, and a scholarship would be great. But either way, I'll see you make it through." George emptied the first bottle, set it down, and gave Harry a quizzical look. "Let's get one person in this family off on the right track. What do you say?"

"I guess I better keep reading," Harry said.

"I hope you'll read your ass off, little buddy," George said, and picked up the second bottle of beer.

13.

The day after Sonny left, George put all of Eddie's toys and clothes into a box and squeezed the box into the junk room; two days later, George took a bus to New York so he could get his flight to Munich from Idlewild. An hour before he caught his bus, George walked Harry up to Big John's and stuffed him full of hamburgers and French fries and said, "You'll probably miss Eddie a lot, won't you?" "I guess," Harry said, but the truth was that Eddie was now only a vacancy, a blank space. Sometimes a door would close and Harry would know that Little Eddie had just come in; but when he turned to look, he saw only emptiness. George's question, asked a week ago, was the last time Harry had heard anyone pronounce his brother's name.

In the seven days since the charmed afternoon at Big John's and the departure on a southbound bus of George Beevers, everything seemed to have gone back to the way it was before, but Harry knew that really everything had changed. There had been a loose, divided family of five, two parents and three sons. Now they seemed to be a family of three, and Harry thought that the actual truth was that the family had shrunk down to two, himself and his mother.

Edgar Beevers had left home—he too was an absence. After two visits from policemen who parked their cars right outside the house, after listening to his mother's muttered expressions of disgust, after the spectacle of his pale, bleary, but sober and clean-shaven father trying over and over to knot a necktie in front of the bathroom mirror, Harry finally accepted that his father had been caught shoplifting. His father had to go to court, and he was scared. His hands shook so uncontrollably that he could not shave himself, and in the end Maryrose had to knot his tie—doing it in one, two, three quick movements as brutal as the descent of a knife, never removing the cigarette from her mouth.

Grief-stricken Area Man Forgiven of Shoplifting Charge, read the headline over the little story in the evening newspaper which at last explained his father's crime. Edgar Beevers had been stopped on the sidewalk outside the Livermore Avenue National Tea, T-bone steaks hidden inside his shirt and a bottle of Rheingold beer in each of his front pockets. He had stolen two steaks! He had put beer bottles in his front pockets! This made Harry feel like he was sweating inside. The judge had sent him home, but home was not where he went. For a short time, Harry thought, his father had hung out on Oldtown Road, Palmyra's Skid Row, and slept in vacant lots with winos and bums. (Then a woman was supposed to have taken him in.)

Albert was another mystery. It was as though a creature from outer space had taken him over and was using his body, like *Invasion of the Body Snatchers*. Albert looked like he thought somebody was always standing behind him, watching every move he made. He was still carrying around that piece of his tongue, and pretty soon, Harry thought, he'd get so used to it that he would forget he had it.

Three days after George left Palmyra, Albert had actually tagged along after Harry on the way to Big John's. Harry had turned around on the sidewalk and seen Albert in his black jeans and grease-blackened T-shirt halfway down the block, shoving his hands in his pockets and looking hard at the ground. That was Albert's way of pretending to be invisible. The next time he turned around, Albert growled, "Keep walking."

Harry went to work on the pinball machine as soon as he got inside Big John's. Albert slunk in a few minutes later and went straight to the counter. He took one of the stained paper menus from a stack squeezed in beside a napkin dispenser and inspected it as if he had never seen it before.

"Hey, let me introduce you guys," said Big John, leaning against the far side of the counter. Like Albert, he wore black jeans and motorcycle boots, but his dark hair, daringly for the nineteen-fifties, fell over his ears. Beneath his stained white apron he wore a long-sleeved black shirt with a pattern of tiny azure palm trees. "You two are the Beevers boys, Harry and Bucky. Say hello to each other, fellows."

Bucky Beaver was a toothy rodent in an Ipana television commercial. Albert blushed, still grimly staring at his menu sheet.

"Call me Beans," Harry said, and felt Albert's gaze shift wonderingly to him.

"Beans and Bucky, the Beevers boys," Big John said. "Well, Buck, what'll you have?"

"Hamburger, fries, shake," Albert said.

Big John half turned and yelled the order through the hatch to Mama Mary's kitchen. For a time the three of them stood in uneasy silence. Then Big John said, "Heard your old man found a new place to hang his hat. His new girlfriend is a real pistol, I heard. Spent some time in County Hospital. On account of she picked up little messages from outer space on the good old Philco. You hear that?"

"He's gonna come home real soon," Harry said. "He doesn't have any new girlfriend. He's staying with an old friend. She's a rich lady and she wants to help him out because she knows he had a lot of trouble and she's going to get him a real good job, and then he'll come home, and we'll be able to move to a better house and everything."

He never even saw Albert move, but Albert materialized beside him. Fury, rage, and misery distorted his face. Harry had time to cry out only once, and then Albert slammed a fist into his chest and knocked him backwards into the pinball machine.

"I bet that felt real good," Harry said, unable to keep down his own rage. "I bet you'd like to kill me, huh? Huh, Albert? How about that?"

Albert moved backward two paces and lowered his hands, already looking impassive, locked into himself.

For a second in which his breath failed and dazzling light filled his eyes, Harry saw Little Eddie's slack, trusting face before him. Then Big John came up from nowhere with a big hamburger and a mount of French fries on a plate and said, "Down, boys. Time for Bucky here to tackle his dinner."

That night Albert said nothing at all to Harry as they lay in their beds. Neither did he fall asleep. Harry knew that for most of the night Albert just closed his eyes and faked it, like a possum in trouble. Harry tried to stay awake long enough to see when Albert's fake sleep melted into the real thing, but he sank into dreams before that.

• • •

He was rushing down the stony corridors of a castle past suits of armor and torches guttering in sconces. His bladder was bursting, he had to let go, he could not hold it more than another few seconds . . . at last he came to the open bathroom door and ran into that splendid gleaming place. He began to tug at his zipper, and looked around for the butler and the row of marble urinals. Then he froze. Little Eddie was standing before him, not the uniformed butler. Blood ran in a gauzy streak from a gash high on his forehead over his cheek and right down his neck, neat as paint. Little Eddie was waving frantically at Harry, his eyes bright and hysterical, his mouth working soundlessly because he had swallowed his tongue.

Harry sat up straight in bed, about to scream, then realized that the bedroom was all around him and Little Eddie was gone. He hurried downstairs to the bathroom.

14.

At two o'clock the next afternoon Harry Beevers had to pee again, and just as badly, but this time he was a long way from the bathroom across the junk room and his father's old cubicle. Harry was standing in the humid sunlight across the street from 45 Oldtown Way. This short street connected the bums, transient hotels, bars, and seedy movie theaters of Oldtown Road with the more respectable hotels, department stores, and restaurants of Palmyra Avenue—the real downtown. 45 Oldtown Way was a four-story brick tenement with an exoskeleton of fire escapes. Black iron bars covered the ground-floor windows. On one side of 45 Oldtown Way were the large soap-smeared windows of a bankrupted shoe store, on the other a vacant lot where loose bricks and broken bottles nestled amongst dandelions and tall Queen Anne's lace. Harry's father lived in that building now. Everybody else knew it, and since Big John had told him, now Harry knew it too.

He jigged from leg to leg, waiting for a woman to come out through the front door. It was as chipped and peeling as his own, and a broken fanlight sat drunkenly atop it. Harry had checked the row of dented mailboxes on the brick wall just outside the door for his father's name, but none bore any names at all. Big John hadn't known the name of the woman who had taken Harry's father, but he said that she was large, black-haired, and crazy, and that she had two children in foster care. About half an hour ago a dark-haired woman had come through the door, but Harry had not followed her because she had not looked especially large to him. Now he was beginning to have doubts. What did Big John mean by "large" anyhow? As big as he was? And how could you tell if someone was crazy? Did it show? Maybe he should have followed that woman. This thought made him even more anxious, and he squeezed his legs together.

His father was in that building now, he thought. Harry thought of his father lying on an unmade bed, his brown winter coat around him, his hat pulled low on his forehead like Lepke Buchalter's, drawing on a cigarette, looking moodily out the window.

Then he had to pee so urgently that he could not have held it in more form than a few seconds, and trotted across the street and into the vacant lot. Near the back fence the tall weeds gave him some shelter from the street. He frantically unzipped and let the braided yellow stream splash into a nest of broken bricks. Harry looked up at the side of the building beside him. It looked very tall, and seemed to be tilting slightly toward him. The four windows on each floor looked back down at him, blank and fatherless. Just as he was tugging at his zipper, he heard the front door of the building slam shut.

His heart slammed too. Harry hunkered down behind the tall white weeds. Anxiety that she might walk the other way, toward downtown, made him twine his fingers together and bend his fingers back. If he waited about five seconds, he figured, he'd know she was going toward Palmyra Avenue and would be able to get across the lot in time to see which way she turned. His knuckles cracked. He felt like a soldier hiding in the forest, like a murder weapon.

He raised up on his toes and got ready to dash back across the street, because an empty grocery cart closely followed by a moving belly with a tiny head and basketball shoes, a cigar tilted in its mouth like a flag, appeared past the front of the building. He could go back and wait across the street. Harry settled down and watched the stomach go down the sidewalk past him. Then a shadow separated itself from the street side of the fat man, and the shadow became a black-haired woman in a long loose dress now striding past the grocery cart. She shook back her head, and Harry saw that she was tall as a queen and that her skin was darker than olive. Deep lines cut through her cheeks. It had to be the woman who had taken his father. Her long rapid strides had taken her well past the fat man's grocery cart. Harry ran across the rubble of the lot and began to follow her up the sidewalk.

His father's woman walked in a hard, determined way. She stepped down into the street to get around groups too slow for her. At the Oldtown Road corner she wove her way through a group of saggy-bottomed men passing around a bottle in a paper bag and cut in front of two black children dribbling a basketball up in the street. She was on the move, and Harry had to hurry along to keep her in sight.

"I bet you don't believe me," he said to himself, practicing, and skirted the group of winos on the corner. He picked up his speed until he was nearly trotting. The two black kids with the basketball ignored him as he kept pace with them, then went on ahead. Far up the block, the tall woman with bouncing black hair marched right past a flashing neon sign in a bar window. Her bottom moved back and forth in the loose dress, surprisingly big whenever it bulged out of the fabric of the dress; her back seemed as long as a lion's. "What would you say if I told you . . . " Harry said to himself.

A block and a half ahead, the woman turned on her heel and went through the door of the A&P store. Harry sprinted the rest of the way, pushed the yellow wooden door marked ENTER, and walked into the dense, humid air of the grocery shop. Other A&P stores may have been air-conditioned, but not the little shop on Oldtown Road.

What was foster care anyway? Did you get money if you gave away your children?

A good person's children would never be in foster care, Harry thought. He saw the woman turning into the third aisle past the cash register. He saw with a small shock that she was taller than his father. If I told you, you might not believe me. He went slowly around the corner of the aisle. She was standing on the pale wooden floor about fifteen feet in front of him, carrying a wire basket in one hand. He stepped forward. What I have to say might seem. . . . For good luck, he touched the hatpin inserted into the bottom of his collar. She was staring at a row of brightly colored bags of potato chips. Harry cleared his throat. The woman reached down and picked up a big bag and put it in the basket.

"Excuse me," Harry said.

She turned her head to look at him. Her face was as wide as it was long, and in the mellow light from the store's low-wattage bulbs her skin seemed a very light shade of brown. Harry knew he was meeting an equal. She looked like she could do magic, as if she could shoot fire and sparks out of her fierce black eyes.

"I bet you don't believe me," he said, "but a kid can hypnotize people just as good as an adult."

"What's that?"

His rehearsed words now sounded crazy to him, but he stuck to his script. "A kid can hypnotize people. I can hypnotize people. Do you believe that?"

"I don't think I even care," she said, and wheeled away toward to the rear of the aisle.

"I bet you don't think I could hypnotize you," Harry said.

"Kid, get lost."

Harry suddenly knew that if he kept talking about hypnotism the woman would turn down the next aisle and ignore him no matter what he said, or else begin to speak in a very loud voice about seeing the manager. "My name is Harry Beevers," he said to her back. "Edgar Beevers is my dad."

She stopped and turned around and looked expressionlessly into his face.

Harry dizzyingly saw a wall of barbed wire before him, a dark green wall of trees at the other end of a barren field.

"I wonder if you maybe call him Beans," he said.

"Oh, great," she said. "That's just great. So you're one of his boys. Terrific. *Beans* wants potato chips, what do you want?"

"I want you to fall down and bang your head and swallow your tongue and *die* and get buried and have people drop dirt on you," Harry said. The woman's mouth fell open. "Then I want you to puff up with *gas*. I want you to *rot*. I want you to turn green and *black*. I want your *skin* to slide off your bones."

"You're crazy!" the woman shouted at him. "Your whole family's crazy! Do you think your mother wants him anymore?"

"My father shot us in the back," Harry said, and turned and bolted down the aisle for the door.

When he got outside he began to trot down seedy Oldtown Road. When he came to Oldtown Way he turned left. When he ran past number 45, he looked at every blank window. His face, his hands, his whole body felt hot and wet. Soon he had a stitch in his side. Harry blinked, and saw a dark line of trees, a wall of barbed wire before him. At the top of Oldtown Way he turned into Palmyra Avenue. From there he could continue running past Alouette's boarded-up windows, past all the stores old and new, to the corner of Livermore, and from there, he only now realized, to the little house that belonged to Mr. Petrosian.

15.

On a sweltering midafternoon eleven years later at a camp in the Central Highlands of Vietnam, Lieutenant Harry Beevers closed the flap of his tent against the mosquitoes and sat on the edge of his temporary bunk to write a long-delayed letter back to Pat Caldwell, the young woman he wanted to marry—and to whom he would be married for a time, after his return from the war to New York State.

This is what he wrote, after frequent crossings-out and hesitations. Harry later destroyed the letter.

Dear Pat:

First of all I want you to know how much I miss you, my darling, and that if I ever get out of this beautiful and terrible country, which I am going to do, that I am going to chase you mercilessly and unrelentingly until you say that you'll marry me. Maybe in the euphoria of relief (YES!!!), I have the future all worked out, Pat, and you're a big part of it. I have eighty-six days until DEROS, when they pat me on the head and put me on that big bird out of here. Now that my record is clear again, I have no doubts that Columbia Law School will take me in. As you know, my law board scores were pretty respectable (modest me!) when I took them at Adelphi. I'm pretty sure I could even get into Harvard Law, but I settled on Columbia because then we could both be in New York.

My brother George has already told me that he will help out with whatever money I—you and I—will need. George put me through Adelphi.

290

I don't think you knew this. In fact, nobody knew this. When I look back, in college I was such a jerk. I wanted everybody to think my family was well-to-do, or at least middle-class. The truth is, we were damn poor, which I think makes my accomplishments all the more noteworthy, all the more loveworthy!

You see, this experience, even with all the ugly and self-doubting and humiliating moments, has done me a lot of good. I was right to come here, even though I had no idea what it was really like. I think I needed the experience of war to complete me, and I tell you this even though I know that you will detest any such idea. In fact, I have to tell you that a big part of me loves being here, and that in some way, even with all this trouble, this year will always be one of the high points of my life. Pat, as you see, I'm determined to be honest—to be an honest man. If I'm going to be a lawyer, I ought to be honest, don't you think? (Or maybe the reverse is the reality!) One thing that has meant a lot to me here has been what I can only call the close comradeship of my friends and my men—I actually like the grunts more than the usual officer types, which of course means that I get more loyalty and better performance from my men than the usual lieutenant. Some day I'd like you to meet Mike Poole and Tim Underhill and Pumo the Puma and the most amazing of all, M. O. Dengler, who of course was involved with me in the Ia Thuc cave incident. These guys stuck by me. I even have a nickname, "Beans." They call me "Beans" Beevers, and I like it.

There was no way my court-martial could have really put me in any trouble, because all the facts, and my own men, were on my side. Besides, could you see me actually killing children? This is Vietnam and you kill people, that's what we're doing here—we kill Charlies. But we don't kill babies and children. Not even in the heat of wartime—and Ia Thuc was pretty hot!

Well, this is my way of letting you know that at the court-martial of course I received a complete and utter vindication. Dengler did too. There were even unofficial mutterings about giving us medals for all the BS we put up with for the past six weeks—including that amazing story in Time *magazine. Before people start yelling about atrocities, they ought to have all the facts straight. Fortunately, last week's magazines go out with the rest of the trash.*

Besides, I already knew too much about what death does to people.

I never told you that I once had a little brother named Edward. When I was ten, my little brother wandered up into the top floor of our house one night and suffered a fatal epileptic fit. This event virtually destroyed my family. It led directly to my father's leaving home. (He had been a hero in WWII, something else I never told you.) It deeply changed, I would say even damaged, my older brother Albert. Albert tried to enlist in 1964, but they wouldn't take him because they said he was psychologically unfit. My mom too almost came apart for a while. She used to go up in the attic and cry and wouldn't come down. So you could say that my family was pretty well destroyed, or ruined, or whatever you want to call it, by a sudden death. I took it, and my dad's desertion, pretty hard myself. You don't get over these things easily.

The court-martial lasted exactly four hours. Big deal, hey?—as we used to say back in Palmyra. We used to have a neighbor named Pete Petrosian who said things like that, and against what must have been million-to-one odds, who died exactly the same way my brother did, about two weeks after—lightning really did strike twice. I guess it's dumb to think about him now, but maybe one thing war does is to make you conversant with death. How it happens, what it does to people, what it means, how all the dead in your life are somehow united, joined, part of your eternal family. This is a profound feeling, Pat, and no damn whipped-up failed court-martial can touch it. If there were any innocent children in that cave, then they are in my family forever, like little Edward and Pete Petrosian, and the rest of my life is a poem to them. But the Army says there weren't, and so do I.

I love you and love you and love you. You can stop worrying now and start thinking about being married to a Columbia Law student with one hell of a good future. I won't tell you any more war stories than you want to hear. And that's a promise, whether the stories are about Nam or Palmyra.

Always yours,

Harry

(aka "Beans!")

MAKING FRIENDS

GARY RAISOR

Jack-o'-lanterns smile their secretive, broken-mouthed smiles as they peer out from behind darkened windows. Eight-year-old Denny Grayson hurries down the sidewalk. He is barely able to contain his excitement. Tonight is Halloween.

A hint of chill hangs in the air and the tang of woodsmoke carries. It's a good smell. The huge yellow moon tags along, floating over his shoulder like a balloon on a string. When he glances up, he sees the man in the moon smiling broadly. Beneath his green latex Frankenstein mask, he smiles back eagerly. He has waited with much anticipation for this night.

A small group of kids pelt by, anonymous in their costumes. Only the patter of their expensive new Adidas and Nikes links them to an exclusive club, one to which Denny will never belong. He watches enviously as they pound on the door. "Trick or treat," they demand in high, childish voices. He turns and scurries to the next house.

A quick stab of the doorbell brings a smiling, silver-haired woman to the door. "My, aren't you scary looking?" she laughs merrily. "Are you going to say trick or treat? What's the matter, cat got your tongue?"

Denny shakes his head and asks, "Ccould I hhaff a ddink of, wwatah, ppleese?" Her smile wavers and she blushes as understanding comes. "Oh, I'm so sorry. Of course you can."

When she goes to the kitchen, Denny reaches into the candy dish sitting so invitingly by the door. He barely retracts his hand before the woman returns with a glass of water. Turning his back, he lifts the mask and takes a short sip. "Ttankk yyoou," he mumbles thickly, holding out his plastic sack. The woman drops in extra candy. After every house on the block has been visited, he climbs on his bike and heads for home, racing the moon from streetlight to streetlight watching the shadows wheel and dart before him.

Pedaling furiously, he soon reaches the section of town where the houses aren't so nice. He weaves the familiar route up the rutted street until the small, rundown house comes into view.

Quietly letting himself in, he tiptoes past his mom who is fast asleep on the couch. As usual, the reek of soured whiskey follows him across the creaky floor.

He barely has time to stuff the mask and candy under the bed before he hears Mom's heavy tread. She enters the room and drunkenly embraces him. "Oh, Denny, I'm so glad you're home. Momma just had the most awful dream. It was full of blood, and children were screaming and screaming . . . "

Denny pulls away from her and throws himself onto the rickety bed. She stares at him in helpless misery. "I dreamed you went trick or treating again," she blubbers wetly, and Denny knows she's going to talk about *it*. "I'm so sorry, baby. I know I let you down. If only I'd checked the candy. Who'd have ever thought someone would be sick enough to put razor blades in a child's—"

Denny turns to the wall and stonily ignores her. Stiffly, she reaches a fluttering moist palm toward him that stops short. "I know the kids at school make fun of your problem. But I talked to Dr. Palmer again yesterday, and he says he might be able to help."

"Hhee ccan't hhellp."

The silence becomes a thick wall between them. For the first time, she notices he is wearing a jacket. Alarm sifts through the alcoholic haze to finally settle on her face. "Where were you tonight, Denny? You didn't go trick or treating, did you?" She yanks him around, trying hard not to wince as the horribly disfigured mouth smiles crookedly at her.

"Nooo, I wass mmakin' ssome neww ffriendss," he utters cheerfully, jumping from the bed and crossing over to the window. He jams both hands into his jacket pockets. His fingers touch a small lump nestled within—it's a candy bar. For a second, he'd almost forgotten he'd placed one in the candy dishes of all the homes he visited tonight.

As he thinks about the kids who make fun of the way he talks, his fingers curl tightly. A sharp flash of pain causes his hand to fill with sticky red wetness. After tonight, he'll have lots of friends to talk to. He stares into the night and smiles a terrible, secret smile. The man in the moon is smiling too; only, this time, a river of blood is gushing from his mouth.

YOU DESERVE

ALEX JEFFERS

Frogs peeped and croaked. Crickets chirped. Mosquitos whined. Ripples smacked against the rowboat's hull and drops dripped off the blades of the oars Rory held up out of the water, raised and poised like a soaring bird's wings—I couldn't really see them but that's how I imagined it. I couldn't really see Rory but I knew what he looked like. There were more stars in the sky than a city boy was used to, millions more, but no moon. Some kind of music floated across the water from the party but all I could make out was bass. "Watch for it," Rory said.

"What?"

"You'll know when it happens."

Then the bonfire on shore exploded and people started screaming.

"*Yeah*," said Rory.

• • •

Back up.

See, when Rory asked if I wanted to go out in the boat, I thought (hoped) it was so we could be alone together and make out. Or something. Despite everything. He was so pretty and I didn't much like or understand his friends. They didn't like me, I hadn't known them all forever and I wasn't their sort. They had their own language that I'd never studied in school and didn't have a phrase book for. But Rory was nice to me from the minute we drove up to the lake house, me and Little Dad in the car with Fitz (the cat) yowling in her travelling cage on the back seat, Big Dad behind us driving the rental van with *everything* from the Boston apartment except the furniture. This handsome, really fit kid in plaid boardies and no shirt was juggling yellow tennis balls

295

on the front lawn where Little Dad pulled up so I wondered if it was really the right house. Cabin, whatever.

"Hey, Stevie!" the kid called when Little Dad switched off the ignition (I'd never heard anybody but Big Dad call Little Dad *Stevie*)—"Hey, Stuart! Mom said you were coming up today. Need some help?" He was still juggling, not even looking at the balls.

"Hey, Rory," Little Dad said, getting out, "good to see you. You're taller." Then he poked his head back in and said to me, "That's Rory. Neighbor. Get out of the car, it'll be fine."

Look. The Ackles Lake summer colony was all people who'd known Stuart Ackles-Echeverría and Esteban Echeverría-Ackles years before Big Dad and Little Dad picked up a teenage son out of the adoption box. Last summer, the summer I moved in, was the first time in forever they didn't go to the lake for a week. Sure I was shy.

But when I looked up there was Rory sticking his right hand through my open window, grinning like he meant it. "You're Max," he said. "Finally. Welcome to Ackles Lake. Mom says you're here for the whole summer—that'll be great. After we get everything unloaded, wanna go for a swim?"

And, see, nobody'd ever flirted with me before but I'd watched movies and read novels, and I was pretty sure (hoping) Rory was flirting all that first week when he was showing me around and introducing me to people and taking me and his dog, Peony, for long walks along the lakeshore and through the woods. Peony was this big, mean-looking pitbull who scared me half to death when Rory brought her over the first time, but she was really a wriggly sweetheart and Rory said I never had to worry about her but if anybody tried to mess with me *they'd* have to worry.

"I think," I said over burgers on the deck because, look, that's half the point of having gay dads, "Rory McDougall is flirting with me."

"Max," said Big Dad.

Little Dad said, "Rory's a really good kid. Unlike some of his friends. Long as I've been coming here with your dad, I've been one of the folks far as he's concerned, not Stuart's fag-spic little jumped-up *friend* in scare quotes. So, yeah, I like him. But I don't know if he's gay. He's never said anything or, like, come to us for advice. Didn't he have a girlfriend summer before last?"

"*I* had a girlfriend every summer when I was his age," Big Dad said, which was something I couldn't imagine. "I dunno, either. What do you mean, *flirting*? Are you flirting back?"

• • •

Back up.

"So Stevie lost his job? That's too bad."

We were sitting on the little dock below Rory's house. (I called it a dock, he said *jetty*.)

"Yeah." I was over, almost over, being worried about it, because Big Dad and Little Dad told me I had to be. "That's why it's the whole summer, not just a week, and why we brought all that stuff. Everything that didn't go into storage. We'll find a new place to live in the fall."

Rory pushed the toggle on his remote-control box and the little speedboat on the lake sped up, making a wide arc and throwing up a white bow wave. "Where?"

"Big— Stuart talks about Hawaii or California. But we can't leave the state because . . . "

"Because the adoption isn't final and those aren't two of the places Stu and Stevie can be married?"

"Yeah," I blurted, relieved not to have to say it myself.

"You know." Rory was glaring at his speedboat out on the water. "I'm adopted too."

"I—I kind of figured. You don't look so much like your mom."

"I dye it," Rory said, putting a hand to his thick, buzzed black hair. "Tinted contacts."

"Pancake makeup to cover the freckles?" Ms. McDougall was a redhead, really pretty. Really not Asian.

"Well, that's out of the way then. But I was just a baby, from some baby farm in China. Not—"

"Hey!" I yelled, "watch your boat!"

It was headed right at us, speeding really fast, faster than a toy ought to be able to go. When it hit a ripple it bounced right out of the water but kept coming, skipping higher and farther and faster with each bounce, and I thought I could hear its motor whining, and I didn't have time to think. I shoved Rory, he went off the dock into the water on his side and I threw myself off the other.

"Wow," said Rory when he came up with a big grin. "I never thought it could actually go airborne."

The boat had smashed to bits four feet down the dock. Jetty. It would have got me right between the eyes.

• • •

Go back.

Little Dad, original suit-and-tie workaholic, came home early, carrying a copy-paper box that rattled when he dumped it on the coffee table. Six inches of his tie dangled out of the left jacket pocket. He looked really happy when he straightened up, pulled off his jacket and threw it at the armchair, grinned at me, and said, "I need a hug."

I hesitated and glanced at the screen where my avatar was fighting for his life without any help from me, then back at Little Dad. There was stuff I didn't understand or trust about living with people who loved me. I *was* about to get up, though, when Little Dad shrugged—he didn't look offended, just kind of manic—and plopped down on the sofa beside me, peering at the TV. "Is that you?" he asked just as an enormous war axe split my avatar's skull open and I paused the game.

"It was," I said, worried maybe he wouldn't approve of the game. It was M for Mature—Big Dad had to buy it for me.

"Sorry—I distracted you. Are you dead now?"

"It's okay." I set the controller down. "I'm not very good at it anyway."

Little Dad put one arm around my shoulders. "It's okay to ask me why I'm home so early, carting every single personal possession I ever left at the office. Including an extremely important World's Best Dad coffee mug."

My stomach went bad. "You got fired." It wasn't a question. My mom got fired a lot, back when I had a mom. It was terrible every time.

"Laid off," said Little Dad. "More unexpected but less demeaning."

"Is that why you need a hug?"

"No. Where's your dad?"

"In the sanctum sanctorum, I think."

He peered around the living room. "That's why you're out here."

"Well, the TV's bigger. But yeah. The sound effects bother him when he's trying to work." My bedroom shared a wall with Big Dad's office.

"Max," Little Dad said. He sounded really serious, like he was about to tell me all the bad things I was trying not to imagine about him not having a job anymore. "That's why we're here, for you to bother. Don't you dare ever forget that."

Then he hugged me because maybe I needed a hug. "Dad," I said, "does Dad know? He doesn't make very much money."

"Baby boy," my dad said, "you're not allowed to worry. That's the rule. First, I know this is going to come as a shock: You—are—not—a—luxury. Second: You are not a luxury like broadband that we could ever do without. Third: You are *not* a luxury. Fourth: I got a decent severance package and I'll file for unemployment. We've got some money socked away. Nothing's going to change right away except I'll be under your and your dad's feet all the time. Maybe you can teach me how to play your game."

Maybe Big Dad's ears were burning. When I looked up, he was standing across the room looking kind of sleepy and content like he'd just woken up from a nap. "Actually," he said, "I'm expecting two rather substantial cheques. And I've been agitating at your dad for I don't know how long to get the hell out of this town, so I take this as an opportunity."

Which meant he knew before Little Dad came home. Which meant he could have prepared me. Which meant trust issues were all ready to raise their heads except Big Dad came around the back of the sofa and plunked down on my other side. The cushion inflated under me and Little Dad so we bounced but Big Dad's arm was already around our shoulders holding us down.

"So . . . whaddya think about the whole summer at the lake 'stead of just a measly week? Then, if it comes to it, which it won't, we can put that place on the market."

• • •

No, further back.

See, what happened was Ramiro, my mom's boyfriend, an extremely handsome man who didn't have a real job so he mostly worked out a lot, decided the way I looked at him when he admired himself in the mirror in just his underpants was queer. Which it was, but that's no excuse. When I got out of the hospital, the group home didn't go so well because the other boys knew why I didn't have a family anymore. The records were sealed and my name had never been in the papers because I was a minor but just try to keep that kind of rumor quiet. Then Stuart and Esteban (mostly Stuart because he had more free time) descended from the heavens like shining angels to tell me they liked me and wanted to get to know me better. I still kind of halfway hoped my mom would get it together because she was what I knew and, you know, my *mom*. But during a mandated and supervised trip to Mickey D's she clutched the new gold crucifix around her neck and said in the steady voice that meant *Don't you doubt that I am clean now,* "I can't help loving you, Aaron, but I can't forgive you either. You're evil—*evil*. I signed the papers."

Evil? I thought back at her even though maybe I believed it but not right that minute because she was the evil one in that Mickey D's. Chewed-up burger and acidy Coke gurgled in the back of my throat and I asked my case-worker to take me back to the home right away. The look in my mom's eyes when I got up made me feel sick. I didn't deserve to feel that. I cried later.

My mom didn't want me but the big guy and the little guy, Stuart and Esteban, they did. I didn't ask them to come to the funeral. I didn't even tell them, they just came. I didn't know if I was crying for a dead mother who never took care of me or the two sweet men knocking down every roadblock the agency and the state threw up just to give me another hug and tell me I was special and *good*.

I felt too good to believe I was happy the afternoon the state said I could live full time with Stuart and Esteban—formal adoption would take another year but this counted. I was sitting in my new bedroom with the video-game system and all the books nobody but me had ever read and a closetful of clothes I'd chosen for myself. I got called out to the living room and presented with cake and pomegranate juice (I didn't really like it). Stuart said, "You certainly don't have to if it'd make you uncomfortable and of course it's not official yet, but it would make us both very happy for you to call us your dads." He was grinning and getting ready to go teary—I knew that about him already.

I said, "There's two of you." You know that was the weirdest, best part for a queer fourteen year old who'd never had *one*. "I'm too big to call you *Daddy* and *Papa*." I pointed at six-foot-six Stuart and said, "Big Dad," then at five-eight Esteban: "Little Dad. That work?"

Big relieved grins, some snuffling, some cake. I said, "How about me? Can I have a new name too?"

•••

Forward.

There was a breeze but it was hot in the back yard. I hadn't seen Rory. Figured he was with his friends who I didn't enjoy spending time with because they made it clear I didn't belong. That was fine. He'd known them longer than me. I didn't know where Little Dad was—Big Dad was in the attic where he'd set up his office, fighting with his deadline. The bigger of those two cheques he'd been expecting was the first instalment of the advance for a new book. He complained about it, in a happy, deranged sort of way: the first book he'd ever sold to a *real New York publisher* (scare quotes), the first book he'd ever sold from a proposal before it was written, the first book that wasn't a novel and that would come out under his real name. It was going to be a memoir when he finished it. About me.

About him and Little Dad and getting married the minute it was legal and wanting a kid together and all the trials of going about getting one and the first year of living with him. That kid. Me.

I didn't like thinking about it. I sure didn't want to read it, though both dads told me I'd have to eventually so if there was something I absolutely didn't want the world knowing about me I could try to argue Big Dad out of including it.

Until then I wasn't going to worry about it (of course I was), but it had made me curious. So I was lying in the back-yard hammock wearing my reading glasses—they figured out I needed them at the group home—with Little Dad's e-reader loaded up with a bunch of Big Dad's earlier books.

Not Stuart Ackles-Echeverría's books. Samantha Argyll wrote girl-boy romances. Sebastian Albrecht wrote boy-boy romances. S.S. Aldershot wrote paranormal romances, mostly girl (witch, weretigress, fairy)-boy (vampire, werewolf, fairy) but the audience liked edgy so S.S. could go a little polymorphous around the edges. Serena Allen wrote BDSM Girl-boy and Boy-girl romances but Little Dad made sure there weren't any of those on the e-reader before he let me borrow it. Sidney Anderson wrote horror stories and dark fantasy.

Big Dad wrote straight-up gay porn too, but I wasn't allowed to know what name(s) he used for that. He said he wanted to try girl-girl romance someday just for the heck of it, and maybe girl-boy-girl and boy-girl-boy, but there were only so many hours in a day and only so many little presses adventurous enough for that kind of thing.

I'd whipped through one of Samantha Argyll's—didn't make much impression—and one of Sebastian Albrecht's—*The Camera's Eye*, about a fashion photographer and a male model. It was pretty dumb but kind of hot, and sweet at the end when they finally figured out they needed to be together and out of the business. Then, for a change of pace, I decided to try Sidney Anderson. I've never really enjoyed scary stories (real life's plenty scary enough), but maybe *Go Down That Road* was dark fantasy instead of horror—Big Dad tried to explain the difference to me once—and I could always stop reading if it threatened to make me unhappy.

Not scared or unhappy. Quivery. I didn't appreciate the cavalcade of dead animals. It gave me a turn when the smoke-demon possessed Kev because I'd come to really like him (I thought he was gay) but maybe he wouldn't be made to do terrible things, or people would realize it was the demon and not blame him, and I was hoping real hard the plan he was working on to get the demon out of his skin would work. The pig-monster was gross, just gross.

Then something like a pig-monster snuffled at my ass hanging low above the lawn and I squealed and almost threw the e-reader and myself out of the hammock—and Peony yapped and Rory laughed.

"Goddamn!" I yelled, hurting Peony's feelings so she whimpered and I had to get down and hug her till she felt better and kissed half my cheek with her slobbery tongue and knocked my glasses off. Rory was still laughing. "You scared the hell out of me!" I said.

"Sorry—sorry." Rory steadied the swinging hammock and sprawled into it, making it swing again. "Whatcha doing?"

"I *was* reading."

"Oh." Pulling the e-reader out from under him, Rory just glanced at it, then said, "Oh, hey, does this thing get internet?"

I gave Peony's ear a last tug and stood up. "No, it's just a reader. Why?"

"Never mind. I'll show you later."

• • •

Wait a minute.

One afternoon, Fitz got out. My dads' ten-year-old tortoiseshell cat they'd had almost as long as they'd been together. She'd been peeved when I moved in but got over it, to the point that now and then I was an acceptable lap. Not a friend. Fitz didn't have friends, but she tolerated me about as well as she did the dads. Then we put her in a cage in the car for an hour and a half, pissing her right off, and took her away to live in a scary, different place. She spent two days under Big Dad and Little Dad's bed. Then she got interested in the windows and the outside world because she'd always lived in the city on the third floor and didn't know what nature was except maybe a pigeon flying by. Little Dad made sure to tell me repeatedly she wasn't allowed out. Very bad to let her out. Keep your eyes open when *you* go out. Latch the door every time. In the yard or on the deck, sometimes I'd catch her staring through the screen like I was nature, a squirrel or a bluejay.

I'd gone out for a walk in the woods.

Okay, alone. It was a thing I did sometimes, a nothing thing. There was a little clearing I'd found, real private, no poison ivy. I'd go there and take off all my clothes and think dirty thoughts about some guy I liked to look at (okay, Rory) and beat my meat.

So I'd gone for my *walk* (scare quotes). For some reason, all those sacrificial small animals from *Go Down That Road* were on my mind so my beat-off

303

session hadn't been as satisfactory as usual. I was almost home, almost right into the back yard, when I heard Little Dad swearing. "Goddamn, goddammit, fucking cat! Stuart! *Max!*"

So I started running, thinking, *Oh, oh no—I didn't—*

Just as I burst through the trees, all ready to start apologizing and begging, Rory called from somewhere, "Got her!" and he came through the trees on the other side, holding Fitz up by the scruff of her neck. For a second I almost hated him. For a second I thought he was grinning at me. "I've got her, Stevie. It's all right. Well—" He held her out farther away from his body. "Well, except for the bird." Fitz hung limp from his fist, her eyes blazing like all the devils in hell and a handful of brown feathers in her mouth.

"God damn it." Little Dad swooped over to Rory (Rory was taller than my dad) and grabbed her and turned around. "Bloodthirsty little fucker—first time she ever gets out." And Little Dad saw me.

I was standing there. Just standing there. Crying. "I—" I tried to say.

"Max." Little Dad saw me, and I knew he was going to say terrible things I deserved having said to me because what if it wasn't a dead bird? What if it was dead Fitz? My tummy hurt bad but I held it in. But Little Dad's voice didn't sound terrible. "Max. Wait—just . . . wait." And he ran up onto the deck hollering for Big Dad, and I heard the screen door slam and something something *lock her in the bathroom and get your ass outside* and I was still crying, I couldn't see I was crying so hard, and my dads were going to send me away and I deserved it because I'm evil—*evil*. Like my mom said before she died.

"Max." Little Dad grabbed me really hard. "Max. Baby." I'm almost taller than him but he was hugging me so hard. "Baby boy, it wasn't you. You didn't let her out, it was *me*, goddammit, Max! It wasn't your fault. Nothing's your fault, baby, you never did anything wrong, *anything*. Listen to me, Max, please, please, please stop crying."

"Please stop," Big Dad said, and he was hugging me too. "Don't cry, Max, Maxie, you don't have to cry, it's nothing, you're everything, Maxwell Echeverría-Ackles, we love you so much, please don't cry, you're everything, everything in the world."

My dads.

My dads.

My dads.

They brought me indoors and put me to bed and gave me ginger ale. My stomach started to feel a little better. Big Dad sat on the floor by my bed holding my hand while Little Dad made an emergency call to the doctor's office in Boston, and then Little Dad gave me the extra meds and held my glass while I swallowed. He climbed over me and leaned up against the headboard so I could lean against him, and they stayed with me until the meds knocked me under, telling me my name again and again and again.

Later that night, after Fitz let me stroke her and call her a wicked bad girl, Little Dad said like it had just occurred to him, "Actually, I think it was Rory left the door unlatched, not me."

• • •

Back up again.

Maybe twenty minutes' walk from the house, along the lakeshore where there weren't any other summer cabins and then a ways back into the woods, Rory started leading me up a slope that got steep fast. Peony wasn't with us this time. I was out of breath when we reached the top of a cliff so high I could see the far shore of the lake, not just the hills beyond. Rory shuffled closer to the edge than I wanted to get, looked down, looked back. "Jump?"

"You're kidding!"

"No." I guess he saw I was about to freak because he came a couple steps back toward me. "The water's deep enough, it's safe, really truly. Scary as fuck, that's the point, but safe. I've done it three times this summer already."

"No." My heart was hammering loud as thunder and he was about to argue at me, maybe call me names, which I didn't want. Not because I wasn't a yellow coward. Because if Rory called me a coward I couldn't be his friend. I was thinking real hard. "Alone? Were you alone those three times?"

"Of course not. Bunch of my friends." Who weren't yellow like me.

"Anybody ever hurt themself?"

"No—I don't know. Not when I did it." He cocked his head, like maybe I was getting my point across.

"It's just the two of us. If we both jump, if we both get hurt, who's going to go get help?"

"You really don't want to do it, do you?" He came back to me, away from that dangerous precipice.

"I really don't."

He punched my shoulder. "I really do." He smiled like it didn't matter and punched me again. "Okay, you be sensible and go down to the bottom and watch me. Here, take my phone—" He handed it to me. "If I break something, call my mom. Take my shirt."

When he pulled it off, his abs made me catch my breath. "You sure about this?"

"Yes, indeedy." Tilting his head again, he got a sly grin. "When you see me survive it, you'll want to do it too." (Not effing likely.) "Go on."

Every minute or two of my clamber down Rory would yell to ask if I was there yet. When I was, not the bottom of the cliff but on some rocks along the shore where I could see him up at the top, he yelled and waved and I waved back. I felt a little sick. He backed up and disappeared. Then he came running, running right over the edge like Wile E. Coyote in a cartoon. My heart stopped and turned to ice when he launched himself into all that air, hollering, arms wheeling, and then he fell. Then there was a big huge splash and it was over.

When his head popped up to the surface I could breathe again. "Whoo!" he shouted and started dog-paddling toward me. Still ten or fifteen feet out, he called, "I bet you didn't take any pictures."

"Oh." I felt stupid.

"'Sokay. Forgot to ask you."

He was climbing out, and I was breathing because he was safe and cheerful, and something sloppy and wet smacked my chest and flopped to my feet. I looked down. Rory's board shorts. I looked up. He was climbing out of the water naked except for his sneakers. I must have looked stupid—he guffawed. "They came undone when I hit the water. Easier to kick 'em all the way off."

I looked at his dick. Of course I did. He saw me look and his hand went down. Not to hide it. Fluff it up a bit because chilly water'd made it tiny. But pretty. Looking away, I crouched for his shorts to toss them back, but he said, "Just us dudes, dude," and kept coming like it wasn't a thing for him to be waggling his pretty dick at me. He took the shorts from my stupid hand, squeezed some of the water out, spread them out on the rock, and sat down to pull his shoes off. He turned them upside down to drain. I was standing there like an idiot. After a moment, he slapped my leg. "You ready to try it?"

"No." *Don't start,* I thought.

"Okay," he said.

I sat down two feet away, looking at the lake, not at Rory, thinking, *It's time, Aar—Max,* but not sure if it was time to say *I'm gay, you know—like my dads* or *I think you're cute,* so I didn't say anything. Maybe it was time to strip my own shorts off and jump in the water, skinny-dipping like country boys did in books—*just us dudes, dude*—but I didn't do that either.

Eventually, Rory put his shorts back on, took his shirt and phone back, stuffed feet into sneakers, and we headed home, him squelching loudly, me tingling.

• • •

What was that.

We were sitting on the dock (jetty) below his house again. Me and Rory and Peony—Peony was lying between us, her tummy warm under my hand, snorfling in her sleep. I don't know what made me say it. I wish I hadn't. "You never talk about your dad."

The temperature dropped forty degrees. Peony woke up growling and pushed against my side, baring her teeth at Rory. "Don't go there, Max," he said, voice like icicles breaking, and stood up.

Peony coughed and bayed and struggled while I held her back, me shocked, babbling, "I'm sorry, Rory! I'm sorry!"

"Fucker. Just don't go there."

Peony stayed with me when Rory stalked away. She howled once, like a broken wolf, and then snuggled up close to tell me I was safe with her.

• • •

Just a goddamn minute. That never happened.

The afternoon before the solstice party on the community beach, I was nervous like you'd expect. It wasn't just the other kids, Rory's old friends who he'd want to have fun with instead of me. It was the grown-ups, who I'd been introduced to, most of them, but didn't know, and if they thought Little Dad was Big Dad's fag-spic little jumped-up *friend*, what did that make me? Little Dad warned me he planned to get drunk and he wanted both me and Big Dad watching him like hawks. Big Dad said nobody would say anything and we'd head home right after the fireworks, and then he said, "I'm sorry, Max, Stevie. We can't skip it, really we can't. I wish we could." It was Ackles Lake and he was the only Ackles left.

Then Rory came by and said he wanted to show me something. So pretty— he was so pretty and cheerful and *nice*, so I pretended to myself again that the time he scared his own dog into protecting me never happened. We went to his house, his and his mom's, which was smaller than ours but newer and *decorated* (scare quotes). We went upstairs to his bedroom. I hadn't seen it before but it was just a bedroom and Rory slept on a twin bed like me except he hadn't made his up again this morning. (Group-home discipline.) He sat on the bed, beckoned me to sit beside him, and pulled his laptop out from under a pillow, flipped up the lid. It had been sleeping.

"Oh, that's not it," Rory said, x-ing out the browser window, but I knew he'd meant me to see it. "Just a second."

I'd seen it. I'd seen the *Boston Globe On-Line Archive* logo and the big, black, bold headline of the old article he'd paid to access. **Hub teen not to be charged in death.**

"Here we go."

He'd brought up his picture viewer. I didn't know what I was seeing right away as he flipped from one photo to the next to the next, because it wasn't possible. Me. In my private clearing in the woods. All my clothes off and my dick hard. My dick in my blurred hand. Me watching my hard dick shoot white stuff four feet across the clearing, my mouth making an *O* and my eyes stupid. Me fallen to my knees, staring at the goop on my fingers, putting them in my mouth, my eyes still stupid.

"*Hot*," Rory said.

He closed the laptop and put it away. He put his hands on me. He put his mouth on mine. There wasn't time to feel sick. I wasn't even there until he brought his hard dick out and put my hand on it. Then I was. Oh, I was. So very *there* for just a little while.

• • •

Way back. Way way back.

The group home.

Esteban and Stuart, the little guy and the big guy, had been visiting me for a while. They'd taken me shopping, bought me things I begged them not to make me take back to the home, clothes and books and a video-game system, because the other kids would steal or break them. They'd taken me for excursions—the Museum of Science, the Arnold Arboretum, a water park in New Hampshire (most fun I'd *ever* had in all my life ever). They'd had me overnight to their apartment where there was a bedroom they said was mine, just mine, only mine, and I could ask them not to come in and they wouldn't.

"Those fags aren't going to adopt you, fag," my roommate said. "Precious little orphan fag. They'll read your file. They'll never adopt you."

I wanted to beat him up because I believed him, I wanted to kill him because he was right, but I didn't. I didn't. I didn't. I was evil—*evil*—but I didn't kill my stinking turd of a roommate.

The group-home *Mom* (scare quotes) said, "Don't get your hopes up, Aaron. It looks good but I've seen 'em back out before." I didn't kill her either.

My case-worker, who was the only one I ever liked, said, "I shouldn't tell you but I know you and you need to be prepared. I think today's going to be the day."

My dads forever and ever said, "Aaron, we've come to love you so much. Will you be our son?"

• • •

Wait. What.

"They said he killed himself," Rory said afterwards, wiping his lips with one hand, his voice perfectly steady. "My dad. When he was fired, before they could arrest him. But it wasn't him. *You* know. I got such a *rush* doing it."

• • •

Now. Nownownow.

The fireworks buried under the bonfire on the beach exploded. People started screaming. I thought I heard Ms McDougall's voice screaming. I thought I heard Peony yelp in pain, then bay, and my stomach knotted up. I thought I heard my big dad howl and my little dad shout, "Stuart! Stu! No! Stu, where's Max? Where's our boy?"

"*Yeah,*" Rory said.

"Where's our son?" my big dad shouted. "Stevie, where's Max?"

"*Dammit,*" Rory said. "Fuck. Bastards, bastards. Smug happy *dad* bastards."

So cold. I felt so cold, so slow, while something fizzed like sparklers in my belly. He wasn't my friend, he'd never really been my friend. Like handsome Ramiro wasn't my friend, or handsome inside. Like my mom. "You don't get to mess with *my* dads, Rory," I said, real low. "I won't let you hurt my dads anymore." Then—I knew what I was doing now—I let the hurting sickness go. I didn't have to touch him, he didn't have to be hitting me like Ramiro, throwing me around my mom's apartment, breaking my nose and my cheekbone and my arm and four ribs. I let the sick go and the pretty boy on the rowboat's other bench who wasn't pretty inside made a shocked little breathy noise. Like he hadn't really figured it all out. When Rory stopped breathing, I didn't feel a thing except flat, empty. It was a lie, another lie, about the rush. The oars slapped into the water.

Then I jumped into the lake and started swimming to shore, to that poor wounded loyal crying dog who needed a hug and my dads, who needed to hug me because I was so cold. My big and little dads. Forever and ever and ever.

THE QUEEN OF KNIVES
GEORGINA BRUCE

Mother tied the crimson school tie at Eva's throat, and turned her around to face the hallway mirror.

"There," she said. She patted Eva's shoulders. "Ready for big school."

The mirror was too grand for the apartment: tall enough to reach the ceiling, and framed in tarnished gold. Eva knew that she must be careful not to smear the glass or chip the frame, as it had been passed down her family, from Mother to Daughter, and so it would belong to her one day. It reflected the bland hallway and Mother's diffident, thin body; the scarlet and gold rug peeling from the floorboards; and everything else, faithful as a mirror should be. But it did not reflect Eva. In her place was someone else, someone who called herself the Other. The Other *what*, Eva did not know. The Other Eva, she supposed. So alike they were, almost identical. But the Other was not Eva. Around her form, a silver aura sparked and glinted with many shards of metal, and the flash of silver blades. There was metal in her eyes, too. *She* had no intention of going quietly to school dressed in that stiff uniform, to sit in a row with her hands folded and recite from a boring book of letters. She would think of something better for Eva to do.

"You look very smart," said Mother, not quite managing a smile. "Shall we take a picture for Daddy?"

The Other smirked at Eva. They both knew Mother was pretending, playing at Happy Families. Father had not been home for days—the last time he had been there, he and Mother had screamed at one another for hours. Eva didn't miss him. She barely thought of him at all, except to remember his penknife with the mother-of-pearl handle; the penknife he had let her play with once. Only once, and then never again. But she had made good use of it, made her first cut.

"Let's take a picture of *you*, Mummy," said Eva.

Eva watched her Mother flinch and turn away from the mirror. Mother didn't like to look at herself anymore. Her pretty scar shone white; it had grown whiter, Eva noticed. It pulled the skin of her cheek tightly around it, dragging the eyelid down: a gouge from eye to lip.

The Other said, *She's scared.*

Eva replied, "Mother is the Queen of Knives."

"Oh no, Eva. We are *not* having this crap! You're starting big school today! It's a new start." Mother pulled Eva away from the mirror, turned her bodily in the direction of the front door. "Let's go."

Mother kept a whole world hidden away from Eva. The Other knew it, and taunted Eva about it often.

Don't you want to know about blood? The Other said.

But Mother had hidden all the knives and locked them away in a secret box, and she wore the key to the box around her neck all the time, even while she slept.

• • •

School was not interesting. Eva had wondered what it would be like, had guessed something much like this, and when it turned out she was right, she was immediately bored. Apparently she was expected to endure this for the next several years. Some of the other children cried when their mothers left them at the school gate, and some of the mothers cried too, and waited outside the railings, putting their faces against the bars to watch the children line up by the door. But Eva and her Mother had parted casually, like a pair of acquaintances leaving a party at the same time, and when Eva turned around in her line to wave at her, Mother had already driven away.

It might have been interesting, had there been something for Eva to do. She could read and write perfectly well, but there were no proper books in her classroom, only letters and pictures. There wasn't anything to do at school, Eva quickly realised, except sit quietly and try not to pee your pants. That was the main thing the teachers talked about: how you had to raise your hand if you needed the toilet, not to hold on until it was too late. Probably the teachers were always cleaning up pee. Two children in her class wet themselves that morning.

At lunchtime, Eva sat alone. The dinner lady tried to coax her, telling her not to be shy, but Eva explained that she would rather sit by herself. Then she took a shiny green apple from her bag and, ever so politely, asked the dinner lady for a sharp knife with which to cut it.

The dinner lady laughed. "Daft child. What are your teeth for? Bite it!"

"But my teeth aren't sharp," said Eva, and she looked so sad that the dinner lady laughed again.

Eva made sure to sit at the back for all her classes. Because she was quiet and continent, it was easy to escape teacherly attention. Late in the afternoon, she finally managed to prise out the blade from her pencil sharpener, and used it to carve her name in her forearm. The best bit was the crimson blood beading on the silver edge, before it ran free. She cut lines down her chest too, and the teacher didn't notice until it was time to go home and Eva stood up with the others, her school shirt ragged and red.

• • •

The Other said blood was her mother tongue. Eva wanted to learn. Every day, she sat in front of the mirror in the hallway, crossed her legs, and tried to understand what the Other was saying.

The Other said, *But how can you understand without a knife?*

Eva's Mother should never have tried to hide the secret of the blood. She should not have locked away the knives, the blades, the razors. But Mother was so careful now, since Father had given Eva the penknife. It had been just the one time. ("Once was enough," Mother had screamed at Father, and Father had screamed back, "It was an accident! She's just a little girl!")

Mother never forgot to put the knives away and lock the box. She never took the key from around her neck, and although Eva watched and waited with great patience, Mother was more vigilant than she.

I'll tell you the stories. But their true telling is in blood. You must have a blade if you want to speak the language.

"Tell me anyway," said Eva.

• • •

Father came home but it wasn't for good. He came for his clothes and books, which he threw carelessly all together into one big suitcase on the floor. Eva stood in the doorway of her parents' bedroom to watch. Mother sat on the bed, straining towards him, as if she wanted to grab him but was holding herself back. Her scar glowed white in the lamplight.

"You'll come and live with me," Father said to Eva. "As soon as I've got the place ready. There's a bedroom for you. You can help me paint it. And we'll visit Mummy a lot. If you want to."

Mother said, "She can't live with you. You're not safe with her. You're not responsible."

"Don't start on this again. She's just a child. A little girl, for God's sake." Father threw some shirts into the suitcase.

Mother twisted her hands in her lap. "Let's not have this conversation now."

"Let's not have it at all." He flipped the suitcase lid over, and zipped it all around. "I'm done."

"Take her, then," said Mother, quietly. "Don't leave me with her."

He looked at her face, and flinched. (It was the scar, Eva thought. He didn't like it.) "God. You really are messed up, aren't you?" He opened his mouth to say something more, then closed it again. He looked at Eva.

Eva lowered her eyes and said, "Daddy, where are you going?"

Father ruffled Eva's hair. "It's just for a couple of days, sweetheart."

That didn't answer her question, but Eva knew better than to act smart in front of her Father. Her Father, who had once handed over the mother-of-pearl knife with its sharp, gleaming blade.

She started to cry. "I don't want you to go, Daddy." He leaned down to her and she flung her arms around his neck and said, "Can I have your penknife, Daddy? I need it so I won't forget you."

"You see?" Mother said. She rose up from the bed and pushed past them, into the hallway. "You see?"

• • •

Apparently the other children had been very upset. There had been phone calls to the school, and phone calls to Mother and Father, too. Instead of going back to school, Eva stayed at home with her Mother. Mostly, Mother stayed in her bedroom, watching television and talking on the phone. Sometimes she raised her voice, and then Eva knew she was talking to her Father, or to the school. "Take her," she would say. "You have to take her." After the shouting, she would cry.

Eva sat in front of the hallway mirror.

"Tell me a story," she said.

The Queen of Knives had many fine scars.

Eva pulled at the scabs on her arms and chest. Would they become fine scars?

The Queen of Knives had so many scars that her skin was shiny. She even had scars on her tongue, lots of them, all criss-crossed, because her words themselves were razor sharp. She knew everything about blood, and her own blood was full of stories. If you spilled her blood, you would know all the stories too.

A thin red trickle oozed from one of Eva's scabs. "What about the princess?"

The princess doesn't know anything yet. She won't know anything until she is the Queen. It passes from Mother to Daughter, in the blood.

There were many stories. Eva began to sit in the hallway all day, from morning until night, and even to sleep there. The first time she lay down to sleep on the rug, she knew that she would wake up in her own bed in the morning. She could almost feel her Mother's arms lifting her, and carrying her to bed in the middle of the night. But the next morning she woke, cold and stiff, in the hallway.

After that, Eva ignored her Mother completely. Mother told her to move, to dress, to get up and wash and go out to play, but Eva simply would not obey. Mother seemed more nervous now that Father was gone. She would stand at the end of the hallway, watching Eva, holding the key around her neck and twisting it round and round, so much so that Eva would look up and wait for the key to twist right off its chain and into her hands, though it never did.

• • •

Father didn't come back. He called Eva, explained it was better if she stayed with Mother for now. Too much change would be difficult for both of them.

He means you'll find the knives in his apartment. He's scared.

"I don't care anyway," Eva said. But she did care about the knives at her Father's apartment, and wondered if she would ever get to see them. She wished she could live with her Father. He would let her have the knives, like he let her have his penknife, that one time.

Mother stayed in her bedroom every day. When Eva pressed her ear to the door, she heard nothing. She might have wanted to go in and put a hand on her Mother's face, to comfort her—but since the scar, she was not allowed to touch Mother's face, or to touch her Mother at all. Before, there had even been kisses sometimes, Eva remembered, but she didn't miss those so much. She just wished she could touch the scar, even once, to trace the cut she'd made.

The Other was contemptuous.

She is a weak Queen. Weak, blunt, and bloodless. A Queen ought to be strong. A Queen ought to be like a steel blade.

"Am I weak?"

Almost as useless as your Mother.

"How can I be strong, like a steel blade?"

Blood makes you strong.

"Mother is really the Queen?"

Mother has forgotten what it is to be Queen.

Eva knew it was true, because she had heard the singing in her own blood. Blood was power, and it made you strong. Mother had forgotten, and she was weak.

Make her remember.

But how could she remember without a knife?

• • •

Mother must not have heard the mirror break, because when Eva crept into her bedroom, she was still asleep on the bed, curled up like a baby.

Everything was in the blood. The past, the future, the Queen's power: all secrets of the blood. Even love was there, a mother's love, vibrant as a jewel. Eva saw it, pulsing under Mother's skin; saw it, and speared it with the glittering point of mirror shard. She pushed her small fingers into the wound in Mother's neck, and scooped out trails of scarlet. Like her Mother had done before her, and her Mother before that, and on and on, through time: she painted a crown of blood over her head.

Eva held up the shard of mirror, and for the first time she saw herself reflected as she truly was. Around her form, a silver aura sparked and glinted with metal, and the flash of silver blades. There was metal in her eyes, too. She wore a cloak of blood, and her hair stood high and stiff, and red like rubies.

Long live the Queen.

THE NAUGHTY LIST

CHRISTINE MORGAN

They got sent in after supper, the other kids.

The other bad kids.

Sent to the basement.

No party for them.

No Christmas party, with crafts and games, songs, cocoa, cookies, and a visit from Santa with presents.

Not for them. Not the bad kids, the kids on the naughty list.

Parties were a privilege. A special reward.

They hadn't earned it. They didn't have enough points.

Minda sat in the corner and watched them come in.

She never got points.

Like Derp. Derp never got points either, though Derp tried. He really did. He tried really hard to play nice and be helpful, turn in assignments, pass tests, keep his room clean, and all that good-kid point-getting stuff. He just couldn't do it right.

Minda didn't try. Minda didn't care.

Derp meant well, that's what her granny would say. He meant well, but he just couldn't do it right. Derp was big and dumb, kind of clumsy, and he scared people. He didn't mean to do that, either, but he did. Even grownups, even teachers, were scared of Derp sometimes. They wouldn't say so, but they were. Minda knew. Minda could tell.

They thought because Derp got frustrated, because he yelled and waved his arms when he was upset, that he must have super-Derp powers. Retard strength, one of the big boys had called it. Derp would snap, and start hitting, and be strong as ten wrestlers or a wild animal.

But Derp hardly ever hit anybody except for himself. He didn't want to be scary. It made him sad.

Being sent to the basement now made him sad too, Minda saw. He came in with his head down and his feet dragging. His froggy mouth turned down in a crumpled wet fold. He snuffled a sigh as he went to a table and plopped onto a chair. There were some crayons and colorbooks on the table. Derp opened a colorbook to a page with trains and started scribbling.

Tess, Jimmy and Spencer were next, clomp-tromping down the stairs in a noisy arguing group. They'd had extra chores for being in trouble. They usually were. Jimmy for stealing and lying, Spencer for being a dirty-messy potty-mouth, Tess for starting fires.

After them came Lamont. He was new to the school. Did he not know the many rules? Or he was too smart to care? Maybe both. Minda had heard that his mom was a doctor, the rich kind, the kind that gave ladies new noses. He earned lots of points by getting best grades on all his tests and assignments. It seemed kind of strange Lamont would be here.

He looked mad about it, too. He glared at Miz Parker like he wished she'd be crushed by a truck.

Miz Parker didn't notice. She just sat at the desk, drinking coffee and playing on the computer. That was pretty much all she did. Solitaire, Mahjong, Minesweeper, Angry Birds. Unless somebody pitched a total fit, she'd ignore them.

Lamont moved his glare around the room like he'd never seen it before. Maybe he hadn't. This might have been his first time to the basement, to the detention hall.

Minda idly wondered what he did. A smart kid with a rich mom, losing enough points to miss out on the Christmas party? Must have been something extra bad.

His lip curled up in a disgusted kind of sneer at the sight of the cruddy old furniture, the low bookshelves crammed with cruddy old books, the cruddy old toys. He glanced at Derp, still scribbling loops in the train colorbook. He glanced at Spencer, who was picking his nose, then at Jimmy and Tess, bickering over what to do first.

He glanced last at Minda, sitting in her corner. She kept finger-combing her long straight dark hair down over her face. She tried to avoid his gaze. Lamont sneered the other side of his lip and went to a chair by the stack of puzzles. He sulked into it with his arms crossed over his chest.

"This isn't fair," he said in a grumbling mutter.

"Yeah, dude." Spencer renewed his digging for nose goblins with a cork-screw motion. "Sucks to be us."

"I didn't want to go to any stupid baby Christmas party anyways," Tess said.

"But there's treats." Derp sighed again, a doleful-soulful sound.

"We'll have snacks," said Jimmy. "They have to give us snacks, they can't starve us in here all night."

"Snacks, right." Tess made a rude noise. "Graham crackers and juice, same as always. Not *good* snacks."

"They get good snacks at the party," said Derp. "Hot cocoa with marshmallows. Frosted snowman cookies. Candy canes."

They all fell silent, thinking about that. In the hush, from beyond the basement, came muffled but cheery holiday music. The party was starting. Footsteps thudded their vibrations as excited kids rushed along the halls and stairways.

Everybody had seen the preparations underway, of course. The school's gymnasium, auditorium, dining room and courtyard being all decorated . . . twinkly lights and glittery garlands, wreaths, ribbons, cardboard reindeer and penguins, construction-paper snowflakes, a real Christmas tree covered in ornaments, a big red chair where Santa would sit to give out presents . . .

"And we're stuck here." Lamont blew out his breath with what was almost a snort.

Miz Parker didn't notice.

"Why're *you* here anyway?" Tess asked the question that had been on Minda's mind.

Lamont scowled and re-crossed his arms.

"I know why." Jimmy flashed a sly grin. "He cut Mikey Nelson."

"No shit?" Spencer perked up. "That was you? Dude!"

"He had to get like ten stitches," Jimmy added.

"What'd you cut him with?" Spencer regarded Lamont with interest as if watching a documentary on television about dangerous wildlife. "A switchblade? A boxcutter?"

"Should've shot him," Tess said. "Mikey Nelson is a turd."

"A scalpel," said Jimmy when Lamont didn't seem to want to answer.

Derp's forehead creased. "A what?"

"A doctor knife, doofus. You know. Like on the shows. Nurse! Scalpel! Forkseps!"

"Forceps," Lamont said.

"Forksex," snickered Spencer.

"Should've shot him," Tess said again. She made a gun-hand and mimed aiming a headshot at Miz Parker, whose oblivious attention remained fixed on the computer. "Pow."

"She always wants to shoot people," Jimmy told Lamont.

"Or set them on fire," Spencer said. "She's a firebug."

"I am not. You're a litterbug and a bug-killer. But I'm not a firebug."

"You set shit on fire."

"That's not why. Jeez. I don't like *fires*, I like *explosions*." She clenched her fists in front of her face and sprang them open. "Ka-boom."

"You're Lamont, right? I'm Jimmy. That's Tess. He's Spencer."

"I'm Derp. My real name's Walter but everybody calls me Derp."

Lamont glanced at Minda again, or at the curtain of hair concealing her face. He lowered his voice. "Who's she?"

"That's Minda." Jimmy paused, his freckled face twisting in thought. "She's . . . uh . . . "

"Weird," said Tess.

"Effin'-A," Spencer said, not without a note of approval. "Minda's one weird-ass *chica*."

Tess nodded. "Even since before her brother died."

Lamont took yet another look. Before he could decide whether or not to say anything else, the detention hall door opened to admit a shrill, complaining whine.

"You can't do this, I'm telling, I'm gonna tell! My mommy's gonna be sooooooo mad at you!"

Miz Parker leaned over from the computer, saw who it was, and pinched the bridge of her nose like she had a sudden ice cream headache.

"You can't *dooooo* this! I'm the Christmas princess!"

"That's enough, Jolene," said Mr. Gregson, the vice principal. "You had plenty of chances and plenty of warning."

He marched in Jolene Sinclair, all sprayed blond curls, chubby pink cheeks, and eyeshadow. Her poofy green satin holiday dress trimmed in shiny gold lace, gold tights, and green velvet shoes with golden buckles reeked of holiday cheer. Wedged under one arm was a stuffed rabbit almost as big as she was, a fluffy white rabbit wearing a curly blond wig and a green satin dress identical to Jolene's.

"Now you stay here and behave—"

"But I'll miss the paaaaaaarty!"

"Yes." There might have been a grim glint of satisfaction in Mr. Gregson's hint of a smile. "You should have thought of that before you pushed Kayla off the stage."

"She was in *my* spot! She's a bratty-bratty-bratty-brat and she was in *my* spot!"

The vice principal turned away from her to have an annoyed-sounding conversation with Miz Parker, leaving Jolene to huff in indignation.

The rest of them watched as she flounced her way to the middle of the room and stood there, pouting.

"What are *you* staring at?" she demanded.

Nobody said anything.

Then Derp spoke up. "That's a really pretty dress."

At once, the pout became a dazzling toothpaste-commercial smile. "Thank you." She skipped to his table. "I'm Jolene and this is Bunny-Hoo-Hoo."

"Bunny what?" asked Jimmy, eyebrows raised.

"Bunny-Hoo-Hoo," repeated Jolene. She had a giggle that sounded like metal screeching on glass. "Because she's a bunny, and . . . " She flipped the rabbit over so that its dress fell up around its head. " . . . here's her hoo-hoo."

Underneath the skirt were no tights or panties, just furry bunny butt and a puff of white tail, and the kids all laughed like maniacs.

All but Minda, of course, who stayed where she was, quiet in her corner, running her fingers through her hair.

Mr. Gregson's phone beeped. He unclipped it from his belt to check the text.

"Of course, to top it all off, the damn Santa's not only late but lost," he told Miz Parker. "I need to talk him through the directions—"

"Oh, great," Her voice was distracted. Miz Parker must not care for any holiday.

"—then figure out what's going on with the choir microphones . . . " He pressed his temples. "Just make sure this bunch stays out of trouble."

"Sure," she said as her attention returned to the monitor.

He dialed and left with the phone to his ear.

"Did you hear that?" said Derp. "Santa's lost."

"So?" Spencer, having worked a fat yellow booger from his nose, squish-wiped it under his chair.

"So, Santa!"

"Not like we were gonna get presents anyways," Tess said.

"*I* am," proclaimed Jolene. "*Lots* of presents. The *best* presents. For me and for Bunny-Hoo-Hoo."

"Are not," Jimmy said.

"Am so!"

"Are not, not now. You're stuck here with *us*, now."

"You get squat," Spencer said. "Jack-shit-diddly-squat."

Her lipsticked mouth made a wounded O-shape. "But . . . "

"They're right," Lamont said.

"But that's not fair."

"Tell me about it."

Spencer shrugged and started picking pieces of rubber from the tattered soles of his sneakers. "We're screwed. Effed in the A. Or in the hoo-hoo."

"While everybody else gets Christmas." Derp drew a sad face in the coloring book.

"I didn't do anything wrong." Jolene fussed with her rabbit's wig.

"Did you really push Kayla off the stage?" asked Tess.

"She was in my spot. She's a show-offy bratty-brat and she thinks she's prettier than me."

"And she gets Christmas and you don't," said Derp.

"The *good* kids do," Lamont said. "The mama's boys and daddy's girls."

"The goodie-goodies." Tess made a face. "The teachers' pets."

"The kissbutts," said Spencer.

"The tattle-tales," Jimmy chimed in.

Another grumpy silence fell as they pondered the ginormous cruel injustice of it all. Outside, the music was the Rudolph song, bright and bouncy. There were laughs and shouts. Vague whiffs of yummy smells—popcorn, gingerbread, cocoa—wafted on the air.

Lamont looked around at the rest of them again. "We should do something."

"Color?" suggested Derp. "Or puzzles, there's puzzles—"

Spencer flicked a speck of shoe-rubber at him. "No, derp-for-brains."

"He means do something about being stuck here," said Tess.

"While *they* have fun at the party," Jolene added.

"Do something like what?" Jimmy asked.

"Bust out?" Tess did gun-hands again. "Never take us alive, coppers?"

"Jailbreak!" crowed Spencer.

Jolene smacked him. "Shut up. Gawd. Tell the world."

Miz Parker, without looking over, raised her voice in a bored not-listening way. "Quiet, keep it down."

"She's not gonna let us go," said Jimmy. "And even if she did, then what?"

"Then we go to the party, duh," Jolene said.

"We'd get in trouble," Derp said. "They'd put us in detention."

"We already are,"

"Oh yeah."

"What else could they do?" Lamont spread his hands. "And at least we'd be able to grab some cookies before they threw us back in here."

"Let's do it." Tess hopped up from her seat.

"What about her?" Jolene pointed at Miz Parker.

"I got an idea." Jimmy wore his sly grin again. With his freckles and his red hair, it made him look like a crazy wooden clown doll. He beckoned, and the others leaned close to hear him whisper.

Minda, from her corner, didn't move. Her ears were good but not that good, good enough to only catch snippets of what they said.

" . . . know how she always . . . "

" . . . yeah in the janitor's closet . . . "

" . . . thinks nobody will . . . "

" . . . won't she . . . "

" . . . how do we get . . . "

" . . . take care of that, trust me . . . "

" . . . let her out, right?"

" . . . worry about it later . . . "

" . . . I dunno, guys . . . "

" . . . want cookies, don't you?"

" . . . well yeah . . . "

" . . . everyone agreed?"

" . . . what about . . . ?"

Minda felt six pairs of eyes focus on her then. She ducked her head, hunched her shoulders, and hid behind her hair.

"She's okay," Tess said.

"She wants cookies too," said Derp.

"She's with us," Jimmy said to Lamont.

"Can she even talk?" asked Jolene. "Can you even talk?"

"She can talk," said Tess. "She just . . . uh . . . "

"Doesn't," Jimmy finished. "But she's cool. Right, Minda?"

Minda did a quick nod, still averting her gaze.

"So, we just wait until . . . ?" Lamont sort of jerked his chin at Miz Parker.

"Yeah. Act regular."

Jimmy's advice was easier said than done; they tried not only to act regular but act innocent, sitting quietly, coloring, doing puzzles. Miz Parker swept them a few suspicious, uneasy looks. Then she went back to ignoring them in favor of Angry Birds or whatever.

Eventually, more or less on schedule, Miz Parker pushed back from the desk. She made a show of cricking her neck side to side. "I'm going to stretch my legs," she said. "I'll be back in a minute, so no nonsense."

What she really meant, the kids knew, was, sneak into the janitor's closet for a cigarette, though the whole school was supposed to be no-smoking. "A Proudly Smoke-Free Zone" the signs said.

Miz Parker stepped out into the corridor. Her shoes clacked on the cement floor. Jimmy, fast like a fox, darted to catch the door before it latched shut. He held it open just a crack, enough for them to peep through.

Light bulbs in wire ceiling cages cast Miz Parker shadows on the painted-cinderblock walls. The janitor's closet was at the far end, past the stairs, the bathrooms, and the ancient drinking fountain with its eternal cold drip.

Jolene tried to elbow her way between Spencer and Lamont for a better view, or to make sure Bunny-Hoo-Hoo could also see. Derp started to say something, too loud, and Tess elbowed him.

Jimmy gave Miz Parker enough time to get settled and light up. Then, still fox-fast, and quiet as a ninja, he zipped down there, pulled a key from his jeans-pocket, and locked her in. Then he spun and did a big beaming "ta-da!" gesture.

"Hello?" came Miz Parker's startled but muffled voice.

She tried the door, but Jimmy had left the key half-turned and half-stuck from the lock so she couldn't open it from her side.

"Hey! Hello? Is someone out there? Hey!"

Rattle-rattle-rattle. Knock. Thump thump.

It stayed shut. The other kids crept into the hall, tentative and amazed, like mice surprised at being let out of their cage. Freedom, but wariness, because what if it was a trick, a trap? What if the cat was ready to pounce?

Minda trailed after them.

"Hey! Open this door! Did you little shits lock me in?"

"She said shits," said Derp, eyes agog.

"Potty-mouth! That's detention for you!" Spencer whooped at the door. He high-fived Jimmy. "You da man, you slick effin' bastard!"

The rattles, knocks and thumps, joined by some hammering bangs, resumed loud and angry, but the door continued staying shut.

"Oh, you're going to be in *so* much trouble!" called out Miz Parker.

"Wow, it worked," Lamont said. "Awesome!"

"Bunny-Hoo-Hoo wants to know what if someone hears her?" Jolene danced the rabbit back and forth.

"Nobody will," Jimmy said. "Not for a while, not with the party and the music and the choir and everything."

"Where'd you get a key?" Lamont asked.

"My dad. He works in the cafeteria, that's why they let me go to school here. He's always losing stuff, forgetting where he puts it, when he's drunk.

Sometimes he gets mad and blames me." Jimmy winked. "Sometimes he's right."

"So let's go already." Tess headed for the stairs.

They went up, reminding each other to avoid the teachers, avoid the prefects and tattle-tales, not make a big deal of it, blend in, and—

"Eat *all* the treats!" Spencer cried, thrusting a fist in the air.

Then Lamont stopped them at the top of the stairs. "You guys . . . " he said. "Look!"

The stairwell came up into a lobby, with the infirmary and nurse's office one way, the school mail room another way, glass double doors opening onto the courtyard, and a glass side door opening onto a parking lot. It was the parking-lot door where Lamont pointed, and when they looked, they saw three people out there by a van with a light-up wreath hung on its front and cartoon reindeer decals along its side.

One of the people was a curvy girl, and another was a short midget guy. It was the third person, the jolly fat man with the white beard and the red suit, that riveted the kids where they stood.

"Santa," Derp gasped.

Santa.

And two of his elves.

The short midget guy wore green pants with triangle hems, shoes with jingle bells on their curled-up toes, a red jacket, and a pointy hat with more jingle bells. The curvy girl had on candycane-striped tights, a short red skirt with a white fuzzy hem, a ruffled white top, candycane earrings, and a cute little cap.

Jolene, clutching Bunny-Hoo-Hoo, uttered a high-pitched greedy squeak as the two elves began unloading boxes from the back of the van.

Presents. The boxes were full of presents! Gift bags with tissue paper blooming out the tops. Packages wrapped in shiny foil or fancy paper, tied with ribbons or topped with bows. So many presents.

"You guys," Lamont repeated. "You guys, I got a better idea."

"Yeah," Jimmy and Tess said together.

"Fuck yeah," said Spencer.

Moments of hasty, hurried planning later, Jolene pranced out the side door.

She pirouetted, made pretty-feet, waved, and chirped, "Santa! Hi, Santa, over here!"

Santa, in the process of poking his white-gloved thumbs at his phone, jumped and looked around. He seemed confused for a second, then put the phone in his coat pocket and went, "Ho, ho, ho, hello there little girl, Merry Christmas," in a full, jolly voice. "Aren't you a pretty darling?"

"I'm Jolene," she said. "I'm our school Christmas princess."

"I can see that you are, ho, ho, ho."

"And this is Bunny-Hoo-Hoo."

"Mr. Gregson said we should meet you out here," said Jimmy, moving up beside Jolene. "In case you got lost again."

"How come you got lost?" asked Derp. "Santa shouldn't get lost."

"Ho, ho, ho," laughed Santa, patting his belly. "Santa's elves are still getting used to our new GPS."

"The reindeer never got lost?" Tess asked.

"That's right, not my sleigh team."

"C'mon in," Lamont said, holding the side door wide open.

"Mr. Gregson said we could help you while everyone else is at the choir concert," Jimmy added, as just then from the auditorium there drifted the sounds of a bunch of kids warbling their way through the first part of "Away in a Manger."

"Well, isn't that nice of you." He chortled and mussed Jimmy's hair. "And what's your name, little boy?"

"Jimmy."

"Jimmy. That's a nice name. These are my helpers, Candy and Jingle."

"Merry Christmas, kids." Candy did a perky bounce that made Jolene's eyes go all squinty and mean.

"Yeah," said Jingle, lots less perky. He slammed the van's back doors. "Merry Christmas."

As they shuffled into the lobby, carrying boxes of presents, Santa went ho-ho-ho some more and asked the others' names, asked if they'd been good little boys and girls. They all introduced themselves and said yes they had. When it was Minda's turn, she just murmured, so Tess explained she was shy.

"It's this way," Lamont said. "Downstairs."

"Downstairs?" asked Jingle. "You mean, like, in the basement?"

"In the rec room," Jimmy said. "It's all set up."

"Santa's workshop, and a tree, and everything," said Tess.

"Why that'll be wonderful," Santa said.

"What's that banging noise?" the candycane elf girl asked.

"Uh, er, um," said Derp.

Jimmy nudged him. "The pipes. Boiler room and stuff."

"You sure?" Jingle looked around. "Sounds like someone pounding."

"They make weird noises. Some kids think the place is haunted."

"Hrm." He didn't seem convinced.

They started down the stairs. Behind Jingle's back, Lamont and Jimmy shared an anxious grimace. If Miz Parker started hollering again, ooh they were gonna get it.

Then she did holler, and things happened fast.

"Hello? Is anybody out there? Help! I'm locked in!"

Santa, already most of the way to the detention hall door, paused and turned.

"What the—?" Jingle began.

Spencer tripped him at the same time as Lamont gave the short midget elf guy a great big hard push. His words turned into a startled squawk. He pitched headfirst down the steps. His box tumbled.

"Steve," screamed Candy, dropping her box too.

Presents went flying, scattering everywhere in the hall. Jingle's jingle bells jingled like crazy. There were some thick snapping sounds as he cartwheeled, and a meaty whump sound when he hit the cement.

"Oh, jeez, Steve, are you okay?"

"Get them in there." Lamont jumped the rest of the way down.

"Ste—"

Jolene smacked Candy in the face with Bunny-Hoo-Hoo. "Shut up!"

Miz Parker banged on the door and hollered some more.

"*This* way, Santa." Derp yanked at the back of Santa's broad black belt.

Caught off-balance, Santa wobbled and fell on his butt. "Oof!"

It took four of them to sort of drag Santa the rest of the way into the room. Some super-Derp-strength would have been really useful.

Santa, dazed, seemed to think they were helping him. He blinked, perplexed, when he saw no special Santa's-workshop or anything. "Wait, didn't you say . . . ?"

They heaved him into a chair.

"What is this?" asked Santa. "What's going on?"

Tess dashed over from Miz Parker's desk with a roll of masking tape. It made long rippy-farty noises as she wound it around and around, taping Santa's arms to the chair arms and legs to the chair legs.

"Now just a—" Santa said, blustering, puffing himself up. "What—"

"It was a trick, stupid," Jimmy said.

"Good little children shouldn't play tricks on Santa. You'll end up on the naughty list for sure."

"We already are," Lamont said. "We already are on your damn naughty list."

"See here—"

"Ow." Candy cried. "Ow, my hair, let go of my—ow!" Jolene had her by a fistful of it, towing her along all bent over and flailing. "Let go of my hair, you brat!"

"I'm not a brat. Kayla's a brat! Kayla's a bratty-bratty-bratty-brat and so are you!"

"This is not funny." Santa said. "Whatever you think you're doing—"

His phone rang in his pocket. Everybody froze like they were playing statue-tag. When Lamont went to fish the phone out, Santa tried to twist away and almost knocked his chair over.

"It's the school," Lamont said, looking at the screen. "Probably Mr. Gregson wondering where Santa is."

He tossed the phone to Tess, who caught it with a gleeful whoop. In the same drawer where she'd found the tape, she'd also found a lighter and a bunch of stuff confiscated from earlier detentions, including one of her own old cap-guns, some firecrackers and a few packets of those snap-pop things. She untwisted the tiny knots of paper and poured until she had a gritty mound of gunpowder or whatever was in them.

In the hall, Spencer cackled. "I think the elf's broken. Watch." He poked.

Jingle twitched and groaned, scrabbling at the floor. Blood oozed from his leg, where a jagged part of bone stuck out through his sock.

"Hey!" Santa wasn't jolly anymore. "Knock it off, kid."

Spencer kept poking and laughing, like he did when he caught a spider or a beetle. Jingle kept twitching and groaning. Each twitch made the bells on his shoes jingle—his hat had fallen off and lay crumpled over by the drinking fountain.

Jolene tugged Candy to her knees. By now, the curvy candycane elf girl was blubbering, still trying to talk but crying as she did.

"Steve's hurt, ow quit it, we have to call 9-1-1, let go of me owwwww."

"I said shut up!" Jolene hauled off and smacked her again, not with Bunny-Hoo-Hoo but with a loud slap that left a vivid red mark on Candy's cheek.

"That's enough." roared Santa. "You kids cut the crap, right now!"

He strained at the masking tape. A few strips popped. Lamont grabbed a pair of scissors from the desk drawer.

"Cut what crap?" he asked, making the scissors go *k-snip, k-snip* at the air.

Santa gaped. Santa sputtered.

Candy, who Jolene and Jimmy were taping to another chair, went on blubbering.

"She's crying," Minda whispered.

Nobody listened.

"Ready?" said Tess, who'd wedged Santa's phone into the pile of gritty powder and surrounded it with a crisscross of firecrackers.

"What are you—hey! Don't! That's my—" Santa said.

Derp covered his ears.

Tess lit it up.

Ka-pang-ga-pow-ka-popopop! Flashes and sparks, the phone flip-jittering until it flip-jittered off the edge of the desk and landed on the floor with grey smoke-streamers drifting up from it.

"Yee-haw!" Tess cheered, doing a victory fist-pump.

Jolene stood in front of Candy, hands on her hips, bottom lip pouted. "Thinks she's so pretty, look at her, thinks she's so pretty, do *you* think she's pretty?"

"Huh?" said Derp, taking his hands down from his ears.

"Stop this, you all just stop this—" Santa said.

"So she's pretty, so what?" Jimmy said.

"Bet you want to *kiss* her, too."

"Kiss her? What?"

"Dooooo you?"

"No. Gross."

"Bouncing around with her big boopiedoops . . . " Jolene hooked her fingers into the front of Candy's ruffled top and tore it open. Candy recoiled so hard her chair almost went over backward, screeching.

"Leave her alone." Santa yelled. "You kids are going to be in so much trouble—"

Lamont stabbed the scissors into Santa's fat belly.

Everybody gasped.

No blood came out when Lamont pulled out the scissors. Only some puffs of white stuff.

"The heck?" Tess asked.

"Hey . . . " Lamont said. His teeth ground together. "It's a *pillow.* He's got a *pillow* under his coat."

"What the hell's wrong with you?" Santa thrashed in the chair. "Are you insane?"

Derp reached for Santa's beard and it came right off. Derp held it, looked at it, and dropped it on the floor. He sniffled.

"Aw, crap." said Jimmy. "All this and he's not even the real Santa?"

"What?" Spencer came back in. "You're shitting me. You're effin' shitting me. Not the real Santa?"

"Hey, look . . . " Santa, or whoever he was, some pudgy man with no chin and brown stubble under the fake beard, tried to smile at them. "Let's not do this, huh? Let's find a way to—"

"You dirty liar." Jimmy punched him in the nose. It didn't go crunch and bleed, but the phony liar Santa yelped and his eyes watered.

Lamont taped his mouth shut and turned to the others. "*Now* what do we do?"

"He'll tell on us," Tess said.

"He better not," said Jolene. "Or we'll tell on *him.*"

"Tell on him what?" asked Derp.

"We'll say he showed us his wee-wee."

Santa choked. "Mmm-hrrgh-hmm."

"He showed us his wee-wee," she continued, "and said if we wanted presents, we had to touch it."

Tess grimaced. "Eew. No way."

"Yeah, no way, I'm not touching anybody's dick," said Spencer.

"Wee-wee," said Jolene.

"Not touching that either."

"You don't have to really touch it. We just *say* that. We say he told us we had to touch it if we wanted presents. Or kiss it."

"Eew," Tess said again, louder.

"Omigod they're crazy they're all crazy, oh God," sobbed Candy. Her head hung down, her hair all messy in her face, her top torn open so they could all see her bra.

"She's still crying," Minda said. "She should stop. She shouldn't cry."

From the hall, there was a struggling, jingling kind of sound. They looked. The short midget broken elf guy was trying to drag himself up the stairs by his arms. His legs, bowlegged to start with and all bent and crooked now, didn't seem to want to move right. They left smears of blood like red snail-trails.

"Wuh-oh," said Spencer. "Some buttwipe thinks he's getting away. Bad Jingle."

He ran over, climbed past the crawling green-suited figure, let him get halfway, then kicked him back down. Jingle bleated. His body went splinter-crunch splinter crunch on the steps. His shoes clinked and dinged. His head clonked on the floor like a bowling ball. He made a long juicy tootling fart.

"Dude," Jimmy said, impressed. "Did you *hear* that?"

"Whew." Spencer waved a hand in front of his face. "Did you *smell* that? Think he shit himself."

Miz Parker wasn't pounding and hollering anymore. Maybe she was afraid to. Maybe she hoped they forgot she was in the janitor's closet.

Santa's eyes bulged. His pudgy cheeks did too. Snot bubbled in and out of his nose.

"And pissed himself," Spencer added, using his foot to roll Jingle over so they could all see the wet splotch on the front of his pants.

"Ste-e-e-eve . . . " Candy kept blubbering.

"Make her stop," Minda said and put her hands over her ears. "She's crying, make her stop."

"So she's crying." Jolene primped her hair and adjusted Bunny-Hoo-Hoo's dress. "So she's a crying-crying-crybaby, so what?"

"My brother cried a lot."

"So?"

She glanced at Jingle. Tess and Jimmy had joined Spencer in the hall, all three laughing as they pushed the crippled elf around with their feet, playing soccer.

"He was stinky, too," she said. "But the crying was worse. He cried all the time." She shook her head as if to rid herself of the memory. "All the time."

Lamont, who'd been listening, raised his eyebrows. "What'd you *do* about it?"

Minda stood up. Calm. She brushed her hair aside and let her gaze slide across them all. "I made him stop."

"H-How?" asked Jolene.

"Yeah, how?" asked Derp.

"I'll show you."

She got one of the gift bags. The tag said 'BOY' on it but Minda didn't care. Inside was a pack of rubber dinosaurs, which she didn't care about either and indifferently tossed away. Derp picked it up.

"Dinosaurs! Can I have them?"

"Sure," said Lamont when Minda didn't reply.

Minda took the tissue paper that had been in the bag. It was holiday tissue paper, white stamped with green tree-shapes. She wadded it up and pressed the wad to Candy's mouth.

Candy shook her head. Her lips were tight-shut now, tight-shut in a line. Minda twisted her dangly candycane earring.

"Ow!"

As soon as she opened her mouth to go ow, Minda stuffed in the wad of tissue paper. Candy tried to spit it out but Minda wouldn't let her.

"Get more," she told the others.

"Open the presents?" asked Derp, with a wide dopey-happy smile. "Really?"

"I'm next, I'm next, I pick next." Jolene snatched up one marked 'GIRL,' found a plastic tiara-ring-necklace set, and squealed. She gave the tissue paper to Minda.

Seeing what they were doing, Jimmy, Tess and Spencer abandoned their soccer game to come help. Jingle had stopped moving anyway, just lay there all limp, so they were bored.

Gift bags and wrapping paper and ribbon and tags shredded in a greedy frenzy, revealing toy cars, fashion dolls, picture books, army guys, paint-by-numbers, bean-bag animals, sidewalk chalks, clay-dough, and more. Some of the gifts contained goodies—tins of cookies, chocolate, spicy Christmas gumdrops, caramel corn, peppermints.

And there was tissue paper. Lots and lots of holiday tissue paper. Red and green and white, plain and patterned, some with trees and some with stars or snowflakes, some with silver and gold speckles.

Piece by piece, wad by wad, Minda forced the tissue papers into Candy's mouth.

Lamont watched, looking both concerned and kind of interested. "Is that what you did to your brother?"

"Uh-huh."

"So you could have more presents?" asked Derp.

"It wasn't Christmas then," Minda said. "There weren't presents. He just needed to stop crying."

At first, when she couldn't spit, Candy tried to swallow them down, but there were too many and Minda was too fast. Candy started to choke and gag. She threw up but the throw-up clogged with the papers. Some trickled out her nose. She lurched her whole body and the chair fell over with her still taped to it. Her face flushed, then turned purple.

Meanwhile, Santa did a huge Hulk-out effort that popped most of the tape holding him. He lunged partway to his feet, strips of tape flapping at his wrists, the chair scraping across the floor where one chairleg stayed stuck to his ankle.

Lamont lunged to his feet, too, with the scissors gripped tight in both hands. This time, he didn't stab the steel blades into Santa's fat pillow-belly. This time, he stabbed them at Santa's face, but missed. The scissors went into Santa's neck.

This time, there was blood.

Lots and lots of blood.

Even Lamont seemed surprised by so much blood. He blinked, letting go of the scissors.

Santa went, "Glurk."

He tottered around in a circle, pawing at the scissor-ends. His legs tangled on the chair. He crashed down. He shuddered. He kicked. He gurgled. Then he didn't do anything at all.

No one spoke for a minute.

They looked at Candy. They looked at Santa. They looked at Jingle, out in the hall.

They looked at each other. Cookie crumbs on their chins, chocolate on their lips, sticky gumdrops in their teeth.

Eventually, Mr. Gregson or somebody would come. Miz Parker would get let out of the janitor's closet. Teachers would be mad, and parents would be called.

But that was eventually. That was later.

For now, the kids on the naughty list still had plenty of presents to open.

THE PERFECT DINNER PARTY

CASSANDRA CLARE & HOLLY BLACK

1. Relax! Guests won't have fun unless their hostess is having fun too.

You walk into the dining room, alone. You're wearing a green shift, pale as grass, and have pulled your hair back into a glittering barrette. You're biting your lip.

"Lovely," Charles says and you look pleased. You dressed up for him, after all.

You explain that you're sorry that your friend Bethenny couldn't come. She had a dance recital and besides, she was too chicken to sneak out of the house. Not like you.

You met Charles the way he always meets girls. He hangs around the mall just like he used to when he was alive. Back then, he wore skinny ties and listened to new wave. He's excited that skinny ties are back. See? He's wearing one tonight.

You look over at me nervously. You probably think I'm too young to drink the bottle of wine you stole from your parents. You think I'm not going to be any fun.

Or maybe you're just wondering what happened to the rest of the guests.

When I smile at you, you look away uneasily. That just makes me smile wider.

When I was a littler girl than I am now, there was this boy who would always hang around. One day, he was over at the house annoying me (he would do this thing where he put his finger on my chin and asked me "what's this?" and when I looked down, he would bop me in the nose and laugh) and I realized the cupboard had a package of almond-flavored tea in it.

337

Since this was back in the eighties, cyanide was in the news a lot. We all knew it tasted like almonds. It was a pretty simple thing to make us mugs of tea—mine, plain, his, the almond-flavored kind.

Then I started telling him how sorry I was that I'd poisoned him. I kept it up until he started crying. Then I kept it up some more.

Our dinner parties always remind me of how much fun that was.

2. A few simple changes to your usual décor will give your house that party feeling.

Charles pulls out the chair for you and that seems to reassure you that things are going just the way you thought they would. You see a pair of teenagers, dressed up in their church clothes, using their parent's good china to have a dinner party in the middle of the night.

A grown-up party, with candles burning brightly in silver candlesticks and glass stemware and napkins folded into the shape of swans. Charles pours from the bottle of wine he's already decanted an hour ago.

You take a big sip. That's the first strike against you. Clearly you have no idea what to do with good wine—how to catch its scent, how to swirl it around the glass to see the color. You glug it like you're washing down a handful of pills.

You put the glass down with a bang on the table. I jump. "That was great!" you say. There's lipstick smeared on your teeth.

Charles looks over at me. I frown at him. Disapproving. He could have done better, my look says.

Charles gets up. "I'll get the first course."

Silence falls between us as soon as he's out of the room. I don't mind. I can be silent for hours. But you're not used to it. I see you squirm in your chair. Put your hands up to fiddle with your barrettes, unclasp them, close them again. Fiddling. You say, "So you're Charles' little sister, huh? How old are you, anyway?"

"Fourteen," I lie. I try to keep the bitterness out of my voice, because there is nothing worse than a disagreeable hostess, but it's hard. Charles is nearly grown, old enough to pass for an adult, while I am struggling to pass for fourteen.

With your flat chest and wide eyes, you look fairly young yourself. Another strike against you.

Charles comes back a moment later with bowls of soup. He places yours down first. That's proper. He's turning into a real gentleman, Mr. DuChamp would say.

"Are your parents on a trip?" you say. "They must really trust you to leave you here alone."

"They trust Charles," I say with a sly smile.

That makes her smile at Charles too, entrusted to take care of his little sister. And it makes me think of my parents, down in the dirt basement, buried six feet under with pennies over their eyes.

Mr. DuChamp said that that was so they could pay the ferryman to take them to the shores of the dead. Mr. DuChamp thought of everything.

3. Choose guests who are interesting, fun, and who will invigorate the conversation.

You pick up your spoon and dig it into the soup like you're scooping out a melon. I am fairly sure that when you do start eating, you will make slurping sounds.

You do. Strike three. I look over at Charles with my eyebrows up, but he is ignoring me.

"So," you say, around your soup, "did Charles tell you where we met?"

I shake my head, although I know. Of course I know. It's always the same. I can't imagine why you think I'd be interested. Mr. DuChamp always used to say that guests should never talk about themselves. They should make polite conversation on topics of interest to everyone.

"It was at a concert." You say the name of a band. A band I've never heard of.

"They were okay," said Charles, "but *you* were amazing."

Only the fact that it would be a massive breach of etiquette prevents me from making a gagging sound.

You both get into a long, dull conversation weighing the merits of Ladyhawke, Franz Ferdinand, Le Tigre, The Faint, and the Killers. Charles forgets himself so far as to exclaim how happy he is that Devo are making another album. Your blank stare is warning enough for him to clear his throat and suggest that you would like more wine.

You do. In fact, you drink it so fast that he pours yet another glass full. A fine bright color has come into your cheeks. Your eyes shine. I doubt you have ever looked lovelier.

Mr. DuChamp always used to say that appearances weren't everything. He said that the way a woman carried herself, the way she spoke, and the perfection of her manners were more important than how red her lips and cheeks were, or how shining her eyes. "Looks fade," he said, "except, of course, in our case." He would raise a glass to me. *"Age cannot wither her,"* he would say, *"nor custom stale her infinite variety."*

Whatever that meant.

I lift the soup spoon to my mouth, smile and lower it again. It was Mr. DuChamp who taught me how to pretend that I was eating, how gestures and laughter distracted your guests so that they'd never notice you didn't take a bite of food.

Mr. DuChamp taught us lots of things. He taught Charles to stand up when a lady entered the room, and how to take a lady's coat. He told me never to refer to an adult by his or her first name and to sit with my legs uncrossed, always. He didn't like pants and didn't approve of girls wearing them. He taught us to be punctual for all social engagements, even though once he moved in with us, the only social engagements we ever had were with him.

When he first came, it was horrible. I woke in the middle of the night because I heard something downstairs. I thought it was my parents fighting—they fought a lot: about the house, which always needed repairs, about her habit of hiding booze and pills, about girls in the office who called him on the weekends. I padded down to the kitchen in my nightgown to see the new Corian countertops splashed with blood.

Mom was on the floor with a strange man hunched over her. All I could see of Dad was his foot sticking out from behind the island.

I must have gasped. Mr. DuChamp looked up. The lower half of his face was red.

"Oh," he said. "Hello."

I made it all the way to the stairs before he caught me.

4.Don't scrimp on food and drink.
Arrange it attractively and let guests help themselves!

Charles clears our soup bowls and returns carrying the main course. It's lasagna, which is the only thing I know how to cook. I know Mr. DuChamp would say I ought to learn more elegant cooking: how to make pâté, clear soups, coq au vin, lamb stuffed with raisins and figs, maybe in a sweet plum sauce. But it's hard to learn when you don't have much money for ingredients, and can't taste what you've made.

The lasagna is a little burnt around the edges but I don't think you'll care. You're too tipsy, and anyway, hardly anyone makes it through the main course.

As you dig into your food, I wonder if you notice that there are heavy curtains across all the windows here and that they are thick with dust. I wonder if you notice the strange scratch marks on the floor. I wonder if you notice that nothing in the house has been updated since 1984.

I wait for Charles to move, but he doesn't. He just grins at you like an idiot.

"Can I see you in the kitchen?" I ask Charles in a way where it's not really a question.

He looks over at me like he's only just remembered I'm here at the table too.

"Sure," he mumbles. "Okay."

We push back our chairs. Mom used to complain about our kitchen because it wasn't the cool, open-plan kind. She wanted to knock down one of the walls, but dad said that was too expensive and, anyway, who wanted an old Victorian house with a modern kitchen.

I'm glad it's the old kind, so I can close the door and you can't hear.

"We don't have any dessert," I tell Charles.

"That's okay," he says. "I'll go down to the corner store for ice cream."

"No," I say. "I don't like her. She doesn't pass the test."

He slams his hand down on the counter. "No one passes your stupid test."

I look at Charles in his skinny tie and shiny, worn shirt. I am so tired of him. He is so tired of me. It's been so long.

"It's a big deal," I say. "Turning someone into one of us. They'll be with us forever."

"*I* want her with me forever," Charles says, and I wonder if you know that, that he feels that way about you. And I wonder if Charles knows that he said "me" instead of "us."

"She's smart," he says. "She's funny. She likes the same music as me."

"She's boring. She has bad manners, too."

"Manners," Charles says, like it's a swear word. "You and your obsession with manners."

"Mr. DuChamp says—" I start but he cuts me off.

"Mr. DuChamp killed our parents!" he yells, loud enough that maybe you might hear. "And anyway, we haven't seen him in months. He's off being vizier or chamberlain or whatever it is he does."

Charles knows perfectly well what Mr. DuChamp does. He looks after the household of the greatest vampire in our state. He has his ear. It is a very lofty position. He used to tell us over and over the story of how he rose from a lowly nestling to planning the state dinners where he entertained members of the elite from New Orleans to Washington. Charles found the stories boring but I was always fascinated.

Even though I didn't like Mr. DuChamp, I liked hearing about how he succeeded in drawing the threads of power around himself. He seized opportunities other people wouldn't even have recognized as opportunities. I liked to think that in his position, I would have seized my chance, too. I guess that's what everyone likes to think.

"Mr. DuChamp taught us how to behave," I say. "Our parents weren't going to do that. If you don't know how to behave, then you're no better than anyone else."

Charles looks stubborn. "Fine, if you want to do everything that guy said, remember that he said we should make more like ourselves."

"Only if they're worthy! He said some people don't care about bettering themselves."

So many lessons. At first, how to hold a wineglass, a fork, not to ever eat with your knife, no chewing gum, speaking when you're spoken to, sitting with your hands in your lap, to say "please" and "excuse me." Later: to kill quickly, to be subtle in finding your prey, not to make others clean up your mess, and the three "B"s: to bite cleanly, then to burn and then bury the remains, unless you wanted more like yourself.

"It's not for everyone," I say. "He warned us."

"This isn't about him," Charles says. "You're the one who doesn't want anyone else around. You're the one who doesn't want more of us. How come I always have to be the one who hunts? How come we always have to eat the girls I bring home? What about your friends? Oh, right, you don't have any."

I make an involuntary sound, like the hiss of air going out of a balloon. "I can't—" I start, then take a deep breath and start again. "When I walk around the mall alone, all the other girls are with their mothers. I used to go into this one arcade, but the boys there wouldn't even talk to me. They're not interested in girls, at least not girls my age. *You* can go out in the world alone. *You* can pretend to have a young-looking face, but I'm a *child* to everyone I meet."

"Look," Charles says. "You know I feel bad for you. I try to be a good brother. I bring girls to your stupid dinner parties and let them sit around like stuffed bears, while you pour out pretend tea. All I want is for tonight to be different, Jenny. Just one night. For me."

"Fine." I whirl around and stalk back into the dining room. I stop short, so short that Charles, just behind me, almost walks right into my back. If he didn't have such good reflexes, he would have.

You are still sitting where you were, at the table, and I think of what Charles said about tea parties. You look stiff as a doll with little red spots on your cheeks like paint. Mr. DuChamp is standing beside you, one hand on the back of your chair. He smiles when he sees us.

"Hello, children," he says.

5. Every party needs an element of the unexpected to make it unforgettable. Think fondue!

"There's a place set for you," I say, even though, really, the place was for your friend.

He laughs, probably unconvinced, and runs his finger through the dust on the sill. "Regrettably, I have already eaten."

"Oh," I say, then remembering my manners, "How do you do?"

He smiles indulgently. "Very well, thank you, excepting one thing." Then his demeanor changes, his face darkens, and he stands, still clutching your hand. You stare at him in horror. "Excepting that you were supposed to bring my master tribute *not six months past.*

"I have tried to contact you and *nothing.* You, my charges, embarrass me. Did I not instruct you better than this? If I, who manage all my master's affairs, cannot manage you, what must I look like?"

I look over at Charles. His expression is determined, but not surprised.

"Charles?" I say. "What tribute?"

He shakes his head. "Six living girls."

I turn back to Mr. DuChamp. He is frowning, like he's trying to puzzle out something. "You did not receive my message?"

"I received it," Charles says. "I tore it up."

"That is unacceptable," says Mr. DuChamp.

"I don't understand." It's you, speaking in your tinny little human voice, like the voice of a fly. "What's going on?"

Mr. DuChamp turns to me. "Ladies," he says. "Perhaps if you were to retire to the parlor, I might speak to Master Charles in private."

I already know you're not going to go along with it. You don't understand that requests for privacy must always be honored. You are already sputtering as I take hold of your arm. I squeeze, just a little, and you turn white.

"Ouch," you say. "Ouch, what are you doing to my *arm*?"

"Nothing," I say. "I'm not doing anything." My mother used to do that when I misbehaved in the supermarket. She would pinch the skin in the crook of my arm and smile a syrupy smile like the one I'm smiling now. Although she couldn't pinch as hard as I can, now. "Ladies retire to the parlor after dinner."

You're looking at Charles. "I'm not going anywhere with your creepy little sister."

"I'll be there in a minute," Charles tells you. "Stay with Jenny."

You go, but not quietly. Whining the whole way.

All the furniture in the parlor is covered in big white sheets. It's more convenient that way. When they get blood on them, we can take them away and launder them and put them back clean. The sofa looks like a fat white iceberg, surrounded by smaller icebergs, floating in the darkness. You cough and sneeze a little, choking on all the dust. There's a fireplace full of dead ashes and windows that have had plywood hammered over them. I wonder if you're starting to realize this isn't a normal sort of house.

I push you down on the couch and go back over to the door. If I stand just behind it, I can hear Charles and Mr. DuChamp, but they can't see me.

"It's not right," Charles is saying. "It's one thing to kill people because we have to, because we've got to live, but those girls were so scared. And I didn't know anything. I hurt that one girl real bad because I didn't know how tight to knot the rope. And another girl just sobbed for the whole five-hour drive. I hate it. I'm not doing it again."

"That is the very point of etiquette, Charles. It instructs us as to how to do things we don't want to do."

"I *won't* do it," Charles says, again.

"That is very rude. And you know I do not tolerate rudeness."

"What's going on?" you say, tremulously, from behind me.

"He's going to kill Charles," I say. My voice doesn't sound all that different from yours.

"What are you?" you ask. You must be sobering up. "What's *he?*" You point at Mr. DuChamp.

I bare my teeth at you. It's the easiest way, really, to show you what I am. I've never done it before in front of someone I wasn't intending to kill right away.

Your eyes go wide when you see the fangs, but you don't step back. "And *he's* one, too? And he's going to hurt Charles?"

You're so stupid. I already told you. "He's going to kill him."

"But . . . why?"

"For not following the rules," I tell you. "That's why rules are so important."

"But you're just kids," you say. You're used to second chances and next-time-there'll-be-consequences-young-lady. You've never had your mother killed in front of you. You've never drunk your brother's blood.

"I'm old," I say. "Older than you. Older than your mother."

I know why Charles didn't tell me about the tribute, though. It's because some part of him still thinks of me as little too. He's been protecting me from that, just like he's been protecting me by staying in the old house, even though he no longer wants to. It's not fair. He was right before when he said he was a good brother. He shouldn't get killed for that.

"Well, do you have a stake?" you ask.

I don't point out that this is like asking a French aristocrat if they have a guillotine around. Instead I point toward the fireplace.

You are surprisingly quick on the uptake. Not sophisticated, of course, but with a sort of rough intelligence. Street-smarts, Mr. DuChamp would say. You grab the fireplace poker and without a second glance head out the door into the dining room.

I lean around the door. Mr. DuChamp has Charles up against the wall. His big hand is around Charles' neck and he is squeezing. He can squeeze hard enough to crush Charles' neck if he wants to, but that wouldn't be fatal. Right now he's just having fun.

When we were just starting to learn how to feed, the hardest part for me was moving out of the stalk and into the strike. There's an awkward moment when you get close to your victim, but haven't actually lunged. It can seem an impossibly gulf between planning and actually doing, but if you hesitate, you'll get noticed.

You obviously don't have that problem. You swing the poker against the side of Mr. DuChamp's head hard enough to make him stagger back. Blood runs down his cheek and he opens his mouth in a fanged hiss.

Before he can get his bearings, I clamp my mouth on his throat like a lamprey. I've never drunk the blood of one of my kind before. It's like drinking lightning. It goes zinging down my throat, and all the time Mr. DuChamp's fists are beating on my shoulders, but I don't let go. He's roaring like a tiger in a trap, but I don't let go. Even when he crashes to the ground, I don't let go, until Charles leans over and detaches me, pulling me off the corpse like an engorged tick so full and fat it doesn't even care.

"Enough, Jenny," he says. "He's dead."

6. Never start cleaning up while your guests are still present.

A lot of people think that when vampires die they blow up or catch on fire. That's not true. As death sets in, our kind subside slowly into ash, like a bowl of fruit ripening into mold and rot on speeded-up film. We all stand in a sort of triangle, watching as Mr. DuChamp starts turning slowly black, the tips of his fingers beginning to crumble.

You start crying, which seems ridiculous, but Charles takes you into the other room and talks to you softly like he used to talk to me when I was little.

So then it's just me, witness to Mr. DuChamp's final end. I take the little broom from the fireplace and sweep what's left of him among the scorched wood and bones.

When you and Charles come back out, I'm standing there with the broom like Cinderella. Charles has his arm around you. You look blotchy and red-nosed and very human.

"We're going to have to run away, Jenny," he says. "Mr. DuChamp's master knew where he was. He'll come looking for him soon enough. I don't know what he'll do when he finds out what happened."

"Run away?" I echo. "Run away to where?" I've never been anywhere but here, never lived anywhere but in this house.

You explain that you have an uncle who has a farmhouse upstate. You and Charles plan to hide out there. I am welcome to come along, of course. Charles' creepy little sister.

This is what Charles always wanted—a real girlfriend, someone who will love him and listen to music with him and pretend that he's a regular boy. I hope that you do. I hope that you will. You might be stuck with each other for a long time.

"No," I say. "I'm okay. I've got somewhere else to go."

Charles furrows his brow. "No you don't."

"I *do*," I say and give him the evilest look I can manage.

I guess he doesn't really want me to come to the farmhouse, because he actually drops it. He goes upstairs to pack up his stuff, and you go with him.

The remains of dinner are still on the table. The glasses full of wine. The four plates, only one of them with food on it. The remains of our last dinner party.

When I'm done cleaning up and I've said goodbye to you and Charles, when you've given me the address in case I change my mind, when you've hugged me, even, my neck so close to yours that I can smell your blood through the pores of your skin, then I'm going to get ready too.

Six girls is nothing to me. I can ask them to help me find my mother in parking lots, to look for lost kittens, to pick me up after I fall from my bike and skin my knee. I don't care if they scream or cry. It might be a little annoying, but that's it.

The hardest part is going to be driving while sitting on a phone book. But I'll figure out a way. If I want the job, I'm going to have to show the Master I'm just as good as DuChamp. I know every detail of the story of his rise to power. I've heard it a hundred times. Everything he did, I can do.

As I leave town, I'll drop this letter in the mail, just so you know what my plans are.

Thank you very much for coming to my party. I had a lovely time.

MAKE BELIEVE

MICHAEL REAVES

I am a very lucky man.

The reason for my saying this is obvious: I'm standing before you, accepting this award for Outstanding Alumnus. But the reason behind the reason is that I became what I wanted to be.

I'm lucky because, for as far back as I can remember, I've wanted to be a writer. Ever since I was a kid, five years old, sitting down in front of our new black-and-white TV to watch *The Adventures Of Superman*. I was hooked the first time I saw George Reeves leap into the air and fly. Actually, he was lying on a board in front of a cyclorama screen with a wind machine blowing his hair and cape, but I didn't know that at the time, of course. I do remember wondering even back then, however, why he always leveled off at a cruising altitude of 30,000 feet even when he was just going a couple of city blocks away.

I'm not what you would call a mainstream writer. I have an unabashed preference for genre fiction—specifically, horror. And, like most horror writers, I've drawn most of my stories from childhood fears and experiences. I grew up in this town—you wouldn't think a place on the edge of the desert would be particularly spooky or atmospheric, but you'd be wrong. The desert can be a terrifying place.

If you'll indulge me, I'd like to tell you about one of those childhood experiences. Oddly enough, I've never written about it, or even spoken of it, before now. I'm not sure why. Perhaps my reasons will become clear—to me as well as you—during the telling. After all, good fiction is supposed to illuminate as well as entertain, isn't it?

I was seven years old, and this took place in 1955. It is probably impossible to convey to you all how totally different a time it was. It was, first and foremost, a much simpler time. You all have console games that tremble on the edge of virtual reality; we had Winky Dink. You have cell phones that can video and text and Twitter; we had party lines. And, of course, you have computers capable of processing gigabytes that you can hold in one hand, and we had UNIVAC.

But it wasn't just the technology that was simpler. It was a more *trusting* time. Back then, parents thought nothing of letting their kids roam all over the neighborhood, as long as they were home in time for dinner. Somehow or other, adults back then were much better at protecting the young from fearful realities. It's true that we were aware of those realities—ever hear of "duck and cover"? But kids were allowed to be kids back then. They weren't exposed to the rampant cynicism and smut that you all imbibed along with your baby food. Don't get me started.

It was spring, I remember, around the end of April or the beginning of May—you'd think that, considering what happened, the date would be burned into my memory. It had to have been a Saturday, because school wasn't out yet. I was playing with a couple of friends—Tom Harper and Malcolm James. We'd gone up into the hills a few blocks from my house to play cowboys and Indians. We were armed and ready for trouble.

When I say "armed," I mean something different than what the word might connote today. I was carrying my trusty McRepeater Rifle, which made a very satisfactory bang when the wheel atop the stock was turned. Tom had a deadly Daisy 1101 Thunderbird, and in addition was packing twin cap pistols. And Malcolm . . . well, Malcolm was carrying his Johnny Eagle *Magumba* Big Game Rifle, which he'd insisted on bringing even though he had a perfectly good Fanner 50 cap gun back in his bedroom. Some people just won't get with the program.

We were hunting Indians, or, as we called them, "Injuns." The term "political correctness," let alone the concept, wasn't exactly widespread back then. It was the middle of the afternoon and, though it was early in the year, it was already hot enough to raise shimmers of heat waves from the dirt road. The hills were still green, but you could see that slowly the vegetation was dying. Another month, and brown would be the dominating color, announcing the beginning of the fire season.

For now, however, it was still pleasant, or as pleasant as those hills ever became. We were walking cautiously through the Badlands of our fantasy, alert for the slightest sound that might betray an Apache ambush. This was more difficult than it might seem, because every few minutes Malcolm would drop into a crouch and spin around, spraying the mesquite with imaginary bullets and going *"Kachow!! Kachow!!"* Tom Harper finally grew tired of this, and demanded to know how we were going to get the drop on the bad guys with Malcolm constantly announcing our presence to everyone in the county. To which Malcolm replied that it was only make believe, and that the most we might hope to flush from the underbrush was a rabbit or coyote.

We knew that, of course. We all knew that. It's important to keep this in mind.

"Knock it off," Tom finally said, exasperated, "or I'll drop-kick your ass into next week."

That got the desired result. Tom Harper's right leg ended in a stump just above the knee—legacy of a car accident. He wore a prosthetic; a hinged contraption made of wood, metal and plastic, and when he ran, he used a sort of half-skip in his locomotion which the rest of us found very amusing. We were careful not to show it, however, because Tom could turn that half-skip into a devastating kick that could easily deliver the recipient as far up the calendar as Tom wanted. Malcolm said nothing more that in any way damaged the fantasy *gemütlichkeit* that we had constructed. And again, it's important to remember that we knew what we were doing.

Malcolm was going on eight, with a seborrheic head of densely black hair and horn-rimmed glasses the exact same shade. He was built like a concentration camp inmate, all sharp, acute angles, with an Adam's apple that leapt about like the bouncing ball in a Fleischer sing-along cartoon. Not surprisingly, he had few friends. Tom had just turned eight; he was handsome, if somewhat bland in appearance, and looked like a future gridiron star—until he began to walk or run with that characteristic hitching limp. I remember once, when we were both younger and I was at his sixth birthday party, seeing his father's eyes fill with tears as he watched his son skip-run across the back yard.

We knew what we were doing. It was play, make-believe. Nothing more.

We were wandering along a dirt road, not far from the ranger station. The shadows were starting to grow longer, and the light more sanguine, as the sun neared the smoggy horizon. "We should maybe turn around," Malcolm said. "We're gettin' too near the cave."

There was no need to stipulate which cave. There was only one in the area—Arrowhead Cave, so named because of the dozens of chipped flint relics found there over the years. It was a tectonic cave, not one formed by gradual erosion. It had come into being thousands of years ago, when an earthquake had shattered a sandstone outcrop and deposited the fragments at the bottom of a ravine. Over the centuries talus and dirt had covered it, and eventually solidified into a roof. It hadn't been a particularly impressive cave, according to rumor, but it had served the local Indians well as shelter for centuries before the valley was settled. It was even less impressive now, after the tragedy of 1938, when four young boys—out, like us, for play—had become lost in the cave.

I never did learn the specifics of the story—when I was a child, the adults had been very tight-lipped about it, even almost two decades later. All I knew—all any kid knew—was that the four boys had died in Arrowhead Cave. A few days later the City Council, acting with an alacrity hard to believe for anyone familiar with local government, had authorized several construction workers to blow up the cave's entrance with dynamite, closing it for good.

Tom and I looked at each other after Malcolm's statement. Neither of us wanted to be thought cowardly. On the other hand, neither of us particularly wanted to get any closer to Arrowhead Cave, as it was supposedly haunted. There had been another minor temblor last week as well, and none of us relished the thought of being near the cave, or—worse—in it, should another quake hit.

As the three of us stood there, momentarily paralyzed by indecision, we—or I, at least—became aware of just how *quiet* it was. I know it's a cliché—I knew it even back then—to speak of an ominous, brooding silence holding dominion over the scene. How many times had I lain on the threadbare rug in our living room, chin cupped in my hands, staring at a black-and-white image of somebody wearing a pith helmet, standing in front of a sarcophagus and saying grimly, "It's quiet—*too* quiet"? Usually this particular trope was immediately followed by the hero being seized around the throat and throttled by an ancient hand wrapped in dry, dusty cerements.

Still, cliché or no, I could suddenly feel my heart pounding. The light had taken on a shimmering, glassine quality, and the air seemed *dead*. It was impossible to get a lungful, no matter how deeply I breathed. There was no nourishment to it.

It would be easy, I suppose, to speculate that we all passed through some sort of *transition* then—a portal to another reality, I guess you could call it. It's tempting to use such a device as an explanation of a sort for what we did next. But the truth, as it usually is, was much more banal. We did what we did because that's what kids did back then.

I started to say something, even though I was somehow convinced that the leaden air would not convey my words. Before I could try, however, a voice shouted, *"Hands up!"*

Now, this is the point. It was fantasy. Make-believe. And we *knew* that. But unless you can remember, *really* remember, those Bradbury days of childhood, the unspoken social norms that we all lived by then, the secret lives and inviolate rules that bound us as fully and completely as office politics and the laws of church and state circumscribed our parents' lives—well, then I have no real hope of making you understand why we did what we did. It wasn't even something we thought about—we just did it. They had the drop on us, after all. They'd caught us, fair and square.

So, all three of us dropped our toy guns and reached for the sky.

"They" were four boys our age, armed with toy guns like ours. They'd come up on us from behind and nailed us good. The tallest one, a kid my age, was wearing bib overalls over a flannel shirt. There seemed to be something odd about his weapon—a carbine, with no manufacturer's stamp apparent—but it was obviously a toy. He gestured with the barrel, a peremptory jerk obviously intended to move us along, while the other three picked up our weapons.

"Let's go," he said. "Shag it."

Arms still upraised, we stumbled along down the road, our captors herding us toward an unknown destination.

Even though these lads represented "the Enemy" (Apaches, space aliens, Nazis, gangsters, the heathen Chinee or a hundred and one other incarnations of Bad Guys), there was nothing in our childhood rules of engagement that prohibited discourse. Consequently, Malcolm attempted conversation. "Where d'you guys go to school?" he asked. "I haven't seen you around—"

"Quiet," one of them, a tall fellow with hair as red as Malcolm's was black, and a face mottled with more freckles than the moon has craters, hissed. And yes, I know it's bad writing to use anything other than "said"—but you weren't there. Trust me; there was less humanity in that one word as spoken by him than there was in a snake's sibilance.

We marched on in silence. And I started to wonder just how they'd managed to catch us so thoroughly off-guard. We'd been standing on the crest of a small hill; if they'd come along the road from either direction we'd have seen them, and there was no way they could've climbed up the side, through the dry creosote, without making enough noise to wake the dead.

. . . *to wake the dead* . . . There are certain phrases that we use a thousand times without thinking, until one day you realize just how hideously appropriate they are.

We went around a bluff's shoulder, down a steep trail, and found ourselves in a high-walled ravine; almost a box canyon. A quarter of the way up the rear wall, at the top of a pile of talus, was what had once been the mouth of Arrowhead Cave. It was little more than a lacuna now, the dynamite having closed it off seventy years ago. Two of our four captors urged us up the ten foot slope.

"Hey, guys?" The nasal quality of Malcolm's voice was rising, a sure barometer of anxiety. "It's gettin' dark—my Dad'll hide me if I miss dinner—"

"Zip it," one of them—short and rotund, with wire-rim specs—said. I got a good look at the clothes he was wearing as I passed him—knee pants and suspenders, a sweater and a flat, button-down cap. There was definitely something anachronistic about the apparel, but what really caught my eye was the toy gun he was brandishing. It was unlike any kids' gun I'd ever seen, and after looking at it for a minute, I realized why. I didn't have the words to describe it at the time, but looking back on it, I realize it was made of stamped metal. It was black, with a red barrel, and on the butt was a stylized sketch of the Lone Ranger. A legend ran in curved script along the bottom of the image; I can't recall the exact phrase, but it was something about listening to Brace Beemer as the Lone Ranger, every Friday.

Why "listen"? Why not "watch"? And who was Brace Beemer? Everyone knew the Lone Ranger was played by Clayton Moore.

As big of a puzzle as that gun represented, however, the one held by the third boy was even more so. It, too, was made out of some material which I didn't immediately recognize. When I did realize what it was, it was enough to make stop and stare, open-mouthed.

His gun was made of cardboard.

There was a slogan inscribed on the side of it, as well—I couldn't read all of it, because his hand partly obscured it. The part I could read proclaimed Geyser Flour to be "America's *top* self-rising flour!"

The boy saw me staring at his paper gun. "Shut yer bazoo, yegg," he instructed me, raising the toy as he did so.

And a strange feeling possessed me; I suppose it made sense in light of later developments, but at the time it was as inexplicable as it was overwhelming. I was, abruptly and totally, *terrified* of that ridiculous cardboard gun. So terrified that I felt in danger of soiling my corduroys.

He reached out and put a hand on my shoulder, pushing me up the slope, and his hand was *cold*. I could feel it through the fabric of my T-shirt.

As we climbed the steep slope, I watched both of my comrades, and knew they'd come to the same conclusion I had about our captors. Tom's face was set in the utter blankness of denial, his gaze as uncomprehending as that of an abused animal. Malcolm's was a hundred and eighty degrees opposite, full of growing realization and horror.

By the time the three of us had clambered up into the shallow remnant of the cave's former entrance, Malcolm had lost it. He was sobbing, babbling incoherently, snot drooling from his nose. I wasn't doing much better myself, but I at least managed to keep a somewhat braver face on. Tom seemed outwardly calm also, but his face was the same sallow hue as that of his prosthetic's plastic skin.

We sat on the sandstone lip that hung above the declivity for what seemed like hours, but was in reality scarcely more than forty-five minutes; just long enough for the sun to disappear behind the western slope of the ravine. I watched our captors. I was only seven, and so I had no idea that all of them were dressed in Depression-era, poor white trash clothes, or that their toy weapons were relics of those same long-gone days. I only knew that there was something profoundly *wrong* about every aspect of them—even the way they moved, and sat, and talked amongst themselves.

MICHAEL REAVES

I say they talked, but, even though I could clearly see them address each other; could even, until the light faded too much, see their lips moving, I heard nothing. It was deathly quiet in the ravine—even Malcolm's crying had, for a time, subsided—and I knew that sound rose with great clarity in still air. But it was like watching TV with the sound off.

"Gh-ghosts," Malcolm blubbered. "Th-they're *ghosts*. They were kuh-*killed* in the cave—"

"Bullshit," Tom muttered.

"—twenty years ago—"

"Stop it." Tom's voice was level and icy, but it was thin ice, covering black depths of hysteria. He stood and faced Malcolm.

Malcolm stood as well. "You *know* it's true! You nuh-know it's—"

"Shut up."

"Shouldn't've let 'em get us, should've *run*, now they're gonna—"

Tom hit him.

It was a short, hard jab, brought up from his waist into the pit of Malcolm's stomach, and it let the air out of him like a nail in a tire. He stared at Tom in utter shock, mouth gaping, making vaguely piscine sounds.

Then he turned, staggered toward the edge of the rocky shelf and, before either of us could try to stop him, he fell.

He rolled down the declivity a few feet before he managed to stop himself. Then he looked up, and Tom and I both heard his moan of terror when he saw the four boys—or whatever they were—surrounding him. His face had been scratched during his fall, and a red streak of blood stood out vividly against his chalk-white skin.

"Please," I heard him say. "Please—I'm late for dinner—"

And they laughed.

I guess it was laughter, though it was the most mirthless, soulless sound I've ever heard. It was the sort of laughter something dead for a long time, long enough to completely forget any connection it had had with life, would make, if it were to somehow be amused.

They laughed, and they moved closer to him. Malcolm made a high, keening noise, a sound of utter despair.

Tom shouted, "You *bastards*! Leave him *alone*!" And he jumped off the ledge.

I don't know what he thought he could possibly do. I doubt he thought about it at all. He just went to Malcolm's rescue—or tried to. He might have been successful, somehow, if he'd had two good legs. I don't know if he forgot that one was artificial, or if he just didn't care.

It was a magnificent jump; it carried him to within five feet of them. He plowed into the loose stone and gravel, and his right leg buckled beneath him; he lost his balance and fell.

He struggled to stand, but before he could, the one with the cardboard gun looked up at him. He was grinning, and it might have just been a trick of the fading light, but for one awful instant it looked like the grin of a naked skull. He raised the gun and pointed it at Tom's chest.

And, softly, but somehow very clearly, I heard him say, "Bang."

That was all; just "Bang," in a quiet voice. There was no puff of smoke, no recoil from the paper muzzle.

But Tom's back erupted in a spray of blood.

He fell backwards.

I screamed.

All four heads swiveled up toward me. Their eyes were like spiders' eyes; black and gleaming.

I knew that following Tom and Malcolm would only get me killed—or worse. There was only one other direction that I could go—back into the cave.

I'd seen before-and-after photos of Arrowhead Cave. The City Fathers had ordered it sealed off, and sealed off it had been, with a vengeance. What had been a dark, mysterious opening into the underworld had been reduced to a pile of rubble, leaving an overhang barely a yard deep.

But there was no place else to hide. I pressed against the unyielding stone, feeling a distant wetness as my bladder let go. I could hear them scrabbling up the slope after me. I turned frantically from side to side, seeking an impossible escape—

And saw, six inches above my head, a lateral crack in the rock.

It was barely wider than my body, and beyond it was unrelieved blackness, yet to me it looked like the gates of Heaven. I jumped, grabbed the flat sandstone lip, pulled myself up and into it, kicking and squirming. There was barely enough room for me to wriggle between the two slabs of rock; I had to breathe shallowly to do so. But I kept crawling.

To this day I've no idea how that providential escape route came to be there. Perhaps it had been overlooked after the blast; perhaps it had been deemed too small to worry about. Or perhaps that temblor we'd had a week earlier had had something to do with opening it. All I know is that, after a lifetime of frantic crawling, I saw light up ahead.

I redoubled my efforts, scooted forward—and felt a cold hand close on my ankle.

I didn't have the breath to scream—it came out as a thin, mewling cry. Whichever one of those things had me began dragging me relentlessly back, down into the darkness. I felt my fingernails splinter on the rock. I kicked back frantically with my free leg, felt my shoe strike what had to be the head of the one that had grabbed me. I gritted my teeth, drew my leg up and kicked backwards with every bit of strength I had left.

His head *splintered*. I felt his skull cave in. But his grip did not slacken.

Sobbing obscenities, I swung my free leg against my other one, as hard as I could. Among the injuries that would be counted up later was a hairline fracture of my ankle—but at the time I felt nothing but a fierce joy when that cold grip loosened for a moment.

I lunged forward, panting, and came to the end of the passage, so abruptly that I tumbled out before I could stop myself. I caught a brief, dizzying glimpse of a hillside below me, scrub brushes barely illuminated by the crepuscular twilight—then I fell. Pain exploded in my head like a roman candle, and I must have passed out.

My last thought before I lost consciousness was: *They're still coming for me.*

• • •

And now most of you are wondering a few different things, I imagine— such as, *Why did he waste our time with this silliness?* or, *He's got quite an imagination,* or even, *Where are the men with white coats and butterfly nets?*

For those of you who wish to know the end of the story—I wish I could tell you. There was front-page material in the local paper the day after that day in 1955, documenting the discovery of Tom Harper's body near Arrowhead Cave. No bullet or gun was ever found, but something very powerful had punched a hole clean through him.

They never found Malcolm.

Me they found at the bottom of the next ravine over from Arrowhead Cave. I had a concussion, and was in a coma for nearly two weeks. When I finally came out of it, I told everyone who asked—and many did, believe me—that I remembered nothing. Which was the truth. My recollection of the events of that long ago day has come back to me piecemeal, during the course of many a long and sleepless night. I stopped seeing therapists after one diagnosed me with PTSD, and wondered why a writer with no military history was so afflicted.

I suppose it's possible that I imagined the whole thing, in an attempt to supply a story that fit the necessary particulars. If it hadn't been for the finding of Tom's body, I would have no reason not to assume that wasn't true. Which, of course, asks the question: What could possibly have happened that was so horrible that I might have made up such a story to normalize the reality?

In any event, I must admit lying to you at the start of my speech. I said I had always known that I wanted to be a writer. That's not strictly true; until I was seven years old, I had no idea what I wanted to be. But after that night, there was no doubt in my mind.

It's how I deal with it.

So, in conclusion, to those of you out there who know without question what you want to be when you grow up, I say congratulations—and be careful what you wish for.

CLASS DISMISSED

Charles Antin's fiction has appeared in numerous publications, including the *Virginia Quarterly Review*, the *Michigan Quarterly Review*, the *Gettysburg Review, Fugue, Unstuck,* and *Glimmer Train,* where he won the award for very short fiction. His writing has also been published in the *New York Times* and *Food & Wine.* He holds an MFA from New York University.

Dale Bailey lives in North Carolina with his family, and has published three novels, *The Fallen, House of Bones,* and *Sleeping Policemen* (with Jack Slay, Jr.). His short fiction, collected in *The Resurrection Man's Legacy and Other Stories,* has won the International Horror Guild Award and has been twice a finalist for the Nebula Award.

Holly Black won the inaugural Andre Norton Award for Young Adult Science Fiction and Fantasy for her novel *Valiant,* part of the acclaimed Modern Faery Tale series. *The Spiderwick Chronicles,* which she co-authors with Tony DiTerlizzi, reached the *New York Times* bestseller list and was made into a feature film. She lives in an old house with a secret library in Amherst, Massachusetts.

Georgina Bruce is a writer and teacher. Her short stories have been published in *Strange Horizons, Ideomancer, Shimmer,* and various other places. She is currently studying for a masters degree in creative writing at Edinburgh's Napier University, and in her spare time undertakes psycho-geographical excursions around the city, sometimes involving whisky. She is often lost. Her blog can be found at georginabruce.com.

The Oxford Companion to English Literature describes **Ramsey Campbell** as "Britain's most respected living horror writer." He has been given more awards than any other writer in the field, including the Grand Master Award of the World Horror Convention, the Lifetime Achievement Award of the Horror Writers Association, and the Living Legend Award of the International Horror Guild. Among his novels are *The Face That Must Die*, *Incarnate*, *The Count of Eleven*, *Silent Children*, *The Darkest Part of the Woods*, *The Overnight*, *Secret Story*, *The Grin of the Dark*, *Ghosts Know*, and *The Kind Folk*. Forthcoming are *The Last Revelation of Gla'aki* (a novella) and *Bad Thoughts*. His collections include *Waking Nightmares*, *Alone with the Horrors*, *Ghosts and Grisly Things*, *Told by the Dead*, and *Just Behind You*. Ramsey Campbell lives on Merseyside with his wife Jenny. His pleasures include classical music, good food and wine, and whatever's in that pipe. His web site is at ramseycampbell.com.

One of the best-selling names in young adult fiction, **Cassandra Clare** is the author of the *Mortal Instruments* and *Infernal Devices* series of urban and, respectively, historical fantasy novels. The first movie based on her work, *City of Bones*, releases in 2013.

Hal Duncan's *Vellum* was nominated for the World Fantasy Award, and won the Spectrum, Kurd Lasswitz and Tähtivaeltaja. Along with the sequel, *Ink*, other publications include a novella, *Escape from Hell!*, a chapbook, *An A-Z of the Fantastic City*, and a poetry collection, *Songs for the Devil and Death*, with a collection of short fiction forthcoming from Lethe Press. He wrote the lyrics for Aereogramme's "If You Love Me, You'd Destroy Me" and the musical, *Nowhere Town*. Homophobic hatemail once dubbed him

"The . . . Sodomite Hal Duncan!!" (sic). You can find him online at halduncan.com, glorying in that infamy.

Formerly a film critic, teacher, and screenwriter, Canadian writer **Gemma Files** is probably currently best known for her Hexslinger series (*A Book of Tongues*, *A Rope of Thorns*, and *A Tree of Bones*), a gay-friendly Weird Western trilogy available from ChiZine Publications. She has also published two collections of short fiction (*Kissing Carrion* and *The Worm in Every Heart*, both from Prime Books) and two chapbooks of poetry, and won a 1999 International Horror Guild Award for Best Short Fiction with her story "The Emperor's Old Bones."

Jeffrey Ford is the author of the novels *The Physiognomy*, *Memoranda*, *The Beyond*, *The Portrait of Mrs. Charbuque*, *The Girl in the Glass*, *The Cosmology of the Wider World*, and *The Shadow Year*. His story collections are *The Fantasy Writer's Assistant*, *The Empire of Ice Cream*, *The Drowned Life*, and *Crackpot Palace*. His short fiction has appeared in numerous journals, magazines and anthologies, from *MAD Magazine* to *The Oxford Book of American Short Stories*. His work has been translated into nearly twenty languages and is the recipient of the Edgar Allan Poe Award, the Shirley Jackson Award, the World Fantasy Award, the Nebula Award, and the Grand Prix de l'Imaginaire.

The late **Charles Grant** was a prolific novelist and short story writer of dark fantasy and horror, who won a World Fantasy Award for his collection *Nightmare Seasons*, as well as two Nebula Awards. Grant also edited the award-winning *Shadows* anthology, running eleven volumes from 1978-1991.

Alex Jeffers seldom feels older than seventeen although he published his first story in 1975. His books are *Safe as Houses*, a full-length novel; *Do You Remember Tulum?* and *The New People*, two short novels; *The Abode of Bliss*, a novel-length story sequence; *You Will Meet a Stranger Far from Home*, a collection of wonder stories; and, this year, *Deprivation; or, Benedetto furioso: an oneiromancy*. His website is sentenceandparagraph.com.

Stephen Graham Jones has eleven novels and three collections on the shelf. He's been a Stoker Award finalist, a Shirley Jackson Award finalist, and has been an NEA Fellow. He has some hundred and fifty stories published. He teaches in the MFA programs at CU Boulder and UCR-Palm Desert.

Michael Kelly is a Toronto-based author, editor, and publisher. He's been a finalist for the Shirley Jackson Award and the British Fantasy Society Award. His fiction has appeared in a number of journals and anthologies, including *Black Static*, *Carleton Arts Review*, *The Mammoth Book of Best New Horror*, *Supernatural Tales*, and *Postscripts*, and has been collected in *Scratching the Surface* and *Undertow & Other Laments* (Dark Regions Press). His next book (as editor) is *Chilling Tales: In Words, Alas, Drown I* (EDGE). He also publishes and edits the acclaimed literary journal *Shadows & Tall Trees*.

One of the most recognized authors in the world since his first novel, *Carrie*, debuted in 1974, **Stephen King** has received Bram Stoker Awards, World Fantasy Awards, and British Fantasy Society Awards among his numerous honors. Even his short fiction is fecund, with "Children of the Corn" inspiring a series of nine horror films. King's most recent release is *Joyland*, from Hard Case Crime.

Joel Lane's publications in the weird fiction genre include four short story collections: *The Earth Wire*, *The Lost District*, *The Terrible Changes*, and *Where Furnaces Burn*—the latter a book of supernatural crime stories. He is also the author of two mainstream novels, *From Blue to Black* and *The Blue Mask*; three poetry collections, *The Edge of the Screen*, *Trouble in the Heartland*, and *The Autumn Myth*; a chapbook, *Black Country*; a booklet of crime stories, *Do Not Pass Go*; and a pamphlet of erotic poems, *Instinct*. Current projects include a collection of ghost stories, *The Anniversary of Never*.

Joe R. Lansdale is the author of over thirty novels and numerous short stories, articles, essays, screenplays, and comic book scripts. He has received numerous awards. Among them The Edgar Award, Grinzani Cavour Prize For Literature, nine Bram Stoker Awards, including Lifetime Achievement, and he has received the Grandmaster award from the Horror Writers Association. He has been awarded the British Fantasy Award, a Golden Lion Award for his contributions to the legacy of Edgar Rice Burroughs, the Mid South Award for Best Novel, two *New York Times* Notable Books, and others. His novella "Bubba Hotep" was made into a film starring Bruce Campbell and Ossie Davis, directed by Don Coscarelli. His short story "Christmas with the Dead" has been adapted into film, screenplay by Keith Lansdale, directed by Terrill Lee Lankford, and produced by Joe and Karen Lansdale. He lives and writes in Nacogdoches, Texas.

Will Ludwigsen's work has appeared in a number of magazines including *Alfred Hitchcock's Mystery Magazine*, *Asimov's*, *Cemetery Dance*, *Weird Tales*, and *Strange Horizons*. He recently released his second collection of short stories, *In Search Of and Others*. He resides in the very strange state of Florida.

Distinguished author **Robert McCammon** has published in many genres, first in well-received and *New York Times*-bestselling horror novels and now in-depth historical thrillers. His latest, *I Travel By Night*, releases this year from Subterranean Press.

Robert McVey attended Sarah Lawrence College, Harvard University, and New York University. He is a psychotherapist in private practice in New York. He is the author of the flash short story collection *We Have Pie*.

Christine Morgan works the overnight shift in a psychiatric facility and divides her writing time among many genres. A lifelong reader, she also writes, reviews, beta-reads, and occasionally edits. She has over a dozen novels in print and more due out soon. Her stories have appeared in several anthologies, been nominated for Origins Awards, and given Honorable Mention in two volumes of *Year's Best Fantasy and Horror*.

An American author of horror and mystery fiction, **Norman Partridge** is best known for two detective novels about retired boxer Jack Baddalach, *Saguaro Riptide* and *The Ten Ounce Siesta*. He is also the author of the book *The Crow: Wicked Prayer*, which was adapted in 2005 into a movie in that franchise. His short stories are collected in the volumes *Mr. Fox and Other Feral Tales*, *Bad Intentions*, and *The Man with the Barbed Wire Fists*.

Gary Raisor wrote the horror novels *Less Than Human*, *Graven Images*, and *Sinister Purposes, Empty Places*, all to great reviews and sold-out print-runs, which, as any writer will tell you, is the true measure of writing success (ha!). Raisor has also written countless short stories, starting back in the '80s with *Night Cry* magazine and *The Horror Show*, working his way into a great many "Best of" anthologies.

Michael Reaves has been a freelance fiction writer for over thirty years. Among other things, he's written for just about all the action-adventure cartoons your eyeballs devoured when you were a kid. He's also written a dozen or so novels (many set in the *Star Wars* universe), short stories, comics, computer games, graphic novels, and movies. He's won an Emmy and a Howie, and been nominated for a Hugo, a Nebula, a British Fantasy Award, and a second Emmy. Currently he's producing a 1940s-style vampire noir movie starring Neil Gaiman.

A retired physician, **John Schoftstall** has sold several stories to *Strange Horizons* and the *Fortean Bureau*. An aficionado of anime and baked goods, he resides in Pennsylvania.

British novelist and short story writer **Michael Marshall Smith** has won the British Fantasy Award multiple times as well as the Philip K. Dick Award. 2013 will see the release of a new novel and short story collection. Smith has also worked extensively as a screenwriter, writing for clients in Los Angeles and London. He lives in Santa Cruz, California, with his wife and son.

When kindergarten turned out to be a stupefyingly banal disappointment for **Peter Straub**, he took matters into his own hands and taught himself to read by memorizing his comic books and reciting them over and over to other neighborhood children on the front steps until he could recognize the words. Soon he had earned a reputation as an ace storyteller, in demand around campfires and in back yards on summer evenings. Not much has changed—he remains one of the more celebrated authors living today for novels like *Floating Dragon*, *Ghost Story*, *Koko*, and *Lost Boy, Lost Girl*, among many other tales. He is a member of HWA, MWA, PEN and the Adams Round Table, and though he is without "hobbies," remains intensely interested in jazz, as well as opera and other forms of classical music.

Lisa Tuttle is an American-born science fiction, fantasy, and horror author. She has published over a dozen novels (including *Lost Futures*, nominated for the Arthur C. Clarke and James Tiptree, Jr. Awards), five short story collections, and several non-fiction titles, including a reference book, *Encyclopedia of Feminism*. She has also edited several anthologies and reviewed books for various publications. She has been living in the United Kingdom since 1981.

Halli Villegas is the author of three collections of poetry (*Red Promises*, *In the Silence Absence Makes*, and *The Human Cannonball*), a book of short ghost stories (*The Hairwreath and Other Stories*), and was the co-editor of the anthologies *Imaginarium: The Best Canadian Speculative Writing* and *In The Dark: Tales of the Supernatural*. Her work has appeared in many anthologies including *Chilling Tales 2*, *The White Collar Anthology*, and *Girls Who Bite Back*. She has also appeared in numerous magazines such as *CNQ*, *The LRC*, and *Variety Crossings*. Halli has received funding for her writing through grants from the Ontario Arts Council and the Toronto Arts Council.

THE TEACHER'S PET

Steve Berman has edited over fifteen anthologies, including quite a few for young adults who have managed to survive the rigors of childhood. His own novel, *Vintage: A Ghost Story,* was a finalist for the Andre Norton Award. He lives in New Jersey, the only state in the Union that has an official devil. He regularly spoils rotten his ginger tabby, Daulton, who has bitten and clawed him on occasion.

PUBLICATION HISTORY

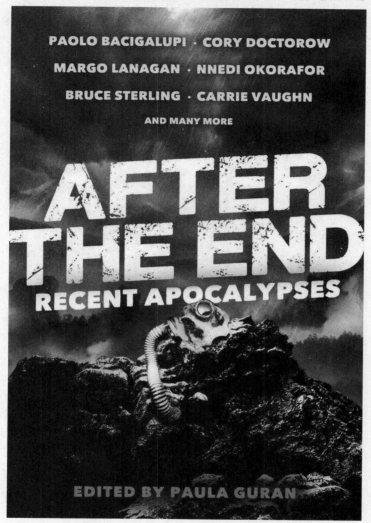

ALSO FROM PRIME BOOKS

IT'S A WONDER
HUMANITY SURVIVED THIS LONG!

ZOMBIES
SHAMBLING THROUGH THE AGES

STORIES BY
STEPHEN GRAHAM JONES
LIVIA LLEWELLYN
JONATHAN MABERRY
AND MANY MORE...

EDITED BY STEVE BERMAN

Trade Paperback | 360 pages | 978-1-60701-395-2 | $15.95

Stories that reveal the threat of zombies are far from recent — from the Bronze Age to World War II — a millennia of thrills, chills, kills, carnage, horror, and havoc wreaked throughout history by the walking dead!

ALSO FROM PRIME BOOKS

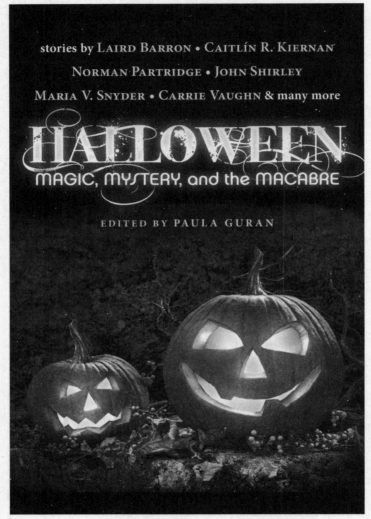

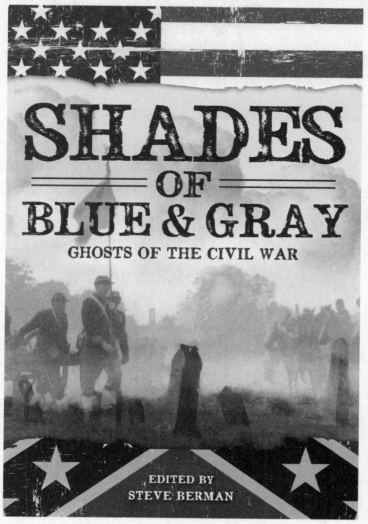